WHO IS MY ENEMY?

Joyce Muriel

ATHENA PRESS
LONDON MIAMI

WHO IS MY ENEMY?
Copyright © Joyce Muriel 2002

All Rights Reserved

No part of this book may be reproduced in any form
by photocopying or by any electronic or mechanical means,
including information storage or retrieval systems,
without permission in writing from both the copyright
owner and the publisher of this book.

ISBN 1 84401 003 1

First Published 2002 by
ATHENA PRESS
Queen's House, 2 Holly Road
Twickenham TW1 4EG
United Kingdom

Printed for Athena Press

WHO IS MY ENEMY?

Chapter One

The unusual darkness of the house struck Paul as he turned his car into the driveway. On this cold, damp November night he would have expected lights to be shining out from the sitting room and from the front hall, especially as it was a Friday when Judith always came home early and prepared a special meal for them.

Quickly parking the car in the drive, he hurried through the car port to the kitchen door at the side of the house. The door was unlocked. Judith must be at home. But the kitchen too was in darkness. As he switched on the bright strip lights, he realised how empty and cold it was.

All the surfaces were clear, but there was no welcoming smell of cooking and, although all the remains of breakfast had been cleared away from the pine table in the dining area, there were no signs of an evening meal being prepared.

The cleared table and the presence of her briefcase assured him that Judith had returned home from her teaching job in the boarding school in the centre of the village, where they lived. But where was she now?

Having convinced himself that the dining room was as dark and empty as the sitting room, he switched on the hall light and called up the stairs. Perhaps she was lying down, feeling unwell? As there was no response to his call, he ran up the stairs and went first to their bedroom. No Judith was sleeping there. Nor was she in any other of the bedrooms or the bathroom. All were empty. Judith was not in the house.

There was no explanatory note on the hall table – no message on the answering machine. Suddenly it occurred to him that she might have mentioned something which he had failed to register in the hurry of leaving in the morning for they had both been late. Nothing, however, was written on the wall calendar in the kitchen. Searching through her brief case, he found her diary.

Friday, 11 November. Yes, there was an entry there but it only mystified him all the more. 'Lawrence?' was all she had written. What could that mean?

Realising that the house was still cold, he turned up the central heating, then switched on the gas fire in the sitting room with its comforting artificial flames. After pouring himself a drink, he sat down in the armchair near the fire and tried to be patient. As he sat sipping his drink, the silence of the house pressed down on him. He felt it was waiting as he was. But for what?

The grandfather clock in the hall struck seven sonorously. He had been home half an hour and still there had been no sign from Judith, who was normally home, at the latest, by five o'clock.

It was so unlike her. In all the six years they had been married, she had never done anything like this. In fact, he had often teased her about the meticulous planning of her time. She was controlled in this as she was in everything. On the rare days when something unexpected had happened, she had always phoned his office in Braxby, where he practised as a solicitor. It was especially surprising that this should happen on a Friday evening which they always spent together, celebrating the end of the week.

Putting down his glass, he stood up. There must be some explanation, if only he could find it. He was being too passive. He hurried to the cloakroom. Her coat was missing, together with the purse in which she kept money and credit cards. Perhaps she had gone to visit someone in the village? A look in the garage assured him that her car was still there, so she could not have gone far since the last bus left the village of St Stephen's at three thirty when she would still be working.

He walked slowly back into the house. At first, he had been merely irritated but now he admitted to himself, as he closed the kitchen door carefully behind him, that he was frightened. And he recognised this fear. It had always been lurking in his mind since the first days of his relationship with Judith. How could someone as beautiful and brilliant as Judith be content to live quietly with him, an average, rather boring country town solicitor? How could she be happy teaching mathematics to mostly unappreciative girls in a small boarding school when she might have been lecturing in London?

She had given him no reason to think that she was not happy and, as the years passed, he had come to accept the unbelievable and he had been happier than he had ever thought possible. Now, it seemed, his dream had collapsed. He felt like someone suddenly awakened out of deep sleep, unsure of himself and his surroundings. Trying to understand what had happened, he forced himself to walk upstairs once more.

It was ridiculous, he told himself, to assume on such little evidence that she had gone. A glance at her wardrobe, however, quickly revealed the truth of what he feared. Many of her clothes had gone, her travel bag was also missing. Her ruby and diamond engagement ring had been carefully placed on the glass tray on her dressing table, together with the eternity ring he had given her on the fifth wedding anniversary. He was finally convinced she had gone, leaving behind anything connected with their marriage. But why? Why do it like this? Surely, she could have told him or left a letter? This furtive slipping away seemed so uncharacteristic of the Judith he had known. Or thought he had known?

Leaving everything as it was, he wandered downstairs and into the sitting room. As he slumped down into his comfortable armchair, he noticed a pile of travel brochures on the coffee table. He had brought them home at Judith's suggestion and they had intended to make a decision that very evening.

A week earlier he had been contentedly drinking his coffee after one of Judith's special meals when she had suddenly interrupted the comfortable silence. 'Don't you think it's time, after six years, that we made our own plans for the Christmas holiday?' From the decisive way in which she spoke, he knew that she had already made up her mind.

'What do you think we should do?' he asked, fearing that she might be about to suggest that they should ignore the established ritual of visiting his parents on Christmas Day and Boxing Day. Since her mother was dead and her father remarried with a new family this had seemed the obvious thing to do.

As she turned her brilliant, dark eyes on him and her red lips curved into her loving but slightly provocative smile, he knew that, as always, he would find it hard to oppose her.

'Don't worry,' she explained, 'I don't want to change

Christmas Day. I simply thought we might go away for the New Year.'

'But, surely, it's too late to book now, isn't it?' he asked, hoping to evade the issue, 'especially as it's the millennium.'

'No, it's just the opposite. The millennium's a bit of a flop or something, apparently and there are loads of vacancies, so you can't get out of it that way.' She smiled teasingly at him. 'It's time we did our own thing, for once. Your family is pleasant but I would like to have you to myself.' She was still smiling, a smile that beguiled and promised. Her voice was always musical and attractive but even more so on occasions such as this. He looked deeply into her dark eyes. He had never been able to decide exactly what colour they were; it seemed to depend on her mood. He felt drowned in their depth and drawn irresistibly across the room to kiss her.

But she held him off lightly with her hands. 'Do you agree then?'

'Of course.' He longed to kiss her. 'It's a marvellous idea. I'll go into the travel agent's on Monday.'

'Good.' Those same hands now pulled him down towards her.

Surely, she had been as happy as he was? Or had it all been a deception? But, if so, why? There must be some explanation, he thought, as he sat alone now. He tried to consider it objectively, as if it had been a case someone had presented to him. It was useless. All he could think of in his bewilderment was his anger and his hurt. It did not seem possible. A nightmare which had always been a possibility at the back of his mind had suddenly become the reality in which he had to live. This room with its memories of so many happy evenings seemed to mock him.

Standing up, he poured himself another drink and took a sip. He must do something. But what? As he sipped his drink, he heard the approach of a car down the usually silent road. To his surprise, it seemed to stop in the road outside his house. Footsteps. Then nothing. Suddenly the front door bell rang shattering the silence of the house. Shocked, he moved swiftly towards the door, then stopped. He did not believe it could be Judith, yet a foolish hope sprang into life. The nightmare might be over. Normality would somehow return.

Quickly, he hurried to open the front door. A stranger stood in the porch. By the light streaming from the hall, Paul could see that he was tall, dark-haired and wearing a raincoat. 'Mr Paul Tempest?' he asked.

'Yes. What do you want?' Even in the uncertain light, Paul was aware of the stranger's keen scrutiny.

'I would like to speak to your wife, Mr Tempest.' His voice was cool and unemotional and he had no perceptible accent.

Paul stared back at him. 'I'm afraid you can't. My wife isn't in.' He tried to appear calm but it was difficult to hide the apprehension he felt.

'Then perhaps I can wait for her, if that is convenient.' The stranger took a step forward.

Paul stood his ground, annoyed at the man's quiet assumption. 'It isn't convenient,' he retorted angrily. 'Who the hell are you? And what gives you the right to come pushing your way into my house, asking for my wife?'

The stranger remained bland and undisturbed, his foot still in the doorway. 'I'm Inspector Barrett from Westford CID,' he said, showing his card. 'Your wife is expecting me.'

Amazed, Paul stared at him. He had not expected this. It seemed totally ridiculous. 'What do you mean?' he demanded, trying to hide the increasing fear he felt. 'I don't see how she can be. I know nothing about it. She would certainly have told me.'

'I rang Mrs Tempest last night to ask if she could give me some information,' the Inspector explained patiently. 'She said she was in a hurry as she had an appointment and asked me to call this evening at about eight thirty. I'm sure she will confirm this, if you ask her.' Again, he made a slight attempt to step forward but Paul held his ground.

'I'm afraid I can't,' he explained. 'Judith, my wife, is not at home and I don't expect her back for some time.' He had no desire to confide his humiliation to this annoying stranger, who could obviously offer him no comfort. But then why was this policeman here at this moment? He must try to discover if his visit had some connection with Judith's baffling disappearance.

'Can I be of any help?' he asked. 'I don't think we've met before, so you may not know I'm a solicitor.' He tried to speak as calmly and normally as he could.

'I have heard your name, sir, although our paths have not crossed before. I'm not sure, however, that you can help me, unless you can give me some idea as to when your wife will be at home, so that I can call again at some more convenient time.' He seemed prepared to go.

Anxious now to obtain more information, Paul opened the door widely. 'Why don't you come inside, Inspector?' he asked, as pleasantly as he could. 'Then we can discuss the matter more comfortably.' After a moment's hesitation, the inspector agreed and followed Paul into the sitting room and, at his invitation, sat down in one of the armchairs and appeared to be waiting.

Finally, Paul broke the silence. 'I was surprised when you said that my wife asked you to call this evening. You're quite sure that it was this evening?'

'I have no doubt of that, sir,' the inspector replied evenly. 'And I'm surprised that Mrs Tempest is not here to see me as she promised.'

'Perhaps you can tell me what it is you want to know and I can give her a message,' Paul suggested, striving to get some explanation.

'Thank you, sir, but I think it would be better if I saw your wife personally. Perhaps you can tell me when it would be convenient?' The inspector took out his notebook and waited.

Desperately, Paul took another sip of his drink and stared down at the intricate pattern of the carpet. Judith's choice. He had always hated it. But why should he think of this now? He lifted his head to find the inspector eyes firmly fixed on him and pen poised.

'That's difficult,' Paul said, realising that in spite of his reluctance, he was now committed to saying more. 'You see, I don't know when my wife will be here.'

'Surely, sir,' the inspector protested mildly, 'you must be able to give me some idea.'

'I'm afraid not,' Paul tried his best to sound cool and unconcerned. 'I'm afraid my wife seems to have gone away.'

'Gone?' The inspector stared at him. 'Are you telling me, Mr Tempest, that you wife has left?'

'It seems she has.' Paul avoided looking at him. 'I arrived home this evening at about six thirty to find the house empty. My wife returned from her work then left, apparently, taking clothes and money with her.'

'And she hasn't left any message?'

'None that I have yet discovered. Whatever you said to her last night, it seems to have had an amazing effect.' When the inspector made no response, he continued sharply. 'Whatever did you say to her? Could she have thought that you were threatening her in some way?'

'I hardly think so, Mr Tempest.'

When Inspector Barrett seemed content to leave it at that, Paul asked again more sharply, 'Then, what did you say to her? Surely, I have a right to know under the circumstances?'

The inspector regarded him thoughtfully. 'I'm quite willing to tell you, Mr Tempest. It's possible, after all, that you may be able to help me. I simply asked Mrs Tempest whether she had had any news recently of an old friend of hers.'

'And who is this friend?'

'Lawrence Reardon. Does that name mean anything to you?'

'I've never heard the name before.' That was the literal truth and Paul did not think it was necessary to mention that 'Lawrence' was the name written in Judith's diary entry for that day. 'Who is he?'

'An old friend of your wife's who has not been around for several years until recently. But, if you haven't heard of him, then it's unlikely that you can help me.' He stood up, preparing to go.

Feeling that he had been given nothing in return for the information he had offered, Paul stopped him with a question. 'But tell me, is this Lawrence Reardon wanted for some crime then?'

'No. We merely wish to get some information from him. One of my colleagues went to see him in Belfast and found that he had left suddenly for England, possibly with a view to getting in touch with Mrs Tempest, so I was about to ask her if she could give me any information as to his whereabouts.' He turned to go.

'Why?' Paul stood up abruptly. 'Why should my wife be expected to have news of him?'

Inspector Barrett turned back reluctantly. 'Because Reardon

and your wife were very close some years ago when she spent several months with her mother's relatives in Northern Ireland. And he might want to see her again now.'

'Very close?' Paul asked suspiciously. 'Are you trying to say they were lovers?'

The inspector hesitated. 'Possibly. I don't know. I was thinking more of certain activities they were both thought to be involved in.'

'Certain activities?' Paul frowned and then an incredible thought struck him. 'You don't mean terrorist activities, surely?' The idea was ludicrous.

'I really am unable to say. Of course, there was never any proof in your wife's case, except that she was friendly with the Reardons.'

Paul laughed. 'I'm not surprised. It's nonsense but even if it were true, why should you be bothering about this now? Haven't you forgotten about the peace process? It's all finished.'

'Not for everyone, I'm afraid. There are some people who don't want peace.'

'And you think my wife is one of those? It's absurd. She is a brilliant mathematician who has taught for the last six years at the public school in the village. She's highly respected both for her integrity and her ability.'

'I don't doubt any of that,' the inspector replied firmly. 'Nevertheless, she is a friend to whom Lawrence Reardon might turn at this moment, or so I have been informed. Mr Tempest,' he continued earnestly, 'I'm not trying to harm your wife. I'm trying to protect her.'

'Protect her? What do you mean?'

'It is thought that Lawrence Reardon and perhaps your wife, too, have important information which certain people who still hope to wreck the peace process want to keep secret. They would not hesitate to kill Reardon and your wife. Believe me, your wife could be in considerable danger.'

Unwilling to accept this, Paul pressed for further information. 'But you're not sure, are you?'

'No. There could be other reasons.'

'Such as?'

'Well...' The inspector hesitated. 'Mrs Tempest and Reardon might merely have decided to renew their once close relationship. In which case it is no great concern of ours. But you can see that we need to talk to them.'

'Of course.' In neither case does it look happy for me, Paul thought.

'I'm sorry, Mr Tempest,' the inspector said, beginning to move towards the door, 'but, I'm afraid I must leave. If I have any information, I will let you know straight away.'

'Of course,' Paul replied. He was numb with the shock. He stood still, afraid that his legs might fail him if he moved towards the door. 'I don't suppose you have any idea where they might have gone?'

'London, I should think is most likely, especially as Reardon has a sister living there.' He paused on his way out. 'If you should have any more news yourself, please ring me at this number. It will always get me.' Tearing a page out of his notebook, he wrote on it and offered it to Paul.

Paul managed to extend his hand to take it. 'Thank you, I will.'

The inspector walked briskly out. The door closed behind him. He was gone.

As he heard the car drive away, Paul stumbled to his armchair and sank into it. He tried to think clearly and logically but that seemed almost impossible. Someone recovering consciousness might feel like this, he thought, struggling to make sense of his surroundings and to reorganise the changed circumstances of his existence.

But his life had been smashed into a thousand pieces that evening. He tried to put them together. Two facts emerged – Judith had gone and gone apparently with Lawrence Reardon. Why? That piece was missing. It might be for love or because she was an accomplice of his. Perhaps, however, there was a third reason, unknown to Inspector Barrett.

'But not unknown to me.' In his misery, Paul spoke aloud. This had always been his secret fear. Suddenly, with exceptional clarity he remembered the evening when they had first met, seven years earlier, when he was twenty-five and Judith two years younger. He had been spending the weekend in London with an old school friend, Anthony, who was becoming known as a promising young barrister. They had been invited to a party given by Anthony's Head of Chambers.

Paul, conscious of being a moderately successful but basically unambitious provincial solicitor, had not wanted to go. I shall dislike them, he thought, and they will be bored by me. Nevertheless, persuaded by Anthony, he went. It was as he expected until he met Judith. He did not expect to be attracted to her for Anthony had just told him that she was completing a doctorate in some abstruse realm of mathematics.

She was standing tall and slender by the window with a glass in her hand, wearing a long simple black dress with copper threads running through it that matched the auburn glints gleaming in her heavy dark hair. As Anthony introduced them, she turned the gaze of her wide, dark eyes on him and her lips curved into a welcoming smile. He was enchanted by her soft, musical voice with its slightest trace of an Irish lilt.

Was she as beautiful and brilliant as she seemed to him? He never gave himself time to consider that for, from the first moment, he was convinced that she was the girl he had long hoped to meet. Miraculously, she seemed happy to spend most of the evening in his company, in spite of Anthony's obvious attempts to compete. As she was leaving, she invited him to come with her to a piano recital the next day, since they had discovered they had a mutual interest in music.

A year later, when she had completed her doctorate, they were married, having been lovers for months. Soon afterwards, to everyone's amazement, she turned down a lectureship and took a teaching post in the public school in the picturesque village of St Stephen's, six miles from the country town of Braxby where his practice was.

For six years they had been happy, or so he had thought. She was different from the people they met and his parents, although they could not honestly find any fault, were never really comfortable with her. This had not upset him for he respected a certain remoteness about her. As a mathematician she must, he thought, at times live in a world he could not understand. This did not worry him, however, for he was happy that she had chosen to live her life with him. And now inexplicably, she had gone without any explanation, as if the six years had never mattered.

He stood up. He could not bear to sit still any longer. He wished he could hate her. Anything would be better than this pain. The grandfather clock struck the half hour again. It must be half past nine. He went to the kitchen. It might help to have some food. After cutting a slice of bread and some cheese, he sat down to eat in the silent, empty kitchen.

Suddenly, shrilly, for the second time that evening, the front door bell rang. He leapt to his feet. Who could it be? He did not want to go and answer it. Loudly and insistently, it rang again and again. Whoever it was was determined to be answered and answered quickly. He hurried to the door and flung it open. By the light of the hall he saw three men standing in the porch. They were tall and wore dark raincoats. For one moment, he thought that Inspector Barrett had come back with two companions but, almost immediately, he realised that these men were different. There was something menacing and sinister about them.

'Mr Tempest? one of them asked quietly.

'Yes. What do you want?'

'We would like to speak to your wife,' the man answered.

Paul stared at him. 'She's not here,' he said.

'I hope you won't mind if we look for ourselves?' the man replied smoothly, taking a step forward.

'Who the devil are you?' Paul asked in amazement.

'Never mind who we are,' the man replied, 'that needn't concern you.' A card was flashed in Paul's face but, before he could look at it, he was pushed to one side as the men entered.

He stood in the hall, unable to believe the evidence of his senses. They went smoothly and swiftly into every room. They were obviously accustomed to this work. He heard them upstairs opening all the cupboards and doors. Then they came back downstairs into the hall where he still stood bewildered.

'Thank you, Mr Tempest.' The same man spoke again. 'We're sorry to have inconvenienced you.' They moved to the door which was still open.

'What do you want?' Paul almost stammered. 'I don't understand.'

'Better not to try, Mr Tempest. Better just to forget what's happened.' His tone was quiet, almost reassuring.

'But what about my wife?' Paul demanded.

'My advice for what it's worth is to forget her too. Goodnight.' They were gone as swiftly as they had come. He heard them drive away.

Chapter Two

As soon as he had heard their car drive away, Paul stood undecided in the hall, now empty and silent again. He was aware that his mood had changed. This second shock seemed to have awoken him from his self-pitying torpor. He had been temporarily overwhelmed by the pain of thinking that Judith had not only left him but had also left him for another man without a word of regret. He had been too ready to believe this because it seemed to be the embodiment of his secret fear that Judith could never really be satisfied with this dull life with him.

This now was unimportant for his last sinister visitors had brought clearly back to his mind Inspector Barrett's warning, until now disregarded. 'Your wife could be in considerable danger.' This last visit made it clear that this was no idle warning. Judith was in danger! He was amazed to think how selfish he had been, thinking only of his own pain and injured pride when her life might be threatened.

At that moment, he was reminded of something she had said to him only a few weeks earlier. After quite a strong disagreement, he had walked across the room to the settee where she was sitting, silently refusing to push the disagreement into a quarrel but still wordlessly resisting the imposition of his will. 'You know I love you, Judith,' he had said, taking her hand. 'I love you more than anyone else in the world.'

She had turned towards him regarding him with enigmatic dark eyes and smiling that friendly but provocative smile that had first attracted him. 'But the real question, Paul,' she had said without emotion, 'is, do you love me as much as you do yourself? As a Christian I was given that as the test of true love.'

After a moment's surprise, he had kissed her, asking her to forgive him and admitting quite truthfully that he had been in the wrong. She had swiftly forgiven him.

Now, however, he realised that he had never tried to answer

her question, never even considered its implications. Had he disappointed her? She had never said so. But he had convicted himself, it seemed in the last two hours by thinking only of himself and scarcely at all of the danger which might threaten her. It was possible that her departure had not been entirely of her own will. He was ashamed of the assumptions he had so readily made. He must now think quickly and clearly and try to plan a course of action.

Deciding that half a cheese sandwich was not a sufficient antidote to several tots of whisky on an empty stomach, he went first to the kitchen and made himself a strong coffee and a more sustaining snack. After about a quarter of an hour his brain was much clearer but he still did not see any obvious solution

It seemed clear that her disappearance was connected with her friendship with Lawrence Reardon. If she had not gone with him, then she must be meeting him. But where? Inspector Barrett had suggested that London might be a good place in which to meet, especially as Reardon had a sister in London. Her address might be in the address book that Judith kept in the desk in the little room she used as a study. He ran upstairs and opened the desk. Thank God, the book was still there. He prayed that it would give him the necessary information.

At first, he thought he had been mistaken but, on his second, more careful search, he found it, not under Reardon but under Barker – James and Maeve – and, lightly in pencil after it as if to remind herself, Judith had written Reardon. The address was somewhere in East London. He would have to look it up in his A–Z. He wrote it quickly in his own diary, then put the address book back.

Hurriedly, he tried to make a coherent plan. He would go to this address in London. Even if he did not find Judith there, he should be able to get more information. Realising that there might still be need for caution, he decided to drive not to Westford but to the smaller station at Braxby where some of the London trains stopped.

A look at the local timetable told him that the first train in the morning was just before seven. This would get him to Euston at about nine in the morning. As the search might take several days, he packed a small bag with necessities and made sure he had adequate cash facilities. After this, before going to bed, he made two necessary phone calls, one to his senior partner and one to Judith's headmistress, explaining that an unexpected family emergency made it essential for them to go to London for a few days. It was much easier to be evasive than he had expected, especially when one had a good reputation!

Everything went according to plan and soon after nine thirty the next morning, he was boarding the bus outside Euston which, he had discovered, would take him to that part of London where Maeve Barker lived.

As he had suspected the address proved to be a council estate of high-rise flats. Concrete blocks towered over concrete paths and outbuildings packed with overflowing dustbins. Here and there were patches of worn, dusty grass. A few young boys were idly kicking balls about, while groups of older youths were gathered in what seemed to Paul to be menacing groups round the dustbins. Drug pushing, he thought. Or was this thought simply the result of media influence? In place of badly needed paint the walls were splashed with violent and brilliant graffiti – the only colour there seemed to be in this grey world. A chill wind scattered around bits of paper and other rubbish.

This was the inner-city land, where an intruder, like Paul, was glad of the disguise afforded by nondescript jeans and a shabby, though warm, jacket. As he made his way with difficulty to the right block, preferring to avoid asking assistance, he reflected on how easy it was for the comfortable middle classes to ignore the existence of these ghettos. Even he had done it, although he had frequently met some of the inhabitants of similar places in his office and in court.

He recalled the anger of his parents some months previously when they had been burgled by three youths from a similar estate in Birmingham. Outraged, they declared that no punishment could be too severe for this sort of thing and were pleased when he reminded them that, in future, many such people might be liable for three years in prison after three previous convictions.

'That's just what they need,' his father declared.

'But will it do any good?' Judith had asked in that quiet, cool way of hers. Indignantly, his parents had brought out all the arguments about encouraging people to commit more crimes by being too soft with them. Judith had not argued with them, for she rarely argued and never with anger. 'But where there is injustice, one has to attempt to put it right,' she said, 'or there will always be conflict. Don't you think so?'

As he entered the right building, Paul remembered that he, anxious as always to avoid conflict, had changed the subject. Nor had he ever attempted to discuss it further with Judith. Why ever not?

The entrance lobby was bare and ugly, except for a few graffiti and small piles of rubbish. The first lift he tried did not work, the second smelt disgustingly of urine but responded to his touch. All too soon he reached the twelfth floor where Maeve Barker lived. Pushing through the heavy door, he entered the corridor leading to the flats. Pausing for a moment, he looked down at the sordid network of streets far below, filled with tiny cars and dotted with people. He shivered in the wind which seemed very cold at this level. How insignificant the busy city below seemed. Suddenly depressed, he wondered once again what he should say, then walked quickly down the corridor.

Stopping before a blue door which bore the right number, he pressed the bell. He heard the sound of quick steps, then the door was cautiously opened. Maeve Barker, for it must be she who confronted him, neatly dressed in jeans and tailored top, was younger than he had expected. Short, black curly hair framed a heart-shaped face. Her skin was very fair, like Judith's, and her eyes bright blue, showing now, he thought, a considerable amount of apprehension as she looked at him.

There was no time for further consideration, so he plunged straight in. 'I'm sorry to bother you,' he said apologetically. 'My name's Paul Tempest and I'm looking for my wife, Judith. I thought you might be able to tell me where she is.'

He was not prepared for her strong reaction. 'Why have you come here with your lies?' she asked angrily. 'Go away and leave me in peace. I don't want anything to do with you.'

She would have closed the door but by putting his foot quickly in the gap, he managed to prevent her. 'What do you mean?' He was outraged. 'Why do you say I'm lying? I am Paul Tempest and Judith is my wife and, or so I thought, a friend of yours.'

'Why do you keep on saying that?' She was furious. 'When we both know it isn't true. I spoke to the real Paul Tempest just over an hour ago. He warned me about you.'

Paul was stunned for a moment but there was no time to waste when these men who menaced Judith were already ahead of him. Quickly, he produced the evidence he had thought to bring with him, his credit card, a university library card which carried his picture and a letter addressed to him and Judith.

Maeve stared at him. 'Oh, my God! He wasn't Paul Tempest then! I thought he must be. He knew so much and was well dressed and spoke so nicely. He looked just like a solicitor.' Her look told him plainly that he certainly did not.

'Whoever he was, he was not Paul Tempest.' Paul hoped that his firmness would impress her. 'Please help me,' he begged her. 'It's even more urgent now.'

She looked at him apprehensively, then said slowly, 'You'd better come in. I don't want to talk here.'

He followed her down the narrow hallway, squeezing past a buggy and a small bike into a large living room, cheerfully furnished and impressively tidy. Children's clothes were airing in front of the electric fire. From the long windows which opened on to a balcony he glimpsed a magnificent panorama of the City. There was no time to waste, however. He must know what had happened. He turned to the waiting Maeve. 'When did he come?'

'At about half past eight. He said he was Paul Tempest and he looked right. He told me where he lived and about Judith. He said he was desperate because she'd disappeared.' Her voice trailed away as she looked miserably at him.

'And you believed him?'

'Yes. I suppose I should have asked him for some proof but it didn't seem necessary.'

'What did you tell him?' Paul asked as calmly as he could.

'I couldn't tell him much except the address where she and Lawrence might have gone.'

'Do you still have it?' When she did not say anything he

21

continued impatiently. 'Please give it to me, if you have. We mustn't waste any more time. Judith may be in danger and so may your brother. I may be too late already but I've got to try. Don't you see?'

Without a word she picked up a piece of paper lying on the mantelpiece and handed it to him. 'Here you are!' She pushed it almost furiously into his hand. 'You'd better go straight away. But don't ever tell them that you spoke to me.' She pushed him through the door and along the hall to the front door. 'I don't want anything to do with any of it. I never did. I hate the whole bloody business. But Lawrence is my brother and he came to me. They gave me this address but they hoped to find somewhere safer, I think. They didn't stay long. I was too afraid to let them. I don't want my husband and our two kids involved in any of this. You do understand that, don't you?'

By now they had reached the front door. Tucking the paper into his wallet, Paul thanked her.

'Good luck,' she said, then added with a sudden unexpected kindness, 'Be careful, for God's sake! Make sure you're not followed. They're evil men, believe me!' Before he could reply the door was quickly shut behind him.

He walked towards the lift, still holding the paper in his hand. He had obtained what he wanted, although he had learned little except that Judith definitely was with Reardon and in even more immediate danger but he felt ashamed when he remembered the fear in Maeve's eyes. It seemed cruel to have pushed her into giving information when she was so obviously frightened, especially when it probably would be of little use since it seemed most likely that the two must either have moved on by now or have been caught. Nevertheless, he must go there in the hope of gaining further information.

Glancing at the paper, he noted that the address was in the region of Finsbury Park. As he took the lift to the ground floor, he decided that he would go straight there, for it would be foolish to waste any further time.

The sky was darker than ever as he emerged from the flats and a light but chilling rain was falling. He looked around cautiously with Maeve's warning still echoing in his mind. The area between the blocks of flats was deserted now, except for a woman pushing a buggy. Even the youths and small boys had disappeared. There were several parked cars but, as far as he could see, they were all empty.

Bending his head and turning up his collar, he strode out into the busy main street. It was a relief to find himself once more among crowds of people. After walking a little way he boarded a bus which took him along Seven Sisters Road. Alighting, he consulted his address again: Flat 1, 29, Cecil Road. He enquired in a nearby tobacconist's and was lucky enough to get clear directions. Within a few minutes he found himself turning the corner into Cecil Road.

He stopped abruptly, remembering once again Maeve's warnings. Twenty-four hours before he had been almost totally unaware of the dangers that could be met in life and, even now, he was so ill prepared that he had been about to walk straight up to the door of No. 29, as if he were making a social call. The road looked oppressive in the dull light obscured by rain. As far as he could tell the houses were gloomy Victorian semi detached, mostly shabby and dilapidated, although a few had obviously been recently refurbished with new windows and bright paint.

He looked cautiously around. The street appeared to be empty of people but there was a row of parked cars, seemingly empty but how could he be sure? Trying to persuade himself that no one could possibly know that he was here, he decided that he would have to take his chance.

No. 29 proved to be one of the shabbiest of the villas, separated from the street by a tiny garden with a few hopeless looking bushes and further embellished with an overflowing dustbin in the middle of its small patch of balding lawn. He pushed open the gate with its broken catch and walked quietly up the path to the front door. The house had a melancholy neglected air. The tiles of the front porch were dirty and cracked, the paint on the front door discoloured and peeling, the stained-glass windows surrounding the door dingy with dust and cobwebs. He would never have associated Judith with such a place.

There were three bells beside the door for three flats. Flat 1 was the only one without a name beside it. He stared at it, realising with surprise that he was tempted to turn away without ringing the bell. That way he would escape from this horrifying nightmare. Nevertheless, he rang the bell firmly and waited.

Nothing happened. The house remained silent. He rang again but still no one came. The flat was empty. He must have come too late. What had happened? Had they escaped or been caught? In either case there seemed to be nothing more he could do. Guiltily, he recognised the sense of relief this thought gave him but immediately it was followed by another – he could not desert Judith. He rang the bell several times, angrily. This time there was a response – hurried footsteps, then the door was opened.

The woman who confronted him was a total stranger. Bewildered, he stared at her. What could this small, plump, grey-haired woman have to do with his quest? Wearing tight striped trousers and a garish jumper, she did not look at all sinister. 'Do you want Flat 1?' she asked, smiling brightly.

'Yes.' Paul felt at loss but she was obviously expecting more. 'I was just going. I thought they must be out. Do you live there?'

'No. I live upstairs but I heard the bell,' she explained. 'I thought I'd better let you in, as they never hear it when they're in the kitchen. Their front door's just down the hall. There's another bell there.' Before he could explain or apologise, she vanished upstairs with another cheery grin.

He walked down the dark corridor until he found the front door of Flat 1. He rang the bell and waited. Again there was no reply. He rang once more. Still, there was no reply. The flat appeared to be empty. Suddenly, he realised that the door was not quite shut. Pushing cautiously, he opened it wide and went through into the tiny, inner hall, which was dark and smelt of damp. There were three doors opening off it. He stood still but there was no sound.

Turning the knob on the door at the end of hall, he silently pushed it open and found himself in what was clearly the living room of the flat. His first impression was that it was sparsely furnished and very squalid. Damp paper was peeling off the walls in several places and many of the ceiling tiles were coming loose. The discoloured, sagging armchairs and settee were so dirty and worn that it was difficult to discover their original colours. On a bare wooden table in the middle of the room there were the remains of a primitive meal. One of the mugs still contained coffee. Picking it up, Paul realised that it was slightly warm. Whoever they were, they were not far ahead of him.

'Good morning, Mr Tempest,' a soft voice spoke behind him. 'Would you by any chance be looking for your wife?'

Chapter Three

Startled, Paul spun round and stared at the man now standing in the doorway. Tall, dark-haired, thirtyish, he appeared to be amused by Paul's reaction. His black casual clothes and his watchful eyes gave him a sombre air which his smile and easy manner of speech seemed to contradict. He advanced a little into the room. 'Sorry to have shocked you but I couldn't resist the touch of drama. Nevertheless, I am right, aren't I? You are Paul Tempest?'

Angry and suspicious, Paul stepped towards him, then stopped. 'What do you want? What are you doing here?'

'I'm looking for your wife too. And I have a strong suspicion that we're both just too late.'

'Who the devil are you?'

Ignoring the question, the stranger walked across the room and opened the door to the kitchen. 'Perhaps we should make sure,' he suggested cheerfully, 'that the birds really have flown.' He peered inside. 'Empty.' He strolled across the room to a third door and opened it. 'The bedroom, I imagine. A bit basic but likewise empty.'

Angry and apprehensive though he was, Paul walked across the room and looked over his shoulder into a cold, damp square of a room. Sparsely furnished with a bed, one chair, a battered chest of drawers and one threadbare rug on the bare boards, it was cold and comfortless. He turned away.

'Depressing, isn't it?' the stranger commented. 'No useful clues either. I suppose we'd better try the bathroom.' He opened yet another door. 'Empty too, thank God! I never like the idea of bodies in the bath.' Apparently deciding to investigate further, he wandered out of sight.

Determined not to follow him this time, Paul retreated to the living room and waited for the stranger to come back, which he soon did still smiling slightly. 'Sorry, no help there either.'

'Who are you? And what the hell has it got to do with you?' Although he resented this man, he did not think he was menacing.

'There isn't time to go into that now,' the other man replied quickly. 'If your wife and Reardon have not been long gone, as this coffee cup seems to indicate, then it's a safe bet that the others aren't far behind. We don't want to meet them – embarrassing to say the least.' He looked quickly around. 'I suggest we make our escape speedily through the kitchen door.' Even as he finished speaking, there was an impatient ring of the porch doorbell. 'What did I say? They're far too quick on their cues. Come on.' He seized Paul's arm. 'There's no time to argue now. I'll explain later.'

Roused by the urgency of his tone, Paul allowed himself to be led into the kitchen, through the unlocked back door, down some steps and into the overgrown garden. They raced down the garden, jumped the low wall and in a few minutes were safely in a completely different street.

'It's a good job I turned up when I did,' the stranger remarked, 'otherwise it might have been tricky for you. By the way, I'm Bill Stephens, a journalist working for the *Daily News*.'

'I should've guessed!' That was his final humiliation, Paul thought. He had missed Judith, had no idea where to look for her and now he had fallen into the hands of the popular press. 'I suppose you think you've got a good story now?'

'Let's leave that for now,' Bill answered quickly. 'We mustn't stand here talking. We'd better make for the tube, don't you think?' Having no better idea, Paul made no objection. 'What are you thinking of doing now?' Bill asked.

'I'm hardly likely to tell you, am I?'

Bill laughed. 'Fair enough, but you don't need to worry. I've no desire at present to make your story known. I'm too busy collecting material for a series of articles on terrorist activities in London, so you can trust me – for the present, that is.'

'I see no reason why I should. How do I know you are who you say you are?'

Stopping short, Bill, still smiling, pulled a slim wallet out of an inner pocket. 'Satisfy yourself. Here's my press card.' He handed it to Paul. 'Take a good look.'

Paul did and then handed it back. They resumed their hasty progress. 'One thing still bothers me. How did you manage to turn up at the flat, right on my heels?'

'Pure luck! The luck that makes a successful journalist. I followed up some odd information and there you were.'

'But how did you know who I was?'

Bill laughed. 'I wasn't sure but it made a good entry. So I've levelled with you. How about you levelling with me?' He stopped as they were approaching the entry to the Underground station. 'What are you planning to do now? Perhaps I can help?'

'The truth is,' Paul admitted reluctantly, 'I haven't the faintest idea. I came to find Judith. I had one clue but I was too late and now I have no idea where she might be. It seems that I have no alternative but to go home and wait to see if she gets in touch with me.'

'Nonsense. You can't give up like that. She may need your help.' He paused and looked thoughtfully at Paul for a moment and then appeared to make a decision. 'I tell you what. You come back with me to my flat. We can talk more freely there. I have my sources, as I said. I may be able to find out something useful. What do you say?'

Depressed and bewildered, Paul did not know how to reply. 'I don't know. Judith probably doesn't want me anyway.'

'You can't be sure of that, so why not see what I can do? We'll have a drink and a chat and I'll make a few calls. Katy, my girlfriend, who is a brilliant cook, will make us lunch and then you can decide. Euston is less than half an hour away.'

It would have been churlish to refuse and he could not resist a chance, however slight, to discover Judith and the truth. While Paul queued for a ticket, Bill never one to waste time, made a couple of calls on his mobile which seemed to please him, although he made no comment.

About thirty-five minutes and two changes later, Paul found himself in a completely different part of London. They stopped outside a large house, obviously divided into flats. Bill's flat, on the second floor, was reached by well-carpeted stairs.

As they entered the hall, a woman's voice called out, 'Is that you, Bill? I expected you about half an hour ago.'

'Sorry, Katy, I was delayed. I've brought a friend for lunch, if that's okay?'

As he finished speaking Katy appeared. Small and slim with short fair hair, fashionably cut and styled, she was wearing tight-fitting black trousers with a vivid cerise-coloured shirt. As she smiled up at him, Paul noticed that her eyes were quite beautiful, deep brown with unusually long lashes.

Bill introduced them as he led the way into his large comfortable living room. He threw himself into one of the leather armchairs and waved Paul to another. 'We've had a somewhat disturbing time,' he told Katy, who was perched on the arm of another chair. 'Even had to run for our lives at one point.'

'Well, it seems you made it.' Katy stood. 'I was going to suggest coffee but, perhaps under the circumstances, something stronger might be more appreciated.' She seemed unmoved by the thought of Bill's possible danger.

'Unfeeling as always,' Bill remarked. 'I suppose you're so blasé, you don't even want to hear the story?'

'Of course, I do but it can wait until we've got something to drink. So what is it to be?'

'Coffee would be fine,' Bill decided. 'How about you, Paul?'

'Coffee, please, strong and black.'

Katy moved towards the door, then stopped. 'Assistance required, Bill. You know our agreement.' With a groan, Bill stood up and followed her to the kitchen.

Left to himself, Paul looked curiously around the large room. It gave an impression of bachelor comfort. Most of the walls were covered with shelves full of books and there were several relaxing chairs and reading lamps scattered around. The most impressive piece of furniture was an antique walnut desk which was so polished and free from clutter that it was clear that Bill did not work in this room. If Katy lived here, there was certainly no sign of her, so she probably didn't. Turning away, he sat down again, suddenly overwhelmed by depressing thoughts. He had failed and there seemed to be little Bill could do.

'Coffee, at last,' Katy announced in her clear, bright voice, as she came through the door, carrying the cafetiere and followed by

Bill with a tray. As soon as she had dispensed three steaming mugs of black coffee, she sat down, obviously prepared to hear their story.

'I don't know how much Paul wants to tell,' Bill commented. 'It's really his story, not mine.'

'I don't believe it,' Katy was smiling wickedly, 'such amazing delicacy on your part, Bill! I can hardly credit it!' Before Bill could reply she turned to Paul. 'However I'll abide by your decision.'

Paul looked at her. 'I'd be glad to know what you think about it. You might understand Judith better than I do'

'And I would like to hear the beginning,' Bill said. Katy looked at him. 'It's all right, I've no wish to use it – not at present anyway.'

It was simpler to tell than Paul had imagined; there was so little he really knew.

'And where do you come in?' Katy suddenly asked Bill.

'I was just following certain information I'd been given in the last few days. You know I'm working on this terrorist story. I heard about Lawrence Reardon picking up again with his one time girlfriend, who surprisingly was the wife of a solicitor, Paul Tempest. I was told they might be at the address where I met Paul and I thought it might be an interesting story. However, it wasn't quite as I expected.' He shrugged, then stood up. 'I'll go and make some of those calls I promised, Paul.'

'And I'd better add a few more vegetables to the casserole.' Katy collected the mugs on the tray and handed it to Paul. 'Visitors are expected to help, I'm afraid, especially when Bill is busy, as usual.'

'That's fine by me'. Paul picked up the tray and followed her into the kitchen where she offered him a vegetable knife. 'Are you a journalist, too?'

'No. I'm a chemist, doing research for a PhD and supporting myself with a little lecturing and marking. I don't live with Bill. I'm a friend, not a girlfriend, although it was different a few months ago but we split up amicably. I always like to get things clear,' she added, seeing that Paul looked a little surprised at her frankness. 'Don't you?'

'I don't think it's ever bothered me much. It certainly didn't when I first met Judith. I was quite sure that she was the person I wanted to marry and all I wanted to know was whether she felt the same. She did, apparently, and so we married.'

'Were you happy?'

'Very – until yesterday. I was very naive, I suppose. She told me nothing about her earlier life and I never worried about it.'

'Did it really matter? After all, you had six happy years and as I read somewhere, "The joys I have possessed, in spite of fate, are mine." It seems to me that you can't assume either that she has run off with Reardon in a fit of mad passion. It doesn't sound quite like that, somehow. Still, I don't think I should interfere, except to warn you against letting your naiveté extend to Bill.'

'Thank you for those words of consolation. It's the first cheering thing anyone has said to me. But what do you mean about Bill?'

'Simply that he's a complex person and a damned good journalist but you should never trust him entirely. I discovered for myself that he always had his own agenda – hence the separation. On the other hand, I'm sure that he can help you now and will, whatever his reasons.' She took the casserole from the oven, added the extra vegetables, put the dish back and shut the oven door firmly. 'It will be ready soon.' She led him back to the living room where Bill was now studying the paper.

Bill looked up as they came in. 'I've got some news. I shall need to follow it up. I'm expecting another call first. I hope lunch won't be long.'

'Ready in about twenty minutes.' Katy gave him an odd look.

It was just as they were ending lunch, which had been one of strained silences, punctuated with supposedly light-hearted badinage, that Bill's mobile rang. He took the call in the hall but quickly came back. 'One of my calls has borne fruit,' he announced cheerfully. 'I've got to meet someone now.' He picked up his jacket.

'When will you be back?' Katy asked. 'I really can't stay much longer, as you know.'

'I shouldn't be longer than an hour, probably less. But you don't have to worry. Paul can look after himself, I'm sure.' He turned towards Paul. 'I think I'm on to something. I hope to come back with some useful information. You're welcome to stay here, with or without Katy.'

'Thanks. I appreciate the trouble you're taking.'

Bill laughed. 'Don't waste your gratitude on me. I probably wouldn't be doing it if I didn't think there was something in it for me somewhere.' Putting on his jacket, he slipped his phone into his pocket and made for the door. 'See you soon with good news, I hope.' After a final wave, he slammed the door behind him.

Katy, who had been collecting the coffee cups, sat down suddenly and looked seriously at Paul. She hesitated for a moment and then decided to speak. 'I hope everything will be all right; I'm not at all sure.'

'What is worrying you? Are you afraid that Bill will bring bad news or that he's making a fool of me in some way?'

Again Katy hesitated before speaking. 'I don't usually interfere in other people's affairs. I've found it more sensible to keep myself as detached as possible. But it seems to me that you've had a terrible shock and could do with a trustworthy friend.'

'Then you really are trying to say that Bill isn't a trustworthy friend?'

'I don't know. I can't be sure. He is first of all a journalist, so you must be wary.'

'But there isn't anyone else, is there?' Paul felt and sounded defeated. 'If Bill won't help me, then I'll have to go home And I don't want to do that.'

'No, of course not. I can understand that.' Katy, having loaded up the tray, moved towards the kitchen. As she went through the door, she called out, 'Do you think Judith wants you to find her?'

Before he could reply, she disappeared. He waited, wondering what answer to give. He turned almost angrily towards her as she came back into the living room. 'What did you mean by that?'

'I should have thought that was obvious,' she replied coolly. 'It must have occurred to you. Why do you think she disappeared leaving you no clue? Surely, she was making it clear that she didn't want you to find her?'

'Perhaps. But may be she was under some kind of duress.' Before Katy could protest, he continued. 'You don't know her as I do. She has always been so loyal and loving. I must find her. I must find the truth.'

'And, if she doesn't want you, what then?'

'Then I'll go home. But I can't believe that is the truth. How can I after six happy years?'

'You've already discovered so much that she hadn't told you,' Katy reminded him.

'Why are you saying these things?' he demanded. 'They don't exactly help. And what has any of it got to with my trusting Bill, which is what we were talking about?'

'I suppose I was thinking that you are too ready to trust people; to believe what they say without questioning. Many people wear masks, you know. They are not always what they seem.'

'I do know that. If I didn't before, I'd be a complete fool not to have realised it by now. As I see it, I've got to trust Bill. There's no one else who can help me at the moment. Even you must see that. I don't even care if he intends to use me for a story in the end. That seems a small price to pay.'

Katy smiled at him. 'If that's so, go ahead, with my blessing. But, in case you do need a friend, without an axe to grind, I'll give you my mobile number and my address.' She took a notebook out of her handbag, scribbled them on a page, then tore it out and handed it to him. 'My flatmate's in the States for a couple of weeks, so I have a spare room if you should need it.'

Paul put the paper away in his wallet. 'Thanks. I'm very grateful, though I'm not sure why you're being so helpful.'

'Neither am I,' she answered lightly. 'Let's say I'm impressed with your courage and loyalty, both rare qualities these days.' She looked at her watch. 'I must go. Let me know what happens, even if you don't want my help.'

'I will,' he promised, 'and thanks again.'

The flat seemed very empty after she had left. He tried to settle down with a weekly political magazine which he read solidly from cover to cover. He looked at his watch. Surely, Bill should have been back by now. He tried to find something else to read but, as the minutes ticked by, his feeling of tension increased.

Unexpectedly, the front door bell rang. He hesitated, wondering whether or not to answer it. It rang again, more imperiously. He walked slowly down the hall. Someone called out. 'Hurry up, Bill. I haven't got all day.' It must be a friend of Bill's. As soon as he opened the front door, he realised his mistake. He had seen these three men before.

As they pushed their way in, it was the one who had spoken the night before who spoke again, mockingly. 'Did you think you had escaped us, Mr Tempest? It's a pity you didn't take my advice last night. But since you didn't, perhaps we'd better take you with us.'

Paul turned and ran down the hall. Blundering through the living room door, he slammed it behind him, turning the key. He hoped he might be able to telephone before they reached him. But it was useless. Even as he felt for his phone, the door was pushed, the lock broken. His hand was grasped and the same cold voice spoke again. 'Don't try anything foolish, Mr Tempest. You don't seem to realise that we're not playing games.'

Paul stared at the spokesman. He was tall, thin, dark-haired and dark-eyed and he spoke with a slight accent. The other two were obviously brothers, shorter, thicker with light brown hair and both were smiling in anticipation. But the dark man was not smiling. His slightly protuberant eyes fixed Paul with an intense, curiously bright gaze. His voice was soft and unemotional.

'What do you want?' Paul demanded.

'We want to find your wife and her companion,' the dark man replied.

'I don't know where they are. And if I did, I wouldn't tell you.' His attempt at defiance sounded futile even to himself.

The two brothers laughed but the dark man neither moved nor changed his expression. 'Don't waste your breath, Mr Tempest,' he said finally, as he loosened his grip on Paul's arm. 'If you're not afraid of us, you ought to be. Sudden death and little things like that don't bother us. You ought to go back where you belong.'

'And if I don't intend to?'

'If that's your last word, then we have no alternative except to take you with us. Once your wife knows we have you – and we'll make sure that the news reaches her – she'll come out of hiding and Reardon will follow her. Of course, you couldn't know it, but it would have been better if you'd stayed at home like a good, little boy. Now just come quietly. It'll be best for everyone.' He released his grip on Paul and then motioned to the other two.

Paul realised that they were quite relaxed because they considered him a weakling incapable of further resistance. But they had underestimated his love for Judith. He could not calmly acquiesce in this treachery. He rushed to the window behind him. His only thought to attract attention. It was locked but he was able to bang on it and shout, just as the dark man reached him. He struggled violently against the brutal grip and managed to shout again. Suddenly, one of the two brothers, standing at the door, called out, 'Someone's coming.' At the same moment a flash of pain blinded him. He felt himself slipping and falling into a gulf of blackness.

Chapter Four

'Paul, Paul, are you all right?' The words seemed to reach him from a long way off. He struggled to reply but the effort seemed too great and it was much easier to sink back into oblivion. 'Paul, for God's sake!' The woman's voice was calling him back urgently. It wouldn't let him escape. With a terrible effort, he opened his eyes and found himself looking into the face of Katy Evans.

'Where am I?' He seemed for some ridiculous reason to be lying on the floor. Whose floor? And how did he come to be there?

'In Bill's flat, of course. But what has happened?'

He struggled to raise himself a little as Katy slipped an arm under his shoulders. A blinding pain shot through his head. He groaned and shut his eyes again, grateful for Katy's supporting arm. After a moment, he risked opening his eyes once more. 'How do you come to be here?' He tried to look around. 'Where are the three men? Did you see them? I thought you'd gone.'

'I had but I've come back, just in time apparently. Now, don't try to talk any more until we've got you up on to the couch.' It was very difficult but Katy was both strong and determined and somehow with her help he managed to get himself on to the couch. He sank back immediately and waited for the agony in his head to subside and for the room to settle down again.

In the meantime, Katy had disappeared but, before he could wonder at this, she reappeared with a glass of water and some tablets. 'Do you think you can take these?' she asked anxiously. 'They're very strong and should do you good.'

He felt he might be sick but, ignoring the nausea, he forced them down and waited. Thankfully, he wasn't sick and after a few moments the pain began to lessen. Finally, he opened his eyes.

'How do you feel now?' Katy asked. She observed him. 'I think I'd better get you some brandy.' She went away and came back with a generous helping. The spirit revived him and he managed to sit up a little. 'Do you think you'll be able to move soon? Because I don't think we should stay here much longer.'

'I'll be all right in a few minutes.' He was puzzled, wondering how much was real. 'Did you see the three men?'

'Yes, it was me who disturbed them. I came up the stairs with a neighbour who lives opposite. We saw that Bill's front door was open, which seemed odd. Then we thought we heard someone shout. I rang the bell very loudly and Mark went into the hall, calling out to Bill. Suddenly, three men came rushing out. They pushed past us and disappeared. Mark chased after them and I came in and found you. I suppose they were the same three men who came to your house?'

'Yes.' As briefly as possible he told her what happened. 'I suppose Mark didn't catch them?'

'No, and I told him not to bother any more. I didn't think you'd want the police around. I suggested they might be some of Bill's less desirable contacts. How do you feel now?' She looked and sounded anxious.

'Better than at first but still lousy. Why?'

'I'm just hoping you'll be able to move soon. I don't think we should stay here much longer.'

He sat up slowly and cautiously. 'Give me a few minutes. Tell me, why did you come back?'

'Intuition, I suppose. I suddenly felt very worried. I am well aware of Bill's facility for disappearing for hours and it seemed to me those three men were too close for comfort. It seems I was right.'

'You definitely were and I can't say how grateful I am that you did.'

'Forget it. The thing is we must go now.' She picked up his jacket and brought it to him. 'Do you think you can get into this if I help you?'

It wasn't easy but he did and finally managed to stand up, clutching Katy. When the room had settled down again, he looked at her curiously. 'Are you still very worried then? Why?'

'I think they are very determined and ruthless and I think you need to disappear as quickly as possible.' She seemed to have no doubts.

'Shouldn't I wait for Bill?'

'No.' She spoke without hesitation. 'I've learned not to trust Bill too much. In the end it's always the story that counts most with him.'

'But, surely, you don't think that Bill had anything to do with it?'

She shrugged. 'I'm not making any accusations but I can't help wondering how they knew you were here.'

'Perhaps they've been following me?'

'Perhaps. But I still think we should get away from here without wasting any more time. It may be the result of some shady deal Bill's made, although he may not have expected them to come here. It's not the first time Bill's made an error of judgement. It's more likely though that he didn't care as long as he got his story. That's the way he is.'

'Do you really believe that?'

'Well, it could be, couldn't it? At least I don't think you should take any more chances. So, for God's sake, let's go – now.'

'Where do you suggest I should go?'

'My flat, of course. If we take the back way out of here, we can take a roundabout route to the Underground. Mark will keep watch at the front, if I ask him.'

'But, if I leave here, I won't be able to get any more information from Bill.' He tried painfully to make a decision.

'What information do you expect to get from him?' Katy began to lead him impatiently towards the door.

'I don't know but he said he would help me. After all, we don't know that it was because of Bill that they came here.'

'We can't afford to waste any more time arguing.' Katy pulled him towards the door. 'Come to my flat first where you should, at least, be safe. We can talk it out then.'

Paul came to a stop in front of the door. 'I can't really think straight, I know, but I've got to find Judith. And Bill's my only hope.'

Katy made a quick decision. 'Come now, at once and I'll leave a message for Bill asking him to ring me.'

'But will he?'

'Sure to. When he discovers you've disappeared, he'll be anxious to find out if I know anything.' Bill's mobile appeared to be switched off, so she hastily scribbled a note and left it propped on his desk in a prominent position.

The journey to Katy's flat seemed to pass like a nightmare. Paul's head ached intolerably and he seemed incapable of coherent thought. He allowed Katy to lead him without question. Her flat was on the second floor of a tall, Victorian terraced house in a quiet turning off a busy high street, somewhere south of the Thames, he guessed.

After leading the way into a large living room, she helped him off with his coat, and then arranged some cushions in a pile on the divan and helped him to lie down. He was only too ready to surrender to her mothering, watching idly while she turned on the gas fire and switched on the reading lamp. 'Take off your shoes and coat,' she ordered him, 'and put this cover over you. The best thing you can do is to rest until you feel fitter, then we'll consider what's best to do.'

His longing for sleep was far too great for him to wish to argue with her. His eyes closed and he drifted off into a welcome sleep, comfortably aware of her friendly presence. In the meantime, Katy settled at her desk by the reading lamp and tried to involve herself in some calculations. She found it difficult, however, not to question her own recent, impulsive actions. Why had she acted in such a way, so contrary to her usual policy of non-involvement? Was it simply her resentment of Bill's casual behaviour, which she had so often experienced herself? Or was it that Paul himself attracted her? That would certainly be ridiculous since he was so obviously devoted to the strangely missing Judith. No, she finally decided it was the puzzle that attracted her, as scientific puzzles attracted her. What was the truth about Judith? At this point she resolutely put aside all such questions and returned firmly to her work.

It was the ringing of her bell which disturbed her about an hour later. She tiptoed across the room, but whoever it was, had slipped into the porch and could not be seen. The bell rang again.

Paul stirred and sat up. 'What's that?' he asked.

'It's only my front door bell. Someone has decided to drop in but don't worry, I'll soon get rid of, whoever it is.' She went quickly out of the room, ran down the stairs and along the narrow, dark hall, as the bell rang again. Opening the door impatiently, she found herself confronting Bill.

'Hello, Katy,' he greeted her cheerfully. 'I got your note.'

'I asked you to ring me. I didn't expect you to land on my doorstep.'

'Don't tell me that I've arrived at an embarrassing moment.' He grinned wickedly at her.

'Of course not. Don't be silly.' She reluctantly opened the door more widely so that he could enter.

He faced her. 'I came because I thought you wanted to talk to me. If you didn't why did you ask me to ring you?'

Prevarication was stupid and would get her nowhere. 'I do want to speak to you.' She hesitated for a moment. 'It's about Paul.'

'I hoped it might be. Do you know he's disappeared? Or did that happen after you left?'

'When did you get back?' she asked him, ignoring his question.

'About an hour ago.' He was clearly impatient. 'I found the flat empty, saw your note and came straight to see you, hoping you might have some news. I thought, in fact, that you might have decided to bring him here for some reason. Am I right?'

She was still unsure how far she could trust him. 'You were a long time away. What were you doing?'

'Trying to get information. What do you think? And meeting some unpleasant characters on the way. What's all this about, Katy? I don't want to waste time. If you haven't got Paul and don't know where he is, just tell me and I'll go.'

'And do what?'

'Look for him, of course. What the hell else? I've got some information he might be glad to have. What's come over you?'

'I just wondering what really matters to you – Paul or the story?'

'Both naturally.' He gripped her by the shoulders. 'Do you know where he is or not?'

'I do.' She pulled herself away. 'I'm simply wondering

whether it's in his interest for you to know.'

'And what is that supposed to mean?' He stared at her, his dark eyes flashing under his heavy brows, his mouth and chin stubbornly set. He could be a formidable opponent, she knew, especially when he kept his anger firmly under control. 'Am I getting the right message here? Have you suddenly cast me as the villain? Why?'

'Come into the kitchen,' she replied, after a moment's hesitation, 'we can talk there.' He followed her quickly up the stairs and into her kitchen. 'How about a cup of coffee?'

He shrugged. 'If you say so.' He sat at the table, watching her while she filled the kettle and spooned the coffee into two mugs. His silence unnerved her. When the kettle boiled, he stood up before she could and filled the mugs, then he looked directly at her. 'It's time for you to stop playing games. What's worrying you?'

'You were away so long,' she answered finally, 'and, while you were away, something happened. I came back just in time to prevent worse.' She paused.

'You'd better explain.'

'The three men turned up, forced their way into the flat, attacked Paul and threatened to abduct him. I turned up just in time with Mark, whom I met on the stairs, and they ran away, leaving Paul unconscious on the floor.'

'So? What has that to do with me?'

'How did they know he was in your flat?' She stared fixedly at him.

'You think I went off and informed them?' He laughed. 'And I thought we were friends! Why would I do that?'

'In return for information perhaps? You have done things before which I've considered wrong.'

'I don't deny it but not this time. I promised Paul to help him and I mean to as far as I can. Perhaps I gave too much away to the wrong person. It's hard to know sometimes. Can I put the matter to Paul himself? Or don't you actually know where he is?'

'He's here in my living room. He's been resting on my divan.'

Bill put down his mug and stood up. 'I'll go and have a word with him then, if you can trust me. Or have you persuaded him not to see me?'

'Of course not. I'm sorry, Bill. It all seems so confusing.' She went ahead of him and, as she opened the living room door, she called out, 'It's Bill, Paul. I think he has something to tell you.'

'If you can trust me, that is,' Bill added as he followed her. 'As far as I know, no three men are following me, but I'm beginning to wonder myself.'

Paul, tall and slim, was standing in front of the fire. He was very pale, his fair hair was tousled and his blue eyes still had an almost vacant look. He was obviously struggling and looked no match, Katy thought, for Bill. He managed a smile, however, as he came to meet Bill. 'Did you manage to get any information?'

Bill looked very directly at him. 'Are you sure you can trust me? If not, I'll just go quietly away.'

'Of course I am. You're my only hope.'

'You're not dealing with nice people. Be warned, Paul. In fact, one bloke told me to tell you to go home and forget it all and they wouldn't bother you any more, or so he said. What do you think?'

For a moment, Paul hesitated, then he replied firmly, 'No way. I came to find Judith and I'm not going back without achieving that. Have you anything else to tell me?'

'Only this and I'm not sure how much it's worth.' He took a folded piece of paper out of a pocket and handed it to Paul. 'Open that and you'll find a phone number written on it. If you ring that number, Paddy should answer and when you tell him who you are he will tell you how to get in touch with Judith, or so I'm told. It might be a double-cross, of course. It doesn't come with any guarantee – certainly not mine.'

For a moment, Paul stared at the paper, then at Bill. He seemed undecided what to do.

'Open it,' Katy urged.

When he still seemed undecided, Bill added casually, 'It can't do any harm to open it. The difficult bit comes next, when you have to decide what to do.'

Opening the paper slowly, Paul studied it for a moment, then refolded it and put it in his pocket. 'Thanks, Bill. That's more than I expected. I'll ring him now. If you don't mind, I'll withdraw to the kitchen, Katy.' As she nodded her agreement, he moved towards the door, only stopping to take his phone from his jacket pocket.

'Remember,' Bill warned, 'it doesn't come with any guarantee. There's nothing straightforward in this business.'

'You mean I could endanger Judith?'

'Possibly or more likely yourself. Don't forget your friendly followers. They are always too close for comfort.'

Paul scarcely paused. 'I understand what you're saying but I must try it. It's the only hope I've got.' He was gone.

'Well, you're not exactly encouraging,' Katy exclaimed.

'There's no reason why I should be. In fact, it's probably better, if I'm not.' For the first time since he had entered the room, Bill sat down. 'Christ, I'm tired.' He leaned back in the armchair and stared moodily at the fire. Katy looked at him with some concern. This was so unlike the Bill she knew.

'Would you like a sherry? Or better still a brandy?' Without waiting for his reply, she went to her cupboard and quickly came back with small glass filled with amber liquid. 'I think this is a brandy occasion. It's more comforting.'

Bill accepted it from her with a slightly mocking smile. 'Good old Katy! Always trying to make things better or, at least, to make them seem normal. I can't help thinking that a frustrated mother lurks somewhere behind that ambitious professional woman's cool exterior.'

'Don't be absurd! Why can't you just accept a simple friendly action?'

'Because in my experience few things are ever simple, even if they seem to be.' He emptied his glass and handed it back to her. 'It's a noble ideal, Katy, but not all broken hearts can be stuck together with sellotape.'

'Don't try to tell me you have a broken heart because I won't believe it.'

'Not broken, just shattered.'

It was not the words but the tone which aroused her concern. 'What's the matter? It seems you've got a great story in your grasp. You ought to be on top of the world. Why aren't you?'

'Even I...' he began to answer then stopped. 'It's not my favourite kind of story. I'd almost rather leave it but I can't.'

'Don't tell me you have serious scruples,' she began, then stopped as Paul came back into the room. 'Did you get him? Did he give you some useful information?' Bill said nothing, she noticed.

'Yes.' Paul seemed jubilant. 'Far more than I expected. He not only gave me Judith's number but also told me to ring her straight away. I can't thank you enough, Bill. I shouldn't have got anywhere without you.'

'What did she have to tell you?' was Bill's only reply.

'She was very cool but then Judith always is. She said she wished I had stayed at home or that I would go back because it would be better for me. I said I wouldn't do that before I had at least seen her and talked to her. She agreed that was fair and then agreed to meet me.'

'That's marvellous!' Katy exclaimed. 'When?'

'Tonight at nine o'clock.'

'I presume she gave you an address?' Bill asked.

Paul hesitated. 'Yes, but I'm afraid she made me promise not let anyone else have it. I'm sorry, Bill.'

Bill stood up and stretched. 'Very sensible of her. It's a wise person who knows his real friends, don't you agree?'

There was an uncomfortable pause. Katy looked at her watch. 'At least we have time for a meal before you have to go. It'll do you good to eat something.'

Bill laughed and put an arm around her. 'Dear old Katy always hoping that a drink or a meal will solve the world's problems. You mustn't disappoint her, Paul.'

'I've no intention of doing so. I'm too grateful to her for everything.' He smiled at her.

For a moment no one moved, then Katy suggested briskly, 'If we are going to have a meal, you two had better realise that you're expected to help. I know it suits Bill sometimes to represent me as a kind of earth mother but, I'm afraid it's only one of his journalistic fantasies.' She moved towards the door.

'Well, I tried,' Bill said, 'but it looks as if we shall have to submit to cruel necessity, Paul, and accept humble kitchen duties.'

'Do you know how to get to wherever it is?' Bill asked suddenly towards the end of a meal during which they had all carefully avoided any mention of what lay ahead. 'Or can we give you some help? If you don't trust me, I'm sure Katy is perfectly reliable and cannot be suspected of having any possible advantage to gain.' He smiled but his tone was unfriendly.

Paul flushed. 'Judith gave me some directions and I have my A–Z. I don't mean to annoy you Bill. I don't have any suspicions. It's just that I think I should keep my word to Judith.'

'Of course you should,' Katy said quickly.

'What about your three far from amiable followers?' Bill asked. 'Aren't you worried about exposing not only yourself but also Judith to them? They never seem to be far away.'

'There seems to be nothing I can do about them,' Paul replied slowly. He was clearly worried. 'Judith seems to think there should be no danger, if I am careful, and I shall certainly try to be.'

'Well, there seems to be nothing more to say.' Bill turned towards Katy. 'Unless you have any ideas?'

'None, I'm afraid.' Katy stood up. 'I can only suggest that Paul has a stimulating cup of coffee before he goes.'

Bill also stood up. 'Leave that to me. I'll do it while you stack the dishes. Paul may prefer to talk to you, in private. And we certainly can't let the condemned man go without a final friendly cup.' He departed quickly to the kitchen.

'I'm afraid I've annoyed Bill,' Paul said miserably to Katy. 'And I can't really blame him, especially when he's done so much for me and I must seem so ungrateful and suspicious.'

'Don't let it worry you too much,' Katy tried to reassure him. 'It's just that Bill hates letting go of a story, even though he's agreed to for the time being.' But she was puzzled. Bill's mood was strange and she was afraid of further difficulties, for she knew how ruthless he could be. She turned to Paul. 'Aren't you scared? After all that has happened?'

'Very. But I don't see what else I can do? I must see Judith and help her if I can.'

'Is that all you feel?' Katy could not stop herself from asking this. 'You don't have to answer,' she added quickly.

'Why shouldn't I tell you? Yes, I'm angry and jealous because of Reardon. And I want to know the truth, wouldn't you?'

Bill's return with coffee cups prevented her from replying. To her relief he seemed to have regained his good humour and made no further comments about Paul's departure, except to check that he had the address and map.

'I suppose you think I'm mad dashing off like this,' Paul asked, looking chiefly at Bill.

'Every man is entitled to his own form of madness,' Bill replied agreeably.

'The truth is,' Paul tried to explain with some embarrassment but considerable determination, 'although it may seem difficult for you to believe now, Judith and I have always been tremendously happy. I have no idea why this should have happened but I love her completely and I trust her.'

'Even after this disappearance with Reardon?' Bill asked.

'Yes, even after that. I'm sure there must be some good explanation.'

'I hope so,' Bill said evenly. 'And may the blessings of the gods be with you.' He looked at his watch. 'I think if my calculations are not too much in error, it's time you should be leaving.'

'I'm afraid you're right.' Paul stood up and took Katy's hand in his. 'Thank you, Katy, for everything.'

Impulsively, she kissed him. 'Take care and let me know what happens. There's a bed here if you want it. Just keep in touch.'

'I certainly will.' He turned towards Bill. 'Thanks again, Bill. I'll be in touch.'

'I shall make sure of that,' Bill smiled a little sardonically. 'I shall be claiming my pound of flesh, don't forget.'

Paul smiled back, then with a last wave he was gone.

'You have actually managed to surprise me, Bill,' Katy exclaimed as they listened to Paul running down the stairs and heard the street door close.

'How so?'

'You've let a possibly great story slip through your fingers without making any attempt to retain control. Is it possible that you're getting soft or,' she looked suspiciously at him, 'do you know something I don't?'

'Leave it, Katy.' Bill sat down. 'Is there a chance of another brandy?'

'You know my maternal fondness won't let me refuse you that.' She laughed, expecting some light-hearted response from him. To her surprise there was none. He merely watched her silently as she poured out the drink and not until he had tasted it did he respond and then not as she had expected. 'It's a story that goes back a long way and it's not one I particularly like. It had a bloody beginning and may well have a bloody end.' He took a further sip of his drink and leaned back.

'Bill? She felt afraid again.

'Don't ask any questions, Katy. I'm not in the mood for them, nor am I willing to answer them. Just say a prayer for Paul, if you still believe in such things.'

Katy stared at him. 'Why are you talking like this? I don't understand you.'

'It's probably better if you don't.'

Chapter Five

Paul walked briskly along the busy high street towards the Underground. Rain was falling quite heavily now but the Saturday evening crowds still hurried past him seeking their pleasures. The brightness of the many lights coming from all directions and intensified by the rain dazzled him, while the mingled noises of cars, buses and people intent on celebration almost overwhelmed him. He was not used to this. Thankfully, he passed into the dimly lit entrance, paused to get a ticket then hurried down the steps to catch his train, which was just pulling in.

Sitting back in the almost empty carriage he had for the first time since he had arrived in London a chance to consider all that had happened. He was soon to meet Judith. This was what he had set out determined to achieve – to find her and to talk to her. Now he was about to do it, he did not feel the happiness he had naively expected. She had seemed so unemotional and distant, as if he were an inconvenient stranger who had been pestering her and whom she was reluctantly agreeing to see so that the nuisance might end.

Suddenly, he was angry, jealous and hurt. He began to consider what he would say, how he could rightfully accuse her of deceiving and betraying him. Until he had spoken to her, it had been possible to believe that it was other people who were getting between them but her cool voice and distant manner had proved to him the unreality of this belief. Perhaps he was simply an immature idiot. He knew from his own professional experience that marriages often ended, that people changed. So why not Judith?

Even Bill who had put him in touch with her had seemed to think that it would be better for him not to bother. Then, what did he know about Bill? Why had he given a stranger so much help? Katy had suggested that Bill was not to be trusted when he was in pursuit of a story. Was she right? How could he know when he had no real knowledge of her? His thoughts returned to Judith. It was bitter indeed to think of her with another man. During the six years of their marriage he had come gradually to feel safe. Now all that was gone. So, how much did he really know Judith?

His head ached and he closed his eyes. He could no longer think of what he would say. He must wait until he saw her. Miserably he admitted to himself how he longed to see her and to be close to her. Was he so weak that he would simply take her back? Probably. What if she did not want to come back on any terms?

He alighted from the train at Russell Square and quickly found his way to the nearby square in which she was living. After a few minutes, he found himself outside the right house. A flight of stone steps led up to the front door. 'Flat One Marshall.' That was what Judith had said. He pressed the bell and waited. Suddenly, she was there framed in the doorway with the light behind her. She was wearing a long black skirt and a loose emerald green tunic, both of which he recognised. It was a shock to see her looking so familiar in these strange surroundings.

For a moment they simply looked gravely at each other and then, without a word or a smile, she motioned him to follow her. They came into what was obviously the main living room of the flat. He was dimly aware of a large comfortable room with heavy curtains and shelves of books but then his eyes focussed on Judith. She was as lovely as she had always been to him and as desirable. He moved close to her. 'You should have gone home,' she said. Her dark eyes were sad, she didn't smile.

'Why? There is no home for me without you, Judith.' As he watched tears came into her eyes and then dripped down her cheeks. He could not remember ever seeing her cry before. Shocked, he put an arm round her and offered her his handkerchief. In the train he had called her to himself 'bloody whore, and fucking bitch'; now he kissed her. What the hell is the matter with me, he thought? How could any man be so weak?

'You must be angry with me.' When he didn't move or answer, she, unexpectedly, returned his kiss. They were close and it

49

was as it had always been, exciting and stimulating. He felt his pulses throbbing and knew that she felt the same. He wanted to lie on the couch with her, take off her clothes, kissing and caressing her and then make love as they had done only two nights before and so often during their six years together.

Then the name Lawrence Reardon flashed into his mind. He pulled himself away. This was ridiculous. She had left him and gone away with another man. Those many wonderful nights and days together had not stopped her. 'You're either a devil or an angel,' he said angrily. 'I'm not sure which but it's probably the former.'

'You are angry and I can't blame you. Good people don't act as I have done. But then I'm not good.'

'Where is he? Your lover? Is he here? If so, we might as well invite him to join us.' He moved towards the door but she took hold of his arm and would not release it.

'He is here but he's asleep. In one thing you're wrong, Paul. He's not my lover – not now. Years ago he was, but not now.'

'Then why have you left me for him? Why are you here with him?' He tore himself away from her. 'I don't see why he should be peacefully sleeping. What sort of a man is he? Isn't he brave enough to face me? Perhaps, unlike you, he has a conscience.'

'Perhaps I'm here because I have a conscience. I thought I'd killed it but it's not an easy thing to do. We may not have much time, so at least let us talk a little before you have to go.'

His head was pounding again It was a nightmare. He sat down heavily on the divan and leaned forward, his head in his hands. Suddenly, the meaning of her last sentence hit him. He looked up at her. 'What do you mean, we may not have much time? Are you expecting visitors? My three followers perhaps?'

'Your three followers? Who are they?'

'How the hell should I know? But everywhere I go, they go. They came to our house on Friday evening to advise me to forget you, after they had failed to find you. They were close behind me in Finsbury Park and they discovered me in Bill Stephens's flat where they kindly hit me on the head, presumably to enforce their message, although I'm not quite sure what it is. They are rather enigmatic, in fact.'

'Perhaps they are the Fates come to warn you of your doom if you insist on knowing me.'

'And Inspector Barrett who came before them on Friday evening.'

'A reminder of the law which you are supposed to uphold.'

'He seemed more concerned to remind you of something. He said you had agreed to meet him.'

'I had.'

'Was that why you went away?'

'I didn't want to meet him but I would have gone away even if he hadn't come. I had already decided that.'

'And when had you decided that? And why didn't you think it was necessary just to mention it to me? Or did you think it was possible that I might not miss you? Good God, Judith what sort of a monster are you?' He stared at her, struggling to control his anger. He wanted to hurt her.

She didn't turn away from his angry looks. There were no tears now. 'To answer your first question I decided to go away when Maeve phoned and told me that Lawrence was coming to England and was determined to see me. I knew I must see him and I didn't know how tell to you. It seemed to me that it was better for everyone, especially you, if you were not involved.' She sat down in the armchair opposite to him. 'I expect I do seem like a monster to you. Perhaps I am. I know I didn't behave very well. I suppose I panicked, especially when Inspector Barrett rang me up. He was bound to think the worst of me because I knew the Reardons.' She was not crying but she was very pale and her hands were tightly clasped as she stared at him.

'And what did you expect me to think, with you missing and then Barrett coming with his incredible story. Surely, it would have been better to have prepared me? Couldn't you trust me?'

'I should have done. I realise now it would have been better but I was afraid of losing your love. Afraid of what you might think when you heard of my friendship with Maeve and Lawrence. It was all long ago but...' She paused and gazed at him with her sorrowful, dark eyes.

He tried to ignore her appeal. 'So Inspector Barrett was right. Your friends are terrorists – murderers perhaps.'

'To you and many other English people but not everyone thinks of them in that way. It is surely a matter of your viewpoint. Some terrorists have become leaders of nations and their sins have been forgiven.'

'But your friends aren't numbered among those – as yet – are they? But frankly I don't care a damn about the politics at the moment. It's you I care about and your behaviour towards me, your husband. I trusted you. I even thought you loved me.'

'Of course I do. Surely you believe that? We've been so happy, how can you doubt it.'

'I didn't. That's why I came after you, even though Inspector Barrett warned me not to. I thought you might have been forced to leave me, in some way. But you weren't, were you?'

'It wasn't physical compulsion but I felt I ought to help the friends who had been kind to me one summer, twelve years ago, when my mother and I visited Northern Ireland to see her relatives.' Standing up suddenly, she came quickly across the room and knelt at his feet. 'Paul, darling, I didn't want you to be drawn into all of this because of my past acquaintances. I thought it might affect your career, that your family would be upset. Most English people know so little about Ireland. Can't you understand what I'm trying to say? It all seemed to happen so suddenly and I was terrified.'

'I suppose I can, although you never seemed to be the sort of emotional person who would panic.'

'That was because you only knew me when I was with you. You made me feel safe, before then I had nobody after my mother died. I told you she had left my father and he had married again, didn't I?'

'Yes, you did but I don't think I realised how much it had affected you, probably because I've always had such a secure life. I expect I've become a bit smug.'

'I had a sort of breakdown after her death. That's why I went to university a year late.' She smiled at him, that well-remembered smile. 'Kiss me, please Paul, then I'll know you still love me.'

Putting his arms around her, he lifted her up next to him and kissed her. She stroked his forehead. 'What a terrible bruise! Does your head still hurt?' She kissed the spot, then snuggled close to him. As he kissed her again and again, certain questions came into his mind but he pushed them away. There would be time for those. One, however, remained. 'What would have happened if I hadn't come after you? Would I have lost you for ever?'

'Don't be silly! I was going to phone you tonight and tell you I was coming back soon. I thought you would wait because of what Inspector Barrett had said.'

'How could you expect me to wait when I thought you might be in danger?' He leaned back suddenly, feeling dizzy and unbearably weary.

'What's the matter?' she asked anxiously. 'Are you ill?'

'It's probably just the effect of a blow on the head and shock. I expect I'll be all right after a good night's sleep.'

'Of course, that's what you want. I'm being terribly selfish, not thinking about all you've been through. Can I get you something?'

'A glass of water and some painkillers would help.' He tried to smile at her.

'Good. I won't be long.' He had scarcely shut his eyes or so it seemed when she was back. He took the painkillers and drank the water. 'Is there anything else I can get you?'

'A bed would be nice – particularly one with you.'

'Where were you going to spend the night? Haven't you got a bag somewhere? Or did you rush off without anything?'

It was very tiring to have all these questions, he thought, especially when he had told her what he wanted; nevertheless, he tried to answer. 'My bag is at Katy's flat.'

'Who is Katy? I don't think I know her.'

'I'm sure I must have mentioned her.' He began to feel confused once more. Judith seemed different again. Or was it his imagination? 'She's Bill's girlfriend who took me to her flat after I'd been knocked on the head. I rang you from there.'

'She's been extremely kind. But surely she's expecting you to go back, isn't she? Won't she be worried?'

'I don't think so. I don't imagine that she's that kind of person. She'll just assume that everything's gone well. But don't worry, Judith, I'm not insisting on a bed with or without you. As soon as the painkillers have taken effect, I'll make my way back. Shall I see you tomorrow'

'Do you want to?' She smiled at him. 'It isn't really necessary now, is it?'

'What do you mean?'

'We've said all that's important. I admit that I was very wrong to go as I did; I simply wanted to stop you from being involved in Lawrence's rather dubious activities. I wish I didn't have to be but he and Maeve are old friends and, although you may not like to admit it, you know that the police always suspect Irish people from Belfast. You know I love you. It would be better, perhaps, if you went home and waited for me.'

'I don't understand. How long am I supposed to wait?'

'Only until I've helped Lawrence to sort himself out a little.'

'He won't want to keep you from your husband for too long, will he?'

'Of course not. In any case I wouldn't allow it. You must know that. Now lie down for a bit.' She rearranged the cushions and persuaded him to lie back. 'You'll soon feel better.' She sat on the edge of the couch and stroked his forehead and hair with her cool, gentle fingers. Occasionally, she bent down and kissed him lightly. It was all very soothing and comforting. He took her free hand in his. The familiar Judith had come back.

Suddenly, he was roused by the sound of the door opening. 'What the fuck are you doing, Judy?' It was a man's voice, rich, musical and definitely Irish. Judith sat up, pulled her hand away and turned towards the door. 'Why the hell is this guy lying on the couch?'

With great difficulty and pain, Paul raised himself up a little and turned towards the door. A man standing in the doorway – clearly seen. Tall, broad, wearing blue jeans with an open-necked thick check shirt. Black hair, cut short but determined to curl. A strong face with good features but very pale. As he advanced further into the room, Paul lay back, feeling dizzy again.

'It's all right, Lawrence,' Judith replied quickly. 'It's only Paul. He's a friend. He came to see if he could help. He's a solicitor, you see. I got a message to him.'

'Sure and that's very friendly of you, Paul.' Lawrence came a little nearer. 'But why are you lying on the couch?'

Judith answered quickly before Paul could collect his still bewildered thoughts. 'Someone who doesn't seem to like us hit him on the head, rather hard.'

'Shit! That's real bad luck, Paul. Let me know if you want him hit back.'

'Thanks but I don't think I know him.' He tried to sit up again but pain stabbed his head and everything went blurred. 'I feel worse now than I did earlier.'

Lawrence came closer and looked at him carefully. 'That's delayed shock. Take it from one who knows.' He bent over Paul and touched the wound with a hand that was surprisingly gentle. It was the face of a hard man with deep lines but the brown eyes as they looked at Paul were surprisingly kind. 'I'm Lawrence, Lawrence Reardon, and you are?'

'Paul – Paul Tempest.' Paul waited for the reaction. There was none.

Lawrence straightened up. 'We'd better look after him, Judy. Make him comfortable.' Paul tried to protest but Lawrence ignored him firmly. 'You need sleep and quiet. Don't stand around, Judy. Fetch a spare duvet or something, while I take his shoes and jacket off.' Judith disappeared without a word. Paul found himself firmly but kindly dealt with.

He tried to resist. There was something he wanted to say but he was no longer quite sure what it was. 'You don't know me,' he managed to mutter, 'you ought...'

'Don't let that worry you. Judy says you're a friend. That's enough for me. Fuck, we don't want to lose a friend, we've too few, as it is.' The door opened once more. 'Give it to me, Judy. I've got more practice than you.'

'Good night, Paul.' The door closed behind Judith.

Paul gave up the struggle. The room seemed to be growing darker, even Laurence's face as he deftly tucked him up was growing indistinct. He closed his eyes. There was something wrong but he could no longer try to think about it.

'That's right. Relax.' Lawrence's voice was soothing. 'You'll feel better in the morning.'

It must have been several hours later when he awoke. The

55

room was very dark, only a little glimmer of street light came through the curtains. At first, he lay still wondering where he was. Gradually, memory came back to him. Slowly and cautiously, he raised himself up to a sitting position. He waited but there was no pain. His head was clear, he felt completely normal.

Groping his way to a light switch, he flooded the room with bright light. Even that had no effect on his head. His watch told him it was nearly five o'clock. The flat was completely silent. There was no need to think. He knew what he wanted to do. He must get away immediately without seeing Judith or Lawrence. He had to sort out his ideas first and he could not do that here. He put on his shoes and slipped into his jacket, making sure his wallet was still there. Being naturally methodical, he folded up the duvet and tidied up the cushions before he left the room, shutting the door quietly behind him.

Carefully, he felt his way to the front door, praying that it would open easily. It did. At last, he was in the empty, silent square. A few minutes' brisk walking brought him to the main road near the tube station. He hesitated for a moment, then decided to take a taxi, giving Katy's address. He must go there to get his bag, he told himself.

It was only when he paid off the taxi outside Katy's address that he realised it was still far too early to call on her. He wandered back to the high street where luckily he eventually found an all-night café. Lingering there, undisturbed, over a snack and several cups of tea, he tried at last to think clearly. The events of the night before flashed vividly through his mind, like a continuous loop of film, over and over while he tried to make sense of them but always he came back to one point – Judith had lied to him. Lawrence Reardon had never heard of him, did not recognise the name of Paul Tempest.

Perhaps he was exaggerating the importance of this? It might have been so if he had not always thought of Judith as an extremely honest person. It might be an unjust overreaction but he simply felt that he did not know her any more. Had he ever known her? His thoughts went round and round and it was a relief when his watch showed him that it was sufficiently late for him to approach Katy without annoying her too much. Perhaps, if he told her as a detached outsider, she might help him to find the truth.

Making his way resolutely back to her flat, he rang her bell without any hesitation.

Chapter Six

After a brief interval he heard someone hurrying down the stairs and along the hall. The door was flung open to reveal Katy, obviously fresh from her shower with damp hair and wearing a crimson towelling bath robe. 'Paul!' she exclaimed, before he could apologise for his early visit. 'Come in. How glad I am to see you. I'd begun to think something dire must have happened and so had Bill.'

'I'm sorry. I would have phoned last night but it wasn't possible,' he explained as he followed her up the stairs and into her living room. 'You'll understand when I tell you about it.'

'I'm sure I will but never mind now. You're just in time for breakfast and you look as if you could do with something.'

'I certainly could. I've been swilling tea for hours in a dingy little café and I could definitely do with something solid and a strong black coffee.' He looked round the comfortable warm room with pleasure. Here he could relax and take refuge from the cold and loneliness outside.

'Good. There's plenty of coffee. And what would you think of scrambled eggs on toast – lots of it?'

'Marvellous.'

'Sit down by the fire then and I'll go and tell the cook we need extra.'

'The cook?'

'Well, Bill actually. He stayed the night. But don't make any rash assumptions. Bill was unusually gloomy. Seemed to think he might have sent you to your doom and I was feeling nervous, so we cheered one another up. He'll be very relieved to know that you are safely back.' She hurried off to the kitchen.

Paul sat down and rejoiced in the cheerful warmth of the gas fire. What a wonderful welcome. He had only known these two for twenty-four hours and yet they seemed like old friends. How differently Judith had greeted him. He leaned back and closed his eyes. Bill and Katy would surely give him their opinion.

He was soon aroused by the smell of fresh coffee and the savour of scrambled eggs. It was a tasty breakfast expertly cooked by Bill who seemed unusually cheerful, relieved as he admitted to see Paul safely back. Finally, as they relaxed over more toast and marmalade Paul told his story. 'What do you think?' he asked them anxiously.

'It seems to me that you've outjudithed Judith,' Bill commented, smiling.

'What do you mean?' It was not the comment Paul had expected.

'I only mean that you in your turn left without a note or any other explanation. Which may be somewhat surprising to your hosts. Judith is now in the position you were in. She doesn't know where you are or even exactly why you have gone.'

Paul stared at him. 'It's strange but I never even thought of that. Do you think I was wrong then?'

'I can understand why you did it,' Katy said.

'But was it wrong?' Paul persisted.

'It rather depends on what you want to happen next,' Bill suggested. 'Do you know?'

'Not really. I was confused, I know, but even so it was clear enough to me that Judith was still lying, certainly to me and perhaps even to Lawrence. She did not introduce me as a her husband and it was obvious that he had no idea who I was and she did not intend to enlighten him.'

'She took a chance, don't you think?' Katy asked.

'I imagine she never expected Lawrence to turn up,' Bill said, 'and when he did she relied on Paul's chivalry.'

'More likely on my confused head. I more or less passed out soon afterwards. And when I woke up, all I wanted was to get away. I don't understand Judith at all. She was like two different persons, even last night. I hoped you might be able to help me, Bill.'

'Perhaps I can. I have some knowledge, which may be helpful, though some of it may not be what you want to hear.'

'I must know the truth before I decide.'

Bill stood up. 'I suggest you have a hot, leisurely bath and a shave to freshen yourself up and then I'll tell you what I know.'

'Thanks.' He too stood up. 'I expect you're right. I need that, if it's all right with you, Katy?'

'Of course.' She began to stack the breakfast dishes on the tray. As she moved towards the kitchen, Bill called out, 'Don't bother with the dishes now. I'd like to have a talk.' He sat down and picked up the Sunday paper as she and Paul both went out of the room.

When she came back, Katy sat down opposite him. 'There's something I'd like to ask you, Bill,' she said. 'Are you really on the level with Paul? Or is this part of your attempt to get a really big story? Because, if it is, I must refuse to help you.' She waited a little nervously for his reply.

'I've thought about this a lot during the last few hours.' He looked steadily at her. 'It was tempting because I knew I could make a big thing out of it. It's right up my street. I know more about Northern Ireland than most other journalists in London but, as I told you last night, it's not a story that I want to deal with. It would be a kind of betrayal for me. I know you haven't a very high opinion of my moral scruples. You made that clear when we parted. But you can trust me on this one. Do you believe me?'

She met his searching glance and smiled. 'I don't know exactly why I do, but I do.'

'I'm glad of that. I intend to tell Paul all the facts I know but only the facts, no rumours or assumptions. Do you think that is right? Or would you rather not be asked?'

'I'm glad you've asked me and I think you're right. You should only tell him what you know to be true. Will it upset him?'

'Possibly. But he can't make a proper decision without some knowledge. Now, before he comes back, I'd like to say something about us – about last night.'

'You don't have to. I'm not blaming you. We both wanted it and we both enjoyed it. But I haven't changed my mind and I don't want to tie you down or try to interfere with your career. Nor do I want you to interfere with my career. Perhaps we should go back to being friends.'

'Certainly, if that's what you wish. I hope you may change your mind at some time.'

'I've been offered an interesting research post in California but I haven't yet made up my mind whether to take it or not.'

'Selfishly, I hope you decide against it. I thought you were happy in your present work, aren't you?'

'I am but there are times when I long to make a completely fresh start.'

'There are other less drastic ways of making a fresh start. I'm still around, for example.'

'Restarting an old relationship with the same inbuilt difficulties would hardly qualify, I'm afraid.' She smiled to take away the sting of the words.

'You're probably right.' He handed her a section of the paper. 'You might as well look at this until Paul comes back.'

It was only a few minutes later when Paul returned, looking considerably refreshed. 'I'm ready for your revelations, Bill,' he said, sitting down. 'I begin to realise I need more knowledge before I can understand, and I do want to understand.'

'Would you rather I went away?' Katy asked.

'No. A woman's opinion might be very useful.'

'It's difficult to know where to begin.' Bill paused then continued as if he had made up his mind. 'Before I start my story, I'd like you to look at a photograph I have.' He leaned over towards his jacket lying on a nearby chair and took from his pocket a wallet, from which he extracted a photograph. He showed it to Paul who studied it carefully. It was, Katy saw, the photograph of an attractive young woman in her late teens or early twenties. It was a lively, intelligent face not easily forgotten.

Paul was staring at it in amazement. 'Of course, she's much younger but this has to be Judith or her twin sister!'

'It is Judith when she was about eighteen.'

'How the devil do you come to have it?'

'I knew her but her name was then Judy O'Hara, and, if you remember Lawrence called her "Judy" last night?'

'Then you knew these people – but how?'

'I was a young radio reporter in Belfast when Judy was eighteen, about twelve years ago. But my knowledge goes back even further. When I was five my father went to work in Belfast, although he was not Irish. We stayed there until I was nearly ten and I went to the same school as Lawrence and met his family and friends too. Judy O'Hara, who came every summer with her mother, was one of these friends. I think they were also distant relations.'

'I don't understand. Judith was Judith Martin when I met her and James Martin was her father. At least, that is what she told me.'

'James Martin was her stepfather. Her real father, Martin O'Hara, was shot and killed by a Loyalist terrorist when she was three. He had come from Southern Ireland but there was no reason for the shooting, since he had no known Republican connections. Unfortunately, things like that happened frequently, still do.'

'Poor Judith.' Katy commented. 'What ever did her mother do?'

'I believe she took a job in Dublin offered to her by a friend of her late husband. There, I believe, she met and married James Martin and moved to the North of England but practically every summer she came back with Judy to see her relatives. People said her second marriage was not very happy. I have no personal knowledge of this and didn't really meet Judy again until that summer twelve years ago when she was eighteen. That was the year, of course, when Judy O'Hara seems to have disappeared.'

'Do you mean that was when she became Judith Martin?' Paul asked.

'I imagine so but I don't really know.'

'But surely some people must have known or must have asked questions,' Katy objected.

'Some may have done but, if they did, they kept it quiet. It was safer that way. The whole business was pretty horrible, even for those times.'

'I think that Judith's mother died about that time,' Paul said. 'She has always told me that and she reminded me of it last night and said she had a sort of breakdown, which prevented her from going to university for a year.'

'If she did, I'm not surprised,' Bill said slowly.

'But for heaven's sake, Bill, tell us what happened,' Katy interrupted impatiently. 'You keep hinting but you haven't told us anything. Don't you really know?'

Bill ignored that. 'I met Judy that year as Lawrence's special girlfriend. They had been close since they were about fifteen but now they were talking of marrying some time but it didn't seem likely since Judy, who had always been brilliant, was about to go to Cambridge, I think, to read mathematics, while Lawrence's future was pretty uncertain. Still they hoped, as we all do when we're in our teens. Judy came in June and intended to stay until late in September. She had some sort of temporary job. Everything was fine when I went away in mid-August on a month's assignment. I could hardly believe what had happened when I came back.' He paused. 'I think I've earned a brandy, Katy. Better give Paul one, too. He might be glad of it.'

'Most people blamed Michael Reardon,' he continued after a few sips. 'A hard man, much involved in the IRA but never caught. He is, at least, ten years older than Lawrence and had looked after him and his sisters and their mother when their father was killed in the seventies. He was Lawrence's hero and through him, Lawrence became involved in a small breakaway group, which Michael directed. In late August, it was decided apparently that three of them, Michael, Lawrence and another man, should rob a bank. All went well, except that the night watchman was injured and that a policeman who had come on the scene had been shot dead. When I came back, Lawrence had been accused of murder. There was some witness, I believe, who claimed to have seen him with the gun in his hand but I don't think the evidence was very strong and he might have got off if he hadn't, amazingly, confessed. He persisted in his confession and was finally sentenced to thirty years.'

'Oh, no,' Katy exclaimed. 'How terrible! And you don't think he was guilty?'

'I'm too cynical these days to say I'm sure but all of us who knew them both thought that Michael was a much more likely killer and had killed before.'

'So Lawrence confessed to save Michael?' Paul asked. 'Is that the idea?'

'Michael and the family whose chief support he was. I expect it interests you as a lawyer?'

'Very much.' He considered the matter for a few minutes. 'I suppose,' he asked finally 'that he has been released recently under the new agreement?'

'Yes, that's how I came to go into it again.'

'It seems the law is interested too,' Paul remarked, 'since Inspector Barrett visited me.'

'Perhaps, though I can't think why. And if they are, I don't think Lawrence will want it.'

Obviously needing time to think over what he had heard, Paul made no response but stood up and walked slowly over to the window, where he stood, looking out with his back towards them. Katy and Bill looked at one another but said nothing, for it was obvious that Bill's story had been a great shock to him.

Finally, Katy said softly, 'I think I'd better wash up the breakfast.' Without a word Bill followed her to the kitchen. 'I never realised it would be quite like that,' Katy said as Bill closed the kitchen door.

'I warned you,' Bill replied, 'and I avoided it for as long as I could, hoping that Judy might tell him herself.'

'She should have done,' Katy agreed. 'I wonder why she didn't.'

Bill shrugged. 'Who knows? There must be plenty of things even I don't know.'

Paul hardly noticed their going as he stared down into the almost empty street of three-storied Victorian terrace houses, now turned into flats and bedsitting rooms. It was a grey, depressing November day with a chilly wind, which instead of leaves, stirred up wrappings, empty crisp packets and other reminders of Saturday night celebrations in the city.

Paul saw none of this. He is sitting with Judith in the garden of the best pub in their village, where they are entertaining a fellow solicitor, John, and his wife, Alison, to lunch. The sun is so bright and hot that they are glad of the protection of the summer umbrella as they eat their meal, chatting idly. He smiles happily at Judith, brilliant in summer shirt and shorts. Suddenly, the picture focuses as Judith says clearly, in response to some remark he no longer remembers. 'Of course as a mathematician my aim is always to discover truth.'

'Surely,' John asks rashly, 'we lawyers can say that too?'

Judith laughs. 'I hardly think so, John. In my experience the lawyer's aim is to establish innocence if he is defending, and guilt if he is prosecuting.'

'But, in order to do that, they must obviously try to discover the truth,' Alison protests, apparently wishing to support her husband.

Judith smiles gently at her. 'Of course we would all like to believe that but, I think, a closer knowledge would soon prove to us that it rarely is so.' She looks first at John and then at Paul, waiting for one of them to challenge her. Receiving none, she continues, 'I'm afraid we must regretfully take silence for consent, Alison.'

The picture fades as Paul remembers thinking then, Why does she say that?

Now as he comes back to Katy's room and the dreary street below, he realises, she must have been thinking of Lawrence even then. Very quickly he came to the thought that Judith who had said her main aim was truth had not spoken the truth to him, not even when they had last met. Had she ever spoken the truth to him? How could he know? What was there left for him to do?

He stared out into the street, feeling the pain of memory. He was angry too. He was quite unaware of how much time had passed when Bill came back into the room. Hearing the door close, Paul turned to face him.

'I'm sorry I had to be the teller of such a story,' Bill said, obviously concerned by the effect it had had.

'Like me,' Paul tried to reply calmly, 'you must be accustomed to stories of people's infidelities and lies. It's harder to be objective about them when they concern oneself, that's all.'

'Yes, I'm accustomed to all sorts of horrors but it is definitely different when you have a personal interest.'

'Do you still have the photograph?' Without a word, Bill handed it to him. Yes, it was certainly Judith, the more he looked at it, and the surer he was. For a moment, he wished he had known her then; she looked so innocent and hopeful. For the first time, he thought she too might be pitied.

'I have another one here.' Bill opened his wallet. 'It shows

Judith with the Reardon brothers.'

Silently, Paul took it. Judith looked very much the same as in the first photograph. That must be Lawrence with his arm round her. 'Prison has certainly changed Lawrence, poor devil!' he exclaimed, comparing the handsome young face with its cheerful grin with the hard-lined face of the man he had met.

'Prison usually does, particularly nearly twelve years in the Maze with some time in solitary confinement,' Bill commented.

Paul was still looking at the photograph. 'Who is this fellow?' he asked suddenly, pointing to a man standing on the other side of Judith.

'Let me look. Ah, I remember him. That's Tom Farrell. Why?'

Paul stared at the third man with his lean, intelligent face and piercing eyes. He was the one who was not smiling. 'He looks formidable somehow.'

'You're right there, he was. A high-ranking IRA man or so everybody said. Cold and ruthless, they also said, but attractive to the girls. How much of this was rumour, I don't know. He was never arrested. In spite of everything I quite liked him. At least, I could have an intelligent conversation with him.'

'Where is he now?'

'God alone knows. He vanished from Belfast just after Lawrence's trial. Personally, I think he was sent to the USA but I don't know.'

'I should recognise him if I met him,' Paul commented.

'It's not impossible that you will. Rumour has it that he left Belfast with Judy.'

'You're not telling me that he was her lover also? I find that hard to believe. If he went to the USA then surely she would have gone with him? It doesn't make sense. But does any of it make sense?' Paul sounded completely weary and bewildered. 'There are so many lies and deceptions that I think the only thing for me to do is to take Judith's advice. Perhaps the only straightforward thing she has said.'

'And what was that?'

'Go home and wait for me. And that's what I think I will do. Go home, but with little hope of seeing her again. I doubt if the woman I married still exists if indeed she ever did.'

'Perhaps you're right. It doesn't look promising for you. I'm a realist; I would take the same point of view myself.'

'Well, you can have your story now, as long as you keep me out of it. Or will the temptation be too much?'

'I want to know the truth. Don't you?'

Paul shrugged. 'I don't see what good it can do me, do you? Though I wouldn't mind meeting Tom Farrell, on more equal terms, of course. Perhaps he's Judith's latest lover?'

'I would say he is incapable of love.'

'Perhaps they all are. But my mind is made up. It will be good to be back at work tomorrow.'

'Paul.' Katy's head appeared round the door. 'You're wanted on the phone.'

'Who the hell could want to speak to me?'

Katy came through the door. 'She says she's Judith and she wants to speak to you urgently.'

There was a long silence. Bill and Katy looked at Paul. He hesitated, then suddenly made a decision. 'It's probably stupid of me but I'll speak to her.'

'She'd better have something convincing to say,' Bill said to Katy.

'Why?'

'Because he's just decided to abandon her and go home.'

'He shouldn't,' Katy said decisively. 'I hope you discouraged him. No, of course, you wouldn't, would you, Bill, unless it made a better story.' She turned away without waiting for his protest. 'You don't believe in love.'

'Why should I? I've never seen many examples of it, if any.' Silently, they waited until Paul came back.

He picked up his jacket. 'I've stupidly agreed to meet Judith at Westminster Cathedral. I'll take my bag with me and then go on to Euston, I expect, so I'll thank you both very much now. I promise to be in touch.' He kissed Katy swiftly, then picking up his bag, went towards the door.

Katy went after him. 'Try to forgive, Paul.'

'How can I without knowing what there is to forgive?' Once again, he was gone.

67

Chapter Seven

He saw her immediately, standing alone, as he entered the cathedral. She was wearing her long, deep purple winter coat and her dark hair with its copper glints fell in loose waves to the collar. Having watched her for a minute, he moved to her side. She turned and their eyes met. He was struck instantly by her unusual pallor. Whatever she was doing, it did not seem to make her happy. 'Shall we go outside?' he asked. She nodded and they moved away together.

As soon as they reached the busy forecourt, he stopped. Taking her arm, he turned her to face him. 'I have only two questions. Firstly, how did you find me? And secondly, and more importantly, why did you bother?'

'The first is easily answered. You gave me Katy Evans's name and I eventually traced her telephone number. The second will take longer.' She paused.

'I haven't much time, I'm afraid.' He looked into her unfathomable, dark eyes and resisted their appeal. She should not persuade him again to reject his reason. Indicating the bag he carried, he continued, 'As you can see, I was about to take your advice of last night and return home though with scarcely any hope of your joining me. Surely, therefore, there is little more for you to say, unless of course you intend to speak the truth for once.'

'What do you mean? Why did you go as you did last night?'

'Because I realised that, in spite of all your protestations of love, you were still lying. Lawrence Reardon had never heard my name and he certainly had no idea I was your husband. I'm pleased, however, that he did turn up, even though it must have annoyed you, because he undoubtedly saved my life by preventing you from pushing me out into the street before I was fit.'

She didn't answer immediately but stood very still, staring past him, then without looking at him, she said unemotionally, 'You seem to think I'm completely heartless. Perhaps, you're right. Why don't you simply continue on your way to Euston?'

'Damn it, I can't, Judith! I wish I could.' He wanted to shake her but instead he said abruptly, 'Is there anywhere where we can eat and talk? There isn't another train for two hours anyway.'

'There's a quiet little Italian place a couple of streets away.'

He took her arm. 'Then let's go there. You look as if you could do with some food. Or must you return to Lawrence? Does he even know you've come?'

Again she failed to answer his question directly. 'He doesn't expect me back for some time.'

'Good.' He took her arm. 'Then lead us to the place.'

Neither of them spoke again until they were settled in a corner table of the half empty restaurant. Once they had ordered, Paul decided that it was time for him, at least, to be honest. 'You don't have to try to invent any stories. I know about Judy O'Hara and something about the unhappy circumstances that seemed to have ended her life about twelve years ago, just before Judith Martin was born. I didn't know last night but I was told this morning.'

'Who told you?'

'A journalist called Bill Stephens, who knew you all in Belfast years ago. I ran into him when I began my search for you. I don't know whether it was an accident or not. But I rather doubt it. There have been too many strange happenings.'

'I remember Bill. It probably wasn't an accident.' She looked directly at him for the first time. 'So you know about Lawrence.'

'I know that you and he were in love, that he was sentenced for thirty years for the murder of a policeman, while robbing a bank. I begin to understand, therefore, what a shock it must have been to you when you were suddenly told that he was being released after twelve years. I still don't understand, though, why you bolted without telling me anything. Perhaps you wanted to see him first and make sure you still did love him before upsetting me? But even so, that was a crazy way to do it, don't you think? I think I'm even more upset than I might have been and certainly angrier.'

'I think I was crazy, perhaps I still am. I couldn't bear to think of facing it all again. And when Inspector Barrett rang up, I was terrified. I knew there was something threatening here. I couldn't face it and I didn't want you to be involved. Can you believe me?'

'I suppose I do believe it as far as it goes. But I'm not just someone, you know, I've been your husband for six years and I love you passionately. You must know that. I thought you loved me in the same way that I loved you. Was I wrong?'

'I loved you in the same way as you loved me and just as much. And I still do.' She smiled at him in the enticing way she had but he felt there was something almost mocking about it.

'What does that mean? I don't think I understand?' He was hurt and angry, feeling as he had sometimes felt before that she was perhaps manipulating him.

'Have you ever seriously thought about love?'

He was exasperated. 'Good God, Judith, this is no time for discussing things like that.'

'It seems to me to be exactly the right time. That is why I asked you to meet me. If we can understand one another then you can help me. If not, or if you don't want to, then you can't.'

'I fell in love with you the first time I met you. I've never changed. In fact, the day you left me I was probably even more in love with you than I was at first. I thought you felt the same. It was a devastating shock.'

'I know and I'm truly sorry.' She put her hand on his, then removed it as the waiter delivered their meal.

'Since you know all this why do you ask me if I've ever thought about love? That's rather insulting, isn't it?' He took a mouthful of food, then pushed his plate away. He wasn't hungry and it was inferior to Bill's freshly scrambled eggs. Sipping his wine, he waited for Judith to respond.

Obviously hungry, she took several mouthfuls before she finally put down her knife and fork. 'It wasn't meant to be insulting; it was a question I needed to have answered. What you feel for me is a very strong physical attraction.'

'Lust, you mean?' He was angry, feeling that she was belittling him and their marriage.

She was unmoved. 'A less delicate way of putting it but very true. I feel the same for you. It's necessary and most people experience it at some time but the surprising thing about us is that the feeling was so powerful and that it has lasted. But I was asking you about something different which people usually call "love". It has many forms, I suppose, but basically it means, I think, caring for someone as much as you care for yourself or at least trying to and willing yourself to make a habit of it.' Picking up her glass, she took a sip of wine and looked at him waiting for his response.

'This is ridiculous.' He tried to justify the anger he felt. 'It's simply a waste of time trying to start a philosophical discussion when our marriage is falling apart.'

'It might be a very good time.'

'Why don't you say clearly what you mean, instead of trying to wrap it up?'

'What do I mean?' She looked squarely at him, no attempt now to entice. Avoiding her glance, he looked round the restaurant, full of self-satisfied customers, overeating and drinking far more than they needed. None of them, he felt, being subjected to this kind of inquisition. 'Can't you tell me?' She was still looking at him.

'It's quite easy,' he said defiantly. 'What you are really saying is that now that Lawrence is back you love him, as you always did, and want my agreement to your going off with him, because that would make you feel better about it. Our marriage can easily be forgotten. Why the hell did you marry me anyway? Wouldn't it have been more honest to have had a temporary affair? Especially since you call yourself a Catholic.'

'I expected our marriage to last.' She was not faltering at all before his attack. 'Love can very often be added to lust to form a permanent attachment. But I admit that I married you in the first place for two reasons – we both enjoyed our sexual life together tremendously and, very important for me at that time, you asked no difficult questions. You were content to take me as I appeared.'

'In other words I was a trusting idiot, easily deceived by my vanity.'

'Rubbish. It suited you and you were happy.'

He could not deny that. 'But now we come to Lawrence. Although for some reason you won't say it clearly, now that he is back you love him. Isn't that right?'

She appeared to consider the question, then replied finally, 'In a way I suppose I do.'

Suddenly, he didn't want to struggle any longer. 'Then have my blessing,' he said, 'if that's what you want. It's hard for all of us – his coming back from the dead, as it were. I'll go home as you suggested and arrange matters as easily as I can.'

'But I don't want that. You're misunderstanding me.'

'You said you did last night.'

'I know but I meant to come back to you, as I said. I thought I should deal with this on my own, even thought I might do it better that way but I can't. And now you've shown you do have some love for me, I'm asking you to stay and help. Please Paul, don't go back, at least not yet.'

'I'm damned, if I understand you.' He looked into her dark eyes; she smiled at him and put out her hand. He wanted to kiss her. How often had this happened? He was probably making a fool of himself again but he didn't care. 'I'll stay, although God knows why.'

'I'm sure he does.' She returned to her meal for a moment, then putting down her knife and fork, she looked long and hard at him. 'Thank you,' she said.

'What for?'

'For trying to understand and for saying that you will stay and help me.'

'Don't thank me. I'm a very reluctant hero. I'd much rather go back to my old life if it were possible. I suppose the shameful truth is that I can't bear to think of being without you, even though I suspect that's what will happen in the end. Am I right?'

She was silent for so long that he thought she didn't intend to answer him, then suddenly she seemed to shiver as if struck by a sudden blast of cold air. 'I can't see the end now. I thought it had ended once before.' She shivered again.

'Whatever is the matter, Judith?' The hand he enveloped in his was cold.

'I am frightened – very frightened I began to be frightened when Inspector Barrett phoned me, then I told myself I was being silly. That it was simply a matter of trying to help Lawrence now that he had so unexpectedly been released. Maeve told me there was no one else now. It had to be me, so I agreed. Maeve was afraid but then she always was, so I didn't think about it too much but now...' She shivered again.

'Has something new happened?' He wanted to comfort her but could not think how it was to be done.

'It was something you told me last night. I only thought about it later.'

'What was that?'

'It was about the three men who followed you and finally attacked you.'

'I asked Bill about them but he didn't seem to have any ideas.'

'Neither do I. That's what's so frightening. I was awake much of the night worrying about it. Then I found you'd gone. Oh, Paul!' She clung to his hand.

'I'm here and I intend to stay unless you tell me to go. We must talk properly but first of all eat your meal. You need it, don't you? And have you glass of wine, then you'll feel stronger.'

She smiled at him and began to follow his instructions. 'You've always bossed me about my food.'

'And you've always needed it.'

For a moment they were happy in the past.

As they heard the front door shut behind Paul, Katy looked at Bill. 'Do you think he will go home?'

'I was pretty convinced he would until he received Judith's phone call and decided to meet her. If he wants to free himself that is a mistake, I imagine.'

'But I don't think he really does, do you? It's obvious, whatever he says, that he's still very much in love with her. I don't think he wants to let her go.'

'I doubt if many men would want to let her go.' Bill sat back in the armchair and smiled. 'As I remember her Judy O'Hara was not only a very lovely girl but she was born with that power that a few women have to attract most men. It's not necessarily a good gift to have, of course, and I don't think she wanted it but even at eighteen it was clear.'

Katy grinned at him wickedly. 'And you, I fancy, were one of those she attracted. Am I right?'

'Perhaps. But even then I wasn't so young and inexperienced to risk antagonising the Reardons. Besides there was a story to be followed.'

'Always the same Bill.' Katy sighed. 'If Judy O'Hara failed what chance could I possibly have?'

'Don't underrate yourself. Sex appeal isn't the most important thing in life. There are times when loyalty and friendship are far more important.'

'Are you saying that Judith isn't capable of anything like that? If so, poor Paul!'

'I don't know that she isn't but I wonder.'

'Nevertheless, in spite of all you fine words, I think she still has the power to attract you. Hence your continued interest in this story.'

'You may be right about her attraction but my continued interest has far more to do with a far less attractive character, whom I'd foolishly almost forgotten.'

'Who is that?'

'Tom Farrell, the third man, as one might say. He's the one who draws me. A dangerous man, I suspect. But whose side is he on?' He stood up and began to put on his jacket.

'You're not going, are you?' Katy looked disappointed. 'I thought we'd have lunch together.'

'Sorry, my love.' Bill bent and kissed her lightly. 'Work calls. I must make some enquiries and see what I can discover about Tom and his merry men.' He moved towards the door.

Katy stood up. 'Nothing has changed, has it? But take care. It's nice to have you around sometimes.'

He turned round. 'For you, I will take care. With luck, I'll pick you up this evening. If, not, I'll be in touch.'

As he watched Judith finish her meal, Paul thought, This isn't real. We're acting our parts again – the happy husband and wife and all that goes with it. But it isn't true. Was any of it ever true? He looked at her, trying to remember all that had been said. One thing was true, he felt sure. She was afraid. But of what? Why did she want him now when before she'd tried to keep him away? 'What was you real reason for asking me to meet you?' he asked as she finished her wine after putting down her knife and fork.

She looked startled. 'I've told you. I need your help.'

'But you didn't last night. So why now? Oh, I know, the evil Tom Farrell.' He almost laughed, wanting her to realise that he was not going to be manipulated. 'But it's not the first time you've come across him, is it? To judge from the snap I saw he was one of your friends.'

'I knew him, that's true and he was one of my friends but not in the way that you seem to imply.'

None of this was entirely convincing. 'So, what's new, then? Why did you take the trouble to phone me when I had conveniently taken myself away? The truth, please, or I go on to Euston.' He took out his wallet and signalled to the waiter. She watched him as he received the bill and paid it. 'Well, are you going to answer or do we go our separate ways?' He had never felt so cold and angry. He did not intend to be humiliated any more by this pretence. He had begun to feel convinced that she was capable of treating all men as she had treated him. It was unbelievable that she should talk of love.

She looked straight at him. Her voice too was cold, as if she knew what he was thinking. 'Lawrence asked me to see you. That is the truth. Are you satisfied?'

'Lawrence?' He stared at her. 'Why?' He was very reluctant to believe her. 'I find that hard to believe.'

'Nevertheless it's true. Remember, I told him you were an English friend, a solicitor, who wanted to help if he could. He believed me and he liked the look of you. And he needs help.' She stood up, slipping into her coat as the waiter presented it. She bent to pick up her handbag and then straightened up to face him. It was obvious that she was preparing to go. 'But I don't suppose that matters to you. He's only a lousy terrorist. Why should he expect you, a respectable English solicitor, to help him? I was right to tell you to keep away. Now go.'

He believed her. She had never spoken so passionately before. He caught her arm, as she was about to move away. 'Wait a minute, Judith. It seemed incredible when you first said it but I do believe you now. But you must admit that it isn't exactly what you said at first.'

'I'm sorry. I wasn't entirely lying. I am afraid because I don't know who is trying to terrorise you or why. And I want your help, if only because Lawrence wants it.'

'Why did you talk about love? What had that got to do with anything?'

'I wanted us to be honest I felt it would be better if we could be.'

They walked through the door and stood in the street. The clouds were growing thicker and it was beginning to rain slightly. Judith shivered slightly.

'I think you're right but we can't stand here talking.' He looked round irresolutely, wondering what to suggest.

'We can go back to the flat and you can at least talk to Lawrence. If after that, you don't want to stay, you will be quite near to Euston. What do you think?'

'All right. I'll go with you but there are several things we must talk about, before I can possibly agree to meet Lawrence. You must realise that.'

'Of course.' She turned left. 'I think this is the way to the nearest Underground.' Unexpectedly, she put her arm through his. 'It might be better if you asked some questions first.'

'I hardly know where to begin.' He looked down at her. 'But there is obviously one thing I must know. What is your relationship with Lawrence?' He waited for her to answer but she continued to walk on looking straight in front of her. 'There it is,' he said finally, 'you won't answer the first question I ask. How can we make progress?'

'I'm not really considering our progress at the moment and I hoped you would be able to forget about it but, since you insist on it, I'll try to answer you, as I did last night. I have no "relationship" with Lawrence at this moment. When you have met him and talked to him, you will probably realise why. He is shocked, I think. He came out of prison unexpectedly and found that neither his brother, Michael, nor any of his family wanted to see him, that his friends seemed to have melted away, so he talked to Maeve. She suggested me and so I met him at her flat. But she is afraid, as you found out, so we left quickly and went to Finsbury Park, an address Lawrence had been given. But in the early hours we were told it would be safer for Lawrence to leave so we came to our present flat, where it seemed unlikely that anyone would find us.'

They entered the Underground station and Paul did not speak until he had bought their tickets. 'That was very convenient. How did you come to know about it? Who owns it?' He realised, even as he spoke, that he still sounded sceptical.

'It belongs to Rhoda Marshall, an old university colleague and friend of mine. She went on a sabbatical in October and sent me the key, suggesting that you and I might like to use it some time, perhaps for the millennium.'

'I see.' They had reached the platform now and the train was signalled. It seemed better to wait until they were seated. The train arrived almost immediately and they quickly found two seats as there were very few people travelling on this wet Sunday afternoon. As he thought over what she had said, he realised that she had told him many more facts but nothing about her feelings. It seemed wiser to ignore that for the present. 'How do you propose to introduce me to Lawrence?' he asked instead. 'Are you going to tell him now that I am your husband or do I have to carry on the pretence? That will make our conversation even more difficult, don't you think?'

She didn't answer at first then said slowly, ' He will have to be told, of course.'

'Why didn't you tell him at first?'

'Because I thought Maeve would have told him.'

'I realised she must know because she was not surprised at the name. But how was that?'

'I kept in touch with her. We were close friends at one time and she came to England to get away from it all as I did. She told me she was married and I told her I was and we both promised not to tell anyone else. But I thought she would have told Lawrence when he turned up. When I realised she hadn't, I couldn't seem to do it. I thought it might be one more blow for him. Now, of course, I realise that was cowardly and stupid.'

'It makes sense but the trouble is that other people seem to know anyway. Do you know how?'

Her answer came quickly. 'No, of course not.'

There was still much that puzzled him but the time had come

for them to change trains. While they were waiting, he used his mobile to ring Katy. Having told her where he was going, he asked to speak to Bill.

'Bill left soon after you,' she told him crisply, 'in search of Tom Farrell and friends. When he comes back, if he comes back, I'll give him your number and ask him to get in touch. I'm sure he will. But the hound is on the scent and nothing will deter him, certainly not me.'

He could tell she was upset although she was determined not to express it.

As the boarded the train, he explained to Judith that he had been telling Katy where he was going but he did not mention Bill's activities. He wasn't sure how Judith would view them. Did that mean, he asked himself, that he still did not trust her? How could he when he was sure that there was still so much he didn't know. He did not, however, want to ask further questions at this moment. She, too, obviously preferred to be silent.

Their train journey was soon over and, as they walked towards the flat, he made a decision. 'I will tell Lawrence. I think that will be easier for all of us.'

She stopped, startled, suddenly realising that he had taken the initiative from her – an unusual situation. 'I see you don't entirely trust me.' She smiled. 'But that's probably a good idea.'

'Not trusting you or telling Lawrence myself?'

'Both.'

They were outside the flat now. For a moment, she hesitated, then with a resolute air she walked up the steps and inserted the key in the door. Paul followed her quickly. As she opened the door, she called out, 'Lawrence, I'm back – with Paul.'

Paul waited apprehensively as he heard the sound of Lawrence's approaching footsteps. This meeting was going to be of great importance but, whether for good or evil, he was not sure. He waited with Judith as Lawrence came quickly down the hall towards them.

Chapter Eight

As the door closed behind Judith, Paul and Lawrence stood regarding one another in the living room where she had suggested they should talk. Paul saw clearly now how Lawrence had changed from the handsome, curly-haired young man of the photograph with his hopeful smile. He looked older than he should have done. The curly black hair was the same but the face was leaner and harder with deep lines imprinted by suffering. His mouth and chin were set in determined lines. He looked a hard, cold man until he smiled as he did now and the earlier Lawrence was revealed not only in the smile but in the glance of those dark brown eyes, whose compassionate glance Paul remembered from the night before.

Lawrence saw a man of about the same age and build as himself but so very different in everything else. Not only was he good-looking with his fair hair, blue eyes and lightly tanned complexion but he also had, in spite of a certain diffidence, a pleasant manner and the confidence of one whom life had treated well, on the whole. His face was unlined, his smile untroubled. Nevertheless, Lawrence reminded himself, he's had the courage to stand by Judith and to agree to meet me. With that thought he returned Paul's smile.

'Sure and I'm glad to see you looking a little fitter than you did the other night,' he remarked as they sat down on facing armchairs. His voice was pleasant with a lilt but without a strongly marked Irish accent.

'I'm glad to be fitter, mostly thanks to your remedial treatment.' Finding the room warm, Paul stood up, unzipped his jacket and removed it. 'I think I ought to apologise for disappearing so abruptly.'

Lawrence shrugged. 'It's no matter. Judy told me you're a solicitor and you're willing to help if you can. It's good of you to think like that. I don't want to be discouraging but I don't think there's much you can do. Some people may object but I've still been officially released like many others.' His tone was coolly neutral. Here was no Lawrence begging for help, as Judith had presented him. But if this was true, why was he hiding in this flat with Judith?

Paul was puzzled. Again Judith seemed to have been lying or was Lawrence understandably suspicious in spite of his apparently friendly manner? He decided to plunge in, without considering where it would lead him. 'Judith told me that you wanted help and she told me that she was frightened.'

'Did she now?' Lawrence presented a grim, unsmiling face. 'Did she say why she was frightened?'

'Not exactly. She seemed to be worried that some other people might be involved. Do you think that might be so?'

'Sure, I do. But why would they be bothering with you? That's what puzzles me. And, although Judy is a very attractive girl, as I know, why would you risk so much for her? It can't do a respectable English solicitor much good to be mixed up with me or even with Judy O'Hara.' The brown eyes Paul had once thought compassionate were now hard and suspicious.

'Are you saying Judith was lying when she said you wanted my help? If so, perhaps you'd prefer me to go?' He picked up his jacket.

'No,' Lawrence said very firmly. 'I do need your help. Not to protect me. That's hardly likely, is it?'

'Most unlikely,' Paul admitted. 'But what then?'

'I have a this feeling, strange as it may seem, that you can help me to sort out what is happening. For a start – how do you fit in? I knew nothing of you until last night and, when I ask, Judy tries to shut me up with one of her fictions. Who the fucking hell are you, Paul?' He leaned back in his chair with a slight smile, apparently completely relaxed. 'Friend or foe? Or just another victim to Judy's charms?'

In spite of himself, Paul smiled back. 'That's rather difficult to answer.'

'Then why not try the truth? I prefer that myself.'

'It might be a bit of a shock for you,' Paul warned him.

Lawrence smiled. 'Try me, I've had plenty of shocks.'

'Your Judy O'Hara no longer exists. Her name now is Judith Tempest. She is my wife and we've been married for six years. When I met her, she'd already abandoned Judy O'Hara and I knew her as Judith Martin.'

'I see.' Lawrence showed no clear sign of any emotion. 'Does that mean then that you knew nothing about her past in Belfast, about her family, or even about me?'

'That's right.'

'Then you're the one who's been shocked, I'd say. That does surprise me. When did you learn the truth?'

'My learning started last Friday evening when I discovered that Judith had disappeared.' After a brief hesitation he told Lawrence the whole story of the puzzling events of the Friday evening. His instinct sharpened by many interviews told him that he could trust this man, even though he had been a terrorist. And perhaps still was. When Lawrence didn't comment immediately, he queried him, 'You're not entirely surprised, are you?'

'Not entirely.' Lawrence's face was suddenly transformed by a wry smile. 'Thanks for telling me, Paul, and for trusting me. I could be a right bastard, you know.'

'Yes, you could be, I'm well aware of that but I don't think you are.'

'You're right. Just a bloody fool. I don't seem to have learned much from my twelve years in prison, do I?'

'I'm not quite sure that I know what you mean.'

'I was a bloody fool then when I trusted some people too much and I was a bloody fool to come to London now to see Maeve and Judy.'

'The authorities do know, I suppose?' Paul was anxious, wondering what difficulties they might be in.

'Sure they do. I'm not such a fool. I told them I wanted to see my sister, the one closest to me and her kids.'

'But you could be in trouble now,' Paul persisted. 'You've disappeared. They don't know you're here, do they?'

'I hope not because, if they do, others probably do.'

'So Judith was speaking the truth when she told me you needed help?'

'Yes. Sure. A bit of legal assistance. Will you, can you help me?

I can pay you.'

'The payment doesn't matter but I think I need to know more before I can answer your question, don't you?'

'What do you know?'

'Only that when you were eighteen you were involved in a bank robbery with two or three others. During this raid, the night watchman was badly wounded and a policeman who turned up was shot dead. Later, you were arrested. The evidence was flimsy. It looked as if you might have got off but instead you confessed and were sentenced to thirty years. Is that correct?'

'Spot on.'

'Many people think you confessed to save your elder brother, Michael, or so I have been told. Is that right too?'

'Of course it is.' Judith's voice came from the open doorway. They both turned round to look at her. Neither was aware of how long she had been standing there. She walked across the room and stood close to Paul, looking directly at Lawrence. 'Don't let him fool you, Paul. He's the bloody idiot who trusted the great hero, big brother, Michael.' Her voice was scornful. Looking up at her, Paul was amazed to see how angry she was. He had never seen her so overcome with emotion. He turned to see how Lawrence would take this and waited for his reply.

It didn't come quickly. For what seemed an interminable time, Lawrence looked up at her. To Paul his expression was unreadable. It was certainly not anger that he showed. After that pause, he spoke quietly and even gently. 'Judy, my darling, you're just as hot-headed as ever and you know it. Calm down.'

'How can I be calm when you will keep telling lies?'

'Now aren't you the one who's stretching the truth a bit? I haven't told Paul anything. He'll tell you that himself, I'm sure.' He turned towards Paul.

'That's correct. I've merely told Lawrence the facts and rumours I have been given. You prevented him from answering me.' Paul was aware that, even if Lawrence remained apparently unruffled, he himself was angry with Judith.

'And what were you going to say?' Judith asked Lawrence.

'I was going to say as I have always said that I confessed because I was guilty.'

'Oh, God! How can you even after all these years?' Judith sounded close to tears. 'I can't think why you wanted to see me again if that is all you are going to say?'

'I wanted to explain, to get you to understand.' Lawrence still managed to sound calm and patient.

'Oh, I understand,' Judith moved towards the door, 'only too well. But it doesn't matter now, does it? I'll leave you to your discussions with Paul.' She shut the door firmly behind her.

Paul and Lawrence stared at one another. 'Poor Judy,' Lawrence said quietly. 'She had too much to bear.'

'I have never seen her behave like that. She has always been very controlled and cool. I think it must be that she cares a lot for you.'

'How long have you known her?'

'Nearly eight years. I met her as Judith Martin who had just received a first class degree in mathematics at Imperial College and was studying for her PhD. When she had achieved that, she agreed to marry me, rather to my surprise, and came to teach at the public school in the village where we live.'

'That's Judy! She was always very bright. When I went to prison she was going to Cambridge and that's where I always imagined her to be. I used to think about it quite a lot. Do you know why it was London instead?'

'She was ill and decided to take a year off. Her mother died also. Her stepfather lives in Manchester but she rarely sees him. That's all I know, I suppose I took the rest for granted.'

'And why not? It seems to have made you both happy.'

'But surely, it must upset you?'

'Upset me? Why?'

'When you were released so much sooner from prison, I thought you might...' Paul stopped, wondering how to express his thoughts.

Lawrence looked puzzled, then smiled suddenly. 'You've been having romantic thoughts, Paul. You imagine me, I suppose, thinking about Judy during all those long years in prison. It isn't like that. At least it wasn't for me. Judy and I parted when I was sentenced. I freed her completely. What else could I do? I couldn't expect her to wait thirty years, now could I?'

'It must have been a difficult thing to do.'

Lawrence shrugged. 'She was angry with me. You've just seen how angry. And that made it easier.'

'That's what I don't understand. Why is she so angry?'

'It would be better if you asked her that yourself, don't you think? I might have the wrong idea, after all.'

'I suppose so.' Paul stood up and wandered restlessly over to one of the bookshelves that lined two of the walls. He stared at the books without registering anything about them, then turned round. 'It seems quite clear to me that her anger springs from her love for you. She resented losing you twelve years ago and now she is resentful that because of her marriage to me she has lost you again. But that too, it seems to me, can be put right. I don't want to keep her married to me against her will.' He waited for Lawrence's reaction.

'Steady on!' Lawrence too stood up. 'You can't possibly make that decision by yourself. And, if you do, my bet is you won't find Judy very grateful. She'll be angry with you then.'

'I suppose you're right.' Paul sat down again, reluctant to agree that his 'noble' offer might not be appreciated.

Lawrence stood, smiling at him. 'And there's another thing. You've forgotten to ask me.' He sat down again. 'Being an honest bloke, I have to tell you that I don't want to marry anyone at present, certainly not Judy who is your wife.'

'I'm a solicitor, you know. I could arrange a divorce quickly.'

'For God's sake, man, stop it. I don't fucking well want to get married. Haven't I made that clear? You must arrange that with Judy if you want to, but don't include me in your arrangements. You've also forgotten that bad lad though I am, I'm a Catholic and I don't believe in divorce. So drop it, will you?'

'I'm sorry. I only thought.'

'I know what you thought but forget it. There are more threatening things to discuss now. The truth is I've been a bloody idiot again coming to London. I wanted to talk to Judy to see if I could sort things out and to see Maeve. It seems that there's nothing I can sort out with Judy, and Maeve's suddenly too scared to talk to me. I think some unpleasant characters want to get in touch with me and so, it seems, do Special Branch. That's where I need a bit of advice and Judy suggested you. I can understand if you don't want to be involved but I wish you'd say straight out. If you don't, you'd better get out now.' He had changed. The smile had gone. The hard man with the firm mouth and watchful eyes had returned. The lines seemed to have deepened on his face. He looked aggressively at Paul. 'I hope you understand me.'

Paul didn't answer immediately. Sitting back in his chair, he recalled their conversation. 'It was my desire to get more information which led us astray, I think.'

'It was more because of Judy jumping in, I reckon. She put us off course, a bit. Still, no harm's done. You know I'm not your rival, so can we forget about that?'

'I don't see why not, at least for now. But I still need more information, you know, before I can commit myself. You understand that, don't you?'

'Sure. But I don't know what I can give you. You'd better ask the questions.'

'Did you really come to England just to see Judith and Maeve?'

'Yes, but I told you I was a bloody idiot.'

'That's fine but why then have you gone into hiding? That doesn't seem like the action of an innocent man.'

He looked carefully at Lawrence to see his reaction but none was obvious as he answered immediately, 'Because I got the impression that some other people wanted to meet me and I was definitely not anxious to meet them.'

'Do you mean the ones who for some reason came after me?'

'Yes.' Lawrence shut his mouth firmly, as if determined not to say any more.

'Have you any idea why they wanted to meet you?' When Lawrence did not answer, Paul became impatient. 'It's no use! I can't do anything for you if you're not willing to be honest with me. Surely you can see that? You're asking too much. I might as well go.' He stood up and picked up his jacket.

He was halfway towards the door before Lawrence spoke. 'Don't be too hasty, Paul. I'm willing to level with you but the problem is I don't know much.' As Paul came back to his chair, he continued, 'I was involved with that mob before I went to prison. They took part in the bank robbery but, since then, I've had nothing to do with them and I don't want to be mixed up with them again.'

'Did you know they were in London before you came?'

'No. Michael could probably have told me but he didn't. I don't know why not. It was a bit of a shock.'

'Why do you think they are here?'

'I don't know but I guess they are part of a breakaway group that wants to cause trouble to upset the peace process and Special Branch will be only too happy if I'm fool enough to get involved with them again.'

'And what do you think will happen?'

'It's obvious. Jesus, surely you can see it? I'll have to give Special Branch information or go to gaol. And, if I do give information, my life will be short.' He leaned forward with his hands clasped between his knees and seemed to be studying the carpet, then suddenly he sat up fixing his eyes on Paul. 'You'd better go. I realise there's nothing you can do. And you'd be another bloody idiot if you tried. Get out, man, while you can.'

It all sounded convincing and honest. But was it? Paul tried to consider all the facets of the situation. 'What about Judith?' he asked finally. Before Lawrence could answer he became aware that his mobile phone was ringing. Fishing it out of his jacket pocket, he answered the call. It was Bill. Excusing himself, he moved over towards the window. 'Have you some news?' he asked Bill, surprised at hearing his voice.

'Not exactly news but, since you left, I've been investigating some pretty murky waters. I haven't met Farrell and the O'Keefe brothers; they are well concealed but I have met two or three people only too eager to warn me about them but too frightened to give me any solid information. One thing's sure – they're up to no good and they're dangerous. It's also clear that they're amazingly well informed, which is why I've rung you.'

'Do they know about this place?'

'I don't think so but who knows how long that will last? Watch your step. Even the most unlikely person may turn out to be unreliable. My advice to you is leave now. I can always offer you a bed.' It was clear to Paul that Bill was not even sure about

Judith. His next words seemed to confirm this. 'Incredible though it may seem, I was going to suggest that, if you had to trust anyone, Reardon might be the best. He may be a villain in the eyes of the law but he's honest, I believe.'

'It had occurred to me. Thanks for the help. I'll decide soon and be in touch.' Putting away his phone, he came back to where Lawrence waited quietly in his chair. 'That was Bill Stephens,' he explained as he sat down again. 'He hadn't much new information, I'm afraid.' He looked across at Lawrence. Could he seriously trust him, especially if that might mean distrusting his own wife?

As if reading his thoughts Lawrence smiled rather mockingly at him. 'I reckon you're wondering how far you can trust me, if at all. Am I right?' Without waiting for a reply, he stood up. 'I suggest a whisky before we go any further. You may not need it but I do. It's a new pleasure for me.' Without waiting for a reply, he moved over to a corner cupboard and took out a bottle and glasses, into which he poured generous measures.

'Don't you think,' Paul asked, as he accepted the whisky, 'that I'd better go and have a word with Judith? I don't want her to feel excluded.'

'Why not? She excluded herself and she can just as easily come back, if she wants to.' Lawrence's tone was curt and decided. 'I'd rather you decided about me, without her help.'

'She does presumably know you better than I do.'

'You've already had her opinion. Do you really want to hear it again? I would rather give you my truth, that is, if you want to hear it. If you don't, then you'd better be leaving.' Finishing his whisky, he put down his glass and waited.

'I do want to hear it,' Paul decided, wondering nevertheless if he wouldn't be wiser to go. But that still left the problem of Judith. Would she come with him?

'Good, then I'll give you my version. The truth, as far as I'm capable of it. You must decide for yourself whether you can believe it. You've had Judy's version…'

'Which others agree with.'

Lawrence shrugged and then laughed. 'Strange, isn't it? I supposing it's quite flattering really this sentimental yarn about this bloody idiot of a youth who took the blame to spare big brother, the hero and mainstay of the family. Can you honestly believe that anyone would keep that up when faced with thirty years in that sink of a prison?' He paused, looking mockingly at Paul.

'It's difficult but people do strange things in a highly emotional situation such as yours was.' Paul realised as he spoke that he didn't want to have to believe anything different, fearing that it might be unacceptable.

Lawrence's smile told him that he fully understood this. 'Sorry, comrade, I can quite understand that you might prefer to think of me as a self-sacrificing idiot. But it's just crap. I confessed because I was guilty and for no other reason.'

'But, as I understand it, you might have got off. The evidence was pretty circumstantial, wasn't it?'

There was a hint of mockery in both Lawrence's smile and his tone of voice 'That's what he told me, my learned counsel, but I had this funny idea. I was pretty sure they were determined to find someone guilty, so I thought it had better be me because I was. Am I making myself clear?'

'I think so.'

'Well, so as to leave no doubt, I'll put it this way. I held the gun, my finger pulled the trigger, I fired the shot that killed the policeman. I don't suppose you care to hear it much but I'm a killer. My friends might put it differently and call me a brave fighter for the cause. I'm not so keen on that any more but at least it's nearer to the truth than Judy's version.' He paused, then looked at Paul, as if judging the effect of his words. 'I think it's about time you decided to go, isn't it?'

Stubbornly, Paul refused to accept this. 'What about the rest of the story? Were you responsible for everything that happened?

'I didn't plan the robbery, I didn't injure the night watchman, I didn't even have a gun until someone thrust it into my hand as the policeman appeared. I shot without thinking. But none of that matters, does it? I was guilty of shooting the policeman.'

'You are saying then that on the whole you were treated justly?'

'Justly?' Lawrence looked sardonically at Paul. 'Did I say anything about justice? I don't remember that I did.'

'But surely that's what you mean when you say you were lawfully punished for what you did?'

'Sure, I did say that. But what's that got to do with justice? Of course I don't know as much about this sort of thing, as you must do but, speaking from my own small experience, I would say that the law hasn't got much to do with justice. Wouldn't you agree?'

For a moment Paul could think of nothing to say. He felt stripped and vulnerable as if he was being forced to take off all his clothes in public and reveal his true, puny body. Had he always practised his craft of law quite blindly or had he slipped gradually into it? Realising that Lawrence was still waiting for a reply, he struggled to find some suitable words. 'I'm not quite sure I understand you. Could you perhaps make it clearer?'

Lawrence smiled a genuine, friendly smile, or so it seemed. 'Sure, and I'm only to pleased to try. With law, as I see it, it's just a matter of knowing the rules and of being punished if you're discovered breaking them. But justice is different. I suppose you might say it means giving somebody exactly what he deserves. That might be a bit rough and ready but I'm not a philosopher.'

'It seems a good enough place to start.'

'Yes, but the trouble is how do you decide that? Where do you start? Take my case. I shot the policeman. I don't deny it. But how did I come to be in that position? Was it perhaps because when I was a kid my father who belonged to no organisation was shot just because he was a Catholic? Sounds convincing but can you leave it there? How about the man who shot my father? He was never punished by the way. But did he shoot my father because his brother was killed by a Catholic who thought the only good Protestant was a dead one? I could go further back than that but I won't. All I want to know is how do you decide what is justice here? I thought a lot about that in prison.'

'And did you come to any conclusion?'

'Not really. The chaplain lent me a book by a bloke called Plato which was supposed to be about justice. Do you know it?'

'Do you mean *The Republic*? Did you manage to read it?'

'I tried but it seemed to me that he didn't get very far either, so I gave it up. I mean if a clever bloke like Plato couldn't solve it there isn't much hope for me, is there?'

Paul suddenly found himself smiling back and feeling relaxed. 'Not much. So what did you do?'

'I looked in a different direction. It seemed to me there had to be a simple answer that ordinary folk could understand and work with.'

'And did you find one?'

'Yes.' For the first time Lawrence seemed to hesitate. 'A clever lawyer like you will probably think it's too simple to be right.'

'Try me.'

'The chaplain suggested it so I read the Gospels for the first time. Of course I always went to Mass, when I was kid but that never seemed to have much to do with the Gospels. Well, the answer's there if you look for it. You've got to start with forgiveness. That puts a stop to it, you see. If you've forgiven the person who's hurt you, then you can't go on to hurt them, can you?' He leaned forward. There was no mockery or irony now in either his voice or his expression. 'I had a good chance to think it through during a spell of solitary confinement. Of course it's not just you forgiving other people, it's asking them to forgive you.'

Paul found himself considering this. Here was no slick preacher but a man who had been to hell. 'But can it be done?' he asked finally.

'Yes. I've done it. I wrote to the woman whose husband I'd killed. Told her a bit about my life and how I felt now and asked her to forgive me.'

'That was brave of you. Did it work?'

'Yes. I expected her to spit on me but she didn't. She wrote back after a couple of weeks and said my letter had made her cry but they were the best tears she'd ever cried. She said I was right. We'd got to stop wasting lives. She didn't want her son to end up dead or as good as dead like me. She promised to pray for me and I reckon she has. Of course, it won't always go like that, I've found that out, but I've just got to go on trying, especially now I've been set free. That was the chief reason why I came to London, you see.'

'What do you mean?'

'I came to see Judy and to set things right with her. I knew she was very angry when I went to prison and I didn't want her to go on feeling like that. It's bad. I didn't know, of course, that she'd made a new life for herself.' He stopped and looked at Paul. 'I don't understand it. She should be all right. Look, I don't want to upset you.'

'You're not. I'm just beginning to realise how right you are.'

'You see, she's angrier now than she was twelve years ago and that doesn't make sense. She won't say anything either. There's something wrong here, Paul. Something that worries me. What do you think she's up to?'

Suddenly, Paul recalled Bill's warning. He stood up. 'I think it's about time we tried to find out, don't you? For both our sakes, mine as well as yours, we shouldn't waste any more time.' He moved towards the door.

After a moment's hesitation, Lawrence began to follow him.

Chapter Nine

The sky was a deep, satisfying blue with soft, white clouds drifting lazily across it. The same summer breeze that moved the clouds gently stirred Judy's hair as she lay back on the rough moorland hillside gazing up between the leaves of the stunted tree which gave her some shade. Why was this juxtaposition of green and blue always so pleasing, she wondered? Had God planned it to please us or did it simply please us anyway? Idly, her mind wandered into many fascinating but useless byways.

The striking of a distant church clock in the valley below reminded her of the passing of time. She had walked further than she had intended and it was a long way back to the farmhouse where she was staying with her mother and stepfather. Every year they came back here to the Yorkshire village where her stepfather had been born. She enjoyed these visits but she was not sorry this summer that the holiday was ending for that meant that in three days' time she would travel to Belfast to visit her Northern Irish relatives and to stay with her father's sister, her Aunt Norah, where her mother would later join her.

She sat up as she realised how near she now was to the bliss she had been looking forward to since Easter. In three days' time she would see Lawrence again and they would be beginning two months together. Life was very good, she thought, as she stood up, dusted down her jeans and set out on the long walk back. At the beginning of October she was going to Cambridge to read mathematics and Lawrence was also going to university in Leeds to study engineering. Then, their real life would begin free from the interference of their families. At the end of their time at university they planned to marry. After that, it was all a little vague except that they would be together.

She had known Lawrence for many years but it was only when she was fifteen and he was sixteen that they had realised that they were in love. She remembered his first shy butterfly kiss that had both shocked and delighted her. Since then their love had grown steadily, in spite of their frequent partings. This, their last holiday before university, would be the best so far, not only because it would be longer but also because it would be a prelude to a freer life in England. She hummed a little tune as she slithered down the steep hillside. How lovely it would be to be with him again!

Their first meeting was just as she had expected. Lawrence came round an hour after she had arrived and had a cup of tea with her and her widowed Aunt Norah who was strict but kind. With her permission, they went out for a walk which quickly ended in a quiet, little bar where they could sit and talk. At first, all they wanted to do was to hold hands and look at one another with delight.

'Oh, Judy, my darling, I've been dreaming of this moment for weeks,' Lawrence said softly.

Her heart beat fast as the touch of his hands and the expression in his dark brown eyes told her so much more. Feeling the need for restraint, she lowered her eyelids, afraid that her own glance might give away too much of what she felt.

Understanding her, Lawrence smiled. 'Don't worry. I'm determined to be well behaved until we are away from here and free to love. Your Aunt Norah will have nothing to complain about, not even my mother who was born thinking the worst of men!'

Seeing that no one was looking in the almost empty bar, he kissed her quickly and then ordered the Coke they always drank. For the next hour he told her news of friends and they discussed their plans for the following two months. Both of them had part-time jobs but that left them plenty of time to spare. After that, with arms twined comfortably around each other, they walked slowly home, convinced that no one had ever been happier.

Looking back, she could not be sure when it was that she first became aware that something was wrong. Almost immediately, perhaps, but it was not until Aunt Norah spoke to her one morning after breakfast that she admitted her doubts to herself. They were sitting in the cosy kitchen of Aunt Norah's terraced house which had scarcely changed in the thirty years she had lived in it. It was crowded, untidy but comfortable and Judy loved every inch of it, especially the rocking chair near the open fire.

How often had she rocked and comforted herself on that as a child. Aunt Norah too seemed to be blessedly unchanged. Her greying hair was still worn in a bun, her spectacles still slipped down her nose and she still wore the medallion of Our Lady of Lourdes on a silver chain round her neck, together with a crucifix.

'I was talking to Bridie O'Keefe yesterday and she's very worried about those boys of hers.'

'Do you mean Joe and Pat?' Judy was surprised. 'I've met them several times and they don't seem any different to me.'

'Perhaps you haven't been noticing with Lawrence around. Bridie's worried anyhow. She says they're always out and she doesn't know where they go.'

Judy laughed. 'Well, they are nineteen and twenty and working in their uncle's wood yard. They just want to have a good time, I expect, like so many of the boys They want to feel independent.'

'That wouldn't worry Bridie,' Aunt Norah replied slowly. 'She's not exactly new to the job. She's brought two older boys up successfully. She just doesn't like the company they keep. They've become very friendly with Tom Farrell lately and others like him.

'Tom Farrell! I know him quite well. He's older, of course, but he's very intelligent and has a good job. I'm surprised he's friendly with them, after all they're not very bright.'

'Brains aren't everything. Goodness is more important. You shouldn't trust Tom Farrell.'

'Why ever not? He's always been really pleasant to me, friendly but nothing more.'

Aunt Norah smiled a little grimly. 'I wasn't thinking of things like that,' she said, without specifying the 'things'. 'I meant his political opinions.'

'Political opinions? I didn't know he had any.'

Aunt Norah looked severely at her. 'It's no good sticking your head in the sand, Judy. Mind you, you were always one for that, even as a child, trying to pretend things hadn't happened, as if that would make them go away. I know you don't live here all the time but you must know how dangerous and frightening it all is. After all, you own daddy was killed.'

'Don't talk about it,' Judy said quickly. 'I don't want to think about it. I always hope that when I come back things will have got better.'

'Well, they haven't.' Aunt Norah began to collect up the breakfast dishes fiercely. 'And that's why Bridie is worried. We all know about Tom and his secret ways and it's not safe to be too close to him.'

'Do you mean he's a member of the IRA?'

'Hush! It's not good to gossip but that's what we all think.'

'Then why hasn't he been arrested?'

'He's one of us, he and Michael Reardon. You don't think any of us would give them away, surely? If you do, you've been too long in England.'

'You said Michael Reardon. Does that mean Lawrence too? No, I don't believe it. We've been friends for years and Maeve's my friend too.'

'Did I say anything about Lawrence? I like him. He's always been a good boy. But Michael is his brother and he's a powerful man, they do say, in the IRA but, as long as Lawrence spends his time with you, you've no need for worry. He's really fond of you, that I do know.' Aunt Norah departed for the scullery, leaving Judy to bring out the rest of the dirty dishes.

For a moment Judy did not move. Was she sure of Lawrence? Now, she admitted to herself that there had been little happenings that had worried her in the days since she had come back. Several times Lawrence had made excuses for not seeing her and it had never been quite clear what he was doing and why she could not be with him. It had not been like that at Easter. No, she dismissed the frightening thought. It couldn't be true. She was sure that Lawrence loved her and that he would never risk their future happiness in this way. Besides he had always agreed with her, or so she thought, that violence never achieved anything and that bitterness destroyed one, as she thought it was still destroying her mother. She went into the scullery to speak once more with Aunt Norah.

'You don't really think that Lawrence is involved, do you?'

For a moment Norah made no move but continued washing up, then suddenly she turned to face Judy. 'I don't but there's some who wonder.'

'There are some people who will gossip about anything, whether it's true or not. You know that, Aunt Norah.' Judy was angry. 'But why should they pick on Lawrence?'

'I suppose it's because of Michael,' Norah replied reluctantly. 'Ever since their father was killed, he's taken everything on his shoulders and Lawrence, being the youngest, owes most to him. It's not surprising the boy thinks he's a hero.'

'I know he loves Michael but that doesn't mean he supports his political ideas. In fact, I'm sure he doesn't. That's one of the reasons why he wants to go to university in England – to get away from it all.'

'I'm sure you're right. After all, you know him better than most. Now, will you pass me those dishes or we'll both be late.' It was quite clear that for Norah the subject was now closed. Judy told herself she was satisfied but, to make sure, she decided to say something to Lawrence at the earliest opportunity.

That evening they spent with Maeve and his mother at his home and there was little opportunity for private talk and, as he walked back with her to Aunt Norah's, she was too happy to be alone with him at last to risk spoiling it with annoying questions, especially as she had decided that it was all most likely idle gossip by people who envied him his charm and his intelligence.

On the following morning, the Feast of the Assumption, they met at Mass and spent a short time afterwards chatting before they went to work. It was then that he told her that he would not be able to take her to the local dance in the evening as he had promised. She was hurt and disappointed and naturally demanded to know why. There was a slight pause before he answered and then he said, 'Michael wants me to help him with a rushed job at the garage.'

'But that's not fair! Surely, it can be done tomorrow when there isn't a dance?'

'No, I'm sorry, Judy. I'm just as disappointed as you are but it has to be done before morning. I don't want to let Michael down, he's always so good to me. You wouldn't want me to, would you, Judy darling?'

'I suppose not,' she said reluctantly. 'But I still think it's horrid of you on this night especially. All our friends will be there and

I've bought a new dress for it. Couldn't you just help Michael for an hour or so and then pick me up later? I wouldn't mind that.' She thought he would yield but he didn't. Even then, she wouldn't have been so angry and suspicious if he had looked directly into her eyes but he didn't. Instead he bent down and kissed her, promising that he would make it up to her. He was very persuasive and she forgave him but the doubts did not quite go away, even when he gave her his solemn word to take her out into town on the next evening.

She told herself that she would not have had these silly suspicions if Aunt Norah hadn't passed that nasty gossip on to her. Nevertheless, she was still so angry and hurt that when Tom Farrell unexpectedly asked her to go to the dance with him, she accepted without hesitation. Aunt Norah was not at all pleased, not because of Tom's supposed Republican connections but because, as she reminded Judy, he did not have a good reputation with girls.

'That's just more gossip, I expect,' Judy retorted. 'In any case, I can look after myself.'

As it turned out she did not have to. Tom was an excellent dancer, amusing and full of flattery but he attempted nothing that she could object to. Even when he delivered her to her home, he did not try to kiss her goodnight but simply thanked her for a good evening. As he was going, however, he suddenly turned back, took her hands in his, whispering tenderly, 'If only Lawrence weren't my friend.' Leaving the sentence incomplete, he left her, feeling flattered but not disturbed.

In spite of her doubts, Lawrence kept his promise by taking her out the next evening and buying her a delicious meal in one of the town's best restaurants. It was a such a happy evening that she asked no questions but surrendered to the joy of being with him. He too seemed happy and relaxed but, as he left her, he made no definite promise for the next day. This, however, did not worry her; she was confident that he would call on her when he was free.

It was quite late when he did turn up. It was hot and humid as it had been all day, the clouds continually threatening rain which did not come. Aunt Norah was out spending the evening with

Bridie O'Keefe. Judy had retreated to the sitting room which was cooler than the kitchen and was trying irritably to do some neglected study when she heard his knock at the door. Tired of being on her own and glad of an excuse to leave her work, she greeted him happily. Almost immediately, she realised that he was in a strange mood. After giving her a quick and almost absent-minded kiss, he followed her into the sitting room but, instead of sitting beside her on the sofa, he wandered over to the window and stared out at the gloomy sky.

'God, I wish it would rain,' he exclaimed irritably. 'This weather drives me mad. I haven't been able to settle to anything all day.'

'Why don't you come and give me a hug?' She smiled up at him but, instead of returning her smile, he stared at her as if he couldn't understand what she was saying. Then, as if waking up, he strode over to the sofa, took her in his arms began to kiss her passionately.

'Judy, darling, I love you so much. I could never bear to hurt you. You know that, don't you.'

She was half lying on the sofa now and he was caressing and kissing her in a way he had never done before. Her whole body was thrilled and excited in a way it had never been before. She did not want to resist him, although part of her knew that she should – that this was madness, the kind of madness they had always been careful to avoid.

'Judy, my own sweet darling,' he kept saying as his kisses and caresses became more demanding. Afraid, she struggled with him, crying out as he hurt her. 'Judy, my own love, don't send me away. I couldn't bear it if you did. I need you so much. I'm so afraid of everything tonight.' Feeling the urgent need of his body now pressed close against hers and her own longing, she could resist no more. It was painful, though wonderful, but she was too ignorant to know exactly what was happening. She felt an unexpected wetness within her as Lawrence suddenly pulled himself away. 'It'll be all right, I promise you,' he said. 'We'll always be together.'

Suddenly in the gathering twilight, she glimpsed over his shoulder the bright light of the votive candle before Aunt Norah's statue of the Sacred Heart. It brought her back to reality as if Aunt Norah stood before her. They had been wrong and foolish. She burst into tears. She had never intended it to be like this! 'Please go,' she begged him.

He tried to comfort her. 'I'm sorry, Judy. I didn't really mean to but it'll be all right. I promise you,' he said again and again.

She wanted to be comforted but nothing could drive away her sense of dread. 'I do love you,' she said through her tears, 'but it's better if you go now.'

Reluctantly, he stood up, remained staring at her for a moment, then said abruptly, 'You're right, Judy. I'm sorry. I'd better go. I must go.' He bent and kissed her and almost rushed out of the room, only pausing to say, 'Don't ever forget I love you. I'll be back tomorrow.'

It was Aunt Norah who brought her the news early the next morning. She was still in bed when Aunt Norah came hurriedly into her bedroom, without knocking as she usually did. Her normally rosy face was pale and her hair was untidy, as if she hadn't bothered to do it properly. 'Oh, Judy, my poor child,' she exclaimed as she stood by the bed.

Judy sat up, suddenly frightened. 'Whatever's the matter? Something terrible has happened, hasn't it?'

'I don't know how to tell you.' Norah's eyes were full of tears.

Judy knew. 'It's something to do with Lawrence, isn't it? For God's sake just tell me.'

Norah nodded. 'He was arrested some time after midnight, he and the O'Keefe boys.'

'Arrested? How could he be? I saw him last night. He didn't say anything to me. It must be a mistake.' But she knew it wasn't. He had been so strange and then he had rushed off. To do what?

Aunt Norah sat on the bed and took hold of both her hands. 'You'll have to be very brave,' she said.

'Please just tell me,' Judy begged her.

Quietly and simply Aunt Norah told her the whole terrible story.

When she had finished, Judy was silent, then she asked in a quiet, little voice, 'Do you mean that the others, whoever they were, got away, except for the O'Keefes and they might get off anyway? But Lawrence,' Judy continued, 'is accused of killing the policeman because he was actually found with the gun in his hand?' She felt she must get it all clear – her mind seemed so confused. Norah nodded. 'Lawrence is a murderer then,' she stated finally.

Aunt Norah tried to evade this. 'Don't say that, my dear,' she protested, holding Judy's hands more tightly, the tears running down her cheeks. 'It must be a mistake. Perhaps we've got the story wrong. People are already saying it's much more likely to be Michael.'

Judy pulled her hands away. 'I don't think so. Michael would be cleverer than that. He promised me he would not get involved but I was afraid that something was wrong. It's no mistake. Don't cry, Auntie.' She kissed her aunt. 'We've all cried too many tears already. Now I must get up. I have to go to work later.' She moved towards the bathroom.

Norah turned and stared at her. 'Judy! You mustn't talk like that. Don't you care?'

'Of course I care. But what is there for me to do? Lawrence has destroyed our life, our future together for a stupid cause that has already destroyed too many people. He broke his word to me. I don't want to cry. I'm going to carry on somehow.' She walked through the door and into the bathroom. This is the worst moment of my life, she thought, there can be none worse.

But you were wrong, Judith Tempest told herself. She got up from the bed where she had been resting. Why had she been forced to revive these memories just because Lawrence thought he could come and put everything right? But she would go no further. She would not look into that final abyss, which she had determined to cut out from her memory. Judy O' Hara had died. She had killed her and she would not resurrect her. There was a sight tap on the door.

'May I come in?' It was Paul's voice. She was relieved to see him. 'I'm sorry if I've disturbed you. I suddenly realised that Lawrence and I had been talking for a pretty long time and I was afraid that you might feel excluded.'

'I was quite happy to be excluded. Have you reached a

decision?'

Paul came further into the room and looked around. 'Is this your friend's study bedroom?'

'Yes, and I have slept here on my own. If you are still wondering there is no relationship between Lawrence and me – now – and never will be.'

'I have already understood that from both of you. But to return to your question. I have reached a decision that I will try to help Lawrence, if I can. I am not experienced enough to know how much that is, however.'

'I suppose not. Have you told him?'

'Not exactly. I would prefer you to be there, if you are not too angry.' He came close to her and, putting his hands on her shoulders, forced her to look at him. 'Why are you so angry?'

'Don't worry about it. It was a momentary lapse. I have recovered.' It was quite impossible to read the expression of her dark eyes as she looked directly at him. He sighed for he had hoped to come closer. Although she heard and understood the sigh, she refused to respond. 'Where is Lawrence now?' she asked instead.

'In the kitchen investigating the food supply. He is hungry.'

'Shall we join him there?' she suggested. 'I would enjoy a cup of coffee myself.'

As they entered the kitchen, they found Lawrence busily engaged in frying bacon for a sandwich. Having declined his offer to make some for them, Judith set about preparing coffee.

'This is one of the delights of life I have had to forget!' Lawrence exclaimed as he placed his bacon between two slices of bread. After cutting the sandwich, he took a satisfactory bite seemingly uninterested in anything else.

'I think Paul would like to explain his position to you,' Judith remarked coldly, 'if you can spare the time to listen to him.'

Lawrence laughed. 'You haven't changed a bit, Judy. You always liked to get things clearly organised.' He turned to Paul. 'Fire away. I'm listening.'

Paul quickly explained his willingness to help but his inability to know how much he could help. 'I think the best thing for me to do,' he said finally, 'is to ring up Inspector Barrett (he gave me a Special Branch number) and to put the situation to him. He may accept my word when he wouldn't accept yours alone. Meanwhile, you'd better continue to lie low.'

'Where?' Lawrence asked between mouthfuls.

'Here, if Judith has no objection.' Paul turned to look at her but she had her back to him as she was drawing the curtains to cut out the growing darkness. 'What do you say?' he asked her.

'I suppose I must accept the situation.' She turned round and began to pour out the coffee. 'But I'm not sure it's the best thing we can do.'

Paul was irritated by her cold attitude but before he could reply his phone rang again. He moved out into the hall to answer it. It was not Bill this time but Katy.

'I have a message for you from Bill, who has gone off I know not where. He says that he thinks trouble is brewing and it would be safer for Lawrence not to stay much longer where he is,' she said.

'And did he have any suggestions as to where he might go?'

'That's the problem. His flat doesn't seem to be safe, so he suggested mine.'

'But I can't expect you to do that for a complete stranger,' Paul protested.

'You may not but Bill does.' She laughed. 'You see what a devoted slave I am!'

'Why is Bill so anxious to keep on helping?'

'What you mean is do I know if Bill is just exploiting all of us for a story? I had my suspicions but I don't think so. I think he was more involved years ago than he has told us, involved personally I mean, not politically. He is worried, so I am happy to help because I find I still have a soft spot for the old devil.'

'I would like to speak to Bill himself—' Paul began.

'So would I,' Katy interrupted him. 'He has promised to come here some time tonight but God knows when. That's all I can say. By the way he also said that you must not let anyone, and he emphasised the anyone, know where Lawrence is going.'

'I think I understand. In the meantime, I'm to give Lawrence your offer of hospitality?'

'Right.'

Paul walked slowly back to the kitchen, wondering how he

could most tactfully get Lawrence away from Judith, since it was obviously Judith who was not to know. The difficulty, however, was solved by Lawrence himself, who declared, as he put down his coffee, 'I've been thinking things over and I've decided that it's best for me to leave.' Paul was too astonished to reply immediately. What had Judith been saying, he wondered?

Before he could say anything, Lawrence continued. 'As I told you earlier, I think I was a bloody fool to come here in the first place. I can't do either of the things I wanted to do, so it's best for me to get out and stop making things difficult for you and Judy.'

'What do you think?' Paul asked his wife.

'I think Lawrence is right,' she replied calmly. 'There is nothing he can do.'

'There you are,' Lawrence said cheerfully. 'I'll just pack my bag and go.'

'But where on earth will you go?' Paul asked. 'You've got nowhere to spend the night.'

'I shall probably find somewhere. If not, I can always sleep rough. It doesn't worry me. I need a chance to be on my own just to think.' He smiled at Paul. 'It's all right, don't upset yourself. I'll go and pack now.'

'Don't you care at all?' Paul asked Judith.

'It might be safer for him on the streets. But, no, I don't care.'

Being unable to think of any suitable reply, Paul poured himself a cup of coffee and drank it slowly. When Lawrence came in the kitchen to say goodbye, he stood up and said, 'I'll see you to the Underground or the bus stop, that might help.' Ignoring Lawrence's protests, he went out with him, merely pausing to tell Judith that he would be back soon.

Chapter Ten

Paul walked back slowly from the Underground entrance, where he had left Lawrence, trying to decide what he would say to Judith, for he was both puzzled and annoyed by her indifference towards the man she had once loved. Having been impressed himself by Lawrence's honesty and apparent repentance, he could not understand why she remained aloof and even hostile.

As he entered the flat he heard the tumultuous arpeggios of the third movement of the *Moonlight Sonata* coming from the sitting room. Judith was a good pianist and he stood and listened with enjoyment for a few minutes without interrupting her before she reached the end. Striking the last chords, she turned round to look at him. 'Mission satisfactorily accomplished?' she asked with a slight mockery.

Then, without waiting for a reply, she began to play a nostalgic Chopin nocturne. Sitting on the sofa nearby, Paul leaned back to listen to her, shutting his eyes. The last incredible forty-eight hours seemed to vanish and he was at home again, listening happily to her as he had often done. It was beautiful and comforting. None of the questions he had been determined to ask seemed to matter any more.

'Would you like some supper?' Opening his eyes, he realised that she had finished playing and was smiling at him. 'How about an omelette with some crusty bread and a glass of wine?' she suggested. This seemed ideal. 'I'll prepare it,' she said, 'and you can choose a suitable CD. Mozart perhaps; what do you think?'

It was definitely like being at home, he decided some twenty minutes later as they sat together on the sofa, sipping their wine and listening to the light-hearted music. He put his arm around her. 'We should go to Vienna some time,' he suggested. 'Perhaps for the millennium?' Putting her wine down, she turned to look at him, her lips parted slightly. Pulling her close to him, he kissed her again and again with growing happiness.

Suddenly, cruelly, it seemed to him, she broke the spell. 'Aren't there some questions you want to ask me? Don't you think I was cruel to Lawrence?' She drew back a little, looking enquiringly at him. 'Or do you think it would be better to forget all that you have discovered and for us to return as soon as possible to our former contented life?'

As soon as she put it into words, he felt that his foolish dreams of a few moments before were impossible to realise. 'I don't deny I would like to but my reason tells me it's impossible. Surely, you don't dispute that?'

'I'm not sure. What did Lawrence tell you? Did he say anything about our relationship in the past?'

'No. He only told me that he was guilty of the crime he had been charged with, in the sense that he held the gun and pulled the trigger. He made it clear that you were quite wrong to think otherwise.'

'And so he thought he was justly punished?'

'He was anxious to make a distinction between what was legal and what was just, and so in prison he decided that he was legally punished but not justly.'

'Why not justly?'

'Because he said that to treat a man justly is to give him exactly what he deserves but in situations such as those existing in Northern Ireland that is impossible because nearly everyone who kills is revenging some earlier murder, probably in his own family. That argument has, of course, considerable force in every disordered society. Nevertheless, the government must attempt to maintain the legal system in order to avoid chaos. Don't you agree? '

'I have thought of these things,' she said coldly. 'Any intelligent person living there is forced to. But does he have a solution?'

Paul could feel her unspoken antagonism. Embarrassed, he tried to explain to her Lawrence's ideas of love and forgiveness and finally how he tried to put it into practice with a surprising result. 'I think that is why he wanted to see you,' he ended, 'to ask for your forgiveness.'

'We have not talked much but he has tried to speak to me of that.'

105

'Then, why are you so angry with him? Surely, that's a good thing to do? I would imagine that you would want to forgive him.'

'Forgive him for what? It was not my husband he killed. I am glad to know that she was good enough to forgive him. Her children may be happier as a result. My mother never forgave my father's killer and I think the bitterness of it killed her in the end. It certainly affected my life and spoilt her marriage with my stepfather who is a kind man.'

'Then, surely, Judith, you of all people ought to believe that forgiveness is very important?' He drew her closer to him. 'I'm sure you do, really. And, if so, why can't you forgive Lawrence?' When she did not answer immediately, he kissed her gently. 'Surely, you can at least tell me?'

'You don't know what you're asking.' She frowned and tried to pull herself away but he wouldn't let her.

'Please try,' he begged her.

'I can't forgive him because he hasn't really asked for my forgiveness.'

'But you said he had and you'd refused it.'

'He said he was sorry he had let me down but he had no idea what he was talking about. He was very relieved when I told him that I had finally continued my studies and that my life was now proceeding satisfactorily. He was sorry that he had hurt me at the time. And that was it. I suppose finding Maeve so frightened and that we were possibly in danger made it difficult for us to talk of anything else.'

'And you didn't encourage him? You didn't even tell him about me?'

'No, why should I? That had nothing to do with him. I simply told him that I couldn't forgive him until he told me clearly where he had offended me. Then and only then I might be able to do it. He was so lacking in understanding that he made me angry.'

'Yes, I realise that. But I still don't know why. He told me that the rumours were untrue and that he had actually killed the policeman. He couldn't say differently, even for you.'

'I don't want him to lie or make up a romantic tale. I want him to tell the whole truth which, I'm pretty sure he still isn't doing.

Most important of all, I want him to look truly at our situation as it was and to realise fully the wrong he did. Without that his "so-called" repentance seems unimportant to me.' Firmly now, she pulled herself away from him and sat up. 'I don't really want to talk about this, Paul. It's still painful for me to recall it. I've tried to put it out of my life but, for your sake, I'll tell you something so you can understand why I can't forgive. Lawrence didn't just hurt me. He betrayed our love and our promises to each other. We had agreed not to get involved in terrorist activities but to spend our life together. Then, without a word to me, he threw it all away for the cause. And he seems to have no idea of what he did and how much that meant to me. How can I possibly forgive him? He hasn't asked me to. Do you understand now?'

As she turned to face him, he saw that she was very pale and obviously deeply upset but she didn't weep. He took her in his arms and kissed her gently. 'My dear love, I don't suppose I understand it all properly but I do want to and, most of all, I want to comfort you. How can I best do that?'

'By simply staying with me and trusting me.'

'That's easy.' He kissed her again. 'You were the one who left, don't you remember? I came searching for you and wouldn't be put off, so you can't imagine that I want to leave you, can you?'

'I know. I acted crazily. I didn't want to see Lawrence. I was trying to decide to tell you but then the policeman rang and I was afraid that I was becoming involved in something unpleasant and I thought I could keep you out of it. But I've told you that before. It doesn't matter now, does it?'

'Of course not.' He stroked her hair trying to soothe her but he still had an uneasy feeling that there was much she was even now not telling him. 'Did you love Lawrence very much?'

'Yes, with all my heart or so I thought then but I was very young. It was like a dream come true. I thought we would get away from the horror and live a normal life. I believed he felt the same. He said he did.'

'But you did at least have a normal life in England with your stepfather, didn't you?'

'A lot of the time we didn't because my mother refused to forget my father and didn't want me to. So often I was forced to remember what happened when I was only three.' As she stopped speaking he felt her trembling and tried to soothe her and quieten her but she insisted on continuing. 'If I tell you now I shall never have to mention it again, shall I? You don't mind hearing it, do you?'

'Of course not. It will make things easier perhaps, if I do know.' He felt very guilty that he had never asked these questions before but had left her to suffer alone.

'I was sitting on the floor playing with my toys. My father was playing the piano – he was a musician. Suddenly, there were three deafening noises, shots. My father slumped forward and hit all the piano keys. There was an incredible jangling noise and then a terrible moment's silence. I ran up to him and called him but he didn't move or speak. Blood was dripping on the carpet. I didn't know what to do. Then my mother rushed into the room and started to scream and went on screaming. I went up to her but she didn't seem to notice me. People came and later someone took me away. Hours afterwards, they told me my daddy was dead. Mother was never the same again – not even when she married my stepfather. She told me that she married him so that I would have a proper home. But I never did, although he was kind. That was why Lawrence was so important. Do you understand? His father had been killed like mine and I thought he agreed with me that it was best to move away from it – never to think of revenge. But he didn't and then I thought I hated him.'

'I feel ashamed that I never asked you, never tried to find out what you had suffered. I was too bloody complacent for words. Content to live on the surface.'

Sitting up, she moved away from him a little. 'Don't be silly. There was no reason why you should have suspected anything like that. In any case I wouldn't have married you if you had. Only this morning, don't you remember, I told you that one of my two reasons for marrying you was that you didn't ask questions? I meant that. Only four years before I had started a new life with a new name. I did not want to think about the old one. Judy O'Hara was dead and I wanted it to remain that way. Don't you understand?'

'But now the situation is different, surely? Lawrence has come back into your life and some of the past has been made known to me. Don't you think it would be better now if you told me the whole story?' He took her hand and tried to look into her eyes but she turned away. 'Please,' he begged her, 'don't shut me out any more.'

She turned to look at him. 'I have told you,' she replied coldly, 'all that is necessary, more, in fact, than I ever wanted to tell. Why do you say that it's better for us to continue talking about the past? I simply find it an unnecessary pain.'

'Because it will strengthen our marriage by bringing us closer to each other. Surely, you must agree that a relationship is stronger when it's based on honesty and understanding?'

Unexpectedly, she smiled at him. 'Dear old Paul! It sounds good and I'm sure it's what a marriage counsellor would advise. But it isn't necessarily true, is it?'

'It seems the best way to me. I don't see why you want to deny it.'

'Don't you?' She bent forward and kissed him, then smiled up at him beguilingly. Instinctively, he returned the kiss. Gently she moved herself away from him. 'Wouldn't you say that we have been happy these last six years? Haven't your friends envied you your marriage?' She waited, smiling. He could not deny the obvious truths. 'I don't see how we could have been happier.'

'But wouldn't you have been happier if you could have talked freely to me? Didn't you resent my complacency?'

'No, and again no. You gave Judith Martin freedom to be herself and she appreciated it. Are we any happier for what you have learned recently? I hope that we can put it behind us now and go on with our lives as soon as we can.'

'But how can we possibly do that?'

'It may be easier than you think. Judy O'Hara is dead and best forgotten. Lawrence has, at last, had the good sense to go away. You can keep your promise to sort him out with Inspector Barrett, if that is possible, and we can then go home.'

'I don't understand you, Judith! You can't really be saying that we can continue our lives as if nothing has happened?'

'Why not? Nothing really important has happened if you look at it rationally. I have been forced to tell you about my unhappy youth and especially about Lawrence with whom I was foolish enough to fall in love and who let me down rather badly as it seemed at the time. I was not involved in any terrorist activities, so why can't I be allowed to forget these unhappy times?'

'Then if that is all it was, why can't you forgive Lawrence? Why are you so angry?

'I'm angry because he forced himself into my life again, so that he could have the luxury of being forgiven. Since it upsets you, I'm even prepared to forgive him as long as I don't have to talk to him again.' She smiled at him. 'Will that satisfy you?'

He looked closely at her; she continued to smile. There seemed little more to say. Miraculously, the Judith he had always known seemed to have been restored again. He tried to put aside suspicions that she was not telling the whole truth. 'All the same I am glad you've told me. You might believe now that I love you. You might even be able to love me in time.'

'You're still worrying about what I said this morning about love. I was trying to be truthful. Love is a word that can have so many meanings and people often deceive themselves with it. Why not just accept the fact that we are happy together because we find such delight in making love? You know you enjoy it as much as I do. What on earth is wrong with that?'

'Nothing. I sometimes worry that it might not last.'

'I believe that it'll last as long as we do. That is the truth about us, so why should you worry about all these other truths, whatever they might be? Forget you're a solicitor and remember you're a very good lover. At least, I think so.' Suddenly putting her arms round him, she pulled him down on top of her and their lips met in a long kiss. 'You can't deny it, can you?' she whispered after a few minutes.

'I don't want to try,' he replied, pulling her even closer.

'Let's go to bed,' she suggested. 'It'll be much more comfortable. It's early; we can make up for the time we've missed recently.' He did not want to stop but reluctantly allowed himself to be persuaded. She stood up. 'I'll take the tray into the kitchen and if you tidy up the music here you can have your reward. The quicker you are, the sooner that will be.' As the door closed behind her, he began to put the CDs away and the sheet music.

He didn't want to waste a minute.

He had almost reached the living room door when the bell rang. He froze. Who could possibly be calling on them? It couldn't be anyone they wanted to see. A strange feeling of dread came over him. The bell was rung again. Slowly, he walked down the hall to the front door. The bell rang again. Whoever it was was impatient. He opened the door. Even in the dim light he thought he recognised the man standing there as the leader of his three attackers, but when the man spoke he realised he was mistaken.

'I'm sorry to disturb you, Mr Tempest, especially at such a late hour but I need to speak to Judy.' He spoke coldly and unemotionally.

'Who the hell are you?' Something in the man's manner angered Paul unreasonably.

'I'm not sure whether you have heard of me. I'm Tom Farrell.'

'I've certainly heard of you. What do you want?' He stood without moving, blocking the doorway.

'As I've already said, I wish to speak to Judy.' He spoke as someone who did not expect to be denied.

Paul tried to hide his anger. 'She's not available at he moment. Surely it can wait till tomorrow? Now will you please go? I have no wish to speak further with you.' He tried to shut the door but with a swift move Tom Farrell stopped him.

'I quite understand your feelings but I have come to speak to Judy. Is she here?' Before Paul could answer, the kitchen door opened and he heard Judith's voice.

'Who is that?' she asked. Turning round, he saw her begin to move into the hall. Before he could answer Tom Farrell spoke for himself. 'It's me, Judy. I thought you would be expecting me.' He moved a step forward. 'Although I'm later than I intended.'

'Why the hell are you pushing yourself in here?' Paul asked furiously. 'Neither of us wants to see you.' To his amazement Judith did not support him.

'It's all right, Paul,' she said, moving forward swiftly. 'I want to see Tom.' She was smiling past him at Tom. 'I'm glad you've come. I thought that something…' She paused suddenly, then added, 'Let's talk in the living room.' After shutting the front door, Paul slowly followed them, realising bitterly that Judith had still been deceiving him even when she had seemed most loving to him.

As he came through the door, Tom Farrell spoke to Judith. 'Since I'm so late, Judy, I won't stay long now. But can I just have a word with Lawrence. Where is he?'

'I don't know,' she replied.

'Don't get soft-hearted, Judy,' Tom said smiling. 'Just tell him I'm here.'

'I can't. He left some time ago. He didn't want to stay here any longer.'

'Where did he go?'

'We don't know. He said he'd wander around and just doss on the streets somewhere.'

There was a silence, then Tom sat down in an armchair. 'In that case, we do need to talk, Judy.' He looked at Paul. 'I'm sorry,' he said, 'I think it might be better if you weren't involved, Paul.'

'So do I,' Paul agreed grimly. Without looking at Judith, he left the room.

Chapter Eleven

Almost without thinking, Lawrence entered the Underground and bought a ticket to the station which Paul had told him was the nearest one to Katy's flat. On arriving there, he disembarked, took the escalator and finally emerged into a busy high street. Then he paused. Paul had given him the directions to Katy's but suddenly he realised that he did not want to go there – at least not yet. He was not quite sure why he had so unexpectedly decided to leave Judith and Paul except that he had an uneasy feeling that it would be unsafe to stay there any longer. Most of all, however, he needed to be on his own and to think.

In the last few hours everything seemed to have changed. He had not expected it to be straightforward when he had decided to come to London. He had known that many things would be difficult, perhaps dangerous, but he had always imagined that it would be possible to talk to Judy.

How stupid he had been! While he had been in prison, cut off by his own wish from his friends and most of his family, so much had changed. He had changed greatly himself, passing from bitterness to resignation, and finally to repentance, and yet he now realised he had expected to find Judy the same eager, passionate girl he had left on that dreadful night. Instead he met a cool, aloof woman who did not wish to talk of the past and who rejected any attempts on his part to ask for forgiveness. She had made it quite clear that her feelings were no concern of his; she had even wanted to conceal her husband from him. Why, he wondered, had she ever agreed to meet him? If she had not done that, he would not have had any hopes. What was there for him to do now?

He paused outside a shop window and stared at the tantalising display of extremely flimsy women's underclothes. Fashions had obviously changed in twelve years. Judy, he was sure, had never worn clothes like those. He wandered on down the high street past a display of greed-inducing chocolates, a cheap jeweller's, a crowded gambling arcade, feeling more and more out of touch. People pushed past him, almost as if he were invisible. Everyone seemed to have a companion or a definite destination. This was lonelier than prison. He turned up the collar of his jacket to keep out the wind and the cold drizzle it brought with it.

Suddenly, he noticed a snack bar on the other side of the road and, at the risk of his life, managed to dash across to it. He was not hungry but it looked warm and inviting and a cup of coffee might help him to think. Finding an empty table, he ordered a coffee and a doughnut. This was an improvement, he decided. It was good to be warm and in the company of people, without any need to talk and explain himself. An elderly woman came up and asked if she might share his table. Smiling, he agreed. She wore a very shabby tweed overcoat with an even more ancient shawl to protect her neck and shoulders. Her face was worn and old like her clothes but her brilliant red woollen cap and her bright blue eyes that looked sharply at him proclaimed that the world had not yet beaten her.

Taking off her mended woollen gloves, she wrapped her hands round her teacup. 'It's a good place this on a cold night,' she remarked smiling at him, 'particularly when you're on your own. Trouble is, even a cup of tea costs a fortune.' In spite of herself, her blue eyes lingered longingly on his fresh doughnut.

Lawrence pushed his plate towards her. 'Would you mind having this? I don't want it. I only bought it as an excuse to stay a bit.' For a moment he was afraid she was going to refuse but hunger overcame her pride.

'Thanks.' She put out her hand. 'I really like a fresh doughnut but you can't afford things like that on a pension. Shouldn't really have this cup of tea, I suppose, but it's nice to get warm and see people.'

'Do you live alone then?' Lawrence realised how much he wanted to talk too.

'Yes, ever since my old man died nearly five years ago. I miss him. I've got a cat but it's not quite the same.' She laughed. 'Though he does cuddle up to me in bed.' She looked at Lawrence. 'Are you on your own too?' When he nodded, she went on.

'Doesn't seem right to me. A good-looking young chap like you on his own on a Sunday night. If I'd been a few years younger, you wouldn't be. What's happened to the girls?'

'I've been away a long time. People forget you – don't want to know you when you come back. You remind them of things they'd rather forget.'

'How long you been away then?'

'Twelve years.'

She looked at him carefully with her shrewd blue eyes, as she carefully chewed the doughnut. 'You been in prison? Just come out?'

'Yes. How do you know?'

'Oh, I dunno. You have the look about you. Pale and kind of cut off. My brother was in prison once. I suppose I remember how he looked. Don't need to worry. You can still make a go of things. My brother, Fred, got a good job up north and he's been fine ever since. Was it a bad thing you did? No, I shouldn't ask. You don't have to tell me.'

'I killed a man. I didn't mean to and I've been sorry ever since.'

'That's all right then. If you're sorry, God'll forgive you and he'll find you something to do, if you ask him.' She spoke with complete confidence.

'You believe in God?'

'Of course I do. Couldn't manage without him. Look at me tonight. I was feeling real down, so I said a prayer and the Lord led me here to you. Someone to talk to and a doughnut as well.'

Lawrence laughed. 'I never thought of myself as an answer to prayer!'

'Don't get cocky, young man! It was my prayer what was answered. You're just God's instrument.'

'In that case, how about another cup of tea and another doughnut?'

'You couldn't make it coffee, could you?' The bright blue eyes twinkled at him.

'Why not?' He went swiftly to get them for her, then sat down again, smiling.

For the next fifteen minutes they talked, at least Doris, as she told him her name was, talked and he listened. She told him a little about her life at present but spoke mostly of the joys of the past when her Arthur was still alive. Suddenly, however, she put down her empty cup and looked straight at him. 'That's enough about a silly old fool like me,' she said. 'What about you? You've got to put the past behind you. Have you decided what you're going to do next?'

It was impossible to evade her. 'I don't know. I need to think but I don't know how to start. It seemed pretty clear in prison but outside it's all different. I don't know where to begin.'

'You need someone to talk to.' She looked at him sympathetically. 'Isn't there anyone?'

'No. I thought there might be. There was a girl I loved when I went to prison but she doesn't want to know. I can't blame her.'

'No. Twelve years is a long time. She's had to fend for herself, you see. It's hard for girls.' She was silent for a moment, then she leaned across the table towards him. 'Why don't you try talking to God, like I do? But perhaps you're one of the people who think they don't believe in him?'

'Oh, I believe in him all right but I'm not sure he still knows me. I don't know how to get to him, you see.'

Doris considered the question. 'There's a Catholic church,' she said at last, 'about five minutes away from here. It's called Holy Cross Church. It's a nice little church. I often slip in there if I feel out of touch. It's warm too. Just say "hello" to Him, then sit there and think. I can't think of a better place.'

'Where is it?' It seemed the sort of place he needed – quiet and warm.

'When you go out of here, just turn right, then take the second turning on the left. You can't miss it. If you go now, they'll just be coming out of evening Mass; it'll be really warm. Father Patrick may be around but he won't bother you. Why don't you try it? It can't do you any harm.'

'I will.' Lawrence stood up. 'But what about you? Can I get you anything else?'

'No. I've had a lovely time out, thanks to you. But you can see me on my way home. I don't live all that far from the church. And a strong arm's always welcome.'

They left together and he parted from her outside the church porch as the last few people were still leaving.

Slowly he went up the steps and through the heavy door, stopping without thinking to dip his fingers in the holy water and make the sign of the cross as he had always done as a boy. The church was fairly dark but there were still a few lights on and rows of candles flickering before the statue of the Sacred Heart. Making his way to the front row, he sat down and gazed at the large crucifix over the altar. What was it Doris had said? Just say 'hello'. It had seemed so easy but now somehow it wasn't.

He stared at that well-known figure of suffering. The eyes of that slightly bent head seemed to gaze into his. 'Well, here I am,' he whispered, 'I wish you would help me, though I don't see why you should.' Feeling a little ridiculous, he bent his head. What had gone wrong? As he had told Paul he had come to believe that repentance and forgiveness was the only way to end the unending repetition of violence and hatred which had darkened his youth. Surely that must be right, for that was what Jesus taught. And it had seemed to work. The widow of the man he had killed had forgiven him. He had felt wonderful then, filled with joy and hope. Hard though it had been, he had tried to treat the people around him differently. Then had come his unexpected release. That had seemed like a sign. He had been forgiven. Life could begin afresh.

But it hadn't been like that. Now he realised how naive he had been. It had seemed to him that if only he could see Judy he would be able to put everything right. He had gone on thinking about her and loving her all these long twelve years and he had imagined it had been the same for her. But had he ever tried to see the truth of her situation? As Doris had said, 'It's hard for a girl, when she has to fend for herself.' He could understand that now, however, he could even accept that she was married but what he could not understand was why she wouldn't talk to him, wouldn't forgive him when he said he was so sorry for letting her down. That seemed far more important than the other people who threatened him. What was there for him to do? He almost wished he had been able to stay in prison.

Feeling it was too painful to think about this any more, he let his thoughts wander back to the happy days he and Judy had spent together. The hours when they had been able to escape from Belfast to a quiet spot where they had been able to hug and comfort one another with their love and with the plans for the future. He almost groaned aloud when he thought how it might have been, if only he had been different.

Lifting up his head, he noticed the priest busy round the altar, making preparations for the next morning's Mass, he imagined. The church was now empty. The priest turned round and caught his eye. For a moment, he hesitated, then he came across the sanctuary, down the steps and approached Lawrence. 'You are a stranger here, I think,' he said quietly. 'Is there any help I can give you?'

Lawrence looked up at him. It was difficult to tell his age, for although his hair was a silvery grey, his face was remarkably unlined and his grey eyes had an ageless tranquillity. So this is how you do it, God, was Lawrence's first thought. 'I don't know,' he said aloud. 'I'm not sure.'

Father Patrick looked down at the still youngish man – about thirty he imagined him, for his black, curly hair was still untouched by grey. The face might be called handsome but the features were marred by lines, which indicated bitterness and suffering. The first impression was that of a hard man but the dark brown eyes looking up to him seemed to show a man deeply troubled. He also became aware of the young man's unnatural pallor and like Doris he realised what that most probably indicated. 'In that case,' Father Patrick replied, 'would you be willing to take a chance with me?'

For a moment Lawrence hesitated, then he shrugged. 'It can't do any harm, I suppose. I do need to talk to someone.' He stood up.

'I imagine it might take longer than five minutes, so shall we go to the presbytery where we can also be sure of privacy?' He began to move towards the back of the church.

Lawrence started to follow him, then stopped. 'Understand,' he said harshly, 'I only want to talk. I don't want confession or anything like that. Just a conversation between two people.'

'That is exactly what I was suggesting, although I also thought

I might offer you a share of my cold supper.'

'I'm not hungry. I don't need charity.'

'Of course not. I wasn't offering that, merely a friendly cheese sandwich and a glass of Guinness while we chat. You may not be hungry but I must confess that I am.' He smiled, apparently quite unmoved by Lawrence's seemingly surly attitude.

In spite of himself, Lawrence smiled back. 'I think I would enjoy that. It's been a long time since I did.'

As they walked towards the presbytery, the priest introduced himself. 'I'm Patrick – Patrick Fitzgerald – originally from Cork but I've been in London for over twenty years.'

'Do I call you "Father"?' Lawrence asked as they went through the door into the hall of the presbytery.

'No. Unless, of course, you want me to call you "Father"?'

Lawrence grinned. 'Lawrence will do – Lawrence Reardon. From Belfast – only just come to London for the first time.'

The presbytery was warm and welcoming but the priest's study into which they went, although comfortable, was only sparsely furnished – a desk with a computer, telephone, two armchairs and a table laid with a simple supper and, of course, shelves of books and piles of papers. Lawrence felt relaxed as he took the armchair offered to him by the fire. Meanwhile, Patrick, having tossed his cassock on the back of a chair, went out, only to come back a few minutes later with an extra plate and glass and two bottles of Guinness. 'The feast is prepared,' he declared, 'come and eat.'

Sitting down at the table, Lawrence watched him while he carefully poured out the drink, then gratefully took the glass offered to him. 'I'm afraid it couldn't be simpler,' Patrick apologised, 'just bread and cheese and an apple if you would like one. Help yourself.'

'You have no idea who I am,' Lawrence protested as he took the offered food. 'I might be a conman, a crook or somebody really dangerous. Don't you think you ought to be more careful.'

'You're a man in deep trouble. You wouldn't have been sitting in the church if that were not so,' Patrick smiled serenely.

'I suppose you're going to say God told you to speak to me?' Why was he being so aggressive and unpleasant, Lawrence wondered, instead of accepting the kindness he wanted so much?

'Perhaps. Do you think he might have done?'

'I shouldn't think so.' Lawrence paused, then went on, 'You might as well know, I'm a murderer. I've only recently come out of prison after twelve years instead of the thirty I expected.'

'The Maze prison perhaps?' He waited but when Lawrence didn't answer, he took a long drink, then, picking up his knife, he began to butter a slice of bread. 'If I'm right,' he asked finally, 'are you a Protestant or a Catholic?'

'Does it matter? Though I can't imagine a Protestant would be in this church, can you?'

'Strange things do happen. But no, it doesn't matter.' He cut a slice of cheese.

'I suppose you'd call me a Catholic. I was brought up one but that seems a long time ago. I was also brought up to hate the Protestants and to revenge my father's death. That seems a long time ago too. And completely pointless.'

'You think that now, do you?'

'Yes, and if you don't, you ought to.' Patrick only smiled and offered him the cheese. Looking at him suspiciously, Lawrence took some, then continued. 'I say you ought to because during my last years in prison I read the Gospels properly for the first time and it seemed to me that Christ had the right idea. You've got to be sorry for the bad things you do and ask people to forgive you and of course you've got to forgive them as well. That's the only way to stop this hating and killing. I suppose I'm trying to say we should love one another or at least try to.'

'You seem to have a pretty good idea of the Christian message. So what has gone wrong? Why were you in my church tonight?'

'I don't really know. I thought I had it right. It seemed to work and I was really on a high for a time, but since I've come out it hasn't been like that. God seems to have disappeared, if he ever was there. The two people I most wanted to see, my one time girlfriend and my sister, don't want to know, they don't even want to talk to me. So what can I do? What's gone wrong?'

'Perhaps it will help if you tell me more of the story. But have a drink and a little food before you start.'

It seemed easy in this quiet room without any fear or tension to tell the story of his love for Judy and of his sorrow for the breaking of the agreement they had made to cut away from their past and start afresh. There was silence when he ended but it was a friendly silence.

Father Patrick seemed to be in no hurry to speak. He seemed to be considering what he had heard or, perhaps, he was praying. Finally, he looked straight at Lawrence and commented exactly as Doris had, 'Twelve years is a long time, you know. You couldn't have expected her to stay the same.'

'I do realise that was just a silly dream but I did hope she would talk to me and we could make our peace. It tortures me that she won't even try.'

'You don't expect her to leave her husband, do you?'

'No, definitely no. I couldn't marry anyone as I am. And he's a decent bloke. I've met him and I like him. I told you that. He cares a lot for her. But he's upset too. Judy had never told him anything.'

'You say she's angry?'

'Yes, very.'

'And she says she won't forgive you? What exactly does she say?'

'She says she can't forgive me because I haven't asked her to. She says I haven't understood the situation properly and that I'm not telling the whole truth.'

'Is she right? Are you telling her the whole truth?' When Lawrence didn't answer, Patrick continued, 'Perhaps you haven't even told yourself the whole truth? Have you considered that?'

'I don't know what you mean.'

'Sometimes we hate the things we have done so much that we hide them not only from others but also from ourselves. We don't even admit them to God, although of course he knows.'

There was a long silence while Patrick waited for Lawrence to answer. He was obviously not going to offer any assistance.

Finally, Lawrence looked up at the priest. 'You're right. There are things I've never told anyone, although they don't directly affect Judy.'

'How can you be sure of that when you and she were as close as you have told me you were? Surely, what affected you so deeply must affect her. Have you considered the possibility that other people may have hinted things to her so that now she considers that you must be lying?'

'I suppose that could have happened. There are always people ready to make trouble, especially because they distrust my brother, Michael. He was a powerful man in the IRA but he never got caught and now he's very much involved in Sinn Fein and the peace process. I imagine some folk consider I'm like him but I'm bloody well not!' He glared angrily at Patrick.

'You don't seem to like him either?'

'Perhaps not. But this doesn't help. I would tell Judy these things if she'd let me get close enough but she won't. I almost think she hates me. I suppose I deserve it, perhaps. I don't know. Since she's happy now why should she go on hating me? I didn't enjoy prison. I've been punished. You might think she could afford to be kind.'

'Perhaps there is a reason you have never thought of.'

'Why doesn't she tell me then? Give me a chance? What the hell am I supposed to do?'

Patrick considered this for a time while thoughtfully peeling his apple. Lawrence finished his drink and then leaned back. He was content for a moment to enjoy the peace of this room and the comfort of talking to someone who cared. This was what he had been longing for. He had stupidly hoped to find this with Judy. He had been living in an unreal world, he now realised, where time had stood still. It had not been so for Judy.

'I think,' Patrick said slowly and quietly, 'that you are supposed to find the answer to the riddle yourself. Perhaps it is something that she cannot bear to tell you or maybe it is that she believes that, if you have to be told, you are not truly repentant. Or perhaps it is both these things. But you have to find the answer for yourself. If you don't think it is worth the pain and trouble, then give it up and go away.'

'I can't give it up. I wish to God I could.'

'Perhaps it is God himself who doesn't want you to. He always has his own agenda and it often doesn't correspond with what we think it ought to be. Remember in Isaiah the prophet says of God, "My ways are not your ways. My thoughts are not your thoughts.'" He stood up and moved across to the armchair by the fire. 'I'm sorry that there is not much I can say. I'm afraid I've disappointed you. But apparently God does not intend you to have an easy solution.'

Lawrence too stood up. He grinned. 'It begins to look like that but I'm very grateful to you anyway for welcoming me and listening to me. I only wish I knew where to start.'

'My feeling,' Patrick replied quietly, 'is that you should start with that time when you last met. You left that young girl without one word of truth and without preparing her in the least for what might happen.'

'Oh God, it was so terrible what I did! I've never been able to face it.'

'But you must for her sake and yours. I have only mentioned what you didn't do, for that is all you've told me but perhaps the answer lies also in what you did do. Have you thought of that?'

Lawrence looked grimly at him, his face even paler, if that were possible. 'I was very selfish, I—'

'We agreed that this was not to be a confessional,' Father Patrick interrupted him gently. 'You must go on your way now. My part is done. But first go into the church and try to ask for further directions before you resume your journey. You have a bed for tonight, I think you mentioned?'

'Yes. And I ought to be there by now. But I'll do as you say first. Good night and thank you.'

'Good night, Lawrence. May God bless you,' was all Patrick said as he conducted Lawrence to the door into the church.

Chapter Twelve

Lawrence pressed the bell labelled 'K. Evans' and waited, still wondering if it would not have been better to go back and make a determined attempt once more to speak honestly to Judy. After a few moments he heard someone running down the stairs. The door was swiftly opened and in the light of the hall he saw a slightly built young woman with soft naturally brown hair and a friendly smile 'You must be Lawrence!' she exclaimed. 'Thank God! I was beginning to think that something must have happened to you.'

Cutting short his apologies, she invited him to follow her upstairs. 'My flat's on the second floor,' she explained as he quickly followed her. She led him along the landing to a large living room, where for a moment they stood and looked at each other. Immediately, without his usual reserve he decided that he liked her. She had no outstanding features except for her large, long-lashed tawny brown eyes and her firm mouth with its ready smile but he had the impression that she was kind and trustworthy.

'Make yourself comfortable,' she said, taking his bag from him. 'Take your jacket off and sit down there.' She indicated a comfortable armchair drawn up near the brightly burning gas fire. 'You look pale and tired. Would you like coffee and food? I can soon provide both.'

'Neither thanks. I've had supper. It's just good to be here.' He had to smile back at her. 'I'm afraid I've interrupted your work,' he said, indicating the working computer on a nearby desk.

'Don't worry about that. I'm glad of the excuse to stop.' She curled herself up comfortably in the other armchair. 'Now tell me what happened. I was expecting you nearly two hours ago. Did you lose your way?'

'Not physically as Paul gave very good directions but you might say I did mentally. My mind was so confused, I just had to try to find a quiet place to think things through or at least to try to.'

'I can understand that. Even to me the last few days seem to have been overfull of happenings. Did you find somewhere to go?'

'A church and a kindly priest who was willing to spare the time to talk.' He stopped being unwilling to say more to someone who, however kind, was still a stranger. Apparently understanding, she sat back, seemingly content to let him say more if he wished or to remain silent. 'I began to wonder,' he said after a few moments, 'whether I had been wrong to run away without trying to sort things out more. Do you think I ought to go back even now?'

'I don't think you should. Definitely not.' The firmness of her tone surprised him.

'You seem to be quite sure.'

'I am. About an hour ago, Paul rang up again. He was expecting to speak to you and was rather worried when I told him you hadn't yet arrived. Nevertheless, he gave me a message for you. He told me that some time after you had left they had a visitor, totally unexpected by him but apparently not by Judith.'

'And who was that?'

'Someone you know well, I think – Tom Farrell.'

Lawrence stared at her. 'Are you sure that he said Tom Farrell? Could you have made a mistake?'

'No. He repeated the name to make sure I'd got it right. He said it was very important that I should tell you as soon as I saw you. He sounded angry but he didn't say anything about that.' She waited for him to make some comment.

Lawrence, struggling to overcome the shock, finally managed to say, 'It simply doesn't make sense. How could Tom Farrell have found out that address? Who could have told him?'

'I'm afraid I can't help you. I'm only an onlooker, friendly but not really involved except through my relationship with Bill.'

'Does Bill know anything about this, do you think?'

'I don't think so but he hasn't been in touch since he suggested that you left Paul and Judith and came here.'

'It seems as if he did know that something was wrong, don't

you think?'

'Possibly, but he didn't tell me and since he asked me to help, I think he might have told me something. But I'm afraid that's often Bill's way. He tends to make use of people.'

'Are you suggesting that Bill might have told Tom himself?'

'I suppose he might have done but I can't think why, can you? Especially as he warned you. No. I think he must have heard something that worried him.'

'It has to be Judy then. There is no one else who could have done it. But why? Why should Judy have done something like that? It doesn't make sense. It obviously upsets Paul as much as me. I don't understand it at all.' He covered his face with his hands, then shook his head as if he were trying to sort out his thoughts. Katy waited, sympathetic, but unable to help. At last he raised his head and looked at her. 'I'm sorry. I haven't any right to bother you, just because you've given me refuge. It's just that I'm baffled.'

'I know what you mean, at least to some extent. Bill makes me feel like that sometimes, when I suddenly realise that I don't know what he's doing or why. I suppose that's why I stopped living with him. I didn't want to take the strain any longer.'

'Do you ever regret it?'

'Sometimes but not enough to go back.'

'Yet you obviously still like him. You only took me in to please him, didn't you?'

Katy considered this carefully. 'That's not the entire truth. I heard about you because of Bill but I took you in because I wanted to help. It was the same with Paul. Of course, you could say that Bill takes advantage of that weakness of mine.' She smiled. 'I expect he does when it suits his own ends.'

'I wouldn't call it "weakness". I'd call it "kindness". And I'm very grateful for it. The trouble is that I'm lost, Katy. I don't know where to go or what to do, so I'm tremendously glad of a temporary refuge.' They were two normally reserved people and yet they were speaking like old friends. It seemed perfectly natural to both of them. 'I felt I could trust you as soon as we met.'

'You can. The truth is I've been a bit lost myself in some ways.'

'You mean because of Bill? Is it that you want to break away from him completely but you can't?'

'I think I do but then I'm not sure. He says he's changed and wants to marry me but I'm scared. I've had the offer of a good job in California and I'm thinking of taking it. Do you think that would be right?'

'You shouldn't ask me to advise you. Most of my life has been a disaster so far. All I'd say is don't do it unless you're ninety per cent sure or something like that.'

Clasping his hands, he leaned back in his chair and closed his eyes. He looked so vulnerable and so weary that Katy had a tremendous desire to help him more. 'Why have you come to London?' she asked gently. 'What did you expect?'

Opening his eyes, he sat up again. 'I don't know. I suppose I wanted to make amends somehow and obtain absolution.' Seeing her puzzled look, he grinned almost cheerfully at her. 'I suppose you don't understand these Papist phrases?'

'I'm trying to but I'm not sure I do. You seem to be implying that you've been a pretty bad sinner, although you're now repentant, I think. Were you a bad sinner?'

'You know I was. I was sent to prison for thirty years for killing a policeman.'

'And what else?'

'Isn't that enough?'

'You've been punished for that, so the slate should be clear. It must have been terrible in prison. Wasn't that enough punishment?'

'It was hell. I didn't think I'd be able to stand it. I tried to think of ways of committing suicide but I was rational enough to realise they wouldn't work and that to try and then to fail would just make life worse. I had to become hard and bitter like the others, outwardly, at least. But inside I was just a frightened, miserable kid who realised that I had thrown away a large part of my life. I thought it would be at least twenty-five years, you see.'

'It must have been wonderful when they told you that you were going to be released.'

'Yes, I felt I had a chance to do something useful in the world but I'd come to terms with life before then. I'd read a lot, talked with the chaplain and become a Christian. That changed everything, I thought. I was happy even in prison.'

'And now you're free but you're not happy? Why is that? Is it just that twelve years is a long time and the world's changed a lot in those years? Aren't you being hard on yourself, expecting too much too soon?'

'It's partly that but it's much more. I've begun to see that bad deeds done are like stones thrown into a pond. You can never know how far the ripples will spread. I've begun to be afraid of consequences I'd never imagined. Consequences of my actions.'

'That is why you talk of making amends and seeking absolution?'

'Yes. You mustn't deceive yourself about me, Katy. I'm more dangerous than you might think, potentially I mean, not at this moment.'

'That's a relief.' Katy smiled and stood up. 'I think I'll get us both a whisky. And don't dare refuse. I need it and, as my friend, you must join me. You are my friend, aren't you?'

'I very much hope so. I need a friend.'

'And so do I.'

After he had left the living room, Paul tried to control his anger so that he could think more clearly. For a few moments, however, he could only remember the cool arrogance of Tom Farrell and Judith's desertion. The whole time they had spent after Lawrence had gone had been an illusion carefully and cleverly created by her. Lulling his anxieties and suspicions, she had convinced him that she was still passionately in love with him. But why had she bothered especially when she knew that Tom Farrell was coming? The answer must be that she had not expected Farrell just then but it was clear that she had expected him at some time. Furthermore, Tom could only have had the address from her.

And what of Lawrence? It seemed that she was not only angry with him but ready to betray him to his enemies. For it seemed clear to him that Tom Farrell was no friend to Lawrence. There was no point in hiding away in the bedroom, he decided. He must confront them both, however distasteful this might be. As he came out of the bedroom and walked down the hall towards the living room, he heard Judith's voice.

'It's no use, Tom. I can't help you at the moment.' He couldn't tell what Farrell said in reply but it was obvious from Judith's next words, 'Of course, Paul might know. But he hasn't said anything to me. Why don't you ask him yourself?'

'Why don't you?' Paul asked angrily as he opened the door and walked in the room. Farrell, still wearing his dark overcoat, was leaning against the mantelpiece. Judith, who was walking towards him, spun round at Paul's unexpected interruption. Farrell, however, simply raised his head a little and looked at him. Neither of them spoke. 'To save you the trouble,' Paul continued, 'I'll tell you. I thought I did know where he was but a phone call has told me I was wrong. He hasn't gone where I expected he might go with the result that I don't know where the hell he is now.'

He sat down in an armchair trying to appear indifferent, although his pulse was racing. There was something menacing about Farrell's stillness. He would have liked to have threatened him violently but he knew that this would only result in his defeat; Farrell was much more accustomed to violence than he was. Instead, he waited for his response.

After a moment, Farrell straightened up. 'I'm sure I can take your word, Mr Tempest,' he said in his cold, unemotional voice. 'That being so, I'll leave you both with apologies. It seems I was misinformed.'

As he began to move towards the door, Paul stood up barring his way. 'I should like you to answer a few questions before you go.' Clenching his hands, he tried to speak as calmly as the other man.

'Why not ask your wife?' Farrell suggested. 'I'm sure she can answer you as well if not better than I can.' He turned and smiled at Judith. 'You shouldn't lie to your husband, Judy. It's a bad habit and leads to trouble.'

Although Tom Farrell's obvious familiarity with Judith angered him even more Paul was determined to persevere with his questioning. 'I think it would be better if I asked you both, don't you?'

Judith looked towards Farrell, obviously waiting for his

reaction. Tom Farrell merely smiled. 'Very well, if that's what you want. It might be the best course. I was never convinced that Judy's plan of action was the right one. Shall we sit down?' He moved towards the other armchair.

Paul remained standing. 'I'm feeling very angry,' he admitted, 'not so much with you as with Judith who, as you suggest, has not been telling me the truth, or so it seems.' He turned towards Judith who had sat down on the settee. 'Why have you invited this man here?'

Waiting for her answer, he stared fixedly at her. She turned away, nervously looking towards Tom Farrell as if seeking some support from him but he gave her no encouragement. She turned back again. 'Why did you do it,' Paul asked again, 'when you must know that I would not want to meet him?'

She looked directly at him and said clearly and firmly, 'Because he is my friend and because I do want to meet him.'

'Your friend? How can you say that? You know he is Lawrence's enemy. You know the police are probably seeking him as a terrorist and a murderer—'

'Please, Mr Tempest,' Tom Farrell interrupted quietly, 'you as a lawyer should know better than any of us how unwise it is to make unsubstantiated accusations. I may not have lived my life as you think I should but I have never been convicted of either of these charges.'

Paul laughed. 'I should imagine you have always been far too clever to be caught but I don't think you can deny that you would be capable of murder if you thought it necessary.'

'You're quite right.' Tom Farrell seemed unmoved. 'I have been trained and I would not hesitate to kill if I thought it was the right thing to do.'

Paul turned to Judith. 'And yet you say that this man is your friend, even though you have just heard what he has admitted.'

'Tom is not a murderer and it was my silly idea, not his, that he could help me more in my present difficulties than you could. In fact, I persuaded him to come to help me.'

'Your idea? Are you trying to protect him or something?' He turned towards Tom Farrell. 'Am I supposed to accept this nonsense? Are you trying to hide behind her or what?'

'Of course not!' Judith's dark eyes flashed. 'It was my idea and I wish it had succeeded. I wish you had stayed away. We would all have been happier.'

Tom Farrell smiled. 'As you must know, Paul, Judy is very persuasive. That is why I now found myself trying to help her, even at the risk of offending you and perhaps endangering myself.'

Paul turned once more towards Judith. He felt bewildered and outraged. 'Have I got this right? Are you actually telling me that this man is your friend? And that it was you who persuaded him to support you instead of me, your husband?'

'Yes. But I didn't intend it to be for your good. I simply wanted you to stay out of this. It has nothing to do with you and you might be hurt.' Her dark eyes were as unfathomable as always and she sounded completely calm.

'I have been hurt. I don't mean physically, but by you. You have lied to me and deceived me not only in the beginning but even tonight when I thought—'

'Paul,' she interrupted him sharply, 'I was not lying to you earlier tonight. I was saying what I have always said but that is between ourselves; it has nothing to do with Tom and the present situation.'

'You're right. If there is anything left for us to talk about, we can do it better on our own.' He turned towards Tom. 'So I have to accept, do I, that you are not my enemy but Judith's friend who was trying to keep me out of all this? I suppose these underhand methods come naturally to you?'

'As a terrorist, you mean?' Tom smiled the mocking smile that Paul recognised so well. 'I'll accept that, if it pleases you.'

'The truth would please me more.' Paul looked at both of them in turn. He waited but neither of them said anything. He sat down, feeling suddenly very weary and hopeless. 'Am I to understand then,' he asked, turning to Judith, 'that all you want me to do is to return to our home and wait to see what happens?'

'It is probably the safest idea,' she replied quietly.

'I see.' He tried hard to hide the pain he felt and to appear as calm as she did. 'I came because I wanted to help you and to stand by you if you were in trouble but obviously that was unnecessary, since you have your champion.'

'What is really worrying you?' Tom Farrell asked suddenly. 'If you suspect that Judy and I are lovers that's not so. We have not met for nearly six and a half years. She is married to you and, although you may not share my views, I regard marriage as a serious bond.' His voice was as cold and unemotional as always but Paul did not doubt his sincerity. 'We are both imprisoned in the past and what we want is to be free. Isn't that the truth, Judy?'

'That's all there is to say,' she agreed.

'I think it might be better for me to go now,' Tom suggested, 'and leave you two to talk.'

'What, about Lawrence?' Paul asked, suddenly roused. 'This fine talk is all very well but you haven't mentioned him. Judith suggested that I might help him but, at the same time, she keeps in touch with you and I'm pretty sure you don't want to help him. That all seems pretty treacherous to me.'

'I don't know what Lawrence has told you—' Tom began.

'The usual story,' Judith interrupted bitterly.

'I'm not sure what you mean by that.' Paul was annoyed by Judith's attempt to forestall his answer. 'He told me that he fired the shot that killed the policeman. He accepted that he was properly punished according to the law but denied that there was any justice in the situation.'

'I see.' Tom's cold grey eyes rested briefly on Paul, then he turned slightly towards Judith. 'Did he tell you, Paul, how or why he came to be in London?'

'I understood it was because he very much wanted to see Judith and his sister, Maeve.'

'I understand that. But how did he get permission to come here so soon after coming out of jail?'

'I supposed it was some kind of compassionate leave, although I didn't ask him.'

'You were very kind to him, weren't you?' Paul flushed. There was no ignoring the hint of mockery in Tom's voice and in his smile. 'But tell me, how did you first learn he was in England?'

'When Detective Inspector Barrett...' Paul stopped abruptly as he realised the significance of what he was about to say.

'When Detective Inspector Barrett told you he was looking for him. That was what you were going to say, isn't it? Paul nodded. 'So it doesn't seem as if Lawrence was acting entirely with official permission, does it? He had quietly slipped away from the law, as one might say and that is why Special Branch is looking for him. Doesn't that seem likely to you?'

'If that is true, then why did he want me to get in touch with them for him? You suggested it, in fact,' he said, turning towards Judith.

'I wanted to know what he would say,' Judith replied indifferently.

'I don't understand any of this,' Paul said impatiently, 'but I do know that he agreed to the plan, which doesn't seem as if he thought he would be in serious trouble.'

'But now he isn't available, is he? At least that was what you said to me recently. But perhaps you weren't being entirely truthful?'

Paul considered his reply. His sympathies were still with Lawrence but now Tom had raised doubts in his mind. Did he understand any of these people? 'The truth is,' he said slowly, 'that I thought I knew where he was going but, when I enquired, he hadn't arrived. I'm not prepared to say any more. For your part are you willing to tell me why you want to meet him?'

'Why? Do you think I might kill him?'

'Perhaps.'

'I might,' Tom agreed smoothly, 'but first of all I want some truth from him, without this religious cant he now seems to be talking.'

'He seems very sincere to me but you don't want to believe him, just as Judith won't forgive him when he asks her. It seems to me that you might be imprisoned in the past but he is trying to break away and you don't want that.'

'What do you mean by that?' Judith's voice was quiet but he could tell she was angry. 'What right have you to judge?'

'None, I suppose. Except that it is quite clear to me that you're determined to pursue him, even if you wreck our marriage. You seem quite prepared to throw away your present happiness because of some wrong in the past.'

'You are very unjust!' Judith was struggling to speak calmly. 'I didn't ask Lawrence to come back. I wish he hadn't. But he has. Perhaps he is not quite as perfect as you seem to think he is.'

Tom Farrell stood up. 'It's time for me to go.' He turned towards Judy. 'I'm sorry, Judy,' he said gently; then, as he turned towards Paul his voice hardened again. 'I will find Lawrence. But I advise you not to contact the police.'

'Perhaps I should contact them about you and your violent friends? I imagine they might be interested.' Paul was amazed at the anger he felt.

'Try it, if it pleases you.' Tom Farrell was quite unmoved. 'But do remember that you have no proof of anything and that you have no easy means of tracing me. When we find Lawrence, as we will, everything can be settled.' As he moved towards the door, Judith stood up and followed him. He paused at the door. 'Goodbye, Paul, and be careful, for Judy's sake if not for your own.'

Paul stood still as they walked down the hall. He heard the front door open, then there was silence. Seized by panic, he rushed to the door with the crazy conviction that if he did not stop it Judith would vanish into the night with this cold man of violence. She had not vanished but what he saw seemed almost as unbelievable. Facing Tom, Judith was looking up at him. He put his arm round her shoulders, then, as Paul looked, he bent and kissed her gently. For a moment she seemed to cling to him, then she slowly drew herself away. They were obviously reluctant to part.

Moving hastily back into the room, Paul walked over to the window. Drawing back the curtain, he looked into the dimly lit silent square. He saw Tom Farrell hurrying towards the corner. He heard Judith shut the front door. She was coming back. What could he possibly say to her?

Chapter Thirteen

Katy's whisky was indeed warm and comforting but not more so than her friendly smile as she curled up opposite him again. Lawrence could not imagine why he had thought her quite plain when he had first seen her. Anyone with sparkling tawny brown eyes like hers and with a smile like hers could only be considered beautiful. He had a ridiculous impulse to stroke her soft brown hair.

Looking at her watch, Katy exclaimed, 'I think I might as well give Bill up! He's obviously forgotten about me. He's probably already in bed and asleep.' For a moment her smile was dimmed, but not for long. 'In which case we might as well drink to each other and enjoy ourselves.'

Lawrence felt uncomfortable for he had imagined that Bill would turn up. 'In that case would you rather I didn't stay the night? I can always find somewhere to doss down, I'm sure.'

'Don't be silly. You can have my divan here and I'll retire with suitable maidenly reserve to my bedroom. I will feel much happier if you're around to keep me safe. I never thought I'd find myself saying that! Please don't humiliate me more by refusing. I don't think my ego would stand it! Forgotten by Bill and rejected by you! How could I explain that away?' She was still smiling brightly but he felt an appeal she could not give voice to. 'You must be my knight in shining armour.'

'Then you are my lady and I will protect you.' He smiled back at her and, lifting his glass, toasted her with the last of his whisky.

'Good.' Finishing her whisky, she stood up. 'Then I suppose we'd better make plans to get to bed. You should find the divan comfortable but I'll put an extra cover out in case you need it. It seems pretty chilly tonight. In the morning, we may hear from Bill with our instructions.'

Deep, dark depression hit him suddenly. Reluctant to move, he huddled himself together in the armchair. In the middle of tidying the cushions, Katy stopped and looked at him. 'What's the matter? You look kind of lost.'

He tried to smile. 'I suppose I feel kind of lost. Nothing has happened quite as I expected.'

Putting down the cushion, she pushed the hair back from her face and regarded him seriously. 'What you need,' she decided, 'is a hug. I'm a great believer in hugs. They say far more than words and we could all do with more of them. What do you think?'

He could not resist the warmth of her voice nor the friendliness of her smile. 'Sounds good to me, though I can't remember when I last had one.'

'All the more reason to try one now.' She seemed to be waiting.

'What should I do?'

'Just stand up and I'll show you.' As he stood up, her arms encircled him, holding him close. It was wonderfully comforting, and it seemed perfectly natural to put his arms round her. The darkness receded; life suddenly held possibilities of friendship and understanding. 'This is the first time I've been close to a human being for over twelve years!' he exclaimed. Still holding her close, he bent slowly and kissed her without passion but with great tenderness. Healing tears flooded his eyes and he buried his face in her shoulder. Still without speaking, she held him even more tightly.

'God bless you!' he managed to say.

It was several minutes before they moved apart. Confused, he muttered, 'If you'll give me what I need, I'll get my bed ready. It's very late.'

Without answering Katy continued to gaze at him. 'I think you'd better share my bed,' she said finally. 'And I mean just that. You need a bit more that just one hug, don't you, Lawrence? And I don't mean anything sexual, just a chance to talk very closely with a friend. Am I right?'

He could not deny it. He knew that, if she left him, the darkness would overwhelm him again. 'Oh, Katy, how do you know so much? But can you really trust me, knowing what I am?'

She smiled. 'I know I can trust the Lawrence I have talked with tonight and that's all that matters. Now let's sort things out.

You're quite right, it is getting late or rather early. Have you got everything you need, nightclothes, and so on?

'In my bag,' he replied, picking it up.

'Good. While you go to the bathroom, I'll sort out the bed.' She laughed. 'I'll put a bolster between us, then you'll know you're safe.'

In a surprisingly short time they were comfortably settled, side by side. The one reading lamp on the table by her side of the bed provided an oasis of light, shutting out the darkness and the threatening shadows.

Katy smiled at him. 'Tell me more about yourself,' she said. As if sensing his withdrawal, she added quickly, 'I mean about you years ago before everything went so terribly wrong.'

He thought and then replied slowly, 'I suppose they always were wrong. I never wanted to be involved in the violence. I think I was a bit of a coward, really.'

'It must have been terribly difficult to try to live a normal life, with the background of the Troubles all the time.'

'It wasn't just the background; it was in my home, after my father was killed in an ambush. My mum didn't intend that we should ever forget, especially when Michael, my eldest brother, became a big man in the IRA. My other brother followed him and that was supposed to be my future. Nothing was said; it was simply made obvious.'

'And you didn't want that?'

'No. I wanted to use my brains. I didn't want to be a mechanic; I wanted to be a design engineer. I actually enjoyed maths. The kids laughed at me at school and my family waited for me to grow up. That's why Judy was so important.'

'How do you mean?'

'She was very bright. Much brighter than I was but we could talk maths and she understood my ambition.' He smiled, remembering. 'But it wasn't only that, Katy. She was beautiful and all my mates wanted to take her out. When we were fifteen, she chose me and my troubles were over.'

'You loved her?'

'Loved her? I worshipped her. And then I let her down!' He was silent, staring in front of him.

Katy gently took his hand in hers. 'We're not going to talk about that now,' she reminded him. 'It was good that you had so many happy times together. I almost envy you. I never had anything like that. Mine was a pretty dull predictable life in a comfortable provincial suburb. I made my way to university in London, studied chemistry, did better than I had expected, so I decided to make a career. And that's me.'

'No love life?'

'Nothing of any importance until I met Bill. He was already a successful journalist; it seemed amazing to me that he should be interested in me but he was. We lived together for quite a time but then I left.'

'Are you willing to tell me why?'

'I'm willing but I don't know if I can. It was I who changed, not Bill. I suppose I could say that I realised that I would never, never come first with him; the story, the job would always take precedence.'

'But surely you must have known that was how it would be? And you had your job which mattered to you, didn't it?'

'Yes, of course, you're right.' There was a long pause. Lawrence waited. She sat up impatiently, almost angrily. 'Of course, you're right. I'm not being entirely honest but I don't want to be unfair to Bill. He's always been kind to me and I've no reason to be afraid.'

'But you are?'

'Yes. He's an investigative journalist, as you know. And they have to be ruthless at times, or so I suppose. I'm just worried that he might do something I couldn't accept and I don't want to risk being involved. Also, I've detected a feeling in myself of wanting to settle down and have a family one day. That would never work with Bill.'

'What does he say?'

'He's asked me to marry him. I've told him about California.' She looked at Lawrence who was lying back with his eyes shut. She laughed. 'I'm sorry. I had no intention of using you as my agony aunt. You won't believe this but I simply meant to cheer you up.'

He opened his eyes and grinned at her. 'And you have by

talking honestly to me and by listening to me. It's years since that has happened to me.'

'Me too. I know lots of people but there's no one to talk to.'

'Not even Bill?'

'No. There has never seemed to be any time. He doesn't need it but I do. Funny, isn't it, how you can suddenly meet someone and know you can trust him?'

'I think it's a miracle.' He bent over and kissed her gently. 'It's time we went to sleep. Good night, Katy. May we sleep in peace.'

It must have been over an hour later that her phone woke Katy. 'Is that you, Bill?' she asked, thinking that at last he had remembered her.

'No, it's Paul. Do I understand that Bill isn't with you?'

'He isn't but Lawrence arrived some hours ago. Shall I wake him?'

'No, there's no point.' Paul sounded very strange. 'Something has happened, Katy. I can't explain now. I'll be in touch in the morning early. In the meantime, don't let Bill know where Lawrence is.'

'Why? What do you mean?'

'I'm not sure myself. It's just that I'm convinced that will be best. You'll have to trust me; can you?'

'I will. I'm pretty annoyed with Bill anyway.' She remembered the fears she had expressed to Lawrence but decided to say no more.

'I'll be in touch in the morning,' Paul promised. He rang off. Switching off her phone, Katy tried to settle herself to sleep again.

As he heard Judith coming down the hall to the living room where he waited, many thoughts rioted in Paul's mind. He would confront her with her treachery; he would force her to see the horror of her behaviour. He would, if necessary shake the truth out of her. To his surprise as she came through the door, he found himself saying with an anguish he could not hide, 'Why did Tom Farrell kiss you?'

'Because he is my friend and he wanted to comfort me a little.' He stared into her eyes which seemed even larger and darker than usual, emphasising the paleness of her face. 'Are you jealous then?' The unemotional quietness of her voice seemed to mock the possibility.

'Of course I'm jealous. I suppose you consider that stupid and ridiculous? Since your feelings are obviously so slight and changeable how can you imagine it?' He moved a step towards her as if he would attack her. She neither moved nor flinched. He dropped his hand. 'Jealousy is hardly an adequate word to express my feelings of total betrayal and humiliation.'

Waiting for her to make some defence, he stared at her but she simply moved back and sat down quietly, apparently waiting for him to continue. She sat in the armchair, directly under the tall standard lamp which illuminated clearly her features. She was as beautiful and desirable as she had been when he had first met her and now, as then, there was something sad, even tragic, about her. It would be only too easy to surrender. Her next words saved him. 'Perhaps you should tell me more clearly what you are accusing me of?'

'My God!' He stared at her. 'Surely, that is obvious even to you? There is so much. I don't know where to begin. I suppose it's easiest to begin at the end. You invited Tom Farrell here, the man whom I've been given to believe is an unrepentant terrorist and Lawrence's enemy. And then you tell me he is your friend and make it clear that you have been in touch with him all along and that he knows more than I do.'

'He is my friend and can help me but, more important than that, I wanted to keep you out of all this. I knew that if it ever happened it would be horrible and, if you were involved, I would lose my last refuge.'

'You mean you wouldn't be able to lie any more, as you have done in all the years I've known you?'

'What is a lie? Are you able to judge truth so easily? But I've forgotten you're a lawyer and you know all about it.' Leaning back, she closed her eyes as if weary of it all.

Anger flooded over him. He, who had always been so calm and controlled as he had thought, had to dig his nails into his palms to prevent himself from attacking her. Sitting down opposite her, he spoke as rationally as he could force himself to. 'Is there anyone, Judith, whom you have ever really cared for?

Earlier you told me pleasantly but brutally that our marriage was not based on love but on lust.'

She sat up suddenly. 'I would prefer to say physical attraction but, whatever word we use, you shouldn't despise it; it's very strong and long lasting and many marriages fail because it isn't there.'

'They also fail because there's no love. But it seems to me that you don't know what that word means. You left me because Lawrence called you. Or, at least, that's what it seemed. It might have been possible that you still loved him a little. But no! Your aim seems to have been to hurt him and then to betray him.'

'What do you mean?'

'I'm no longer entirely sure. It's difficult to disentangle all the threads or to make any kind of sense of this game you seem to be playing with us all. First you want to keep me out, if I'm to believe the nonsense I've been told and then, when that fails, you apparently decide to use me to give Lawrence a false sense of security by putting forward the idea that I can help him. Although the truth, of course, is very different.'

'What then have you decided is the truth?'

Her strangely calm, almost detached, attitude disturbed and surprised him. If he was ever to reach the truth, he felt, he must tear her calm to shreds. 'It's very difficult to know, isn't it? You ask me to help Lawrence, then you tell me he is lying and try to convince me that you almost hate him and cannot forgive him even when he asks you. What sort of a woman does that make you? A pretty unpleasant one, it might seem. He has lost so much, has so little and yet you want to deny him that small comfort.'

'What the hell do you know about it all, Paul? What right have you to say these cruel things?'

Without allowing her to deter him, he carried on remorselessly. 'Which brings me to the latest actor in this weird melodrama created by you. I mean Tom Farrell, of course. Another victim, perhaps? I don't know. All I know is that, although you have not met in six years or so you say, you are very close. He has been behind the scenes all the time apparently and now it seems you are prepared to hand Lawrence over to him, his worst enemy. But are you though? Even that isn't clear. Tom turns up but Lawrence has gone and you did nothing to stop him.' He paused and stared at her but she only gazed defiantly back at him. 'Now I ask myself who is to be the next victim? Tom or me? Perhaps you wouldn't mind telling me?'

When she still did not reply, he stood up. 'I'm beginning to think that it might be wiser for me not to wait to find out but to go back home and carry on with my life. When you want a divorce, perhaps you'll let me know.' He turned as if to leave the room. 'I'll take the first train in the morning.'

Before he could move any further, she jumped up and caught hold of him. 'You can't go now! Please, please, don't go now, Paul! Not in this way!'

He removed her hands from his arm firmly but gently. 'Why ever not?'

'Because I need you. Because you are my husband. We have been happy. You said so yourself.'

'I thought we were. But, Judith, how can I be sure of anything now? I don't know who you are or what you are. And I'm not sure you do either. Was anything in our years together real?' Looking at her, he saw her eyes fill with tears, which rolled slowly down her cheeks. Deathly pale, she sat down in the armchair as if she had no strength left.

Moving across to her, he offered her a handkerchief and waited it until she was calm enough to speak. 'They were as real as I could make them. The longest settled time I've ever had. I began to hope that what has happened would never happen. I even came to feel quite safe. I don't even understand myself. So, how can I possibly explain it to you?'

'I don't know but I wish you'd try.' He sat down on the arm of her chair and put his arm around her.

'You don't really want to leave me, do you? We were so close and so happy earlier this evening.' She looked up at him, her eyes again luminous with tears. The copper lights in her dark hair gleamed as they had done when he had first met her. The old magic began to work. Instinctively, he bent down and kissed her. Yielding, she clung to him. Suddenly, angry at his own weakness and remembering her recent closeness to Tom, he moved away and stood up.

'It's no good, Judith! Don't tempt me.'

'What do you mean? I don't understand you. We could be very happy just as we always have been. You're still in love with me, aren't you?'

'Yes. I can't deny it. But it's no longer enough.'

'What do you want?'

'Honesty, I suppose. I want to be sure of you. I want to know you properly. Don't you understand?'

'I think I do. But what can I say? How can I make you understand? Your life has been easy and straightforward. Mine was broken in half. There are some things so horrible, Paul, that one doesn't want to remember them. Judy O'Hara died, you married Judith Martin. When I met you, I really came alive again, at last. But, if you'd asked questions, I wouldn't have married you. The pain of remembering would have been too agonizing. I don't suppose you can really understand but please don't leave me now. Not now.' She stood up and held out her hands to him.

Moved by her appeal, he took her in his arms. 'I still don't understand but I won't go.'

'Try not to judge me. There is so much involved here. One day I may be free from the past. Then I may be wholly what you want but at present this is the best I can give you. I don't know what would happen to me if you left me.' It seemed as if Tom no longer mattered.

What right had he to judge, he asked himself as he held her close. Had he not been satisfied until now? Did he even want any more? For a moment, however, he wondered if this might not be the right time to ask some questions. As he hesitated the doorbell rang, startling them both.

'Whoever can it be at this hour?' Judith stared at him with frightened eyes.

Reassuringly, he said, 'It must be a mistake.' But even as he spoke, the bell rang again more demandingly. 'I'd better go,' he said, releasing her. 'I don't suppose it's anything to be afraid of. Perhaps Lawrence has decided to come back.'

'I hope it's nothing else.'

Smiling at her to hide his own apprehensions, he went quickly to open the door. Immediately, he recognised the tall lean figure in his dark overcoat. Tom Farrell! 'What the hell are you doing here?' Furious, he barred Tom's entrance.

'I do apologise, Paul, for returning at this unseemly hour, particularly when I know I'm very unwelcome.' The voice was cool and quietly mocking as usual but there was a hint of something different.

'Then why the devil have you come?'

'To seek sanctuary, I'm afraid. It's sad but at this moment I cannot think of anywhere else to go.'

As Paul still hesitated Judith's voice rang out clearly from behind him. 'Come in, Tom.' She held out her hand to him, causing Paul to move aside. 'Something bad has happened, hasn't it?' she asked, putting her arm through his and leading him to the living room. After closing and locking the door Paul followed them just in time to hear Tom answer, 'You're right, Judy. Something pretty bad has happened or so it seems.' He looked questioningly at Paul.

'Paul will treat you as my friend,' Judith said confidently.

Chapter Fourteen

Closing the door quietly behind him, Paul ignored Judith's conciliatory remark which seemed irrelevant to him. 'Why have you come back?' he asked Tom. 'I can't imagine any reason why you should think you would be welcome, at least not with me.'

Before Tom could reply Judith intervened, 'Tom is my friend, as I have told you. I think you should at least give him a chance to explain himself. You're not always right, you know.'

Without answering her, Paul turned towards Tom, 'Well? What did you mean about seeking sanctuary?'

'Just that. I can't think of anywhere else to go at the moment.' His voice was as cold and as unemotional as always but he was extremely pale and Paul had the feeling that he was exercising great restraint with difficulty. 'I also think what has happened might also be of considerable interest to you both.' Without waiting to be invited, he took off his overcoat, placed it carefully on the back of a chair and sat down on the settee. To Paul's annoyance, Judith sat down next to him, as if asserting her allegiance.

After hesitating for a moment, Paul sat down opposite them. 'Perhaps you'd better explain.' He tried to make his voice as unemotional as Tom Farrell's.

'I walked towards Southampton Row from here and towards the river, hoping to get a taxi in the Strand. As I walked towards the bridge I saw that it was closed and that there were police cars and ambulances on the bridge. A bystander told me that a bomb had been discovered, although no one seemed to be quite sure whether it had exploded or not. Deciding that this was no concern of mine, I walked on a little way and took a taxi to my home in South London going by Chelsea Bridge. Stopping him at the end of the road, I walked on a little to my address where I again saw a small group of people around two police cars. The door to the upstairs flat which I rent out was open. A man standing by told me he believed that the police had arrested two terrorists, so I walked away. I decided that the best thing to do was to make my way back here.'

'Why?' Paul asked grimly. 'I can see no possible reason why that should be the best thing to do. Surely you don't imagine that I will want to give refuge to a wanted terrorist. It's ridiculous! Can you possibly give me any reason why I shouldn't phone the Special Branch number I was given or even the ordinary police?' As he finished speaking, he took his phone out of his pocket.

'There are several reasons, if you're willing to listen.' Tom looked coldly and steadily at him. 'That is, if you still have some interest in truth and justice.' He looked steadily at Paul and waited for his response.

'Please, Paul,' Judith pleaded, 'you don't want to make a terrible mistake. Remember, you don't know everything.'

'Give me one good reason,' Paul replied to Tom, putting his phone down beside him.

Tom smiled with irritating mockery. 'I'm not a terrorist,' he declared.

Paul laughed. 'Surely, you don't expect me to convinced by that? What else would you say? I need a bit more proof than that.'

'What proof have you that I am a terrorist?'

'Firstly, the facts I have been given about you, and secondly, your pursuit of Lawrence Reardon who, now he is reformed, desperately wants to avoid you.'

To Paul's irritation Tom smiled his familiar mocking smile. 'Firstly, for "facts" would it not be fairer to say "rumours"? Secondly, I agree that Lawrence wants to avoid me but why does that prove I am a terrorist?'

'He obviously thinks you are leading a breakaway group in London, just as the police apparently do, and he doesn't want to be involved.'

'If he thinks that why doesn't he betray me himself to the police?'

'Perhaps that is exactly what he has done. Don't you think that is the likeliest explanation? He obviously realised that you were getting close to him, thanks to Judith, so he decided that the time had come to forget old loyalties and go to the police. I can't say I blame him.'

'What the hell do you know about it, Paul?' Judith demanded angrily.

'I'm afraid you're not thinking straight,' Tom said coolly.

'What do you mean?'

'Lawrence has had no means of obtaining my address. Who could have told him? Judith hasn't done so and you don't know it.'

Paul couldn't deny that. 'Someone must have done,' he said weakly.

'Who is this person? Where is Lawrence now?' Tom asked. 'You both told me earlier that you didn't know.'

'I don't.' Judith said quickly. She looked at Paul. 'You must know.'

'I gave him Katy Evans's address and he was supposed to go there. But when I rang up later, Katy said he hadn't arrived, so I left a message with her, assuming that he had somehow been delayed. When you asked me, therefore, I actually didn't know where he was. And I still don't know.'

'Perhaps the police have picked him up,' Judith suggested. 'But even if they have, he doesn't know where Tom lives.'

'Nor would he know anything about a bomb, unless he's greatly deceived you,' Tom said grimly. 'Who is Katy Evans? I've never heard the name?'

'She's the girlfriend of Bill Stephens, the journalist, whom I met accidentally on Saturday. Three men attacked me in his flat while he was out. It was Katy who found me semi-conscious and took me to her place. She's very kind and pleasant. I have no suspicions of her.'

'I see no reason why you should have. But I think it is somewhat gullible of you, Paul, if you still imagine that anything happened "accidentally" as far as Bill Stephens is concerned. He is too much of a journalist for that to be true. If he isn't, he's changed since I last knew him.'

It was then that Paul suddenly remembered the photographs Bill had shown him. 'But, of course, you all knew him in Belfast, didn't you? I remember he showed me some photographs.'

'Yes, he was a junior reporter then working for the BBC. I met him in the course of my work and introduced him to the Reardons and, incidentally, Judy. He was charmed by Judy as we all were.'

'I wasn't aware of it.' She looked very surprised.

'No, in those days you were too absorbed with Lawrence. But I don't think you need worry about it. I think his main idea was then, as now, to get a story if he could and he sensed that one or two of us, especially Michael Reardon, were close to the heart of events.'

'Do you mean,' Judith said, shocked, 'that he wasn't a friend at all but a sort of spy? You don't mean that surely, Tom?'

'Of course I do,' Tom smiled at her indulgently. 'But, of course, he didn't see it like that. He liked us but his burning ambition was to be a great journalist and he wasn't going to let any of us get in the way.'

'Why should he?' Paul challenged Tom. 'I imagine he saw you as possible terrorists and hoped to expose you and save lives.'

'Of course,' Tom agreed, 'it simply depends on what side you're on in any of these disputes. Bill was a true Brit and saw it as you see it, I expect. Fortunately or unfortunately, according to your viewpoint, he didn't succeed. But now it seems to me that he thinks he's got another chance to tell a fascinating story and bring it right up to date.'

'Am I right in thinking then,' Paul asked slowly, 'that you are suggesting that he's still in some way acting the part of a spy or "agent provocateur"?'

'Exactly. Have you ever asked yourself how those men knew you were in Bill's flat? Who could possibly have told them?'

Paul frowned. 'Are you telling me that Bill himself told them? I find that difficult to believe.'

'Who else?' Tom laughed. 'I don't imagine that he knew what the result would be but he probably thought it fun to pull the strings. Or perhaps he simply gave away the information and the wrong people picked it up. Actually, it seems to have turned out rather differently from what he expected, as it brought his girlfriend into the action.'

Paul stood up, walked restlessly across the room, then sat down again. He could not sort out his ideas, feeling as if he had entered into a nightmare world with no rules, in which friends became enemies and enemies friends. What was Judith? She looked exactly the same as she sat there with her beautiful dark eyes fixed on him and her red lips faintly smiling as if to encourage him. But was she? Had he ever known her? He turned to look at Tom Farrell who no longer seemed cold and cruel but almost friendly. And what of Bill? 'I don't think I understand anyone any more, not even myself!' he said.

'I sympathise,' Tom said, 'but the most important problem at the moment seems to be Lawrence. I think he ought to be kept from Bill. Don't you agree?'

'I really don't see why that should worry you, since it has always seemed that you're no friend of his. Or have I got that wrong too?'

'I can't say whether I'm his friend or his enemy until I've spoken to him and had some truth from him. Judy also wants some truth from him and he seems strangely unwilling or unable to give it to us. The difference is that Bill simply wants a story and he won't worry who suffers as along as he gets it.'

'What story?'

'It's a story both political and personal. Bill wanted it twelve years ago and he wants it even more now. He appears to be convinced that it could be his big break. It might, however, be ruinous and heartbreaking for others, including Judy. The best thing we can do now is to try to keep Lawrence away from him.'

'Is this true? Do you agree?' Paul asked his wife. She nodded. He stood up. 'It might be already too late but I'll ring Katy and warn her. I'm sure she'll help. She broke up her relationship with Bill because she disliked a certain ruthlessness in him.' It was then that he made the call which woke Katy. 'It's all right,' he told the others. 'Bill hasn't turned up yet and she'll do what we suggest. I promised I'll be in touch in the morning, though God knows what I'll tell her.'

'The truth, perhaps,' Tom suggested.

'Which is?' Paul looked to Tom for enlightenment but Tom merely shrugged and smiled, as if it was no longer any concern of his.

'You can surely remind her,' Judith suggested impatiently,

'that Bill is no true friend of Lawrence or of any of us. Ask her to tell Lawrence what you have heard from Tom and leave him to make his own decision after that. He can't run away for ever.'

'I'll do that, although I'm not sure exactly why I'm doing it.'

Standing up, Judith looked at the exquisite brass carriage clock which stood on the marble mantelpiece. 'It's time we got some sleep. There's nothing to be done before morning.' Without allowing Paul to express his amazement at this idea, she turned towards Tom. 'You can sleep here on this couch. I believe it's quite comfortable.',

'I can vouch for that,' Paul agreed, 'having spent a few hours on it myself.' As he said that he had a vivid recall of Lawrence covering him up so gently with the duvet and of his kind brown eyes which had been so consoling in that painful hour. He suddenly prayed for Lawrence's safety, wherever he was, for, whatever he might have been, he was now, Paul was sure, just a man trying to be good. 'I'll get you a duvet and an extra pillow,' he said quickly to Tom.

When he came back Judith had already straightened out the couch and rearranged the cushions already there. They were standing close together and suddenly Paul felt like an intruder. Then Judith turned to him. 'I think we need a nightcap, all of us.'

'Whisky for me, please,' Tom replied promptly, 'if you can supply it.'

'The same for me,' Paul agreed.

'It's a good thing that my friend is a somewhat hard-drinking woman,' Judith said as she went to pour out the whiskies. 'I think we shall have to stock up before we leave.' As she handed the drinks to them, she announced that she would have hot milk. 'I shall take it to bed and you can join me, Paul, when you've settled Tom.' Without any further words of explanation, she departed for the kitchen.

The two men stared at each other in some surprise at her abrupt departure, then Tom laughed. 'She doesn't seemed to have changed very much!'

'I wouldn't know,' Paul responded stiffly, 'but I would have imagined that she had changed a lot since you last saw her, if that was in fact six and a half years ago.'

'It was six and a half years ago and I hope she has changed since she wasn't very happy then but I'm pleased to see that there's still plenty of the old Judy left. Just look at the way she's left us to sort ourselves out. She's not a girl to get between men and their boring disputes.'

Sitting down opposite him, Paul looked long and hard at Tom as he calmly sipped his whisky. 'I never imagined a few hours ago that I would be offering you hospitality,' he remarked finally as he took a sip of his own whisky.

'And I never imagined that I would be asking for it. Sometimes, however, life takes us by surprise and we have to see things differently.'

'It sounds melodramatic, I suppose, but I thought of you as the enemy.'

'Hardly surprising since everyone seems to have cast me in that role, though for different reasons.'

'I can't understand why you accepted it.'

'Too difficult to explain now in full. But it's obvious really – the terrorist whom every good Brit must hate and the old friend from your wife's past. I'm still your enemy really, aren't I?' He finished off his whisky with his usual sardonic smile.

Paul considered this. 'I don't know. I'm not really sure about anything any more. It's probably time I was shaken up a bit. But you were a terrorist, weren't you?'

Tom smiled. 'You surely don't expect me to indulge in my confessions. I was an idealist fighting for justice and freedom, although I rarely killed anyone. Now I'm a successful accountant. I've been in the USA for years.'

'You would be capable of killing, I think.'

'Possibly.'

'Do you want to kill Lawrence?'

'I want the truth from Lawrence. I've waited eleven years and now I'm determined to have it.'

'The truth?'

'Yes. The truth about my youngest brother's, Liam's, death. I think he knows it. Liam was very important to me. He was one of the two people I've ever cared about.' He put down his empty glass and stood up. 'Time to go to bed, I think.'

Draining his own glass, Paul stood up. 'Judith wants the truth from Lawrence, I think.'

'Yes. But a different truth, although they may be connected.' It was obvious from his tone that Tom did not intend to say any more, so, after showing him to the bathroom, Paul went to join Judith.

She greeted him with a smile. What shall I say to her? he wondered as he began to undress. Earlier in the evening they had been about to make passionate love, later he had rejected that as being no longer what he wanted. What now? 'I think I'm beginning to like Tom Farrell,' he said as he got into bed, 'or at least to respect him.'

'You're not giving up your principles, surely?' She was still smiling.

'Principles! Prejudices more likely. You know I'm not sure I've ever thought about anything critically. I've just gone along with the prevailing opinion. That's a shameful admission, isn't it?'

'You've never had to before.'

'That's hardly a sufficient excuse, is it? He's done things which I would have condemned but I never gave a thought to other things which should have been condemned. That's been my trouble, Judith.'

'That was you.' She turned towards him. 'I need comforting now.'

He hesitated. 'What does that mean?'

'Just a friendly hug, no more.'

Although disappointed, he felt unable to protest. As soon as they had kissed, she turned away and seemed to fall asleep almost immediately, while he tried vainly to follow her example.

Chapter Fifteen

As she switched on the radio for the early morning news, Katy called Lawrence cheerfully. 'Toast and coffee are ready, if you can persuade yourself to come to the kitchen.' Rolling up her brightly coloured blind, she caught a glimpse of chimneys and roofs against a grey lowering sky which threatened rain. Picking up the kettle which was boiling, she crossed the room to pour the water into the cafetiere, then stopped suddenly as a news headline caught her attention. 'A bomb was discovered in the early hours of the morning on Waterloo Bridge. The bridge is closed and the Terrorist Branch has been called in. The police say that it is too soon yet to say whether the bomb is the work of a breakaway section of the IRA. We hope to have further details later in the programme. It is believed that two men were arrested for questioning but have since been released.'

Katy became aware of Lawrence standing immobile in the doorway. They stared at each other for a moment but neither spoke or moved until Lawrence walked quickly towards the radio, switched it off and sat down at the table. 'I suppose you are wondering if I have anything to do with that?' His brown eyes were sombre as he looked at her.

'Of course not! Don't be ridiculous!' Pouring the water into the cafetiere, she sat down opposite him. 'Why ever should I think that?' Passing the toast to him, she smiled, trying to ignore his still sombre look.

He took the proffered toast but still did not smile. 'I can think of several reasons why you might, the most important being perhaps the fact that I was at least two hours late arriving here.'

'But you explained that,' she protested quickly.

'And you were generous or gullible enough to believe me. That's what many people would say.'

'I don't care a damn what many people would say. I trust my own feelings. You can't convince me, Lawrence, that you would be so treacherous. You may have been a villain once but you're not now. Admit it, you aren't, are you?' she challenged him with her bright friendly glance.

Suddenly he smiled at her. 'I don't think I ever was much of one, certainly I wasn't a successful one. I was just afraid when I heard the news that you might be suspicious. And I couldn't really blame you.'

'Rubbish! We're friends.' Before saying any more, she pushed the plunger down in the cafetiere, then poured out their coffee. 'Drink that. It'll clear your head.' She took a quick drink of her own coffee, then put down her mug. 'I suppose it explains Bill's silence. He would obviously be kept busy.'

'It's possible,' Lawrence suggested slowly, 'that Tom Farrell may have something to do with all this.'

'No, definitely not. I was going to tell you about that.'

'About what?'

She told him about Paul's phone call and his surprising suggestion that Lawrence should be kept away from Bill. 'Amazingly,' she concluded, 'he and Tom Farrell seem to have become quite friendly. He said he would ring and explain. I hope he does. I'm baffled.'

Lawrence slowly buttered his toast. 'So am I.'

'I had a feeling that Tom Farrell was supposed to be the villain or at least that everyone suspected him. But then I don't know much about any of it, and Paul may be mistaken,' Katy admitted. 'I know even less than I thought I did now that Bill seems to be considered unreliable too.'

'Perhaps the truth is that nobody knows the whole truth and that everybody is suspicious of everybody.'

'That sounds very uncomfortable.'

'It is uncomfortable being a terrorist, even an amateur one like me. You never know who is your enemy.'

The ringing of Katy's phone prevented further conversation. She jumped up and rushed round the kitchen. 'Oh God, where did I put that phone?' Lifting up a pile of papers, Lawrence uncovered it and handed it to her. 'Thanks. I expect it's Paul.' From her first words, however, Lawrence realised that it wasn't Paul and, quickly understanding why she put her fingers to her lips, he listened and remained silent.

It was obviously Bill, and he was making his excuses. 'You don't need to waste your efforts, Bill,' Katy replied sweetly. 'I've just heard the news and I realised immediately that you must have been busy, far too busy to worry about me.' She listened. 'Of course I can understand that.' More was said by Bill, then with a little frown and a note of slight surprise, Katy replied, 'Lawrence? I can't help you there, I'm afraid. He's not here and I've no idea where he is. Should I have?' Lawrence could not but admire the subtle perfection of her lies and yet he would have sworn that Katy was a truthful person.

He could imagine Bill's reply from Katy's answer. 'Of course I know that, like you, he was supposed to be coming here. Like you, he didn't, nor did he let me know. Since I've become accustomed to this sort of behaviour, I didn't let it worry me but decided to enjoy my solitary evening. I can't help you any more, I'm afraid. Is it important?' Smiling slightly, she listened. 'There's no point in your coming round here this morning. I have to go into college, as you know and again this afternoon. I can meet you for a quick lunch in the usual place but, if it's Lawrence you urgently want to speak to, I can only suggest you try Paul.' She waited, then ended, 'Okay, I'll ring you later and we can perhaps fix something.'

After putting down the phone, she immediately picked it up again to dial Paul to acquaint him with the situation. After that she listened then with a quick 'Goodbye' put down the phone again and turned to Lawrence. 'You're welcome there, if you want to go but what they really want, I can't tell you. I'm not sure they know themselves. It all seems to be a bit of a bloody mystery and I hate mysteries. I can't deal with them.'

'You seem to deal very well with Bill.'

'You mean I lied to him successfully. I don't usually lie. That's something else I hate. But Bill irritated me. I don't trust him and I don't intend to be manipulated any more.' She finished her coffee then buttered a second piece of toast vigorously.

'I'm sorry. You're angry and it's all my fault. I've involved you in this situation you hate.'

'Not you. Bill. He tried to use me as he often has. I lied

because we are friends and I feel you need help. I'm right, aren't I?'

'Yes. You're completely right and I appreciate it.' He took her hand in his. 'I really appreciate it, Katy.'

She smiled at him. 'Well, let's relax then. Have some more toast and coffee.' She stood up then put more bread in the toaster.

'I'll accept your hospitality willingly but not your suggestion to relax. It's time for me to do the things I have to do, to face the things I've shirked and to stop running away.'

She turned to look at him, surprised at his serious almost grim tone but, without further words, she understood him. 'That means you're leaving here, doesn't it?'

'Yes. There are people I must talk to and matters I must try to put right. I don't know how it will turn out.'

'But I will see you again, won't I?' She was suddenly afraid.

'I very much hope so but I'm not sure that I can even promise that.'

'I don't want you to go, Lawrence, you know I don't.' She moved across the room as if to prevent him leaving.

He stood up and faced her. 'I don't want to go, Katy. I don't know how to say this. It might seem crazy after such a short time, but I believe I love you.' Without moving, he waited for her reaction.

'It doesn't seem crazy to me.' Her voice was soft but her eyes met his directly. 'Although I suppose it is crazy but the point is, I feel the same way.' She laughed suddenly. 'I feel as if I've suddenly walked into a new world and become a new being. I'm terrified but I'm wonderfully happy, aren't you?'

He put his arms round her. 'I can't tell you how happy.' He smiled, relaxing the grim lines of pain the years had put on his face and suddenly she saw the handsome, idealistic young man he had once been. 'From the first moment I met you, only twelve hours ago, you have been kind and understanding and, most important of all, you have given me hope. Thank you, Katy, and thank you for believing in me.' He kissed her gently.

For a few moments they stayed close together, giving one another comfort and strength, then he released her reluctantly. 'I can't stop you from going, can I?' she asked.

'No. If I'm to be worthy of you, I've got to stop trying to escape and face up to the past. There are things I must try to put right.' He sat down to finish the coffee and toast she had offered him. She sat opposite him. 'After all, that's why I came but Maeve is frightened and doesn't want to talk to me and Judy seems to hate me, although she's happily married.' Abruptly, he turned his attention to the food. 'I must go soon,' he said.

'But that's not all, is it?' Katy looked searchingly at him. She expected the truth and he knew she should have it. 'Maeve's frightened, Judy's angry, Tom Farrell pursues you but secretly. Why?' Their eyes met. 'Do they think you've become an informer?'

'Perhaps.'

'Are they right? Don't worry. I won't stop loving you if you are. There are never simple solutions in these situations, I'm sure.'

'I want to be truthful with you. You must understand, Katy, I'm not a hero. I allowed certain assumptions to be made by certain people so that I might have the chance of coming here.'

'I see.'

'I didn't intend to be a traitor. I thought Tom might be guilty of going against the peace process but I wasn't sure, although Michael, my brother, seemed pretty convinced.'

'So you might have led the police to him?'

'Possibly. But I don't see how since I've been trying to avoid him. I didn't want to be dealt with as an informer, which is how he would see me if he really were the leader of some breakaway group. I just desperately wanted to see Judy again. I stupidly thought that since I'd been released so much earlier we might still have a chance. But she seems to hate me.'

'Why?' Although she was convinced that Lawrence was trying to be honest with her, Katy felt that there was still much here that she could not understand.

'I can't answer that, can I? Not before I've persuaded her to talk to me.' He paused, staring past her through the window, then looked directly at her. 'But, please, Katy don't forget the facts. I couldn't bear it. Don't forget that I allowed myself to be put into a position where I killed a man. I was violent and angry in prison for years. Then the chaplain, a very understanding man, persuaded me to read and think and brought me to repent of what I'd done. When I became a Christian, I realised that, although all of us are capable of evil, we are capable with God's help of even greater good. God loves and forgives us and we must love and forgive others and ask for forgiveness for the harm we have done. That's the only hope the human race has got, or so it seems to me now. Can you accept that? Can you accept me as I have been and as I now am? I tried to tell you some of this when we were talking last night but I feel you ought to know it all now.' He waited for her to reply.

'I'm not at all sure I understand everything yet but I'm sure I will and, until then, it doesn't seem to matter.' She paused, trying to find the right words. 'I don't know how to explain it,' she said at last, 'but I know I love you, Lawrence. It's not logical but when I met you I felt as if I had been waiting all my life to meet you. It's like coming home. I seemed to recognise you straight away. Can you understand?'

'Of course I can. I feel the same.' He stood up. 'I must go but I'll be back. I promise you, Katy. I'm sure now. Nothing can keep me away.'

'Where are you going?'

'I don't know exactly but I must talk to Judy. I feel I've injured her deeply and I must try to help her, even though she doesn't seem to want me to do so.'

'But surely she's trying to make it clear that's all over now. You have no place in her life. She's married to Paul.'

'Then why did she agree to see me?'

'Because she thought it would be fair to let you know. I expect she got angry because you persisted too much.'

'I don't think so. She isn't happy. And I think I'm the only one who can help her to sort it out.'

'What if she refuses to see you again?'

'She must. Somehow, I must persuade her. But first I've got to sort things out – things I've been determined not to remember. When I've done that, I must see her on her own. The trouble is, you see, I can remember scarcely anything clearly from the time I went to see Judy to the moment when I stood there with the gun in my hand, knowing I had killed a man. It's a terrible feeling to realise that you've done something that can never be put right. There may be some other wrong I have done and I must find out so that Judy and I can free ourselves from the past but I don't know how to bring it about. We need to be able to talk in peace.'

Katy stood up. 'Why not persuade her to come here? I'll be out till five o'clock. You can have my spare key. Ring her when you're ready and try to get her here. In fact, why not stay here? I shall be going soon.'

'No. I shall go back to the church. I can think there.' Nevertheless, after a moment's hesitation, he took the offered key, kissed her and went out without looking back. She heard his footsteps going down the stairs and then the front door shut behind him. She shivered. The flat was suddenly empty and cold without him. Mechanically, she cleared away the breakfast dishes and tidied up the kitchen. The words she and Lawrence had spoken to each other seemed unbelievable.

After knowing him for twenty-four hours she had calmly accepted his declaration of love and had admitted her own deep feeling for him, begging him to come back to her. She shrank from the thought of Bill's mockery. She had known Bill for over three years. They had lived together, had been lovers since and yet she had never felt so sure about him as she did about Lawrence with whom she had exchanged nothing more than warm hugs and friendly kisses. How could she be so sure? What future could they possibly have? As she prepared to go out, she admitted that she who loved logic had no logical answers. She was simply sure that he would come back if he possibly could and then the future would be good.

Chapter Sixteen

Judith did not sleep well that night and she was greatly relieved when the bedside clock told her that it was 6.30 a.m. Paul was sleeping soundly and did not stir as she slipped out of bed. Without pausing to put on a wrap or slippers she walked quickly to the living room where Tom was sleeping. Opening the door, she called out quietly but clearly, 'Tom, are you awake?'

He sat up immediately on the alert as she had expected. 'Is that you, Judy?' He switched on the bedside lamp.

Shutting the door behind her, she walked to the divan. 'I must speak to you, Tom. It was so good to see you again but terrible not to have any chance of talking to you. That's why I went to bed. I couldn't stand it.'

'I thought as much.' Lifting up the duvet cover, he invited her to join him. 'For God's sake, woman, get in before you freeze in that ridiculous garment.' When she hesitated for a moment, Tom laughed, then turned the searching gaze of his dark blue eyes on her. 'Surely you don't believe I'm going to lead you astray? It's not the first time, is it? We're old friends, remember?' Without another word she got in, grateful for the warmth of his body and the shelter of the duvet.

'I was so glad to see you!' she exclaimed. 'I was afraid that something terrible might have happened and that I'd been very wrong to persuade you to come.'

'There's no need to blame yourself. I would have come to see Lawrence anyway. But why did you really ask me to come?'

'You know why.'

'I'm not sure I do now. You told me you were unhappy and needed my help and advice. But when I do arrive I'm surprised to find your devoted husband still with you and you not exactly repelling him. If you are happy – good. But if you're not, what exactly is the situation? I want the truth now. No more games, Judy!'

'It's not like that,' she protested. 'When Inspector Barrett rang me, I panicked and rushed off several days before I'd intended to. I never imagined that Paul would follow me after he had learned some of the truth from the inspector. When he did, I was terrified that he might do something disastrous. You heard how hostile he was to you.'

'And so you used your charms on him.' Tom sounded a little sardonic.

'Yes,' she agreed miserably. 'But you do understand, don't you, Tom? I was afraid for Lawrence but most of all for you.'

'Oh, I understand, Judy – only too well and that's why I say this can't go on any longer.' Drawing her closer to him, he stroked her hair.

'What do you mean?'

'You can't run away any more. You do see that now, don't you? First of all, you must confront Lawrence with the truth.'

'No. I can't bear to do that. You know I can't.'

'You must, Judy. If you don't, you're not only being cruel to yourself but also to him. You both need to be freed. I'll stay and support you.'

'And, if I speak to him, what then?'

'You must tell Paul. As your husband he has a right to know the truth. He may surprise you by being more loving than you expect.'

'That's not likely,' she said bitterly. 'Why pretend, Tom, when you now know that our marriage has been a sham?'

'You turned me down for that sham six and a half years ago. I accepted your decision, painful though I found it. Now I think that I have some right to ask you to do what may well be best for all of us. None of us can have a proper future until the truth is known. You owe me something, don't you think, Judy?'

'More than I can possibly repay,' she answered slowly, 'and because of that, I'll do what you suggest. But you don't despise me, do you, Tom?' She looked almost fearfully at him.

He kissed her gently. 'How can I possibly, knowing as I do what you have suffered? You're the only person now that I have to care about and I want you to be true to yourself.'

'I'll do my best,' she replied, as she returned his kiss.

'Good. That's all I want.' He removed his arm from her reluctantly. 'Now you'd better get back before Paul misses you.'

'You will help me, won't you?' She didn't want to move away.

'I promise.' He gave her a final kiss. 'Now go. I'll see you at breakfast.'

It was nearly two hours later when a smiling Judith offered Tom toast and coffee as he entered the kitchen in search of breakfast. She looked composed and elegant in a jade green housecoat with her dark hair piled high and swept back off her face.

'Thanks.' He sat down on one of the tall stools regarding with considerable disfavour a large clock with a brilliant yellow frame and an equally brilliant yellow toaster. In fact, yellow seemed to be the predominating colour in the kitchen.

Judith smiled. 'It is a bit overwhelming, I agree. But my friend likes to introduce a little brightness into what is, I suspect, a somewhat dull and ordered life.' She passed the butter and marmalade towards him.

'You look very elegant. Very much Mrs Judith Tempest this morning. I'm not sure I can live up to it. I'm too much of an outsider.'

'Don't be silly, Tom. I'm only trying to boost my morale.'

'Who are you intending to conquer?' He smiled a little mockingly. 'It can't be me, so it must be Paul, poor fellow. Where is he incidentally?'

'He's phoning his office. He seems to have a few problems. I don't really suppose he needs to worry but he's very conscientious.'

'There are times when a man needs to be.' Tom poured himself some coffee. 'Even I must make a phone call soon. Even if the business could proceed without me, it's not in my interest to let my inferiors realise that. Surely you can understand that, even if you despise it.'

'So you really are a business man and not a…' She stopped abruptly.

'And not a terrorist. Is that what you mean? And I believed you had faith in me!'

'I have as a person but I've never been sure about how you

exist.'

'I work very hard most of the time and I have certain qualities that big business appreciates, especially in the USA. But you know that.'

'Of course but you're not denying, are you, Tom, that you have had other important activities?'

'No. But I've not been involved in quite the same way during the last few years.'

'That's not very clear, is it?'

'I didn't intend it to be.'

'That's what I thought but you're still anxious to meet Lawrence, aren't you? You don't sound like someone who is completely detached from it all.'

'Are you?'

'You know I'm not, especially since you convinced me this morning that I must face the truth.'

'You're not angry with me for saying that, are you? I don't want to dominate. I only want to help.'

'I know and I'm grateful. I need your strength.'

'You'll have to learn to be strong yourself.'

'And if I can't, what then?'

While Tom was still considering his answer to this, Paul entered the kitchen. He too was well shaven and well groomed, although with only casual clothes to wear. He greeted them both while appropriating the last slice of toast and the last of the coffee.

'No urgent problems, were there?' Judith asked.

'No, because I did warn Martin that I wouldn't be in on Monday but I really must be back by tomorrow afternoon. Mrs Goodwin has suddenly developed one of her problems.'

'But, surely, someone else can deal with her for once?'

'According to her, there is no one else, so I haven't much alternative.'

Catching Tom's sardonic glance, Judith turned away quickly towards her husband. 'You said you would help Lawrence,' she reminded him.

'I was thinking about that when I woke up this morning and I don't think that there is anything useful I can do. It seems to me very unlikely that Lawrence could have come here without making some kind of deal with the police. And it's not a good idea for me to help him to mislead them, if that's what he wants to do.'

'But surely he wouldn't have done that,' Judith protested.

'Perhaps not but I'm not convinced. There are too many things unexplained.' He turned towards Tom as if inviting his opinion.

'You've sketched out a very likely scenario,' Tom agreed. After finishing his coffee, he put his mug down firmly and stood up.

'Are you too going to desert him?' Judith asked.

'Of course not.' Tom's voice was hard and cold. 'But only because, like you, I'm determined to have some truth out of him. You would be wise, Paul, to keep out of all this, if you can. Now, if you'll excuse me, I'll make a call to my office and then return to my flat.'

'Tom's quite right, you know,' Paul said to Judith, as soon as Tom had left the kitchen 'and if you're sensible, you'll come with me.'

'How strange that you should be agreeing with Tom. Only a few hours ago, you thought he was a dangerous terrorist.'

'I still think he may be but that doesn't stop his advice to me from being sensible. We don't belong among these people, Judith. You may have done once but you don't now. Once we get back home, everything will soon be as it was before. We were happy, weren't we?' They stood, now facing one another. Putting his arms around her, he drew her close, bending to kiss her. She returned his kiss. It was as it had always been, he thought. 'We can have some time together and then we'll catch the evening train.'

'There are things we should do,' she tried to protest but his kisses stopped her. Everything else was forgotten as he pulled her desirable body close to his and it was only the ringing of the phone which brought him back to reality.

Judith went to answer it and to his surprise it was several minutes before she returned. 'That was Lawrence,' she told him.

'Why didn't you tell me?'

'He didn't want to speak to you. He has asked me to meet him so that we can have a proper talk. He says that he has just realised how much more he has to say to me.'

'Isn't that a little unnecessary now? You have told him what you think.'

'I'm not sure that I know any longer. In any case I have agreed to meet him.'

Although he recognised the quiet decisive tone, which meant that Judith was not prepared to argue, Paul suddenly felt himself determined to oppose her on this occasion. 'We have only just made our plans for today,' he reminded her, 'and they did not include your spending time with Lawrence.'

'I didn't agree with those plans. I'm sure that you have to return but I have no wish to go with you. I had a purpose in coming here and I've not yet achieved it.'

'You've seen Lawrence and you said he only made you angry, and convinced you that he was lying, so why waste time seeing him again?' He tried to hide his irritation.

'Because I think he's now prepared to tell the truth and I need to hear it. It's very important to me, Paul, please try to understand.'

'Oh, I think I do understand only too well. Lawrence obviously matters far more to you than I who have been your husband for six years. It is quite clear that your present responsibilities mean nothing to you. You have become obsessed with the past. Surely, you can see how foolish it all is, Judith?' He put his arms around her and continued more tenderly. 'I'm sure, if you think about it, you'll realise that you don't really want to destroy our happiness for a romantic dream long past.' He tried to draw her close to him but she was unyielding.

Finally, she drew herself firmly away from him. 'You have no need to be jealous of Lawrence. There are no sexual feelings between him and me. But you and I can never be happy again if I don't see him. I must release myself from the past. Then perhaps I will be able to tell you what you want to know.'

'That doesn't make sense. Why can't you tell me now?'

'Because I don't know myself yet. You'll simply have to trust me. Now I must get ready to go.' She moved quickly towards the door only to be confronted by Tom who was coming in.

'Surely you can tell me where you are going?' Paul asked. 'Tom might be interested since he too wants to meet Lawrence for some reason. Or is that to be another secret?'

Judith hesitated, then she turned to Tom, as if wishing to exclude Paul. 'I have agreed to meet Lawrence to talk to him. He didn't say anything about you, I'm afraid. I don't even know where we are going but I am to meet him in a café in Clapham.'

'You don't have to tell me,' Tom replied unemotionally. 'I shall meet him when I'm ready to.'

'In the meantime, perhaps, you'll tell me when you'll be back, Judith.' Paul turned pointedly towards his wife.

'I have no idea.'

'Then how can I make any plans for us?'

'I think you should make your own plans and leave me to make mine. It would have been better if you hadn't come. I tried to dissuade you from getting involved, as you know.'

'I came because I love you. It seemed to me that you might need help and I wanted to be there. It was stupid of me, I suppose.'

She moved back towards him. 'Not stupid,' she said softly, 'just very kind. I don't suppose it will be long before I'm back. Please don't worry, Paul.' She smiled at him. 'Kiss me and just be patient.'

He would have lingered over the kiss but, as she pulled herself away, he said, 'I'll try to be patient but do remember that I really do have to be back by lunchtime tomorrow.'

'I will. Now I must hurry.'

'If you're going to Clapham,' Tom said unexpectedly, 'we can travel part of the way together.'

'Thanks. I'll be very quick getting ready.' She hurried away.

Paul looked at his watch. 'I must make a phone call. I'll chuck Judith out of the bedroom too.'

In a few minutes Tom and Judith were walking to the tube together. As they turned the corner of the square, she put her arm through his. 'You don't need to go out of your way just make sure I get on the right train.'

'I know that. Are you sure you know what to do at the other end?'

'Oh, yes, Lawrence gave me very clear directions.'

'Make sure he tells you the truth and that you do too.' Tom took a firm hold of her arm as they entered the station. ' It's time you were happy again. And don't lie to me again, Judy.'

'I'm sorry I've let you down.'

'You haven't but I thought you were ready to start afresh when I left.'

'I couldn't do it, Tom. I wasn't strong enough. I needed someone.'

'God forgive me! I should never have left you but I'm not going to this time. When you've seen Lawrence, come to me if you need me, as I think you may. Don't let yourself be destroyed again.'

"I won't,' she promised. 'I'll be in touch whatever happens.'

'Good. Now I'll make sure you get on the right train.' He took her to the platform and kissed her as she boarded the train.

Chapter Seventeen

Lawrence walked briskly towards the church as soon as he left Katy's flat. He had a firm, although irrational, conviction that he would be able to think clearly now. His meeting with Katy had given him a conviction of his own worth which he had lost since leaving prison. For the first time he felt that he might be able to face Judy's anger and discover the reason for it. First of all, however, he must have time to remember.

The church was quiet and dark except for the flickering candles at the side altars and a light illuminating the large crucifix hanging over the high altar. A sudden remembrance of his childhood made him walk first to the Lady Chapel with the usual statue of the Blessed Virgin and Child. Pausing for a moment, he put a coin in the box, picked up a candle, lit it, then placed it in an empty holder. The words of the Hail Mary came back to him and he recited them softly. A meaningless ritual perhaps – but it seemed to him he needed all the help he could get.

Turning away, he walked to the middle of the front pew where, if he looked up, he could clearly see the crucifix. Christ had suffered too but then he had been guiltless. But I have confessed my sins and asked for forgiveness, he said to himself, so why does Judy refuse to forgive me? How can I start life afresh until she does? What have I done? He stared up again at the Christ figure and it was then that it happened. He seemed to pass into another place, another time. He was aware of himself walking along a street on a sultry August evening. The air was very heavy, there was a rumble of thunder in the distance. He longed for the threatened rain.

But most important of all, he was aware of the fear which gripped him. Why? Then he realised he was walking along the street in Belfast which would bring him to the house where Judy was staying with her aunt. And he knew now that it was that terrible August night twelve years ago. He wanted to escape from it but he couldn't. He was going to see Judy as he had promised and he had to see her.

For a few moments they were wonderfully happy together as they always were but then he remembered that now was the last chance he had to tell her of the promise he had made to Michael. She would think him weak and treacherous to have made it and she would be right. But there was another side. Michael had always been like his father and he could no longer deny the rights of his family. But Judy had no family like that. She only had him, so how could she understand? In his turmoil he walked over to the window. There was a louder peal of thunder. 'I think it must rain soon!' he exclaimed. 'I hope so. It makes me so tense and irritable.' But that was only his excuse.

'Forget about it.' Judy smiled at him. 'Come and hug me and we'll decide what to do.' She was sitting on the settee. She had never been so beautiful and desirable. Suddenly, he realised why all the boys envied him. She was his and she would comfort him in this terrible moment when he could not speak the truth.

Sitting in the church, Lawrence stared with horror at this sudden view of his nineteen-year-old self. Overcome with fear and lust, he seized Judy and embraced her as he never had done before. He desired her. He must have her or he could not bear what was to come. At first she did not understand but suddenly she was struggling with him, begging him to stop. 'Don't, Lawrence,' she appealed to him. 'You know we never intended it to be like this.' She was crying and struggling with him.

'It's all right, Judy,' he replied, 'I love you. I won't do anything to harm you. You know that but, if you love me, let me be really close to you tonight. I can't bear it, if you don't.'

'Please, Lawrence. Don't. You don't know what you're doing.' She didn't have the strength to stop him. He had what he wanted. Suddenly, he leaped to his feet, away from her. She was right. He was not in control. The memory faded suddenly but, even as he sat in the empty church, it seemed to Lawrence that he could still hear her sobs as he left, left because he might be late for his appointment with murder. 'Oh, God,' he said, 'I raped Judy.' For what else could he call what he had done? 'I raped her and left her.' What could he have done that could have been more terrible? And all these years in shame he had hidden it away from himself.

How could she forgive me? he thought. How could she bear to listen to my self-righteous talk? He had thought himself a repentant sinner. Now he saw that Judy had seen only a black-hearted hypocrite. And that was the truth. But God had chosen this moment to reveal it to him, so that he now must meet Judy with the truth of his sin before him. Would she believe him? Would she even listen to him? He thought she might if he could only persuade her to speak to him. If he approached her humbly perhaps she would. But none of that mattered. He must go to her, confess fully and hope that she might be able at some time to forgive him.

After a few moments, he left the church, found the nearest phone box and rang the number of Judith's flat. To his relief she answered. Stumblingly, he tried to explain his need to speak to her, his realisation that there was much more for him to say. She did not interrupt him or help him in any way, and when he had finished there was a pause. He waited, expecting her to refuse but all she said was, 'I will meet you but you'd better tell me where.' He suggested the café where he had met Doris and gave her exact directions.

Now he was sitting at a table near the door where she could not miss him. It was ten minutes past the time and he began to wonder if she had changed her mind, then he saw her coming towards the door. The eighteen-year-old Judy had been so clear in his mind that it was a shock to him to see this elegant young woman with her dark and copper hair beautifully dressed, wearing a long purple coat and elegant black boots. He waved and she saw him as she came through the door.

She didn't smile but sat opposite him, looking gravely at him while she put down her black handbag and took off her fine black leather gloves. He was aware of his heavy jacket and jeans and the his rough black curls which never would remain flat. She was even more beautiful than he remembered but she had changed much. Her face was thinner so that her high cheekbones and the smooth sweep of her jawline were more noticeable. The large dark eyes were unchanged, however, as was the irresistible curve of her mouth Her complexion was flawless but she was very pale, much paler than the Judy of his recent vision. It seemed to him that he had not really looked at the new Judith until now, just as he had not allowed himself to remember the past. If he had looked he was sure he could not have failed to see how remote and how sad she seemed.

He did not know how to begin so he offered her a cup of coffee, which, to his surprise, she accepted. After a few moments she said quietly, 'You said you had something new and important to say to me.'

He put down his cup. He could put it off no longer. 'I have a confession to make and, after that, if you'll let me, I should like to beg for your forgiveness properly. I have only just realised how much I have been deceiving myself.'

She looked round the café which was filling up. 'This doesn't seem to be a very good place for that kind of conversation.'

'No, of course not. I realised that, so would you come with me to Katy's flat? It's quite near; she's lent me the key and she won't be back before five o'clock. It's all right. She actually suggested it.'

Judith picked up her bag and gloves. 'She seems to be a very kindly person. It was she who helped Paul, I believe.' She was already moving towards the door, so he hastily followed her. As they walked to Katy's, she did not speak at all and he was afraid to say anything until they were in Katy's living room. Even then, he switched on the gas fire first and helped Judith off with her coat. She sat down in an armchair and he stood beside her near the fire. She obviously did not intend to help him or to encourage him in any way.

Without any apology or introduction, therefore, he told her as simply and as clearly as he could the fullness of truth that had been revealed to him in the church. 'I don't know if you can believe it but I had somehow wiped the final moments out of my mind, together with other things that happened on that terrible night. No wonder you despised me with my easy words. How could you have failed to be angry?'

'What are you now saying?' For the first time she looked at him directly.

'That I realise that what I really did that night was to force my so-called love on you. To put it really truthfully, I raped you, the girl I had promised to love and care for. And then I left you, in spite of all my promises, to commit murder in support of a cause I knew you hated. The only excuse I can possibly give is my fear. But how can that ever be enough? Oh God, Judith, can you possibly begin to forgive me?' Without thinking, he knelt before her and took one of her cold hands in his.

As she did not move, he laid his head down on her hands, partly to hide the tears which had come into his own eyes and partly to escape the gaze of those unfathomable dark eyes which seemed fixed on him. She did not move but he felt a terrible tension in her.

'I'm so, so sorry,' he murmured. How inadequate the words sounded! How inadequate they were, in fact. 'I can understand how angry you must have been but can you now begin to try to forgive me now that I have really confessed the truth of the wrong I did to you?'

For several moments she neither moved nor spoke; then, as he raised his head to look at her, she answered him in a strangely lifeless voice, 'If only that had been the end, Lawrence.'

He stared at her. 'What do you mean, Judy?'

Again there was silence for several moments until at last she answered him. 'You said you were afraid that you almost lost control of yourself and that was why you leaped away from me so suddenly. I'm afraid it wasn't "almost", you actually did.'

Horrified, he looked at her. 'What do you mean?'

'You began to ejaculate before you withdrew. I felt a wetness but I didn't know what it meant.'

'Holy Mother of God! Judy! No, not that.'

She suddenly sat up more and removed her hands as if she wanted to push him away. 'Just that, Lawrence. About four weeks later with the scraps of information I gleaned from a book, I realised that I must be pregnant. I was just preparing to spend my last two weeks at home before I went up to Imperial College. I had no idea what to do. Obviously, I could not tell my aunt, she would have died of the shame. My mother was already ill, though we didn't know how seriously. I think I went a little mad. I couldn't eat or sleep. I felt very sick. I spent hours in my room, pretending to my aunt that I was working. People, of course, thought I was naturally upset about your going to prison, so they didn't ask questions. After a few days I knew what I wanted to do but I couldn't see how to do it. I had no knowledge, little money and no one to advise me.'

Lawrence stood up slowly, sick and ashamed. 'What was it you wanted to do, Judy?'

She looked at him scornfully. 'What do you think it was that I wanted to do? What else was there for me to do? I wanted an abortion as soon as possible.'

'But, Judy, we'd always agreed that was a very wrong thing to do. Anything but that, you used to say.'

She laughed. 'Spare me the pious arguments. I know them. I agree with them but sometimes you have to choose between two evils and, when I looked to the future, abortion seemed to me the lesser evil. I hated the baby which would destroy my life but most of all I hated you. I'm not sure that even now you can begin to understand that. Can you? Are you man enough to?' She stood up, facing him. She was deathly pale and trembling. Her dark eyes were bright but there were no tears in them.

He did not know how to reply. Shame and misery overwhelmed him. 'I had no idea. If only I had known.'

'And what could you have done if you had known?' she asked him scornfully. 'You had put yourself in prison. Do you think your family would have welcomed your bastard, any more than mine would have done? They're all good Catholics, aren't they?' When he did not reply, she continued. 'Fortunately, I found a friend just in time. I went to church and prayed, and my prayer was answered.'

'Thank God for that, at least. Judy, I'm so glad you did. Did your aunt take pity on you? She was always a good woman.'

She smiled, mockingly. 'It certainly wasn't my aunt or any other woman. It was the last person you or anyone would expect. It was Tom Farrell.'

'Tom Farrell!' He was utterly amazed.

'Yes, Tom Farrell, the terrorist as many said, the womaniser, as others, including my aunt, said. He discovered my situation and gave me all the help it was possible for anyone to give, far more than many would have done.'

'But how did he discover it? I know he was always quite friendly but not in that way.' He found it almost impossible to believe.

Judith sat down again, leaning back in the armchair and resting her hands on the arms. 'He discovered simply by asking and by refusing to be put off. I almost bumped into him as I came out of church and he caught hold of my arm. He asked me what was the matter and when I tried to pretend I was simply upset about you, he wouldn't accept it. He said, "It's more than that. You look ill, Judy. Can I help?" He sounded so kind and concerned that I burst into tears. And then he took charge. Tom's like that, you know.'

Lawrence sat down himself. 'I don't think I ever really knew him, only that Michael always said he was a brilliant organiser.'

'He organised me that day and I was so grateful. He took me to a quiet spot and got the story out of me, bit by bit. I was too ashamed to tell it properly but he filled in the details himself. And he simply accepted it without passing judgement. And I can't tell you how much of a relief that was. Everyone around me always seemed to be so ready to pass judgement on others. And I knew only too well what they would have said if I had dared to tell my story.' She sat silently now, staring straight in front of her waiting for his response.

Lawrence did not know what to say. He was overwhelmed with a sense of his own guilt and failure. And he had to admit with shame he was almost angry that someone like Tom Farrell had been the one to help her. But perhaps that made some things clearer. 'Was it Tom who suggested the abortion? I suppose he would know about things like that?'

Judith turned to look at him. Half scornfully, half pityingly, she asked, 'Is that meant to excuse me or to vilify him? Don't waste your time. The abortion was my idea. Tom was against it at first but he accepted my reasons. Do you think I should have written to you and asked your permission?'

'You despised me and I deserved it. I couldn't have offered you anything, I know. I had almost destroyed you anyway. Why should you bother about me?' He was sure that there could be no shame greater than that which he felt.

'I had no time. There was so much to do. Tom helped me to write a letter to college, asking them to defer my entry because of family troubles. They were very understanding. I wrote a letter to my parents, saying that I was so upset about what had happened that I was deferring and was going to get a job in London with a friend. And would see them at Christmas. Then I went to London with Tom, who was going to work there for a time. He already had a flat and he introduced me as his sister. He arranged for the abortion and lent me the money to pay for it. And that was that. I went to college the following autumn and proceeded with my career, as Tom had encouraged me to do. He was in the USA by that time. So that was the end of our story and the beginning of mine. My mother died suddenly in the New Year and that meant I was finally able to kill off Judy O'Hara. It seemed to me better that she should die with her child. I took my stepfather's name, now that my mother was no longer alive to oppose the idea and finally freed myself, as I hoped, from the past. Five years later I married Paul.'

'And he knew nothing about Judy O'Hara?'

'Nothing. And I wanted it to remain that way.'

'And so my coming back was something you definitely didn't want and that you were determined at first to keep secret?'

'Yes. And it might have been better for you too if you hadn't been determined to find me and to talk to me. Don't you think so? It might have saved you a lot of pain, as well as me.'

Lawrence leaned forward, his hands clasped between his knees. He bent his head so that she could not see his expression. He was struggling with so many different emotions that he seemed unable to find any words. At last lifting up his head, he looked at her and tried to speak honestly. 'As far as I'm concerned, Judy, you're wrong. I don't just want to make a fresh start. I've become a Christian, as I told you, and so I have to try and act like one. An important part of that is trying to see clearly what I have done wrong and asking for forgiveness. The trouble is that by doing that I seem to have involved you in more pain and I never wanted to do that. I honestly didn't.'

After a few moments she replied in a gentler voice. 'I don't believe you did. And I'm not sure that you have. It is probably better to face the truth, if only one is brave enough. I tried to pretend that some things had never happened. That was the best I could do then but perhaps I might do better now. I don't know yet.'

'But can you possibly begin to forgive me?' His face was drawn and his brown eyes expressed the anguish he felt.

Suddenly Judith remembered the boy he had once been. He had obviously suffered a great deal and was still suffering. Following a sudden impulse, she leaned forward and took one of his hands in hers. 'How can I not forgive you now that you have admitted the full truth? We were both victims and neither of us could escape from the pressure of the society around us. We mustn't let the men of violence win. You can now start afresh and I hope you will.'

He took her hand and kissed it. 'I'll try but what about you?'

Gently releasing her hand, Judith stood up. 'That's my problem and I must deal with it. The account is closed between us. I hope you will have a happier future. Now I must go.'

He accepted the dismissal, realising that there was no more for them to say to each other. As he helped her into her coat, he kissed her gently as a sign that he accepted what she had said.

Stopping at the door, she turned to him. 'You've done well so far. But there's still Tom. He wants to speak to you and you won't be able to avoid him. He's very formidable.' Before he could think of an answer she had gone.

Chapter Eighteen

As she turned the corner into the high street Judith paused, wondering what to do or where to go now. Until this moment she had not stopped to think, aware only of the need to get away. Now, in the midst of all this bustle of purposeful people and the incessant noise of the traffic, she felt like an alien landed suddenly on a strange planet She had not been properly programmed. She was empty, lacking all the normal thoughts and feelings. It seemed she had finally killed off Judy O'Hara. But what was left?

Turning right into the high street, it occurred to her that she should perhaps have stayed longer with Lawrence; he had certainly been shocked and distressed. But what more could she have done? She had tried hard to extend to him some measure of forgiveness and reconciliation but she was incapable of anything more. She hoped that there might be someone to help him. In the meantime, however, she also needed help. Remembering Tom's invitation to get in touch with him, she took out her mobile, then hesitated. It was Paul, she told herself, whom she should speak to first. It was as if she was trying to remind herself of an almost forgotten acquaintance.

Paul was her husband, she told herself firmly, and this whole story should now be made known to him. He believed in honesty between husband and wife, or so he had told her. The only trouble was that she did not want to tell Paul; she didn't even want to see him. Slowly, she dialled Tom's number. He answered almost immediately as if he had been waiting for her. She told him as quickly as she could what had been said by her and Lawrence. 'What shall I do now?' she asked him.

'Obviously, you must go back and tell Paul the full story.'

'Why? I don't really want to.'

Tom's reply came instantly. 'Because he is your husband. You must give him a proper chance to know you.'

'I'm afraid he won't like me much when he does.'

'That doesn't matter.' Tom was definite as always. 'You mustn't run away. You must try, Judy. You know I'm right.'

She tried to consider seriously. 'I'll try,' she said finally, 'but if he doesn't like it, what shall I do?'

'Come back to me,' Tom replied firmly. 'In the meantime, do you think you can find your way back to Paul? Are you sure how to get back?'

'Not really but I'll take a taxi. I'll be in touch.' She switched off her phone and looked for a taxi.

It took longer than she had expected but at last one stopped. The driver, a friendly, young Afro-Caribbean advised her that the journey might be slow as there were several traffic hold-ups that morning. 'It doesn't matter,' she assured him, 'I'm not in a hurry.' As he swung out into the traffic, she leaned back and closed her eyes, glad to relax. She felt she could travel through this strange-seeming city without any feeling of responsibility, with no need to plan. Her past seemed to have vanished and the future was unsure.

All too soon, they arrived in the quiet square and stopped outside the correct house. She paid the driver and regretfully watched him drive away. Now she must take action bravely as Tom had said. She walked briskly up the steps, took out her key and opened the front door. As she did so, Paul came out of the living room to meet her. This tall, good-looking young man with his fair hair and grey eyes, looking immaculate even in his casual clothes, was her husband, she reminded herself. She smiled tentatively. He smiled back.

'I hope you've been able to sort everything out with Lawrence?' he asked.

'We have dealt with most things,' she replied.

As she took off her coat, he received it from her and hung it carefully on the hallstand. 'That's good. Now that's settled, we can plan to go home either tonight or in the morning early. Which would you prefer?' he asked.

She stared at him as if he were speaking in a foreign language, then without a word in reply, she walked past him into the sitting room and sat down on the nearest armchair. He followed her, obviously puzzled. 'What's the matter?' he asked.

'Don't you want to know what we talked about?'

'Only if it concerns me and if you want to tell me.'

'I don't particularly want to tell you but, as you're my husband, I think it does concern you. You were anxious to know about Lawrence earlier, weren't you?'

He sat down opposite her. 'But that's natural, isn't it, when your wife runs off suddenly to meet another man. Anyone would be concerned. But now that I've met him and know the story, I just think you should make friends again or whatever it is you want to do, so that we can get back to our normal life as soon as possible. Isn't that right, Judith? I simply can't wait to have you to myself again. I thought you felt the same.'

She stared at him. 'I doubt if that is possible.'

'What isn't possible? What do you mean?'

'I'm not sure that we can just get back to our normal life again. I'm not sure that I want to. And I'm not even sure that you will want to when I tell you the whole truth.'

'Seeing Lawrence and talking to him has obviously upset you. I can understand that. It's never easy to look back. Why don't you relax while I get some lunch? We can talk about it later at home when you're less upset.' He stood up and made as if to move to the kitchen.

'Sit down, Paul,' she said. 'It can't be avoided any longer. We've both been cowards too long. You've talked a lot about truth, now I'm afraid you'll just have to listen to some. Nothing else is possible.'

At first he stood still obviously puzzled and undecided, then finally he sat down again, waiting for her to speak.

'You've never asked me much about my life before I met you', she began. 'It didn't apparently interest you very much—'

'Surely you're not objecting to that,' he interrupted her. 'Only yesterday you told me that was one of the reasons why you married me, that you preferred me to accept you as you are. Surely you're not going to deny that?'

'No. I said it and it was true. But it's not really much of a reason for marrying anyone, is it? Did it satisfy you?'

'Of course not, but that wasn't all you said. You also said that you were as madly in love with me as I was with you since the first moment we met. And that it worked and had continued to work.'

'You preferred to use the word "love",' she reminded him. 'But I didn't agree. That might have annoyed you, did it?'

'Not really. We're happy so why should it matter that we use different words?' He looked at her closely. 'What's the matter, Judith darling? Has Lawrence said something or done something to upset you? Are you still angry with him?'

'No. I think I'm sorry for him. I've forced him to remember something which he had managed until this morning to wipe out of his mind. It was terrible for him. I comforted him as much as I was able but it was also terrible for me, so I left. I hope there is someone who can help him.'

Paul stared at her. 'Judith darling, whatever are you talking about? What have you done? Why have you done it? Surely, it wasn't necessary now?'

She looked at him with a puzzled frown. 'I don't understand you. Surely, it's more necessary now that it ever was? But I didn't actually do it all. He'd already begun to remember. I simply filled in the details, which were worse than he had imagined. I told him the whole truth as far as that is possible. Why should you object? I thought you believed that honesty was important? You were anxious for me to forgive him, because he had changed. I have, as far as I can, but this was the only way it could be done.' She was shivering suddenly and her eyes were filling with tears, which began to roll down her cheeks. Paul moved over to her immediately. Kneeling before her, he tried to encircle her with his arms, pulling her close to him but she wouldn't yield to him. 'Give me your handkerchief,' she asked him, 'then sit down again. As soon as I can, I'll tell you the story I have to tell. If I had been braver, it would never perhaps have been hidden but I wasn't brave enough. If Lawrence hadn't been released and if Bill had not been intent on finishing the story he began to unravel years ago, we still might have avoided all this. But perhaps it's better this way.'

Going back to his chair, Paul watched her as she wiped her eyes and her cheeks. She was very pale still but she had stopped shivering. He tried to remain calm but he felt afraid, afraid that he had made too many easy assumptions and meddled where it would have been better not to have done so.

'As I suppose you've realised by now the story goes back a long time. By the time we were fifteen Lawrence and I were close friends. We spent most of our time together when I was on holiday in Belfast and we wrote to each other during term times. By that summer, twelve years ago, when he was just nineteen we knew we were very much in love. We planned to go to university – I was going to Imperial College, Lawrence to Newcastle. Once away from Northern Ireland we would be able to meet, spend time together and eventually marry. We both agreed that we hated the violence, which our families encouraged, and intended to start a better life and perhaps work for peace in some way. As you know now, it didn't work out like that.' She paused and looked at him.

'No. As you've told me, Lawrence let you down badly and without any warning. I think I have some idea of how devastating that must have been for you. I suppose both of you had underestimated the influence of his elder brother.' He tried to speak sympathetically but he was still puzzled. 'But you've already told me all this and it does seem to me, darling, that twelve years later, when you are happily settled, it should be possible to forgive him, especially since he has been punished.'

'Put like that,' she replied coldly, 'what you say seems very reasonable but, unfortunately, that wasn't the whole of the story nor the end of it.' She stopped suddenly, looking down at her tightly clasped hands. Then, as if making a determined attempt, she raised her dark, sad eyes to his and continued. 'It's horrible to have to tell this story again, after nearly twelve years of forcing myself to forget it.'

He did not know how to respond to the tragic gaze of those eyes. He only wanted them to be happy again, for things to be normal as they had been. 'Perhaps, it would be better if you didn't. You've spoken to Lawrence and that was what mattered. I love you. Can't I just comfort you and help us to be happy again as we have been?'

'No,' she said violently. 'If you had stayed away as I wanted you to, it might have been possible but it isn't now. You said you wanted the truth. Well, it can't be just the part of it that satisfies you, it has to be the whole of it. Then you'll know me as I am. You may not be sure of your love then. Are you brave enough to risk it?'

'Of course I am. I only wanted to spare you.'

Then she began to tell him the story that she and Lawrence had recalled, earlier that morning.

'In effect then,' he asked with horror, 'he raped you that night before he went off?'

'Yes. But that was not the end. A few weeks later I discovered that I was pregnant.'

'My God! You poor kid! Whatever did you do? I suppose your family helped you? But it must have been terrible, particularly after what had already happened.' Words seemed more than usually inadequate but something had to be said. He only wished she would let him approach her. Knowing their strong Catholic beliefs, he began to imagine that somewhere there was a child of Judith's, alive but adopted. No wonder she had wanted to forget. But perhaps nature had been kind and the child had naturally miscarried.

Judith looked at him almost pityingly. 'Obviously, you have no idea. I could not have told them. Fortunately for me, I was saved from suicide because someone did help me – someone rather unexpected – and I had an abortion, in England, of course.'

'An abortion!' He stared at her. 'but I thought—'

'I know what you thought. I thought then and I still think that abortion is usually wrong but, sometimes, perhaps there are greater wrongs. I don't know. I only know I hated Lawrence and I hated the child. I couldn't injure Lawrence but I could have the child destroyed and I did.' She continued to look at him without flinching. 'That is the sort of person I was and perhaps I still am. I hated as strongly as I had loved. But, most of all, I was determined not to be a victim any longer. I wanted to live my own life. Do you think you can understand?' She waited for him to reply.

Paul's thoughts were in a turmoil. He had never expected anything like this. He had imagined a youthful romance, abruptly ended by Lawrence's stupid attempt to placate his brother. The passion, the hatred revealed by Judith's words almost frightened him. As she waited he struggled to find some response. 'What do mean by saying you didn't want to be a victim any longer? Of course, I can see,' he added quickly, 'that you were Lawrence's victim but you make it sound as if it was more than that. What do you mean?'

'I suppose you can't be expected to understand. Even I didn't see it all twelve years ago but now I can see that Lawrence and I were both victims. Being a girl I was more vulnerable, as girls always are, but we were both being moulded by our families. Lawrence's brother, Michael, was determined that he should support the sacred cause, which his father and his uncle had died fighting for. Lawrence thought he could escape but he couldn't. As for me my life was shaped by my mother's fanatical determination that I should never be allowed to forget that my gifted and beautiful father had been shot by the bloody Protestants and that her life had been ruined. That was why she insisted that I keep my father's name and that is why I killed Judy O'Hara when I finally broke free and became Judith Martin.'

'Wouldn't it have been better if you had told me? Particularly after we decided to marry.'

'Why? You didn't want to know. If you had wanted to, you would have asked surely. And if I had told you, would you have been able to cope with it? You married Judith Martin and you were happy with her. Judy O'Hara was rather different, wasn't she? You don't know how to deal with it now, do you?'

'Are you saying that our whole life has been a pretence? That I have not been living with the real you but with an image you have chosen to project? Surely you can see that it's very difficult for me. There is so much that I never knew.' He paused and looked at her. 'You say you're now being honest, but even now there's an awful lot you haven't told me, isn't there?'

'I don't think there's any more you need to know.'

Paul was angry. 'I can't accept that, Judith. If you say you're telling me the whole truth, I want the whole truth.'

'I wonder if you really do. But what is worrying you most?'

'I should have thought that was obvious. You've told me you were poor and friendless, contemplating suicide, then suddenly you're in England and having an abortion, all of which must have cost quite a lot of money and organising. So, although you may well still have been wretchedly unhappy, you're no longer alone in the world. How did this happen? I think that if you're supposed to be telling me the truth, then you should tell me this. Surely, you can see that?'

When she did not answer immediately, he continued. 'Was it your stepfather? If so, why not tell me?'

'It wasn't my stepfather. He knew nothing. How could I tell him? My mother was still alive and ill with the cancer which eventually killed her. They knew nothing. It wouldn't have helped if they had.' She still hesitated.

'For God's sake who was it then? You can't hold back now. I suppose it must have been some man,' he continued bitterly, 'and you don't want to tell me that he became your lover in return for services rendered.'

'What a low opinion you really have of me! Do you really think that I would sell my body in order to procure an abortion? I would rather have killed myself.' She laughed. 'It doesn't fit very well with your protestations of love for me, does it?'

Paul jumped to his feet and moved a step towards her, almost as if he might hit her. Frightened, she too stood up and moved away but he stopped abruptly, his hands clenched. He was pale with anger but somehow he managed to control himself enough to speak quietly. 'Does nothing matter to you? For nearly seven years I've loved the person I thought you were, the person you yourself presented to me. You've just destroyed all that and all you can do is mock me. How can I know what sort of person you are?'

'I'm still the same attractive woman you enjoyed making love to. I've simply told you more about myself, that's all.' She looked at him with her beautiful dark eyes and smiled at him as she had so often done. 'You could decide to forget it and still enjoy making love to me. You could still love me, in the same way as you did before. And we could be as happy as we were before'

He stared at her, trying to get to the real meaning of her words. 'But you've made that impossible now. You know that.'

'Why? Because I've told you the truth about certain things?'

He still felt she was mocking him, although she wasn't smiling. He turned away for a moment as if intending to abandon the discussion but, changing his mind, he turned back towards her. 'Because I know now that wasn't the real you and more important than that because I realise now that you weren't happy. You were simply pretending for some reason.'

'No, I was as happy as I was capable of being. You attracted me too. You know you did. Don't make matters worse than they are.'

He felt that she was deliberately escaping from him again. 'There's no point in discussing any of that,' he insisted, 'until you've told me the full truth. Who was the man who helped you? What was your relationship?'

'There was no relationship in the way you mean it. He helped me because he was my friend.'

'And are you trying to tell me that he wanted no reward for this generosity? He must be a remarkable man. I should like to meet this paragon of virtue.' He laughed.

'You have met him, several times recently.'

'You're not trying to tell me it was Bill, are you?' he asked. His incredulity was obvious.

'Of course not. It was Tom – Tom Farrell.'

He stared at her. 'But he's a terrorist and a murderer probably!'

'Some people see him in that way, others differently. But I don't see that it makes any difference to the facts. He was the man who helped me. He persuaded me to tell him what was wrong and then when I told him what I wanted to do, he arranged it all. He took me to London as his sister, paid all the costs and stayed with me for over four months until he had to go to the States. By that time, he had persuaded me to re-apply at university and convinced me that I could put it all behind me and carry on with my intended career, which I did, as you know. We parted then and I didn't see him again for several years. I knew how to get in touch with him and I let him know when Lawrence returned as I'd promised.'

'And that's all? He wanted nothing in return?'

'Nothing, except my friendship which was his anyway.'

'That sounds fine, Judith but it's not the whole truth, is it? I'd have believed you once but you yourself have taught me not to be so naïve. That's not the whole story of Tom, is it?'

'If you're trying to suggest that we were lovers during those four and a half months we spent together, then you're completely wrong. Tom was far too understanding to inflict sex on me at such a time. We lived together as friends. Although that may seem impossible to you, it isn't, I assure you.'

Stung by her half-expressed contempt, he hit back. 'That all sounds fine and it may be true but I'm sure that there's more to the story of Tom than that. Looking back, I realise that he not only knew you were in London but where you were and you were expecting him. I'm right, aren't I?'

'I told you I'd promised to tell him if Lawrence was released. There's nothing for you to be concerned about. Tom and I hadn't met for six and half years until he turned up the other evening.'

'So he mentioned to me. But after all that time you still trust him, although he's probably a terrorist and a murderer. But I suppose you'll tell me I'm being judgemental and that he never was anything of the sort.'

'You are always ready to judge without knowing the full facts. There is much more to that story than you have heard. Why do you think Bill is so interested?'

'It has puzzled me. But you're surely not trying to tell me that Tom had no responsibility? That he never was a terrorist?'

'I didn't say that. I don't know the full truth myself. But I trust Tom. He is my dear friend.'

'Which I'm not. That's what you're saying, isn't it?'

'That depends on you but you must see that circumstances have now changed.'

'Even I can see that. But does that have to mean that you're definitely not coming back with me?'

'At the moment, no. But do you even want me to? It couldn't be the same as it was. For one thing I realise now that I want to live my own life. I can no longer be content to be a part of yours.'

'And what the hell is that supposed to mean?' He was angry again.

'I can't tell you exactly until I've had more time to think.'

'And am I supposed to wait around meekly while you make your decision? God, Judith, you've got a nerve.'

'Of course not. We'll discuss the situation as soon as I'm ready to. At the moment, I can't possibly see things clearly. I thought I had successfully killed my past self but I hadn't. No one can, I suppose. Now I don't seem to know what sort of person I am. I feel guilty again and afraid. Can't you see how terrible it all is for me? I need help.' She looked appealingly at him.

He was not willing to give it to her. Perhaps he was unable to do so. 'I need a bit of help myself,' he said finally. 'But I must be back tomorrow. If you're not coming with me, what are you going to do?'

'I shall stay with Tom. He has a spare room.'

At that he exploded. 'Do you expect me to accept that as well as everything else? You must think I'm incredibly naive. Why can't you stay here? This flat is yours for another week?'

'I can't bear to be on my own. I need someone to show me where I went wrong and what is the right way.'

'And you choose Tom Farrell of all people instead of me, your husband.'

'Do you think you could do it? Do you think you even want to do it?' she challenged him. 'Wouldn't you much rather that I came back with you and we carried on as if nothing had ever happened? Be honest, Paul, please.'

There was a long silence. Paul walked over to the window and looked out, as if seeking inspiration. Finally, he turned round and looked at her. 'I suppose I can't stop you, if you're determined. I shall catch the eleven o'clock train tomorrow morning. After that, you know how to get in touch if you want to.'

'And is that all you have to say? Do you mean that I must decide to come back to the same old life or stay away? Is that your love?'

'What do you expect me to say when you have just told me that you are going to another man, a terrorist, or so it seems? It's quite obvious that you prefer your old terrorist friends! Bill quite clearly thinks that Tom Farrell is a danger to the peace process. But you're going to put yourself with him. Do you understand how that looks?'

'I don't care a damn how it looks! Do you know I actually thought that you, as a lawyer, might be interested in justice. But you're too prejudiced. You can't wait to find out the full facts.

Believe me or not, I am staying not just because Tom can help me but because I may be able to help him. At least, I can show him my loyalty. He deserves that from me. How can I think otherwise when I remember what he did for me?' She was desperately pale and shivering. 'Don't try to stop me. I'm going now.' She moved quickly towards the door.

'Judith!' He caught hold of her arm. 'Surely, we can talk more?'

She wrenched her arm away. 'It's useless! Unless you can change. And there's no time for that now, even if it were possible.' She almost ran down the corridor to the bedroom. He followed her. She was packing her travel bag, tears rolling down her cheeks.

'Isn't there anything I can do?' He begged her. 'Please Judith.'

'Yes, there is. You can get me a taxi.'

In less than five minutes she was gone. He watched the taxi turn the corner, then returned to the empty flat.

Chapter Nineteen

The flat seemed strangely quiet and alien now that Judith had gone. He did not belong here any more; in fact he never had belonged here. Judith had been right. He flung himself despairingly into one of the armchairs. She had gone and he suddenly realised that he did not even know Tom's address. He was in no better position than he had been four days before when she had suddenly vanished to meet Lawrence. He had tried to help her; he had only set out on this adventure because he had wanted to help her. Where had it all gone wrong?

He remembered how bitterly Judith had said, 'You don't even want to help me. You just want us to go back and carry on as if nothing has happened.' He supposed that in a way she was right but she should have given him more time. She appeared to have no idea of the shock her unhappy story had been to him and perhaps even more so the revelation of Tom Farrell as her saviour. Now she had gone to Tom Farrell seeking the consolation that he, her husband, was supposed to have failed to give. He thought bitterly that it was probably how she had planned it. What was more likely than that she and Tom had been lovers twelve years ago? She had obviously been in touch with him many times since then. Perhaps they had always been lovers and she had never been really faithful.

This interpretation of events was comforting to his sense of grievance; for it absolved him from guilt. He had loved Judith, still loved her. He had thought that they were really happy but, obviously, she had only pretended to feel the same and at the first opportunity had discarded him and returned to her earlier lover. Of course it was a shocking thing that had happened to her but, perhaps, even then she had not been as innocent as she now pretended. If she had been, why had she not told him before instead of throwing it at him now and then leaving without giving him a chance to understand? The thought that she had chosen

Tom Farrell in preference to him was most galling. She had admitted that she didn't even know if he was still a terrorist, as if she considered it to be a matter of no importance.

He remembered how she had said that she no longer wanted to be his "victim". How could she say that when he had always cherished her and tried to give her everything she could want? He not only loved her passionately but he had given her a security she had never had before and she had pretended to be grateful. God, what a fool he had been! Unable to sit still any longer, he stood up and began to walk towards the kitchen without any clear idea of what to do.

As he entered the hall, the front door bell rang. Perhaps Judith had repented and come back? As he hurried towards the door, he decided that he would take her back but not before he had made her understand how much she had hurt him. To his chagrin, it was not Judith who stood outside but Bill.

'I hope I haven't come at an inconvenient time,' he said smiling easily, 'but I'm in the area and at a loose end, so I thought I'd chance it and call before you could think up an excuse to avoid me. Which seems to be my fate at the moment.'

'Not at all. Come in.' It seemed to Paul at that moment that any companion would be better than none. 'What do you mean about everyone avoiding you? I wasn't aware that I had.'

'Well, perhaps not you personally but Lawrence Reardon and Tom Farrell have successfully eluded me, with some assistance from you, I suspect. But the final blow was Katy. She promised to lunch with me so that I might make my suitably humble apologies for not turning up last night. Now she's simply cancelled without a reason, so I thought I might seek consolation from you and Judith.'

'From me certainly but not Judith, I'm afraid. She's not here at the moment.' Paul tried to match his guest's easy smile and cheerful manner. 'Sit down and we'll have a consoling drink. What do you prefer?'

'Whisky, if you can manage it. I need something strong.' Settling himself comfortably in the nearest armchair, Bill leaned back for a moment and closed his eyes, only opening them again when Paul offered him the whisky. Immediately, he took a deep gulp.

'Thanks. I certainly needed that.'

'I gather you had a difficult night?' Paul went to get himself a whisky, feeling that he too needed something strong.

'Yes, and quite uselessly. All because some idiot got his story wrong or deliberately gave false information. But I'm used to that. Katy's behaviour's more upsetting.' He took another sip of his whisky.

'Perhaps she's just tired of being stood up,' Paul suggested.

'Maybe but I don't feel it's just that. She agreed quite cheerfully to have lunch with me then suddenly she says she can't make it. Not only that. She's very evasive and refuses to say when she will meet me. It's not like Katy. If she doesn't like something, she usually says so quite bluntly.'

'It seems to me that you can never be sure that you know a woman, even after years.' Paul sipped his whisky, reflecting bitterly on Judith's behaviour.

Bill looked at him with sudden interest. 'What's wrong?' He looked more closely at Paul. 'Is it something to do with Judith? Has something happened that I don't know about?'

'She went this morning. Refused to come back home with me. Said she wasn't ready.' He paused, realising that he must not risk telling Bill too much. There was no knowing what he might make of it.

'You're going tomorrow?'

'I was. I need to, in fact. But I'm not sure now.'

'Where's she gone?'

'I'm not exactly sure. But she's taken all her things. Says she'll come home when she wants to, not just because I'm ready to go.'

Bill looked at him intently. 'That's not much of a story,' he remarked finally. 'She must have told you a bit more than that or you wouldn't have let her go, surely? I thought you were quite devoted. What's happened? Have you had a quarrel?'

'Not in the ordinary sense of the word – more a basic disagreement, initiated by Judith who seemed determined to have an excuse to go'. Trying to avoid Bill's scrutiny, he offered another drink.

Bill declined. 'No, thanks. You've aroused my curiosity. I'd like to know more of the story. What has caused this change?'

Paul suddenly decided to throw caution to the winds. He needed to confide in someone and why should he worry what use Bill made of the story? Judith didn't seem to care. 'You ask what happened. Well, first of all it was Lawrence Reardon who happened. He rang Judith this morning, saying he wanted to talk to her and, to my surprise, she agreed to meet him.' Finishing his drink with one angry gulp, he went to the cabinet, came back with the bottle and, after refilling both their glasses, sat down again.

'Surely you're not telling me that Irish blarney has prevailed again and she has gone back to her first love? Inured as I am to the ways of this world, even I find that amazing.'

'No, it wasn't that.' Paul hesitated. Angry and hurt, though he felt himself to be, he could not repeat Judith's wretched story, especially not to Bill. 'They went over the events of the past more completely and he was apparently so penitent this time that he managed to persuade her to forgive him.'

'Surely that's not a bad thing? I don't see why you should quarrel about that.'

'That wasn't the cause of our disagreement. Going over the past in such detail upset her more than I realised. She thought I was unsympathetic and suddenly announced that she was going to see Tom Farrell who, she said, would understand her, since he was the only person who helped her twelve years ago when she was in a pretty bad state.'

'Good God I had no idea. I wondered what had happened to her when she disappeared but naturally assumed that she had gone home. Tom Farrell, you say? That opens up some interesting possibilities. So, do you know where he is?'

'Sorry to disappoint you but I don't,' Paul was pleased to be able to reply. 'She failed to tell me that but just went with her case. I don't know where she is or whether or not she intends to come back.'

'You can't leave it at that! You've got to do something about it.'

'There doesn't seem to be much I can do and I'm not even sure that I want to do anything. Apparently I can do nothing right while Tom Farrell is the heaven-sent saviour, the only man who has ever understood her.' He made no attempt to hide his bitterness.

For a moment Bill seemed nonplussed but then he answered slowly, 'I used to think that Tom fancied her in the old days but she had no time for anyone but Lawrence. In any case there were plenty of other girls ready to console Tom. Not that he had much time for them. I always imagined that his interests lay elsewhere, although I never really knew. A bit of a mystery man was Tom. Still, now you remind me he did disappear from Belfast about the time Judith did. He was supposed to have been offered a good job in Chicago but I suspected that his chief work was fundraising. Now he's back he's still of a bit of mystery man. Doesn't that worry Judith?'

'Apparently not.'

'Perhaps she doesn't know the rumours about him?'

'She says she doesn't care if he is a terrorist, she knows he is her friend. And I must admit he does seem to have been a good friend to her twelve years ago.'

'And it doesn't worry her that he apparently dumped her?'

'No, because I don't think he ever did. She seems to trust him far more than she trusts me after six years of marriage. It doesn't say much for her so-called love, does it?' Finishing off his drink, Paul stared gloomily at Bill.

'Don't take it too much to heart. I don't think it's a grand passion. It's the past they share which brings them together. I probably understand this better than you because I was there, although I was not really one of them, of course. I see Lawrence as the catalyst.' He was silent for a moment, obviously thinking, then he asked suddenly, 'Where is Lawrence? And don't tell me you don't know because I don't believe you. He was here and then he vanished. Where did he go?' He looked keenly at Paul. 'Even though you are a lawyer, you're not very good at lying, so why try? We can help each other here.'

Paul surrendered. 'I'm not sure where he is now but he went to spend the night at Katy's because Tom was coming here. And what's worse, Judith seemed to be expecting him.'

He was interrupted by Bill's laughter. 'God, they've played a wonderful game with us both, haven't they? And now Katy's involved and we're in the same boat – both dumped. Lawrence has a lot to answer for, hasn't he?'

'Judith is not in love with Lawrence. I'm quite sure of that. I'm not really sure what she feels about Tom but I'm quite sure of that.'

'I believe you. It seems he's busy charming Katy now, drawing her in. But don't make the mistake, Paul, of thinking that this is all about sex. It's about loyalty and treachery. Matters that you haven't been much concerned with in your quiet life.'

'I think I'm beginning to be aware of that. I believe now that I dealt with Judith very badly. I should have listened more, I suppose, and judged less. I must admit that the whole business frightened me. I wanted to forget it, to pretend that these things never happened and to get back to what I consider normal life, as quickly as possible. Stupid, wasn't it?'

'Possibly but understandable. You've never really been aware of what you were dealing with.'

'I should have asked more questions. I should have tried to understand. After all, I do have experience in getting information out of people.'

'But do you think Judith wanted you to? I don't. There was nothing to stop her confiding in you when you were married or when she heard recently from Lawrence. Instead, she did all she could to keep you out of it. Remember?'

'Yes, and even when Tom turned up last night, she didn't say anything to me, although she had plenty of opportunity. I thought he was a cold bloke – difficult to talk to.'

'And yet Judith had obviously confided in him.'

'And now she's gone to him.' Paul stood up and collected the glasses. 'What the hell do you suggest I do now?'

After looking at his watch, Bill stood up too. 'I suggest lunch,' he said casually. 'There's a quiet little Indian place about ten minutes' walk away. I can guarantee it.'

Irritated by his tone, Paul began to walk towards the door with the glasses. 'I wasn't thinking about lunch. I have rather more important things to consider. Surely even you can see that?' He disappeared through the door.

Smiling slightly, Bill followed him to the kitchen. 'You think I'm an unsympathetic devil, I suppose.'

'I know you are. It goes with the job, doesn't it?'

'Maybe. But I do have experience in dealing with crises and, believe me, there are times when the best thing to do is to relax over a quiet meal and think things over with a friend. You haven't a clue what else to do, have you?'

'Not really, except that I believe that it's time that Judith and I got to know one another better.'

'I expect you'll manage to do that eventually, though I advise you not to be too sure that it'll solve all your problems.'

'Why not? Surely, it's a good idea for two people to get to know one another better?'

'Isn't it more usual to do that before you get married? Or hasn't it occurred to you that you might not like the real Judith when you get to know her?'

'You're not exactly encouraging, are you?' Paul replied despondently as he rinsed the glasses and put them away.

'I might be wrong. After all, I'm not married. But cheer up, let's go and get that meal.'

As he started towards the front door, Paul somewhat reluctantly followed him. They scarcely spoke on their way to the restaurant and at Bill's suggestion they did not speak of their problems until they had finished eating and could relax over a cup of coffee.

'I think,' Bill said suddenly, 'that you must get in touch with Judith as soon as you can. Don't think of leaving before you have done that.'

'I suppose I could try her on her mobile and keep trying until she answers.'

'Good idea. I wish you luck. Of course, there's always a chance she may repent and ring you. But you must stay where you are for the time being.'

'Are you going to do anything?'

'I'm going to visit Katy straight away. If she isn't there, I'll wait for her. I don't intend to lose her to Lawrence, if I can help it.' Offering his credit card to the waiter, Bill smiled across at Paul.

'I didn't realise that you were so keen.' Paul was surprised.

'I want to marry Katy. I've been to bed with lots of women but Katy's different. I like her. I like her honesty and her ideals. It took me some time to appreciate that but I do now.'

'I'm sure she likes you a lot. You don't really need to worry.'

'Very consoling but I know my Katy and I don't intend to let Lawrence have too much time to appeal to her maternal instincts. Action is necessary now. So come on.'

'I only wish I had your confidence. I can't even say I know my Judith.'

'This is where you have to "boldly go". I wish you the luck of the gods. I'll be in touch.'

Paul watched for a moment as Bill strode off towards the tube, then he turned and made his way back to the empty flat.

Chapter Twenty

As she ended her story and wiped her eyes, Judith looked up at Tom. From where she was sitting on the settee he seemed to tower above her as he leaned on the end of the mantelpiece where he had stopped after lighting the gas fire. Since they had parted in the morning he had changed into dark suit trousers with an immaculate white shirt and a surprisingly conservative tie. Clean-shaven now, his black hair was smoothly brushed.

She tried to smile. 'You certainly look like a successful business executive now.'

'Naturally I do, since that's just what I am.' He gave her his usual somewhat mocking smile but his dark, blue eyes were fixed on her with a look she could not understand but which made her uneasy.

'You're not angry with me, are you? You don't mind my coming here, do you?' She twisted the handkerchief in her hands nervously.

Moving quickly, he sat down next to her. Gently taking her hands in his, he held them still. 'No, to both questions. How can I be angry when I understand how bitter it was for you to talk to Lawrence and recall the past? And when I suggested myself that you should come.'

'I knew you would understand. You always do.' She rested her head on his shoulder.

'You must remember that it's easier for me, Judy,' he replied after a moment. 'I was there when it happened. We shared a great deal at that time and I could understand because I had my own grief about Liam.'

'I know.' She was silent for a time, enjoying the comfort as he lifted one hand and gently stroked her hair. Suddenly she lifted her head. 'But I'm not sure that you are really pleased that I have come here. Would you rather I hadn't?'

'You know you're welcome, I've told you that. You can stay in my spare room, as long as you want. But are you sure that is what you want? What about Paul? What about your job? You probably have other commitments too. Do you really want to walk away like that?'

She moved away from him quickly, her dark eyes flashing. 'Why not? I've told you Paul doesn't understand. And what's worse, he doesn't want to understand. He simply wants me to go back with him pretending that everything is just as it was. How can I do that? How can he possibly expect it? Surely, you don't think that he is right? It's not even sensible. It's childish.'

'It may be all those things but you shouldn't be too hard. You've destroyed his happy dream. He doesn't like the cruel world you've just introduced him to. He didn't grow up with it, as we did. Remember we are called to be merciful.'

'I don't think anyone has ever been merciful to me, except you, Tom. You saved me when no one else cared.'

Tom smiled mockingly. 'Not many people, if any, would apply that word to me. Ruthless would be more likely. You're forgetting who I am and what I've done. Don't get sentimental, for God's sake, Judy.'

'I'm not.' She was angry. 'You're just pretending. I hate it when you do that. It doesn't matter what other people think. I know you.' She turned towards him, forcing him to look into her eyes. 'Please don't put a barrier between us, Tom. I can't bear it.'

'You know the truth, Judy. And it's not me who is putting a barrier between us. You have already done so. It's called Paul. Why did you marry him? Did you really think it could work?'

'It seemed to work for nearly six years.' It was her turn to avoid his glance.

'I see, a truly perfect union, made in heaven, which suddenly disintegrates when faced with a few difficult truths.' Tom's tone and smile were both mocking. 'Who are you trying to deceive? I don't imagine you think you can fool me so it must be yourself. Isn't time you faced a few truths?'

'How can you say that when I've just faced Lawrence and told him the whole truth and then told Paul? You know the result of that. I thought you understood.'

'I do understand. It was very hard but you were right to do it. I am glad you did it. But it's only the beginning. You must search for more truth. You can't stop there.'

'Don't you think that's what I am doing?'

'I'm not sure what you're doing. And what is worse I don't think you are.' Standing up suddenly, he walked away back towards the mantelpiece. This time, however, he remained standing with his back towards her and his head bent.

She was filled with an unbearable apprehension. 'Don't desert me, Tom – not again!'

He turned round swiftly. His dark blue eyes were coldly penetrating as he looked at her. He gripped her fiercely by the shoulders. 'What do you mean by "again"? I'm not aware that I've ever deserted you.'

'Twelve years ago you left me after we had spent four months together and I had come to depend on your love and friendship. I don't suppose you realised how hard I found that?'

He did not relax his grip on her but continued to look deep into her eyes, as if he were searching into her very soul. 'We discussed it,' he said finally. 'You know we did. When we admitted our love for each other before I had to leave, we both agreed that it was the best thing we could do at that time. You said you were strong enough now that you knew I loved you. You're not denying that, are you?'

'No, I can't.'

As she spoke, he released her but still stood looking at her. 'You went to college, which was obviously the best thing for you to do. You worked hard and got the brilliant degree I knew you could get. I went to the USA and started on the difficult and dangerous job I had to do. You knew that had to be done. So why do you speak of my deserting you?'

When she did not answer, he continued. 'Did you really feel like that? If so, why did you after what we had agreed? If you did, you could have told me when you wrote to me. I had assured you that if you wanted me badly, I would come. In fact I did come for a month after you had taken your degree examinations. We lived together as lovers and we were happy, or so I thought. In fact, do you remember, we planned to marry in a couple of months' time when you were to come to the States? Unexpectedly, you then wrote that you not only had a brilliant First but also this wonderful offer of research which you very much wanted to do. I was reluctant but finally our marriage was postponed at your wish. Perhaps you have forgotten?' He paused, waiting for her answer.

'No, Tom,' she whispered, scarcely daring to look at him. 'How can I forget?'

'We met briefly,' he continued, 'a couple of times after that. On the last occasion you seemed unchanged, although you mentioned Paul casually. Then, about two months later I got your letter, telling me that you had decided to marry Paul. All you said when I asked for some explanation was that you had come to realise that you were more attracted to the kind of life he offered you. You told me that you were both very much in love and you were sure that you could be happy, although you begged me to remain your friend. Was that how I deserted you?'

'No, no, Tom! I shouldn't have said that.' She stretched out a hand towards him but he ignored it and moved away.

'No, I don't think you should, especially as I am here now.'

She sat down again on the settee. 'That's when it all went wrong after my degree. Working for that which I knew you wanted me to do had sustained me but now perhaps because I had postponed our marriage I felt so lonely and so empty then I met Paul. He fell madly in love with me at first meeting. He was so attractive and attentive that I fell in love with him. And I was tempted to think that the life Paul offered would be far happier and easier for me than the one I might have with you. Surely, you can understand, Tom? I'm very weak, and selfish, I suppose.'

'I can and do understand.' His tone was gentler now. He came and sat next to her, taking her hand once again in his. 'But that isn't really when it went wrong, Judy. It had gone wrong long before that, hadn't it?'

'I'm not sure I understand you? What do you mean?'

'I think it went wrong when you tried to kill off Judy O'Hara and put Judith Martin in her place. You didn't discuss that with me. I wouldn't have agreed to it. You instinctively knew that, so you didn't tell me.'

'Yes, I suppose I knew you wouldn't like it but it seemed a good idea to me.'

'When did it actually happen?'

'It was about three months after you had left when my mother died. She would never have agreed. She had never wanted me to forget my father and my Irish heritage. But now she was gone and it seemed to me a good time to do so, especially easy since I was just about to start a new life at university. My stepfather had no objections. He had always wanted that.'

'And you never thought what you were really doing?'

She looked at him apprehensively. His glance was kinder now but she still felt that he was looking into her soul. She clung to his hand and he did not attempt to withdraw it. 'I don't think I understand you, Tom. What do you mean?'

'I mean that you were in fact repudiating the whole of your past life, not just Lawrence but your father, your mother, your Irish background and even me and our friendship.'

'Oh, no, I would never repudiate you.'

'But you did, in fact, Judy. Paul, your husband, knew nothing about me until I came back ten days ago to help you, as you begged me, when you felt your marriage had failed. You couldn't tell him about me, because if you did, you would have to tell him about the real you and all the rest. For, in spite of all your efforts, Judy O'Hara is the real you, isn't she? Or am I wrong, is it already too late?'

'I hope not. I don't want it to be.' She was very pale and her hands were tightly clasped as if she was trying to control herself.

'In that case we must go back to the original question but put it rather differently. We shouldn't ask why did you marry Paul but what had happened to persuade you to think that it could be a good idea?'

She lifted her head and stared at him with her wide, dark eyes but made no reply, so he continued, 'You are capable of being logical, so if you force yourself to think truthfully, you will realise that your rejection of me was made almost inevitable by all the other changes you made. It was Judy O'Hara that I loved and who loved me, not Judith Martin.'

'But I was already Judith Martin,' she protested, 'when you came back after I had taken my degree and you didn't object, at least not much. It might have made a difference if you had.'

'It might have done,' he admitted, 'but I was weak. We were so happy together that I didn't want to spoil it. Our love was tremendously important to me at that time.'

His sad tone and the words 'at that time' were terrible to her. 'Oh, Tom!' she exclaimed. She could say no more.

'But there were already changes, weren't there? I sensed them but foolishly persuaded myself that when we were married it would all come right.'

For a moment she was silent but, as she met his searching gaze, she knew the truth must now be told. 'You're right! I'm a much worse person than you know. I'd not been entirely faithful to you during those three years. I tried to justify everything to myself but the truth is – I was a bitch!'

'Stop judging yourself. Leave me to form my own opinion. Simply try to tell the truth, without attempting to hide anything from me.' He put an arm round her shoulders to reassure her.

Suddenly the words burst out of her. 'It started when I went to college. Now, I was just Judith Martin without any background or family. I tried to be like everyone else but I couldn't manage it. I had never realised how hard it would be and how lonely. I longed to talk to you but that wasn't possible. Somehow I had to make contact with other human beings without revealing myself, so I made use of my chief asset.'

'I'm not sure that I know what you mean.'

'The physical attraction I've always had for men. I'd never tried to use it deliberately before but now I found it so easy. It was always possible to have a brief affair with someone, ending it when it began to pall or when the man seemed to be getting too serious. When you came back I put it right out of my mind; it seemed to have nothing to do with our relationship. It seems dreadful to me now. How can you possibly forgive me?'

'Don't worry about that now, Judy. It would have been better if you had told me. I think I would have understood.'

'But I didn't, did I? I think it was perhaps because the pleasure-seeking, security-desiring Judith Martin was already gaining the upper hand. It sounds a bit mad but I think that was the truth.'

'And that was perhaps one of the unrevealed reasons behind

your decision to postpone our marriage?'

'Yes, I think now it must have been, although I was telling the truth when I said I very much wanted to do that research. It was a splendid opportunity. But, again you didn't probe into my reasons, as you might have done.'

'No, I came to see you to try to persuade you against it but as we talked I came to see how important this must be to you. My work was very important to me so I could appreciate your feelings.'

'Yes. Your work, your real work, you mean. I wasn't quite sure what it was but I was convinced that it was still dangerous. Was I right?'

'There were still certain dangers,' he admitted.

'And there was my final reason for marrying Paul, more important than any of the obvious ones. True, he was pleasant and attractive, madly in love with me but he also wanted to marry me. I was in love with him but that wasn't important because I'd discovered that it was easy for me to fall in love. Now, however, I persuaded myself that if we married this could be made to last, provided I played my part well. The truth that I admitted to no one, not even myself, was that I was terrified of the thought of marriage with you. I didn't want to endure what my mother had endured and I didn't want a child of ours to suffer as I had suffered. It was cowardly and wrong but perhaps you can understand?'

'How can I not understand, knowing all that I know?'

'I let you down. I'm sorry.'

'No, that's not strictly true. We both made certain choices that helped to part us.'

'You're not being fair to yourself. You hadn't much freedom, Tom, had you?'

'No, I was so far committed that it was too dangerous to try to go back. I had to risk going forward.'

'I guessed that,' she said quietly, 'and I couldn't face it. But I treated you cruelly. How can you possibly forgive me completely?'

At this question he stood up abruptly and walked over to the window, where he stood for a moment looking out. He was apparently considering his answer.

'Forgiveness is very important,' she persisted nervously. 'You told me it was necessary for me to face Lawrence and try to forgive him. I did my best. Now I need your forgiveness. Can I possibly have it?'

Turning to face her, he walked towards her. As she stood up to meet him, he put his hands gently on her shoulders. 'True friends have no need to talk of forgiveness.' Then, as she still seemed anxious, he added, 'Would I be here if I hadn't?' Bending his head, he kissed her tenderly.

'But do you still love me as you did?' she wanted to ask but dared not. Instead she said, 'When I realised my marriage was failing, I thought of you as my only true friend and that's why I dared to call on you.'

'Let's sit down again,' he suggested. 'There is something else I need to ask you.'

'What is that?'

'Why did you decide to eliminate Judy O'Hara? Was it because of Lawrence? I thought when I left you that you were now quite stable. If I had thought otherwise, I would have tried to stay longer, although it would have been very difficult. Was I wrong?'

'No I thought so too. I thought it would be difficult without your help but I knew it would be safer for you to leave England. For a while I managed then it all came back, in my dreams and even sometimes when I was awake. There was no one I could tell. I had to escape somehow.'

Tom put his arm around her. 'But I thought you had put Lawrence behind you, terrible though that was for you to do.'

Suddenly she began to weep, pressing her face against his chest. He felt her tears soaking his shirt. 'It wasn't Lawrence so much,' she sobbed. 'It was the abortion. I kept dreaming about going to the clinic and coming home and realising what I had done. I knew too that you had only agreed because I had threatened to kill myself. I kept thinking it was my decision, my fault. I killed that baby because I hated Lawrence and I hated it. That was a terrible thing to have done. I couldn't face it so I decided to eliminate it all. People may think it can't be done but it can be, for a time at least. The trouble is that the past caught up with me. I didn't know what to do! I still don't.'

He held her comfortingly for a moment, then lifted her face up. 'Wipe your eyes.' He offered her his handkerchief. 'I would much rather you used this than my shirt.' He smiled at her.

He comforted her for a while, then wiped her eyes with his handkerchief. 'Now is the time to stop crying. You've made great progress already. You've talked to Lawrence and in the end forgiven him. Now, you have to look into your own soul, admit the worst and then forgive yourself. You can do this if you remember as I'm sure you do that God always forgives those who are sorry.'

Surprised, she looked at him. 'Do you really believe that? Can it be done?'

Tom stood up. 'I know what I'm talking about. I've had bigger things than that on my conscience.' He walked across the room, opened a drawer in his desk and, taking out a revolver, he showed it to her. 'In my teens I was taught to use this by men I thought were my leaders in a just war. I used it and I was proud of the fact. Even worse than that, you may think, I used my intelligence to plan operations and to raise money.' Putting the revolver back, he turned again to face her.

'So all the rumours about you were true?'

'Yes. They probably didn't go far enough.' He came back to her. 'Does that upset you?'

She put out her hand to him. 'Not really. I've always known the good part of you. And anyway, you've changed, haven't you? Just as you said you wanted to twelve years ago.'

'I think I have. My last big temptation was to revenge Liam's cruel and useless death. But, thank God, I suddenly saw the futility of it all, especially when I saw how you and Lawrence had been made to suffer. We can justify our violent deeds with all kinds of plausible reasons but the truth is that violence always breeds further violence and further innocent suffering. Trying to face this taught me a lot about myself and other people. Admitting the wrongs I had done was a great relief. You can do it as well, Judy and free yourself.' He sat down next to her and took the hand she offered him.

For several minutes neither of them spoke, then Judith lifted her head slowly and looked him full in the eyes. 'You're right. I, who had always said so confidently that hatred and violence were wrong, suddenly felt quite differently when I was hurt personally. I hated Lawrence and his brother and, since I couldn't hurt them, I killed the baby. The hatred was wrong and I'm sorry for it. I suppose I began to realise that when I spoke to Lawrence this morning. He was so changed, so much older. He had obviously suffered a lot. I couldn't hate him any longer. I just felt sorry for us all.' He put his arm round her and for several moments they sat together without speaking, until finally Judith said, 'I feel much calmer now, much happier. Thank you. But the trouble is I still have to think about the future.'

Tom looked at his watch. 'That's true but I think we can postpone that while we think about lunch. Are you hungry?'

'I hadn't realised it but I am – very.'

'That's a good sign. Would you like to go out?'

'I'd rather stay here. Couldn't you produce one of your omelettes? I always liked them.'

Tom laughed. 'How can I resist that? Someone who admires my cooking!' He stood up and made his way to the door. 'Let's go and see what we can find in the kitchen.'

The kitchen was small, beautifully equipped and immaculate. 'This is much better than the kitchen we had in that dreadful flat twelve years ago,' Judith remarked as she sat down at the table and watched Tom assembling the ingredients for their simple lunch.

'You're not supposed to be just an onlooker!' He handed her a bowl. 'Do you think you can beat the eggs up in this?'

'I'll do my best.' Suddenly, she felt that, whatever her future difficulties might be, she was happy at this moment as she watched Tom deftly cook the omelettes and slip them on to their plates. As they ate this simple meal it almost seemed as if the last six years had never been. At the end they took coffee and fruit back to the living room. 'That was very good!' Judith exclaimed as she settled herself comfortably again on the settee. 'I hope you enjoyed it too, even if you did do most of the cooking?'

'I certainly did.' He sat down next to her and sipped his coffee with enjoyment.'

'It's amazing, isn't it, how the best pleasures are usually the most simple ones?'

'A lot depends on the person you're with, don't you think, Judy?'

'I'm glad you've come back.'

'I said I would if you wanted me and, when you said you did, I came on the next available plane.'

'I know and I was grateful.' She paused for a moment then looked directly at him. 'But, if we're being strictly honest, Tom, you didn't only come because of me, did you?'

He did not answer immediately and, when he did, his tone was colder. 'You're quite right. I had two reasons for coming. One was to help you, if I could, and the other was to discover the truth at last.'

'What truth exactly?'

'What really happened on that night of the bank robbery and why Liam, who should not have been there, was there, and why he was gunned down two days later by an IRA gunman.'

'Are you sure it was that way?'

'Of course I'm not sure, but I have some very strong suspicions and I'm determined to discover the truth not only to clear Liam but also myself.'

'Why have you waited until now?'

'Because I'm sure that Lawrence is the one person who could tell me, if he would. I'm determined to make him tell me.'

'I don't understand.' Judith was bewildered. 'I can't believe Lawrence is really a treacherous person; he's not like that.'

'The Lawrence you know probably isn't. But you're forgetting the other Lawrence – Michael Reardon's youngest brother and his greatest hero-worshipper. Why do you think he really came to England? Why do you think he was even allowed to come to England? It was hardly likely that it was just to see you and Maeve, was it? Whatever he says I intend to know the truth because it obviously affects me.'

Tom's voice was cold. His whole manner had changed. Judith shivered. 'Tom, don't. You're frightening me. You're not going to be violent, are you? After all you've just been saying. I couldn't bear it.'

He took her hand. 'I hope not, Judy, I really do. But the truth must be revealed.'

'Hasn't it occurred to you that some people might not intend the truth to be revealed?' She felt more frightened now.

'Of course. That's why I have to act before they do. Fergus warned me this morning and that's not the first warning I've had. There may be people who want to pin the recent happenings in London on me.'

'But that's ridiculous! I don't understand. How can they without…' The ringing of her mobile phone prevented her from finishing her sentence. She took it out of her pocket and answered it. It was Paul.

He wasted no time on preliminaries. 'I think I should warn you and your lover.' She winced at his description of Tom but made no protest. 'Chief Inspector Barrett, I imagine you remember him, is on the warpath. I had an urgent message from him via my office to ring him on the number he gave me. He wishes to see both you and me for reasons which I suppose are obvious and has made an appointment for eight thirty this evening here in this flat. I hope you will be able to be here. I should tell you that I have no desire to put myself on the wrong side of the law for you and your friends. I think I have already risked more than I should but now you have made your allegiance clear, it is foolish for me to risk more. Can I assume that you will be here?'

Judith paused to think for a moment but there seemed to be nothing useful for her to say except to agree. 'I'll be there. But I must see one or two people first.' As Paul rang off, she turned to give Tom the message. To her surprise, he seemed almost relieved. 'Good, I'll be with you.'

'Do you think you should be?'

'Why not? I'm not going to run away. But it would be better to see Lawrence first; in fact it's essential. Can you tell me where he is?' He looked directly at her with a piercing glance.

For a moment she hesitated. This was the moment she must make her choice. Paul? Lawrence? Or Tom? It did not take her a moment to decide. 'I can take you there. We might as well go straight away, don't you think?'

As she turned to retrieve her coat from the chair where she had left it, Tom came behind, putting his hands gently on her shoulders. 'Thank you, Judy,' was all he said but there was no need for more words.

Chapter Twenty-One

It was only too obvious from Katy's expression that she was not only surprised but also disconcerted by the appearance of Bill on her front doorstep. Bill waited smiling slightly. 'Aren't you going to invite me in? It's too cold to stand here for long.'

'I can't think why you're standing there, anyway. I cancelled our lunch date. Or don't you remember?'

'But not every date, surely? It's now about three o'clock. Even the most indulgent luncher should have finished. I hoped I might be welcome now. Surely, you're not going to turn me away, Katy?' He tried to look appealing but he was still irritatingly unruffled.

She continued to bar his entry. 'I already have a visitor, who wouldn't want to see you.'

'I guessed that. That's really why I'm here. I think you may need a little support.'

'What do you mean? Why on earth should I need your support? I'm quite capable of looking after myself.' She was angry now.

Ignoring her protestation, he replied quietly, 'I'm sure you are usually but this person is different. It's Lawrence, isn't it? Please don't lie to me, Katy. You don't usually.'

'I won't be so stupid as to lie to you. You're right. Lawrence is here. Paul sent him last night, hoping that he would avoid both you and Tom Farrell.'

'I've had lunch with Paul. He seems to have changed his mind.'

'I don't understand.' Undecided, she moved back slightly.

'There's a lot you don't understand. That's why I'm here. No other reason.' Pushing past her gently, he began to move towards the stairs.

Before he reached them, she clutched his arm and forced him to turn and look at her. 'If this is just because you want a story, I'll never forgive you, Bill. I mean it.' As she fixed her wide, brown eyes on him, he could see that she wasn't just angry now, she was deeply in earnest.

'It's not a story. It's more important to me than that.'

She laughed. 'Surely you don't expect me to believe that anything can be more important? I stopped expecting that long ago.'

Shaking off her hand, he began to mount the stairs. 'This is – whether or not you believe it. There's a lot you don't know, even about me.'

He had reached the top landing when she overtook him. She caught hold of him again. 'Please, come into the kitchen. I must talk to you.'

'I intended to do just that.' Opening the kitchen door, he walked into the narrow space that was glorified by the name of 'kitchen'. As always it was tidy and clean but depressingly old-fashioned. Sitting down at the small table with its shabby plastic covering, he looked briefly out the window. On this cold November day the view of chimney pots and roofs was etched with cruel clarity against the grey sky. 'God! Why do you insist on living in this depressing dump?'

'You know perfectly well I can't afford anywhere else.'

'You could have gone on living with me and been comfortable.'

'The price was too high.' She sat down opposite him. 'But we have other matters to discuss now. Or have you forgotten? Like your invasion of my privacy.'

'You lied to me and that's not usual. So naturally I want to know why.' He looked at her steadily and waited for her reply, which was slow in coming.

At last, she said, 'I shouldn't have lied. You're right but I thought it was all meant to be kept secret. I wasn't sure I could trust you. I did intend to have lunch with you but I knew Lawrence was meeting Judith. I could see he dreaded it, so I rang up to see if he was all right.'

'And he wasn't?'

'No. He didn't say much but I could see he was very upset, so I thought I should come and help him if I could.'

'Why? Why should you feel it's your duty to help him?'

'I talked to him a lot last night. He's been through a dreadful time and he's very insecure and unhappy.'

'So you thought you should mother him? Has it ever occurred to you that he might deserve to be unhappy? That others are unhappy too?' He stood up and walked over to the window, looking out at the depressing prospect. 'Don't you think you should make sure of your facts before you rush in?'

'Why are you so angry?' When he did not answer, she walked across the room towards him. 'You're not jealous surely? After all, I've only known him since last night.'

'And where did he spend the night? In your bed?'

'Yes. But we only talked. I wanted to comfort him. Not that it's any business of yours.'

Bill turned round to face her with a slightly mocking smile. 'I apologise, Katy, for thinking that I had any right to be concerned about you. It was foolish of me to think that our long relationship meant anything. Lawrence has aroused your pity and I cannot compete there, nor would I wish to. But I won't bother you any more. Give me a ring some time.' He moved towards the door. 'I can see myself out.'

'Don't you even want to see Lawrence?'

'Not particularly. It was you I came to see.'

She was puzzled. 'But what about your story?'

'What story?' He laughed. 'You don't believe a word I say, do you, Katy? I can only hope that you will be half as sceptical with Lawrence. All I can do is to remind you that things are not always what they seem. Lawrence has suffered but he has also caused considerable suffering to others and I'm not sure that he isn't still continuing to do so.'

She stopped him as he was about to leave the room. 'Please don't leave like that, Bill. I'm sorry. I didn't mean to hurt you. I really didn't.'

'But you just can't help yourself, can you, Katy darling?' Turning unexpectedly, he put his arms around her. 'You're an absolute idiot where people are concerned but I still love you.' He kissed her before she could reply.

'Don't go.' She looked up at him. 'I expect you're right. All the same Lawrence does need a bit of mothering but, if you're right, it's all the more important for you to come and protect me. Don't you think so?'

'To please you I will.'

'Promise not to be too hard on him. Meeting Judith seems to have upset him terribly.'

'You may be interested to know that, according to Paul, that meeting upset Judith so much that she quarrelled with him and left to see Tom Farrell.'

'Tom Farrell! But I thought that he was a terrorist.'

'As I said just now things are not always as they seem. This is not for you, Katy. Believe me. I knew these people. Tom was the friend who introduced me to them. I liked him and I still do.'

'Does that mean you've seen him recently?'

'We've been in touch.' He obviously did not intend to say any more. 'Now shall we go to Lawrence?'

Before he could move, she suddenly put her arms around him and, pulling him down towards her, kissed him. 'I'm glad you came. I wasn't happy lying to you. The trouble is you know me too well.'

'It's a good thing I do, don't you think?' As they walked along the short corridor towards Katy's main room, her bell rang again. 'Who on earth can that be? I'm not expecting anyone. Wait here and I'll go and see.'

Running quickly down the two flights of stairs, she opened the front door. Two people, a man and a woman, stood together on the steps. She didn't know them, yet she felt that she had seen them somewhere before. 'I'm Katy Evans,' she told them. 'Do you want me or have you rung the wrong bell?'

'It's all right, Katy,' Bill's voice came from halfway down the stairs. 'I know your visitors.' Almost with one bound he reached her side. 'Let me introduce them. Judith Tempest and Tom Farrell.' Katy was too shocked to say anything and it was Bill who took the initiative. 'Come in,' he said, 'it's too cold to stand out there.'

As Bill greeted them Katy had a moment to study the two people about whom she had heard so much. Her first thought was that Judith really was that rare creature, a truly beautiful woman, naturally attractive to men. Even Bill, she noticed, was not immune. Neither, she sensed with surprise, was Tom Farrell, although it was hard to decide anything about him, perhaps because she had already cast him as the villain of the story. Suddenly, as if reading her thoughts, he turned and looked directly at her with the most piercing dark blue eyes she had ever seen. She felt almost afraid and then foolish as he apologised for his intrusion and asked if it was convenient for him to speak to Lawrence.

'I don't think he wants to talk to anyone at the moment,' she replied, lulled into a false sense of security.

Those blue eyes surveyed her again, then Tom smiled a little mockingly. 'How very noble of you to wish to protect him from me but to no avail, I'm afraid, since we must talk and Lawrence knows that we must. If he doesn't talk to me, then he will have to talk to Special Branch, I'm afraid. Perhaps you'll show me the way.'

She was angry but was not sure how to protest against this assurance. Before she could speak, however, Bill intervened. 'Don't bother, Katy, I'll show Tom the way. Why don't you take Judith to the kitchen and I'll join you there for a cup of coffee.' Before she could think of a suitable reply, he was halfway up the stairs followed closely by Tom.

She turned to the silent Judith. 'They seemed to have settled that,' she remarked bitterly, 'whether or not I agree. But perhaps you're used to that kind of behaviour.'

'I'm sorry you're annoyed but it is very important for Lawrence and Tom to talk. That is why I brought Tom here. I would never have done so otherwise.'

'It seems then,' Katy replied ungraciously, 'that we have no alternative except to do as Bill suggests.' Without another word she led the way upstairs to the kitchen, while Judith followed her silently. The kitchen looked shabbier and drearier than ever in contrast with Judith's elegance, as she stood hesitating in the doorway. 'I'm afraid it's not very comfortable but it's clean. Do sit down and I'll put the kettle on.' She was very conscious of Judith's unhappy silence while she busied herself in the necessary preparations. Bill's entry was a relief. She smiled at him. 'I thought you might be some time.'

'I left them together as soon as I'd shown Tom in. It wouldn't be wise for me to get in the way, at least I didn't think so.'

'You're quite right.' Judith smiled at Bill as he sat down opposite her. 'Tom is very angry.'

'Then why on earth did you bring him here?' Katy burst out. 'Surely you of all people must know how unhappy Lawrence is at this moment. Do you think it's right to inflict Tom on him?'

'Katy!' Bill warned her quickly. 'You mustn't go on imagining that you know everything. I've already told you that Lawrence's is not the only point of view to be considered.'

'I didn't ask to be involved in any of this.' Katy was still indignant. 'But since I am, I think I might be allowed to decide who I invite into my own flat, although I imagine that doesn't concern you, Bill. You're probably just thinking of the story you might get out of this.' She knew she was being rude and unjust but she felt so angry at Bill's desertion that she didn't care. Slamming the jar of coffee on the table, she glared furiously at them both.

'Katy,' Bill warned her quickly, 'don't you think you're being somewhat rude and inhospitable?' He turned towards Judith. 'She's not always like this. It's simply that Lawrence has made her feel protective. And you can never resist the opportunity to help a lame dog over a stile, can you, Katy?'

'That seems a very good quality to me,' Judith said quietly. 'And I'm sure that Lawrence does need help.'

'If you really mean that, why did you bring Tom Farrell here?' Katy retorted. 'You must know that Lawrence definitely doesn't want to talk to him.'

'They have to talk.' Judith was unmoved by Katy's anger. 'And this may be the best chance they will have to do it without interference' She turned towards Bill. 'Don't you agree with me, Bill?'

'Of course, he will. He's made that obvious already.' Katy was irritated even more as Bill smiled at Judith, the more so as she realised that she was jealous.

'If what Tom said about the police is correct, then you definitely are.'

'Inspector Barrett has made an appointment to come to the flat tonight. And he doesn't just want to see Paul and me.' Judith turned towards Katy. 'Please try to understand that I only want to help Tom. When Lawrence nearly destroyed my life, Tom helped me and now I want to repay him a little. Lawrence is chiefly unhappy at the moment because of the wrong he did me, which was greater than he had known. It will be good for him if he can help Tom.' She stopped suddenly and Katy realised that her eyes were full of tears.

'I'm sorry,' Katy said quickly. 'There's obviously a lot I don't know. You were right, Bill.' She looked at Bill appealingly, hoping that she might have his support again. 'I'm just a fool rushing in.'

Bill grinned warmly at her. 'Don't be too humble, Katy, or you'll embarrass me. Why don't we drink our coffee and relax? We may have a long time to wait. How about those cakes you made at the weekend? I'd enjoy one of those if Lawrence hasn't already eaten them all.'

'Of course, he hasn't,' Katy replied indignantly. 'I promised to keep some for you.' As she offered her cakes with Bill's approval, she suddenly felt it might be possible, after all, to like Judith.

When Bill had left, Tom closed the door behind him and then stood with his back to it, saying nothing. Lawrence who had been sitting by the fire got up quickly turning to face him. For a few moments they stood and looked at each other. 'You've changed much more than I expected,' Tom remarked at last, almost with pity.

'Twelve years in prison do have a somewhat ageing effect. You, on the other hand, seem hardly to have changed, except that you look even more prosperous and successful.' He paused for a moment. 'Why have you come?' he asked finally.

'We had to meet. You know that. It was stupid of you to try to avoid it. Why have you?'

'I've always been a bit of a coward. You should know that.'

Moving away from the door, Tom crossed the room and sat down on a chair facing Lawrence's. 'Why don't you sit down again? We've a lot to talk about. It may take some time.' His voice was cool and unemotional but there was something about his whole manner that intimidated Lawrence for a moment, almost as much as it had done twelve years before. Then he had believed it was because Tom was ruthless as people said, but now, as he remembered what Judith had said about him, he was confused. He sat down nevertheless and waited.

Tom, however, remained relaxed but silent, apparently content to gaze at the gas fire. Irritated, Lawrence remembered this as one of his control techniques. 'Well, what have you got to say?' he asked at last. 'For God's sake, Tom, surely you don't have to play games with me now, do you?'

'I've no intention of doing so.' Tom turned his icy blue eyes on him for a moment, then turned away again. 'I found it difficult, I suppose, seeing you again. All I want are some truthful answers from you.'

'Truthful answers about what?'

'First of all about events that occurred twelve years ago, the night you were arrested. You know as well as I do that the full truth has never been told. I don't believe you were ever a killer.'

'Perhaps not as successful as you,' Lawrence replied bitterly, 'but I did kill a man that night, not just any man but a policeman. Or are you trying to make me say as some people did that someone else did it? Because if you are, you're wasting your time.'

'I'm not so foolish. I'm quite sure that you held the gun and you pulled the trigger. But how did you come to have a gun? You knew, as well as Michael did, that guns were not a part of the original plan. I was always against inexperienced people carrying them on such occasions. It only increased the risk. If there is to be killing, it should be carefully planned.'

'Is that something which makes you proud? I don't think it should. It makes me ashamed now to remember what I once believed.'

'Unlike you I am not ashamed of something I once sincerely believed but I expect that both of us have changed. I'm not concerned with that. I am only stating what was true then. Don't you agree?'

'I have to. You were very definite about that.'

'What happened then? Did Michael change the orders without consulting me?'

'Not that I'm aware of.' Lawrence was obviously reluctant to say more. Tom gazed fixedly at him and waited. 'But someone did come with a gun and, in the confusion, when the police arrived, it was pushed into my hand and I like a bloody fool fired it. And for the first time I hit my target!'

'It's a good try, I suppose, but not the truth or at least not the whole truth.'

'It's all I've ever told anyone else. What more do you want?' Lawrence leaned back, closing his eyes, trying to avoid Tom's sudden sharp look.

Tom didn't hesitate. 'Who was that someone? Why did he bring a gun? Did Michael give him permission? I have a right to know because I was, I believe, suspected of betraying my own plan.'

'No. Michael didn't give him permission. He didn't ask for permission. I know you'd like to blame Michael but it wasn't his fault.'

Tom turned to look at him. 'That's irrelevant.' His voice was very cold. 'Who was the man and why did he bring a gun?'

'I don't suppose you can begin to understand!' Lawrence spoke with sudden fury and for the first time turned to look into Tom's eyes. 'It was the first time he'd been on a mission and he was afraid, so he had a few drinks and then borrowed a gun to make him feel better, I suppose. How should I know? All I know is that when someone gave the alarm he pulled it out. I told him not to be a bloody fool and snatched it from him. Suddenly, everyone had disappeared and I was there with the gun in my hand when the policeman appeared. He had a gun. He stared at me, shouted something but I didn't take it in. I didn't know what I was doing. I thought he was going to shoot me, so I pulled the trigger. I just stood there when he fell down. I couldn't move. I knew somehow that he was dead. They arrested me, as you know, but the others escaped. I couldn't really understand anything except that I had killed a man and I was finished. I'd only intended to come on this raid to prove to Michael that I wasn't the coward he thought I was. I'd imagined going to England after that with Judy. Now I realised this would never happen. This was for real.' He buried his face in his hands. 'You really can't understand, can you? I don't suppose you've ever been afraid.'

Only for a moment did Tom hesitate before continuing his

relentless questioning. 'You still haven't told me who the bloody fool was who did this. Who was it who wrecked your life and ruined a good plan? I only hope he had a suitable punishment?'

Lawrence uncovered his face. 'He did. But that didn't comfort me. After all, he was my best mate.' He looked straight at Tom.

For the first time Tom didn't look at him but turned away, then, suddenly looking at Lawrence, he said in a voice icy with rage. 'For God's sake, Lawrence. Who was it? Why are you playing about like this?'

'You know really, don't you? But even the ruthless Tom can't bear to say it, can you?'

'It was Liam,' Tom said in a hard, cold voice. 'My brother. You told Michael and that's why he was shot.' He laughed suddenly. 'It's ironic. Michael was trying to push you into the movement. I was trying to keep Liam out of it. Neither of us was exactly successful, were we? Just another futile business, that's all there is to be said. Did it at least satisfy you to know that Liam got what was due to him?'

'It wasn't like that. I tried to keep him out of it. That's why I said nothing. Anyway, it wouldn't have saved me, would it?'

'If you said nothing, then why was Liam executed? Why wasn't I informed?'

Lawrence preferred to answer the second question. 'You were away. Don't you remember? You went off to be briefed about something, the day after I was arrested or so Michael told me. At least that was the story. Michael was angry. He wondered about you. A lot of people did. I did too a few weeks later when I was told you'd gone off to England with Judy. I knew you'd always liked her. I couldn't really blame her but I hated you.'

'I was obeying orders when I went to London. Michael knew that, if you didn't. I went to the USA four months later for the same reason.' Turning suddenly, Tom looked Lawrence straight in the face. His dark blue eyes were blazing. Even though his voice was still calm, he was obviously very angry. 'I was told it was a Loyalist shooting. I didn't believe it but there was nothing I could do. But are you now trying to tell me that it was Michael's revenge for Liam's leaving you with the gun?'

For a moment Lawrence wondered if he was safe, even here in

Katy's London flat but with a visible effort Tom turned away, answering his own question. 'But you've already told me that you told no one about that. So, presuming that you're speaking the truth why did it happen? Why was Liam shot?' Once more he turned his blazing eyes on Lawrence. 'For God's sake, man, why won't you tell me?'

The words seemed to stick in Lawrence's throat but there was no avoiding Tom now. The truth must now be told what ever the consequences might be. 'It was all Liam's fault, at least that's what they decided when they tried him' He stopped. He was afraid to go on.

'What was Liam's fault?' Every word was like a whiplash.

'He ruined the whole bloody business.' Lawrence was shaking visibly. 'It was his fucking fault that the police were there. That's what they decided, so they executed him.' The silence that followed his words was even more frightening. He looked down at his hands, afraid to look at Tom.

Tom stood up. Walking slowly across the room, he went to the window and looked out into the darkening street. 'Do you expect me to believe,' he asked quietly, 'that my young brother not only took part in a robbery but was also a traitor? Don't you know that I'd made every effort to pay for his education, so that he, at least, could get away from our wretched home? I intended him to go to England and to university. I wanted him to be free, as I couldn't be at that time.'

In spite of his control, his pain was so obvious that Lawrence wished he could have denied it but it was too late now. The truth had to be told. Tom deserved that. 'But he didn't want that, you see. He wanted to be a hero, a man of iron like you, his elder brother. He begged Michael to let him take part.'

'And so Michael let him. I expect it rather amused him.'

'Sure it did. He said Liam and I should have changed brothers. He found it funny.'

'Why didn't Liam say something to me?'

'He was afraid, I guess. He was always afraid, really. That's why he drank. He didn't want you to know that either.'

Tom came back to his chair and sat down again. 'It seems I was a bit of a fool, only seeing what I wanted to see.'

'No. Liam was the fool, I think. He betrayed everybody.'

'What did they think he did, my fool of a brother?' Tom made not attempt to hide his bitterness.

'He got drunk one evening with a few friends and talked about the plans for the robbery. Somebody wasn't a friend and the police were informed.'

'Did they discover the informer?'

'No. But they thought it might have been Bill Stephens, the reporter. People were used to his hanging around and he is a Brit, but there was never any proof. Of course he's still hanging around. Doesn't that annoy you?'

'Why should it? He's only doing his job and, if I'm fool enough to trust him when I shouldn't, the blame is mine.'

'You seem quite friendly with him.'

'I always have been but I observe the limits.' Tom seemed to be his normal self again and Lawrence began to feel that he might relax. Then, without warning, the next question came. 'Why did you come to London?'

'To see Judy and Maeve. I desperately wanted to put things straight.'

'And Special Branch gave you their blessing?' Tom smiled mockingly. 'Perhaps I should have asked more accurately, why were you allowed to come?' When Lawrence did not reply, he continued, 'It was connected with me, wasn't it? I expect it was Michael's idea, that you, the friend of my dead brother, might help the police to investigate my alleged activities. Michael, of course, would know that I was coming to London. Am I right?' Was that something like your mission?'

Lawrence nodded. 'But I'm not intending to do it, Tom. As soon as I met Judy, I went missing. The police are trying to find me now as much as you.'

'Yes. I have noticed that.'

'It was Paul who made it difficult. I didn't know Judy was married and so I didn't expect him to be around.'

Tom laughed. 'Judy tried to keep him out of the way. She left without telling him anything but it wasn't any good. He had more determination than she thought. It's made everything more difficult.'

It was Lawrence's turn to ask a question. 'Why did you come to London, Tom?'

Tom smiled again. 'To see Judy, of course. She wanted me to help her. Why do you think I came?'

'Michael suggested, and I agreed with him, that you were coming with money from the States for the Real IRA and that you were going to help to organise the group in London.'

'And that would have seemed wrong to you?'

'Of course. I'm a Christian now and I believe that violence is totally wrong and misguided. I wanted to stop you.'

Tom laughed. 'My God, I hope you don't think I was responsible for that disgusting muddle on London Bridge last night? You don't think I would ever fall so low, do you?'

Lawrence remained serious. 'No, but that just proved how much they needed you, didn't it?'

'Perhaps but that doesn't mean that I came for that reason, does it?'

Lawrence looked at him very seriously. 'You don't have to tell me anything, Tom. I shall tell this policeman that I was quite wrong – a victim of Michael's paranoia – as I've been before. I shall say that I am sure you came to see Judy because you care a lot for her and she begged you for help. I didn't know that before now, you see. You saved Judy's life after I had wrecked it. I owe you a debt.'

'Nevertheless, it didn't stop you from suggesting that, if they found the O'Keefes they might find me. That misfired, however.' Tom stood up. 'I think we understand one another. Old bitternesses have to be forgotten. Now, perhaps I should return to Judy.'

'I'm sorry about Liam.'

'I misunderstood him, that's all.'

'That's your trouble isn't it?'

Tom stopped. 'What do you mean?'

'You're brilliant with money and plans but you don't understand people. You didn't understand Liam and you don't understand Judy.' He hurried on before Tom could say anything. 'You should have married her as soon as you could. She needed you and when you weren't there, she married Paul.'

'She has told you, I suppose.'

'Of course not but it's obvious when she talks about you. You shouldn't let her go again.'

'Perhaps I won't,' was all Tom said as he moved towards the door. As he was going out, he added, 'I expect we shall meet again later tonight.'

Chapter Twenty-Two

Hearing Tom's footsteps coming along the corridor, Bill went quickly to the door and disappeared through it. On seeing him Tom stopped. 'Did you get all the information you wanted?' Bill asked with a friendly smile.

'I think so.' Tom did not return the smile. 'Lawrence, as I expected, was able to tell me the exact circumstances of Liam's death. It seems he was indiscreet and someone decided to report his indiscretions. He apparently thought he was among friends but obviously someone wasn't a friend.'

'I see.'

'It wasn't you, was it? Lawrence seemed to think you were there.' Tom looked coldly at him.

'Would you hate me if I had done it?'

'Why should I? It would be a natural thing for you to do, as a British reporter. I only want to know the truth.' Neither of them noticed that Katy was standing in the doorway, listening.

'The truth is,' Bill smiled as he spoke, 'I didn't. I decided not to use that story. It seemed to me that Liam was apparently just a boastful young fool. I was wrong but I'm glad I didn't use it.'

'The whole story is yours now plus Lawrence's reasons for coming to London. He wanted to prove that I had come here to organise the Real IRA. At least that's what he apparently told the authorities. He seemed to think – probably Michael had something to do with this – that it was time I had my just deserts.'

'And was he right? Did you come for that reason?'

Tom did not seem to be at all disconcerted. 'And I thought you were my friend!' He smiled sardonically. 'Surely you would have expected me to do a better job? Still, it doesn't matter now. After talking to Judy he decided that I was not the villain he'd thought I was. He has no evidence to give when he reports to the authorities as he intends to do. We can all go back to our normal lives and you have a story if you want to make something of it.'

'I don't want to. These events affected me and I wanted to know the truth.' He looked into Tom's cold blue eyes. 'But I'm not at all sure that I do know it, even now.'

'I doubt if any more will ever be learned.' Tom smiled a little mockingly. 'Now I must find out what Judy wants to do.' Moving quickly past Bill, he entered the kitchen.

As Tom disappeared, Katy came forward towards Bill. 'I heard you say it – actually – that you didn't want a story! And that it wasn't the first time!' She smiled up at him.

Bending down, he kissed her. 'Admit you've misjudged me!'

'Willingly.' She returned his kiss.

'Now will you take my proposal seriously?'

'I might! It depends.'

Judith stood up as Tom came into the kitchen. When he did not say anything but stood regarding her with a remote look, she asked him, almost nervously, 'Was Lawrence able to tell you all you hoped to know.'

'It wasn't exactly what I hoped but unfortunately I think it was the truth.'

'What do you mean? Why do you say it was unfortunate?'

'I suppose I mean that I hoped for something more comforting.'

He seemed to be completely withdrawn and he obviously did not intend to say any more, even to her. Nevertheless, she tried to persevere. 'Were your suspicions right? Was he allowed here so that he might lead the authorities to you?' She looked anxiously at him. She didn't think that she had ever seen him before in this mood. 'You haven't quarrelled with him, have you?'

'Of course not. We understood one another. I need to think about it all, Judy. He is going to report in, as he failed to do last week and I expect he will have to return to Belfast. Are you ready to leave now?'

'Do you mind waiting? If Lawrence is going to have to return to Belfast, I would like to say goodbye to him. I won't be long.' Tom didn't reply but simply sat down at the kitchen table. He seemed like someone who had had a shock. What had happened, she wondered? Perhaps Lawrence would be able to tell her? Without another word, she went out, and hurried along the

225

landing to the living room.

Lawrence was standing by the window but, as she entered, he turned round, greeting her. 'Judy! I hoped I might see you again!' He walked towards her then took her hands in his. 'I want to be sure that you really have forgiven me for everything. Is it possible?'

'I think it is possible now. The more one understands, the harder it is to blame. Don't you agree?'

'The hardest thing to do is to forgive oneself.' Lawrence spoke sombrely. 'But knowing that you can forgive me will help.'

'I know I find it hard to forgive myself.' She looked into his dark brown eyes. 'Can you forgive me for killing our child?' In spite of herself, the tears filled her eyes.

Without speaking, he bent and kissed her gently. 'How can I blame you? I'm simply glad that Tom was there to help you.'

'I think he saved my life. But whatever have you said to him? He doesn't seem to want to speak to me. He almost seems as if he's in shock.'

'He was very upset, I think, although he didn't show it, to hear the truth about Liam's death. He would have found it easier to be able to hate me, as I once wanted to hate him. Now I think he blames himself, although I don't think he should. You must speak to him.'

'Why me?'

'Who else is there?' He stared at her. 'Surely you must realise how much he cares for you?'

'We are good friends.'

'I don't mean just that. Good God, Judy, the man loves you. I knew that when I was nineteen. You seemed to be the only person who wasn't aware of it. That's why I hated you both when I heard you'd gone to England with him but gradually I realised that might be the best thing for you. It still might be. You suit each other.'

'I think you're being a bit romantic! You seem to have forgotten I'm married!'

'Only you can decide how much that means to you. But you owe Tom a lot.'

'I know I do.' She moved away from him towards the door,

then stopped. 'What about you? What are you going to do?'

'I have been offered a chance by a religious organisation to work with young people from both sides helping them to get to know one another and to come to terms with the peace process, especially those who have already got into trouble.'

'Is that a Catholic organisation?'

'No. Catholics and Protestants run it. A priest I met in prison put me in touch with them. I really want to do this, Judy. It's our only hope, I think, of getting a good future and it means that my years in prison won't be wasted. I can't think of anything better for me to do. Pray that I will have some success, won't you?'

'I certainly will.' His enthusiasm and hope impressed her. 'I almost envy you. Why didn't you say this when we first met again?'

'Because I wasn't able to do it until I had talked to you and got your forgiveness. But you shouldn't envy me. You have so many more talents than I have. There is a lot you can do.'

'Perhaps.' She felt sad. 'But I don't seem to have done much with them in the last few years.'

'Then start now.' He smiled encouragingly at her. 'Make a start with Tom.'

'I'll try.' She smiled back. 'Though I have a suspicion that your advice may be sinful.'

'I don't think that loving someone can ever be sinful. Keep in touch, won't you? Michael's address will always find me. I want to hear about your progress.'

'I will write but don't be too hopeful.' She was definitely going now.

'And make quite sure, won't you, Judy, that Tom understands that I won't tell the authorities anything that could harm him. I owe him that.'

'What do you mean?' She was startled. 'Do you mean something about why he came here?'

Before either of them could say any more the door was pushed open gently and Katy came into the room. 'I'm sorry,' she said. 'Would you rather I went away?'

'Of course not,' Lawrence answered her. 'We have said all we need to say. Ask Tom, if you want to know more,' he added turning to Judy.

'I will,' she promised. 'Which reminds me I'd better go back to him before he gets too impatient.' After she had opened the door, she turned to Katy. 'Thanks for everything. I hope we'll meet again.'

'So do I,' Katy returned. 'If you're looking for Tom, however, he left a few minutes ago with Bill.'

'Left?' Judy stared at her. 'But he was supposed to be waiting for me.'

'He said he'd walk with Bill to the tube station and wait for you there. I think he and Bill wanted to have a chat.'

'I see. Well, I'd better hurry then.' With a last hasty smile she disappeared.

'I thought Tom was being a bit odd,' Katy remarked, 'as you came further into the room and made herself comfortable in one of the armchairs. Did you upset him somehow?'

'The truth upset him. But he'll cope. Tom's pretty tough.'

'I expect so.' She ran her hand through her short brown hair as if to get rid of unpleasant thoughts. 'It's all been a bit upsetting.' She smiled at him. 'But it all seems to be over now. Why don't you come and sit down instead of standing near the door as if you were going to run away at any minute?'

Moving across the room towards her, he sat down on the arm of the nearest armchair. 'The trouble is, Katy, that I have got to run away. I'm sorry.'

'What do you mean? I thought you were going to stay for a while. You seemed to mean that this morning, at least. Or was that just "Irish blarney" as Bill told me it was. Or is simply that you've seen Judith?' She spoke sadly but without bitterness.

'No, it isn't any of that.' Standing up, he moved towards her. For a moment he looked down into her lovely but troubled brown eyes, then taking her hand, he spoke gently. 'I love you for your kindness and generosity. You comforted me when I most needed comfort but there are now things which I must do. And more important there is a lot I must tell you about myself before we go any further.'

'I don't think I understand but I want to.'

'I'll try to explain.' He sat down again, this time on the arm of her chair.

As she walked quickly towards the station, Judith's thoughts were in a tumult. Why was Tom behaving so oddly, she wondered. What had Lawrence meant about not telling the authorities? As she drew near to the tube she was struck by the disturbing thought that Tom might not after all be there. Perhaps he had simply decided to go out of her life. As she came round the bend in the road, she saw him, however, standing there, apparently lost in thought and unaware of the people jostling by him.

He was so abstracted that she was able to come right up to him without his seeing her. 'Tom,' she exclaimed. 'I'm so glad I've found you!'

Surprised, he turned and smiled at her. 'I wasn't aware that I'd ever been lost! I told Katy I would wait for you here.'

'I know it was ridiculous but I had this silly fear that you might somehow have vanished and I would never see you again.'

'It might have been better for you if I had.'

The bitterness of his tone both surprised and shocked her. 'Whatever makes you say something so horrid? You know I would hate it.'

'Would you? I wonder. Perhaps for a little while but then perhaps you could be as happy with Paul as you were before. It might be a safer option.'

She seized his unresponsive arm. 'Don't say things like that! We've always been friends. Why are you trying to hurt me suddenly?'

Ignoring her question, he followed his own thoughts. 'It's five o'clock. It might be more sensible if you went back to Paul and talked with him before Inspector Barrett arrives. Don't you agree?'

She looked at him, her eyes flashing. 'I'm coming back with you! It's you I want to talk to. You know that. Why are you being like this? Whatever did Lawrence say? I helped you to see him. You can't shut me out now. I won't let you.'

He looked at her then unexpectedly smiled. 'The same old fiery Judy! You're right of course. It's about time we talked but not here. We'll take a taxi. But don't say a word until we're back in the flat.'

When they arrived at the flat after a silent and much delayed journey, Fergus O'Keefe was standing in the porch. He was carrying a couple of bags and had obviously been waiting for Tom, since he came forward greeting him with considerable relief. 'Just a minute.' Tom waved him aside. 'I'll see Judy into the living room and then come and have a word with you. Wait here in the hall.' As soon as Judith was settled, Tom went out again, shutting the door behind him.

Judith wondered not for the first time why Tom bothered with men like the O'Keefes. Of course, in the Belfast days they must have been useful as willing though humble comrades. That did not explain, however, why he had installed them in the top flat of this house he had acquired some years ago in south-west London. Apparently, he still found them useful, though in what she could not imagine.

She suddenly became aware that the conversation in the hall was not proceeding as quietly as it had begun. Tom was coldly angry. 'Why the hell didn't you get rid of them as I told you to on Saturday?' She could not hear the words of Fergus's reply but it was obviously some kind of excuse. It made Tom even angrier. 'You were bloody lucky then that the police did not search the garage last night.' Fergus's muttered reply was inaudible but Tom's was even clearer. 'Then get rid of them now. I told you what to do. For God's sake, don't waste any more time, you can't be sure they won't come again. And, if they find this stuff, I can't help you.' She heard the front door open. Fergus was obviously going. After a few moments, it was slammed shut and she heard Tom coming down the hall.

Standing up quickly, she began to put on her coat again. After what Lawrence had said to her it seemed all too miserably clear. She spun round as Tom opened the door. 'What are you doing?' he asked her. 'Why are you putting on your coat again? I thought we were going to talk?'

'There's no point, is there? I might as well go and see Paul.' She stared miserably into those penetrating dark blue eyes which now seemed so cold.

He didn't move but continued to stand with his back to the

door. At last, he said, 'What do you mean? When I suggested that, you turned me down completely. Why have you changed your mind?'

'You know why. Don't make things worse.'

'I don't know what you mean.' Then he shrugged his shoulders and smiled slightly mockingly. 'Why don't you simply say that you've changed your mind? Cut out the drama and admit honestly that you've realised that life with Paul is much the best option for you. I won't blame you.'

'Don't dare to talk to me like that. How can you when you know you've lied to me and abused my trust in you? You know I always believed in you.'

'Lied to you! What are you talking about?' He took a few steps forward until he stood in front of her. 'Judy, what are you saying?'

'Please don't make it worse. I heard you just now talking in the hall with Fergus. You haven't given up violence. You didn't come here just to help me. Lawrence was right, wasn't he? You came here…' In spite of her efforts her voice broke in a sob. 'After the way you talked to me this morning. You didn't have to do all that surely? I can't believe that you could be like that.' She stared at him through her tears. Life seemed utterly desolate now.

'Then don't believe it.' He gripped her shoulders hard. 'I don't pretend to be a good man but I'm not such a villain either.' Suddenly, he pulled her close to him. 'Don't cry like that, Judy, my love. You don't need to.' He led her towards the settee. 'Let's sit down together and talk. There's a lot I want to say to you, if you'll only listen. I think it's time I gave my version of events. There's a lot I'd like to tell you. Will you give me the time?'

Wiping her eyes with the tissues he produced, she looked long at him. 'I think it's about time you did talk,' she said at last with a slight smile. 'You can't expect me to understand if you never do, can you?'

Chapter Twenty-Three

'Where do you want me to start?' Tom leaned back as if to make himself comfortable but Judith could sense that he was very tense.

'Why don't you have a whisky first?' she suggested. 'And get a white wine for me.'

'Good idea.' He stood up quickly and walked over to the drinks cabinet. 'This has been a difficult day.' He smiled slightly. 'And it's by no means over yet.' Watching him as he poured out the drinks, she noticed that he was still unusually pale and that his face when he was not smiling was set in unhappy almost grim lines. After handing her the glass of wine, he sat down again and took a large gulp of the whisky before setting down his glass.

'It's often best to start at the beginning,' she remarked coming back to his question.

'True but the question then is – where do you want me to put the beginning? I think I've given you most of the sordid details of my early life – drunken, unemployed father, embittered by the injustice that he, as a Catholic, or so he believed, could never obtain another job. At sixteen, as you know, I escaped owing to the generosity of a prosperous friend of my father's who offered me a home, training as an accountant and, at the same time, introduced me to the IRA. I served both apprenticeships with equal zeal being determined to escape from poverty and to work for the independence and freedom of a united Ireland. I suppose you remember some of this?'

'Of course. I couldn't forget how harsh your early life was. There seemed to be no love at all in your family.'

'Well, my brothers took mostly after their father and my two sisters were as defeated as my wretched mother, who struggled from one pregnancy to another without time or energy to care for any of us. The only one I cared about was Liam, my youngest brother. He was intelligent and ready to listen to me. I did all I could to encourage him to do well at school and planned to pay for him to get to England or Dublin to complete his education. He was the only person I had any affection for until I met you. It seems however that he might have better without my "so-called love".'

Startled by the bitterness in his voice, Judith interrupted him. 'Whatever do you mean? 'What did Lawrence say to you?'

'He told me the truth about Liam's death, which was very different from the fable I had invented to excuse myself and to give me a reason for blaming Lawrence. I suppose that proves your accusation. I was not entirely truthful when I spoke to you this morning. I still had one hatred.'

'But you wouldn't have killed Lawrence, would you?'

'Probably not but that was never in question for, as the truth was revealed, it became clear that it would have been more just to have killed myself. It seems that I was the real culprit.' Taking up his whisky, he stared into the depths of the glass and then took another drink. 'It was my selfishness that killed Liam.' He turned to look at her but his usually piercing blue eyes were clouded.

Disbelieving, she stared at him. 'I don't believe you! You were always so kind and generous to him! Whatever did Lawrence say?'

Slowly, he told her in a hard, cold voice, struggling to control his deep feelings. 'So you see,' he said finally, 'I was really responsible. I failed to understand him. All my kindness and love really amounted to was an attempt to impose my will on him, to make him happy in the way I thought was best. I never asked him what he wanted. I was sure that I knew. That can't be called love. He was too scared of me, even to tell me. And the most terrible irony of it all is that what he most wanted was to be like me! He thought I was a hero!' He put his glass down and, leaning forward, he covered his face with his hands.

Full of sympathy, Judith instinctively put her arm around him. 'You shouldn't blame yourself so much. Everyone, including Liam, has the right to make his own decision. Liam made his. What he did in the end was wrong. And he can't blame your example for it certainly wasn't anything you would ever have done. You mustn't feel guilty. What you tried to do was good.' She waited a few moments but when Tom did not move, she gently pulled his hands away from his face and kissed him. 'I know how kind you can be,' she told him.

Sitting up abruptly, he looked at her almost angrily. 'Don't say that!' As she stared at him, he stood up and walked away towards the fireplace, where he stopped leaning on the mantelpiece with his back towards her. 'In the final count, you have very little to thank me for. I was too self-centred to understand you too. Lawrence made that clear. He said that one of my greatest faults was my inability to understand people.'

'What rubbish!' Judith jumped up and went quickly towards Tom. 'What the hell gives him the right to say things like that? Just because he says he's "a repentant sinner" he thinks he has a right apparently to criticise everyone else. He'd do better to look at himself!'

'Thank you for your support, Judy.' Tom smiled at her. 'But do sit down and listen. We are now getting to the "beginning" you mentioned.'

Reluctantly, she sat down. 'I'm not sure I understand. Where exactly are we?'

'At the point where we had spent just over four months together helping one another, for you helped me almost as much as I helped you. I was about to leave you to go to the States. It is at this point, I think, that Lawrence criticises me again.'

'Why?'

Moving quickly across the room, Tom then sat down beside her. 'He says I should have told you at that time how much I loved you, and should have taken me with you instead of leaving you in limbo.'

She looked at him, surprised. 'How could you possibly say that if, like me, I don't think you were sufficiently sure of this new love?'

'But I was.' He was very calm and definite. 'I have loved you since I first met you when you were scarcely eighteen. It was during the Easter holidays.'

'I can't think why you should have done,' was her unexpected reaction. 'I never imagined you as a victim of my physical charms!'

He laughed. 'I wasn't, although I appreciated them. When I first met you I was impressed by your temerity in arguing with

Michael Reardon and a couple of his friends that violence was wrong and inevitably caused further violence. And when someone cruelly reminded you that you ought not to feel like this because "your daddy" had been shot when you were three, you were not daunted but actually had the further courage to say that was why you did not want another child and another mother to suffer as you had done. How could I not admire such brave honesty?'

'You didn't support me,' she reproached him.

'You didn't need my support. And, furthermore, I hadn't yet made up my mind about this question.'

'It would have been foolish of you in your position to have supported me.'

'Quite, but let's get back to the point which Lawrence made. He says that I behaved wrongly when I left you. I had to go, as you knew, and I thought that we had both agreed that it was best for you to stay in London and study for your degree'. He waited a little for her reply but she was silent. 'You do agree, don't you? Or was I mistaken even about that? Please tell me, Judy.' He took her hand in his.

'That is what we agreed,' she replied slowly. 'But you know now what happened to me. I was academically a success but personally a failure.'

'If I had told you how deeply I loved you, would that have made any difference?'

'I'd like to pretend it would have but I'm not at all sure. I might have felt guiltier but I doubt if I would have behaved differently. The truth is, I suppose, I still needed your support and you weren't there. But I'm not blaming you. That was the situation and I had no right to expect you to be there.'

'This is where I make my real beginning then. I will try to tell you the truth you have asked for about the last few years.' She looked up to meet his penetrating glance. 'Will you believe me?'

'Of course.'

'The trouble is,' he smiled slightly, 'I've never been a romantic hero. When I left you I had two great loves – you and Ireland.'

'Wouldn't it perhaps be truer to say Ireland and me?' She smiled back to soften the implied bitterness of her words.

'It may look like that because I left you but this is where I misunderstood you and where Lawrence is right. I thought you had faced and largely overcome the impact of the agonising events of that August and were now ready to return to your mathematical studies and to your obvious ambition for a brilliant academic career.'

'You were right about my academic ambitions but wrong about my personal life. I hadn't realised myself how much I depended on your strength, but almost as soon as you left I began to run away from my problems. This became much worse after my mother's painful death. There seemed to be no one now. That's when I changed my name, ignoring your advice. Finally, I sacrificed even my academic career for what I thought would be a comforting security. You loved me, you said, we had even planned to marry but, at no point, even when I postponed our marriage, did you make any determined attempt to oppose me. Why not? What had happened to you?' At this point taking her hand from his, she stood up and walked over to a nearby armchair. Sitting down, she gazed earnestly at him. This was to her the most important question and she wanted to make this obvious. He understood this and didn't turn away. 'What are you? What is the truth about you?'

'That will soon become obvious, I hope.' He was cool and controlled. 'When I left you I had begun to agree with you that violence was non-productive. This view was at that time far from popular in IRA circles and I spent nearly four years in difficult and sometimes dangerous situations. Then, unexpectedly, it was made known to me that several people, including some of the top men, shared my viewpoint and more importantly felt that I, with my US connections, could be useful in certain very secret negotiations.

'During the last few years I have been on several missions to Belfast, and Dublin and then back to the States. At the same time I was pursuing my career, often working very long hours and earning far more money than I deserved. But, I insist, although I never forgot you, I believed you were happy and I didn't believe that I had any right to try to over-persuade you.' As he finished speaking, he stood up and moved towards her.

Wide-eyed and utterly amazed, she stood up and faced him.

'Oh, Tom, I never guessed! That explains so much. And Lawrence isn't always right, thank God!'

'Damn Lawrence and his suspicions! It's you I care about! What do you think?'

She looked up at him with her wide, dark eyes and her red lips smiling seductively.

'Stop it, Judy! You don't need to use those methods on me. You're wasting your time. I think I deserve something better than that, don't you?'

She laughed, her eyes sparkling as she accepted his point. 'Kiss me, Tom! Not as you have done lately but as you used to and as you really want to!'

'You're a very wicked woman, Judy O'Hara! And what's worse you know it!'

'And you're a very reluctant lover, Tom Farrell! Are you afraid to compete?'

In reply he took her in his arms and kissed her as he had never done recently, firmly and passionately. 'Does that convince you? Or shall I try again?' Without waiting for her to reply, he kissed her again with even greater ardour. Putting her arms around him, she returned his kiss. Finally, they drew apart a little. 'Are you satisfied now? Was that good enough?' he asked in a matter-of-fact tone.

She moved closer to him again. 'I've been a complete idiot, I think! I believe I've really loved you ever since that night you took me to the dance when Lawrence let me down. Do you remember that?'

'Every minute of it. But you gave me no encouragement.'

'That was where I was such an idiot! I still believed (I was very young) that if we weren't both starry-eyed and romantic it couldn't be love. It was all your fault! As you admitted just now you are not a romantic hero.'

'Would it help now if I ordered you a dozen red roses?'

'It's too late for that. I've decided that I'll just have to love you as you are!'

'Good. That's a relief! But there's still a lot more we must say to one another. Sit down, Judy.' Startled, she obeyed him and sat down on the settee. 'First, are you sure that you do know me as I am? Or are there more questions you would like to ask? Think carefully.'

'What can there be? You've told me what you've been doing. I know that other people's suspicions are unfounded. If they knew the truth, they would be ashamed.'

'They must not know the truth yet, Judy.'

'I understand that but I wish it wasn't so.' She considered his question a little longer. 'What about the O'Keefes?' She asked finally. 'Your conversation with Fergus seemed suspicious. Why are they here anyway?'

'That's easily explained. Soon after I bought this place, about seven years ago, I heard from Fergus that, although they were skilled tradesmen, they were unemployed and penniless, probably because of their rumoured association with me. Feeling responsible, I lent them a little capital and offered the top flat at a minimum rent on condition that they looked after the house. Until now, it's worked well.'

'What's happened then?'

'I discovered that those idiots had got themselves mixed up with some very dubious characters they'd met in a pub. They'd been persuaded to take some bomb-making equipment from them and hide it for a few days. Yesterday morning, I told them to get rid of it. They apparently did and when the police came last night they found nothing in their flat. But this evening I discovered that they had hidden it all in my garage! I was furious as you heard and told them how to get rid of it and to avoid these men or leave my flat. They'll get rid of it.'

From his cold tone, she was convinced they would. 'But that has nothing to do with you?

'Nothing.'

'You're no longer involved in anything dangerous?'

'Of course not. I've retired from being a hero and am aiming to become a politician. And politicians, whatever else they may be, are never heroic.' Smiling, he paused for a moment. 'Well, that about brings us to the end, I suppose.'

Surprised, she looked at him. 'What do you mean? That sounds ominous.'

'Don't be upset. I only meant the end of my story up to the

present, not I hope the end of our story.'

'I'm glad. You had me scared. But what happens next?'

'That rather depends on you, doesn't it? You know the truth about me. You also know I still love you and you have said that you love me. But how much does that mean, Judy? You've got to make a big decision now, one that will last. No one can expect to continue to get fresh chances.'

'But I've already told you that I don't want to go back to Paul.'

'What you actually said was – "I can't go back to Paul." But now you're feeling calmer that may not seem so bad. At least you know what that life is like. It must have many temptations for you.'

Without attempting to reply she sat thinking for several minutes. At last her mind was clear and calm. She looked up at him. He had now returned to his former place, leaning on the mantelpiece. 'There's something you haven't mentioned.'

'What's that?'

'What are you going to do? Are you going back to New York soon? I think you should tell me that. Or do you think it shouldn't matter to me?'

He seemed unexpectedly aloof as he stood there in his immaculate dark suit and white shirt. His black hair was smoothly brushed. His face with its strong, clear jawline and his firm mouth was impressive rather than handsome. It was not until he flashed his brilliant blue eyes on her and smiled as he did now that she felt his attraction and the power of it. Moving swiftly, he came across the room and sat next to her. 'I'm leaving New York. I've already resigned. My apartment is up for sale.' He spoke calmly as if unaware that his news was so startling.

'You haven't told me.'

'There hasn't been time until now.' He took her hand in his. 'Naturally, I was going to tell you.'

'But why are you doing this? I thought you had a brilliant job there.'

'I had but some things are more important than money. I want to return to Ireland. Anyone who believes in peace must give their support now. There's a lot of work to be done and, like Lawrence, I want to play my part. There are people who will hate me but others will welcome me.'

'What about me? she whispered.

'I would like you to be with me.' He put his arm around her. 'Are you brave enough, Judy, to face the ghosts and be yourself?'

'Oh God!' She moved away from him, burying her face in her hands. He waited. 'Now I understand why you suggested that I might after all decide to go back to Paul. You're cruel! How can you give me hope then take it away?'

'That's not what I mean to do, Judy darling. I'm trying to tell you that we can only be happy by freeing ourselves from our fears and by having the courage to be what we truly are and being loyal to what we believe. Judy O'Hara and Judith Tempest can't coexist. You've got to come out of this prison, this imaginary world you tried to create with Paul. You should set him free too. He'll be happier in the end.'

'I expect that's true. But there's a third alternative. I can return to my academic career and live my own life without returning to the place I most dread.'

'You can and that would be better and truer than the present. But I hope you won't because I love you very dearly and I'm sure that we can have a good life together. But you'll have to decide for yourself. That's the way I want it. That's the way I've always wanted it.'

'I know, but I still don't know what to do. Please help me, Tom.'

'I wouldn't if I could. You'll have to brave and there's no time now anyway.' He stood up. 'If you're to keep your appointment with Paul and the inspector you must go now.'

'But aren't you supposed to be there too?' She stood up, facing him.

'I don't think I'll be required now, if Lawrence has kept his promise. The play is over.' Picking up her coat, he held it out for her to put on. 'I'll ring my favourite taxi man, an honest friend of the O'Keefes.'

After smoothing her hair, she put on her coat and gloves, then waited while he fixed the taxi. 'He'll be here in a few minutes.' He took her in his arms. 'I'm here whenever you want me.'

They kissed as she clung to him. 'I still don't know what to say.'

'Say the truth.' Tom was very firm. 'And decide what you want to do. That's important. Don't think about what I want or Paul wants.' He kissed her again. 'Don't look so tragic. It will pass. Everything does.'

'Don't be so bloody cool and rational.' She kissed him fiercely. 'You really do want me to come back, don't you?' Ignoring the bell, she kissed him again.

'What the hell do you think I've always wanted?' He laughed as they moved into the hall. 'I'll come and kidnap you if you don't return.'

'But I'm still free to make my choice?'

'Of course but make sure it's the right one.' He took her out to the taxi and gave her one last kiss as he helped her into it. With a final wave, she was gone.

As soon as the taxi had gone out of sight, Tom went back into the flat. After picking up their two glasses, he took them into the kitchen where he washed and dried them methodically. Then he heated up some coffee left over from their lunch, poured himself a cup and returned to the sitting room. He would have preferred to have accompanied Judy had he not believed that it was more sensible to allow her and Paul another chance to talk together. Her decision must be definite and unforced, he told himself.

Nevertheless, as he sipped his coffee he felt far from being satisfied with himself. Had he been too harsh at the end, he wondered? Was Judy right when she said he was cruel? He had certainly never intended to be. Perhaps he should have made more allowances for all she had suffered? But how could he not speak the truth when he was convinced that her best future as well as his lay in Northern Ireland? One question alone remained unanswered and significantly unasked – would he still be determined to return if it meant leaving Judy once again? He felt unable to face this at the moment, preferring to hope that it wouldn't be necessary. This was their last chance, he knew. His sense of purpose was strong as always but in his late thirties his desire to find a secure happiness at last with Judy was almost overwhelming. All he could do was wait.

★

As she sat in the taxi Judy's thoughts were in turmoil. She had been so happy when Tom had told her that he still loved her and when she had at last realised how deep were her feelings for him. But how could he have been so cruel as to ruin it with that terrifying suggestion that they should return together to Belfast? She didn't feel that she could even contemplate it. But could she now contemplate the thought of life without Tom again? She had spoken boldly about an academic life but she knew only too well that she was not fitted to live alone.

That left Paul. She acknowledged that this had its temptations as Tom had suggested. But how could she possibly go back? Tom had no right to put this terrible alternative before her. She was very angry. If he really loved her, she thought... but then he might equally say if she really loved him...? She could make no clear decision and it was a relief almost when the taxi came to the end of its journey. Nothing need be decided yet.

Chapter Twenty-Four

After showing Inspector Barrett to the door, Paul returned quickly to the living room where Judith was waiting. She was sitting gracefully in an armchair illuminated by one of the many standard lamps in the room. Her smooth dark hair with its gleaming copper glints framed her oval face. In contrast with her deep purple dress her eyes seemed darker and more beautiful than ever, her lips redder and more tempting. As he studied her from the doorway, he realised that since she had arrived and especially during the interview with Inspector Barrett, his wife, Judith Tempest, seemed to have returned to him. She appeared to him to be more desirable than ever but his instinct urged him to be cautious.

'That went surprisingly well, don't you think?' he asked, moving towards her. 'No really awkward questions. You obviously charmed the man.'

'I should imagine it was more because Lawrence has voluntarily reappeared and sorted out several difficulties.' She was cool and distant but she had often been like that in the past.

'He appears to have removed suspicion from your friend, Tom.'

'That's quite reasonable since Tom is not involved in any terrorist activities. He came to London to see Lawrence and to support me.' She looked up at him suddenly as if challenging him to disagree.

Determined not to, Paul sat down in a chair opposite her. 'I thought that Tom might come with you to meet the inspector.'

'He knew that there would be no need since he and Lawrence had talked.'

'I see. They came to a mutually satisfactory agreement, did they?'

She looked sharply at him but answered quietly. 'Yes. After he had spoken to me, Lawrence understood that he had no great reason to hate Tom and when Tom heard how his youngest brother, Liam, had really died then he knew he had no particular reason to be angry with Lawrence.'

'So everything has been satisfactorily sorted out. And life moves on. Is that right?'

'I suppose you can say so.' She sounded very sad. 'Lawrence will return to Belfast to take up youth work, hoping to help to reconcile Protestants and Catholics.' She stopped speaking.

'And I suppose Bill and Katy will carry on much as usual, putting this interlude behind them. What about Tom? Has he any plans?' He waited anxiously for her reply.

'Tom doesn't intend to stay much longer in London.' Her voice was even and quiet, her expression calm, no emotion visible.

Paul felt a great sense of relief. There seemed to be no reason now why he and Judith should not return to Braxby, to their normal life. Obviously, Judith had been overwrought earlier but now she had returned to her familiar calm. He was, nevertheless, unsure as to what he should say at this moment. Suddenly, he remembered something that still puzzled him. 'There is one thing I still don't understand.'

'What's that?'

'Why was Maeve so frightened that she turned you and Lawrence away on Friday night?' When Judith frowned slightly but made no answer, he continued, 'And who was it who called on her on Saturday morning before I did?' Seeing that he had Judith's full attention now, he went on, 'It couldn't have been anything to do with Tom because she said he looked like me, only more respectably dressed. No one could possibly consider that Tom and I resembled each other.'

'She would have recognised Tom since she knew him well years ago. That can't be the answer.' She leaned forward a little towards him. 'You're right, though. She was very frightened.'

'What about Lawrence? He was frightened too, wasn't he?'

'Yes, but I thought that was because he was afraid to meet the police or Tom.'

'That may be the explanation but there are other somewhat mysterious matters. When I arrived at the address Maeve had given me, Bill was already there and seemed to be expecting me. Was that simply a coincidence?'

'I doubt it.' Judith smiled slightly.

Feeling a little annoyed, he asked sharply, 'So am I to assume that it was arranged by you since you knew the address? Were you in contact with Bill?'

'No, but Tom might have been. I had talked to him. It's not really important now, is it?'

'Perhaps not to you but what followed might be. As we were looking round the flat, some other people arrived. They definitely sounded threatening and Bill suggested that we escape through the back door while we still had time. Who were they? Was that anything to do with Tom or with his friends?'

He certainly had her full attention now. She sat up and stared at him. 'I don't know anything about them. It certainly wasn't Tom.'

'Are you sure?'

'Yes.' Her voice was very soft and he felt that she was frightened by what he had told her.

'Can it be possible that other people are involved in the happenings of the last few days? People even you are not aware of? I know that you have all been duping me, but could it be that you also have been duped?' His own persistence surprised him. He had had no intention of saying anything like this. His intention had in fact been to woo Judith back, but when he realised that all the mysteries were not solved he felt forced to probe.

'It must have been some branch of the police, trying to pick up Lawrence,' she suggested after some hesitation. 'You know, don't you, that he had escaped from their surveillance? There is no one else it could have been.' Her voice became stronger as she spoke but he still sensed that she was worried.

'I expect you must be right,' he agreed. He had no desire to pursue this further. It was getting late and he must come to terms with Judith. After a moment's uneasy silence, he returned to his original plan. 'Have you decided what you are going to do?'

'I told you earlier.' She sounded very distant. 'Have you finalised your plans?'

'I've booked two seats on the ten twenty train tomorrow

morning. It's the best morning train.'

'Did you say two seats?'

'I'm hoping that now everything is satisfactorily settled, you'll change your mind and return with me. You don't want to be away from work too long. And it seems to me that the sooner we return to normal, the better it'll be for us. Don't you agree?' He waited with some anxiety for her reply.

'Not really.' Her voice was cool. 'Surely you realised I was serious when I said I didn't want to return with you tomorrow? We can't go on pretending. It won't work any more.'

'I'm not pretending. I want you to come back with me. I know I reacted stupidly this morning and I'm very sorry for that. It was one more shock and I simply spoke without thinking about your feelings. I should have been more controlled, I admit. But surely you can forgive me? Especially when you say you have forgiven Lawrence.'

'Oh, I can forgive you. I didn't behave particularly well myself.' She sounded sad and weary. 'But that's not the real reason why I'm not coming back with you tomorrow. I don't really want to come back at all, although I suppose I'll have to and give my notice properly. I don't want to cause any unnecessary gossip and make matters even worse for you.'

'What the hell do you mean? You're not making sense at all! Have you gone out of your mind, Judith? We've been happily married for nearly six years. Why shouldn't we go back together and be as happy as we were?'

'Do you really think that's possible?' She looked and sounded surprised. 'Are you really saying that nothing has changed?'

'Nothing important has. I admit we had a nasty row this morning, which we've never had before. We were both overwrought and said things we didn't mean. I was particularly insensitive but you just said you'd forgiven me. And last night before Tom intruded...' He broke off and looked angrily at her. 'That's it, isn't it? Tom! I should have expected it but I didn't because I've always trusted you. But now, your old lover's come back, you don't want me. At least, you might tell me the truth.'

'I haven't tried to lie to you. Meeting Tom again has affected me although not perhaps in the way you think. It's not what you suspect. It's just that we share so much background. It's simply that talking to Tom has made me see many things more clearly. He knows me and understands me.'

'And I don't. Is that what you're saying?' He sat down, suddenly feeling defeated.

'Yes, but it's not entirely your fault. In fact, it's hardly your fault at all. I was a fraud. I deceived you when I married you by pretending to be someone very different from what I was. It was a wrong thing to do but you made it easier by never asking any questions.'

'I remember you said yesterday that you married me because you found me attractive and because I didn't ask any questions. I didn't believe you could be entirely serious. I thought you still wanted to hurt me for some reason. Are you saying that you were actually telling the whole truth?'

Instead of answering, she asked a question. 'Why did you marry me, Paul? Have you ever thought about it seriously?'

'Of course I have! What a ridiculous question to ask! You seem to think that I'm nothing more than an infatuated idiot.'

'You still haven't answered my question, have you?' As she fixed her dark eyes on him, the fear that had always been there returned as strongly as it had on Friday night when he had discovered that she had gone. He had sometimes suspected that she might leave him one day. Except when they made love, she had always been a little remote and, even then, on occasions. They had never argued fiercely, he realised now, because she had never cared enough to do so.

Nevertheless, he tried valiantly to give a convincing answer. 'Surely, it's quite obvious? I married you because I loved you. You must have noticed that.'

For a moment she did not answer but appeared to be considering what he had said. Finally, she spoke, looking directly at him. 'I am sure that you have always found me very attractive but can you possibly say you love someone you don't know?'

'If I don't know you, whose fault is that?' He turned angrily towards her. 'I would have listened, if you had ever been prepared to talk to me.'

'And perhaps I would have talked if you had been interested

enough to ask questions. But you weren't, were you? Apart from enjoying music together, you were content for us to go our separate ways, as long as we could make love frequently, which we did.'

'Surely, that's important, isn't it? In my experience dealing with divorce cases many couples separate because they don't enjoy their sex life. And now it seems you want us to separate because we do. Aren't you being rather perverse?'

'If I had said just that, I would be, but I haven't. I'm simply saying that it's not enough by itself for a lifetime. Do stop fencing, Paul. I'm very serious.'

'I have been happy with you. What else can I say? I even thought you were happy, too. Are you saying now that you weren't?'

'At first I thought it was enough. I was very lonely when I met you. I had thought it was best to shut the door on the past, to change my name and start afresh. I had never understood, however, how frightening and empty life could seem in those circumstances. When we fell in love, it transformed everything and I snatched at the chance. It's easy to see why I did but it wasn't right or sensible. To be truthful, I was acting a part all the time and it became harder as time passed. When Lawrence reappeared, I couldn't continue and I couldn't now tell the truth, so I selfishly ran away. I'm very sorry but that's the truth.'

'God, how can you sit there and say these things? Don't you realise what effect you're having or is it that you don't care how much it all hurts?

'I do care very much but I can't go on lying. I have to speak the truth now.'

'But it's not the whole truth, even now, is it? It wasn't just Lawrence who returned, it was also Tom. And strangely enough, you haven't mentioned Tom. Isn't he perhaps the real reason for your wanting to leave me?'

'I won't insult you by pretending that Tom is unimportant but you mustn't deceive yourself. Tom has not forced this on us. He has told me to make up my own mind and to do what I want, without too much regard for his opinions or yours. Lawrence's return forced me to look again at the past and to try to understand the truth about myself and my actions. When I left you this morning, I talked it all over with Tom and he helped me to see how foolish I had been to believe that I could deny my own self and pretend that Judy O'Hara had never existed.' Pausing, she waited for him to reply.

He was, however, too hurt and too angry to make a reasonable reply. 'And so you expect me to believe that Tom is the noble knight, who without any ulterior motives always comes to your rescue?'

'What do you call "ulterior motives"?' She, too, was angry now. The coolly distant Judith had vanished suddenly. 'Can't you ever believe that anyone can ever have decent motives for what they do? Tom is my friend as I have already told you and I trust him.'

Paul laughed bitterly. 'Isn't it time you gave up this pretence? How about some truth for a change?'

'I thought you'd had enough truth.' She flashed at him.

'About Lawrence but not about Tom. Surely you don't expect me to be such a fool as to go on believing that Tom is simply the friend who turns up after nearly twelve just as you want him? Be reasonable, Judith, please.'

'You're right.' She considered him carefully. But are you sure you want to hear the whole truth? You've never been keen to do so before.'

'I thought I was secure. Now I see that I've been living in a fool's paradise and I want to know why. How much have you been deceiving me?'

'You were only deceived because you wanted to be deceived but it's not as bad as you now suspect. Tom and I haven't met for six and a half years, not since I agreed to marry you, in fact. He's the one I treated badly, not you. We had been lovers after I took my first degree and I'd promised to marry him but I left him for you. You were the winner, if that's the right word.' She seemed almost to be mocking him.

'I see.' He tried to understand what she had told him. It was quite reasonable for her to have had a previous lover and there was no reason for him to be jealous. 'But that wasn't the end of the story, was it?'

'It was meant to be and it was until recently.'

'And then what?' Her answer was another shock to him.

'I realised some months ago that our marriage was sterile and was likely to become more so. We had little in common and we had no children. I wasn't even doing the work I wanted to do. I had no congenial friends. My life seemed empty and meaningless. I tried once or twice to talk to you but you didn't want to listen. You seemed to think that bed would solve everything. I decided, therefore, to leave you and come to London. I knew I could stay in this flat for a while.'

'As far as I'm concerned you never gave the slightest indication!' He stared at her. 'I don't believe I've ever known you at all!'

'Probably not! But did you want to?' She was quite calm. 'It was all intended to be done properly. I gave my notice in at half term. I was going to tell you and leave some time after Christmas. It's horrible, I suppose, but that's how I am.'

He could find no suitable words with which to answer her at first. 'Where does Tom fit in?' he managed to ask at last.

'I rang Tom at some length. We'd always kept in touch. I felt I needed his help and advice. He said he thought he could manage a trip to London in the New Year.'

'He was still willing to do that after the way you'd treated him?'

'He knows me as I am and still cares for me. That amazes me but I know it's true.'

'I suppose he expected to get his reward at last?' Paul could not hide his bitterness.

She looked at him coldly. 'How little you understand. We talked as the friends we have always been.'

'But none of this happened. Why?'

'Lawrence and Inspector Barrett happened. I couldn't face it. Believe me, I did want to spare you the scandal. I rang Tom and told him I was running away. He said he would come on the first available plane. I gave him this address.'

'So that's why you weren't surprised to see him. You'd been expecting him.'

'Yes. I'd hoped that he would come sooner.'

'I see. So you're going to leave me now for him? There's

nothing noble about it, is there? You're just the same Judith wanting a bit of excitement. I suppose I've been a bit boring lately?' He stood up suddenly. 'But it doesn't have to be like that, does it, Judith?' As she stood up to face him, he moved towards her. She had never seemed more beautiful or more desirable. 'We can be happy again as we have been. I'm still very much in love with you and I think you still find me attractive.'

Taking her in his arms, he began to kiss her passionately, her lips, her cheeks, and her throat. At first she seemed to yield and return his kisses but suddenly she pushed him violently away. 'Leave me alone! I don't want it any more. Don't you even begin to understand? It's a sham and I can't bear it any more!'

Puzzled, he stared at her. 'Why not? I don't understand. Whatever do you mean?'

She sat up and looked steadily at him. 'I don't believe you've listened to a word I've been saying. That's what's wrong with us. There's only one way we communicate. On the whole we do it very well. I'd almost forgotten how delightful it can be and how tempting. But it's no longer enough. I'm sorry.'

He sat down, feeling cold and afraid. Was this what he had so often dreaded? 'So, it's Tom, isn't it? You really meant it when you said you loved him. So much so that you don't want me to touch you, even though part of you still enjoys it. You're going to go away with him, aren't you?' When she didn't answer, he appealed to her again. 'If you are, at least tell me.'

Suddenly, she stood up and walked over to the piano where her fingers struck a few familiar chords. Was she trying to evade him or was she using music as an attempt to communicate? Irritated, he went swiftly across to her. Seizing her by the shoulders, he swung her round to face him. 'Don't do that! Just tell me!'

'I don't know, Paul. I simply don't know.'

'Do you love him? Are you sure of it?'

'Yes, I'm sure I do.'

'Then, that's it, isn't it? There's no more to be said.' Turning away from her miserably, he went back to the armchair. After a moment she followed him and sat opposite him on the settee. 'When are you going?' When she didn't answer him but remained looking down at her tightly clasped hands, he asked again, 'When?'

'Perhaps never. I don't know if I can do it.'

'Whatever do you mean? Why can't you? I won't stop you if that's what you really want. You'll probably enjoy New York. It's bound to be more exciting than Braxby.'

'Tom isn't going back to New York. He's going to Belfast and he wants me to go with him.'

Paul stared at her in disbelief. 'Then he must be mad! But, perhaps not. It begins to look as if you were wrong to think he is no longer involved with the terrorists.'

'He isn't. He believes that all of us who oppose violence should work for peace while there's still time. That's where we belong and that's what we ought to do.'

'God, how can he be so cruel, especially when he knows only too clearly what terrible memories you must have. After all you've suffered, you deserve to be made much of and to have a comfortable, secure life. That's what I tried to give you. And we can have it again. Surely, you see that, Judith. You can't want to go back there!'

'I don't but in spite of myself I do know that I belong there. I was born there. My father died there, my mother was always there in spirit. I did much of my growing up there, falling in love and suffering.'

'I'm not denying that but that doesn't mean that you have to go back there and suffer more. Surely, if Tom loves you as he says he does, he'd want to keep you away from all that. He'd want to protect you.'

'You don't understand. How could you? He does love me. He saved me from suicide. I owe him a lot. He knows me as no one else can. He doesn't think I need protecting. He remembers me as the brave Judy O'Hara who dared to tell the terrorists that violence was wrong.'

'Then why are you hesitating? Perhaps you don't really love him enough? Or are you perhaps secretly afraid that it'll be like Lawrence all over again? Is that it?'

'No, not that. I'm not sure I'm brave enough to do it. I don't know what to do.' She looked at him appealingly.

'I want to help but you really shouldn't ask me. I'm biased.' He was about to say more when the phone rang.

'That must be Tom wondering what has happened to you.' Picking up the receiver, he listened apparently puzzled, then handed it to her. 'It's not Tom. It's someone called Fergus who says he wants to speak to you urgently.'

As she took the phone, Judith was suddenly afraid. Was danger still lurking out there?

Chapter Twenty-Five

Although he could not see any reason for it, Paul was aware of Judith's fear as he handed her the receiver.

'Hello, Fergus. This is Judy. Why have you rung me? Has something happened?' She listened to the reply while Paul waited, watching her fingers tighten on the phone. 'I understand,' she said at last. 'I'll come at once. Get what information you can and look out for me at the main entrance.'

'What is it? Is something wrong?'

'Tom has been shot. They've taken him in the ambulance to St Thomas's, where Fergus is now.'

'Shot! When? Why?' Paul found it hard to believe but a glimpse of Judith's pale face and tragic dark eyes convinced him. She looked as if she might faint. 'Sit down for a moment.' He tried to lead her gently back to her armchair but she resisted him.

'I'm shocked but I'm perfectly all right and I must go straight away. Fergus doesn't know much.' She hastily put on the coat he offered her. 'It happened about three quarters of an hour ago.' Her fingers were trembling as she tried to fasten her coat. 'Fergus heard some shots, rushed down and found Tom lying in his porch. His brother rang for an ambulance. Tom was bleeding badly and soon became unconscious but, before he did, he managed to ask Fergus to ring me. Oh, Paul, it's so horrible! I thought everything was going to be all right this time. What a fool! I should have known better!'

He handed her handbag and scarf. He wanted to comfort her but did not know how. 'It may not be anything like as bad as it sounds. I know from experience that people often exaggerate.'

'I doubt if Fergus would. He's seen shootings before.' Winding her scarf round her neck, she turned to him. 'Could you help me to get a taxi? It should be possible in Southampton Way.'

'Of course.' Taking hold of her arm he led her towards the front door, retrieving his jacket in the hall. 'But I shan't leave you there. I'm coming all the way with you.'

'You don't have to. I can manage if you get a taxi.'

'Don't argue,' he replied firmly, shutting the door behind them. 'I'm determined.'

'Thank you.' She tried to smile but her eyes were full of tears.

He made no reply but merely held her arm more firmly. He was determined not to mention the fear that had come into his mind that Tom might be already dead or dying. Instead he encouraged her to hurry. Fortunately, they obtained a taxi quickly and the streets were almost empty on this wet November Monday night, so they were able to travel much faster than usual. Judith did not speak except once to exclaim, 'I can't think who can have done it. Years ago, perhaps – but not now!'

They saw Fergus as soon as they got out of the taxi, a short, burly man with reddish hair looking anxiously around him. Fergus scarcely noticed Paul. 'Judy!' he exclaimed hurrying towards her. 'Jesus! I'm glad to see you.'

'Is there any news?' Judith asked as they followed him towards the casualty department.

'Not a lot. They've put up a drip and a blood transfusion because he's lost a lot of blood. Then they took him up to X-ray. They said they might have to operate. I don't really know.' Fergus seemed bewildered by the events.

Deciding he should take charge, Paul suggested to Judith and Fergus that they should sit on a nearby bench while he went to the reception desk to discover what fresh news there might be. The receptionist was unable to add any more information to that which Fergus had already given them. She agreed, however, to try to find a doctor who might be able to tell them more. While Paul was still waiting, Judith joined him unable to sit passively any longer. 'It shouldn't be long,' he tried to reassure her. 'Fortunately, as it's not the weekend, this place is almost empty.' He looked around him. There had been an attempt to brighten up the casualty department with vivid murals and lively notices but it still seemed as depressing to him as hospitals always did and nothing could disguise the antiseptic smell.

A youngish man with dark hair growing thin on top and wearing casual trousers and jacket approached them. His round, rosy face creased into a friendly smile as he gave the greeting of a casual acquaintance. It was not until he introduced himself that Paul realised that he was a doctor. The X-ray, he told them, had revealed that one of the bullets was still in Tom's chest and dangerously close to the heart. They were, therefore, just about to take him to the operating theatre to remove the bullet and to discover the exact amount of the damage. Two other wounds, he said, in the head and in the upper left arm were less serious. The operation was tricky but it was fortunate that Mr Davis, the most senior surgeon, was available to perform it. He finished his report with another cheery smile.

'He will be all right, though, won't he?' Judith turned towards the young doctor with the full force of her tragically beautiful dark eyes.

'We hope so, of course. He has lost a lot of blood but I'm sure he has a strong constitution and that should help. Are you related to Mr Farrell?' He was obviously wondering somewhat belatedly whether Judith was entitled to be given information.

'No, but he's a very old and dear friend of mine and I am deeply concerned.'

Understanding the difficulty she was having in maintaining her self-control, Paul intervened. 'Mr Farrell has only just come to London from the USA after several years' absence. He has been staying with us and we are not aware that he has any other close contacts in this country. We naturally want to do what we can.'

The young doctor seemed to be reassured. 'In that case,' he suggested, 'perhaps you would like to see him before he goes into the operating theatre?' As he began to lead the way, they followed him. When they were about to enter the cubicle, he stopped. 'I should warn you that he is barely conscious and will probably not recognise you.'

Paul held back while Judith went quickly towards the trolley on which Tom was lying. His head was bandaged and he was connected to a drip and a blood transfusion. He was so pale and still that Paul wondered if he might not already be dead or dying.

Judith, however, without any hesitation went straight up to him. 'Tom! It's Judy here. Can you hear me? Fergus rang me and I've come'. Her voice was clear but soothing with no note of panic. 'Can you hear me, Tom?' When she stopped speaking, she took his left hand in hers and waited. When he made no response, she bent and kissed him gently. 'Tom, it's me, Judy,' she whispered.

Something had reached him in his darkness. With a tremendous effort, he slowly opened his eyes a fraction. When he spoke his voice was scarcely audible. 'Judy, I'm glad...' His eyes were closed again but he struggled to say more. 'Stay, won't you, I...' But the effort was too great. He returned to the darkness. 'I will,' she promised as she gave him a final kiss.

They watched as the trolley was wheeled towards the lift, then young Dr Fletcher turned towards them. 'It'll be some time, I'm afraid.'

'How long do you think?' Judy asked.

'It's difficult to say. It's a tricky operation and there may be complications. I'm sorry. But if you can make yourselves as comfortable as possible, I'll bring you news as soon as I have it.' He began to hurry away then turned back, 'I think I should mention that the police have been making enquiries but I've told them they can't possibly interview Mr Farrell.'

They walked towards the seats where Fergus sat gloomily with his head in his hands. When Paul told him the news, he didn't move but said gruffly, 'I'll wait then.'

Paul and Judy sat down silently near to him. After a few minutes Judith spoke. 'There's no need for you to wait, too, Paul. It's nearly midnight and you have to be ready to leave in the morning.' Touching his hand lightly, she smiled at him. 'You've been very good and I'm grateful.'

Her calm strength amazed him. Even though she did not need him, he was very reluctant to go, for it seemed impossible to leave her in this unhappy position without a friend except the taciturn Fergus. He made one last effort to stay a little longer. 'I'm not going till we've had some food. You must be starving. I know I am.'

'I'm not really hungry but I would appreciate a cup of coffee, though I can't imagine how we're going to get it.' She looked round the deserted area hopelessly.

As if in response to his cue, Fergus sat up suddenly. 'Leave that to me. That's right up my street. I'll scrounge some coffee and sandwiches or my name's not Fergus O'Keefe.' After taking the note which Paul offered him, he strode off purposefully.

'He'll do it,' Judith said. 'He'll turn on his Irish charm and his best brogue, just wait. Both of the O'Keefes would do anything for Tom.'

'And for you too, I imagine.'

'Only because of Tom. He let his flat to them and helped them to establish themselves as honest plumbers and decorators.'

'That was very decent of him. I had no idea.'

'There was no reason why you should have had any. You scarcely know Tom.' Sighing, she seemed to withdraw into her own thoughts.

At this point, Paul decided firmly that he must use this opportunity – perhaps the last one he would have – to talk to her. She was still his wife. Was it not his duty to try to stop her? He had yielded to her too soon, accepting too easily her idea that they could not possibly go back to their old life. With Fergus out of the way, he had another opportunity which he should not waste. He must make her realise how precarious her future without him might be. She must be made to understand the real threat to her of this attack on Tom. 'Have you any idea who might have shot Tom?'

She looked up slowly. 'None at all.'

'He hasn't given you any indication that something like this might happen?'

'No. Why should he? He had no reason to expect it.'

'Are you sure?'

'What do you mean?' Her voice was so quiet that she scarcely seemed to be interested.

'Surely he must have had some idea that there are some people around who hate him enough to want to kill him?'

'If he did he never said anything about it.' Her voice was quiet and listless.

'Perhaps, Judith,' he began, then hesitated. Would he be wiser, he wondered, to stay silent but, as she turned her dark, sad eyes on him, he decided he must speak. He must save her from further suffering, if he could. 'Perhaps,' he started afresh, 'Tom hasn't even yet told you everything?'

She studied him for a moment. 'I'm sure he's told me all that matters,' she said at last.

He wanted to shake her, to shout at her, to do anything that would make her aware of her situation but he restrained himself. 'You should think much harder, Judith, before you commit yourself finally. Tom has asked you to go back to Belfast but if this sort of thing can happen in London, what kind of life can you expect there? Do you really want to go back to that?' He hated himself when he saw her flinch but she soon rallied.

Her voice was strong now and her eyes flashed at him. 'Don't say any more! It's very wrong of you! Tom, whom I love, is very ill, perhaps dying. How can you try to persuade me to leave him at such a moment? Don't you think it's rather despicable?'

'I only want to help you,' he protested.

'Then leave me now!'

'Are you sure that's what you want?'

'Yes. Quite sure.'

'All right, Judith.' He stood up. 'But I'll stay in London until you tell me what is happening. You may still need me.'

She stood up too and seemed about to move away but he caught hold of her arm. 'I'll go if you promise to let me know how Tom is.' She looked angrily at him. 'Please,' he added. 'You owe me that, don't you?'

'I promise,' she replied reluctantly. 'But please go now, you can't help me at this moment.'

When he returned with sandwiches and coffee Fergus made no comment about Paul's absence apart from asking what he should do with his change. When Judy suggested that he might as well keep it, he pocketed it readily, remarking cheerfully, 'Well, that's all the more for us then!' He would have divided everything equally but agreed to her suggestion that he should eat the extra sandwiches, while she drank the extra coffee. They scarcely spoke during their small meal and, after he had disposed of the litter, he lay down comfortably on the next bench, using his jacket for a pillow, suggesting that she should make herself comfortable too as they might have a long wait. In a few minutes he appeared to be asleep and, apart form a few people coming and going, Judy was alone in the large, empty waiting room, with its hard bright lights and mockingly cheerful murals.

It was a long time, she thought, since she had been so alone. Now everyone had gone, leaving only Tom who was fighting for his life. All the reluctance she had expressed about being with him seemed so childish and weak now. If he died, there would be no one. He must not die. She would not allow him to die. She would not think of the empty future, which might be hers but would concentrate on this moment, this present time which was all she had. She had been taught to pray when she was a child and had never given up the practice completely. She must pray now with her full being.

Leaning forward, she closed her eyes and clasped her hands. What she had to do was to put herself in the presence of God, words were unnecessary. She plunged into the darkness of God. She did not know how long afterwards it was when she found herself being forced to concentrate on Tom. She was aware of bright lights and of Tom lying on a table beneath them. Ignoring the people around him, she glided forward and took his hand, willing her strength and spirit into his. 'Tom,' she whispered, 'it's me, Judy. If you want to live, cling on to me and fight. I'll help you.'

The scene gradually faded, the darkness returned. Suddenly she became aware of Fergus speaking to her. 'Wake up, Judy. The doctor's just coming.' Opening her eyes, she sat up. She saw by the clock that over two hours had passed. She was relieved to see that young Dr Fletcher was still smiling but perhaps he always smiled? She hurried towards him. 'How is he? Has the operation gone well?'

'Mr Davis is pleased with the final result but it was very tricky, I gather. Would you like to see him? They've just taken him to a ward.'

'I knew Tom would be all right,' Fergus remarked unexpectedly. 'He's always been a tough fighter.'

As they reached the ward, Dr Fletcher beckoned them to come in. 'He's not properly conscious but he might respond to you. I'm afraid you can't stay long. Mr Davis will soon be here to have another look at him. If you can wait, you might get some more information.' Still smiling, he left them.

This pale, motionless man with bandaged head and arm, attached to many tubes was barely recognisable as Tom. After taking one look and whispering, 'Keep fighting, Tom,' Fergus retreated. Judy went up to the bed and sat on the chair. 'Stay a bit,' the kindly looking sister invited her, 'and talk to him. He might hear you, even if he doesn't answer.'

She was alone with him. 'Tom, darling, it's me, Judy. You're doing fine. I hope you can hear me because I want you to know that I love you and I'm fighting with you so we can be together.' She took his hand, willing her strength into him. Suddenly, miraculously his eyelids lifted momentarily and she caught a familiar, piercing look from those dark blue eyes. Just as quickly it was gone and she might have thought she had imagined it had not his fingers tightened on hers, telling her that he understood.

As she sat there she was unaware of the passage of time so absorbed was she in trying to make Tom feel her love and her hope. Suddenly she realised that Mr Davis, the surgeon, had entered the room and was conferring in low tones with the sister. She began to stand up but he quickly motioned her to stay where she was as he began a rapid examination of the patient.

When he stood up she spoke to him. 'Will he be all right?' Her eyes implored him for good news. Looking at her with great kindness, he said slowly, 'He has come through the operation well. But it was very tricky. There was more damage than I had expected. The next twenty-four hours or so will be crucial.' He turned towards the sister and said, 'He must be kept very quiet. No visitors except this young lady who seems to have a good effect.' Turning back to Judy, he added with a kindly smile, 'I have done the best I can but I'm not God. If you believe in prayer, now is the time to pray'. With that he was gone, leaving Judy staring at the sister.

'Mr Davis is a Christian, 'the sister explained. 'He means exactly what he says but don't worry he will also consider it his duty to give Tom the very best treatment. He always does.'

'I'm sure of that. What you've told me makes me feel very confident.' Bending over Tom, she made a quick sign of the cross over him and commended him once more to God. It was far too long since she had done anything like that, she thought.

The sister, who was about to leave the room, suddenly stopped. 'I've just remembered. Your friend, Fergus, is sitting on a bench in the corridor and he's asked me to tell you that he will wait to see you safely back whenever you want to go.'

For the first time Judy realised how exhausted she felt. Looking at the clock, she saw that it was just gone half past three. The night was nearly over. 'I don't know what I should do.' She looked towards the sister. 'I'm very tired but I don't want to leave Tom in case…'

'He should continue to sleep now for several hours,' the sister advised her. 'Mr Davis has given him an injection. Why don't you go home now and get a few hours' sleep, then come back in the morning? Give me your telephone number and I promise to let you know if there is any change. Though I don't think it's at all likely.'

'Thank you. I'm sure you're right.' Bending over Tom, she gave him a final kiss. 'I'll be back, so you have no need to worry.' She then followed the sister out of the small ward into the corridor where Fergus was waiting.

As they walked away she told him what Mr Davis had said. 'God be praised!' he replied instantly. 'Me and Joe'll pray for him. We'll also look after you, Judy, and make sure you're safe, as Tom would want us to. That's the least we can do, since all this is partly our fault, we reckon.'

His last sentence puzzled her but she was far too exhausted to question him, longing only to sink into sleep and oblivion for a few hours.

Chapter Twenty-Six

For the next three days Judy felt herself to be existing in a nightmare world, all the more frightening because it was real. Alone in Tom's flat, she was afraid most of the time, although she knew that the O'Keefes, who visited her regularly, were keeping a close watch on her. If neither of them was free to come with her to the hospital, their friendly taxi driver friend, Seamus, took her there and brought her back.

She spent hours each day in the hospital, not only because she wanted to be with Tom but also because she felt safe there in a secure and ordinary world. Although she was assured that Tom was making progress, it seemed worryingly slow to her. He lay still and quiet most of the time for it was obviously a great effort for him to speak, although he always greeted her when she arrived and returned the kiss she gave him. There were many questions she wanted to ask him but knew she must not. Nevertheless, she found it comforting to sit quietly there holding his hand, feeling the love between them which didn't need words to convey it.

Occasionally, he would express anxiety about her and her safety but she would try to divert him from this with amusing stories about 'Nanny' Fergus and 'nursemaids', Joe and Seamus. Never did she admit her fear but as his hand tightened on hers she was sure he understood it but respected her wish not to dwell on it. Once he raised her hand to his lips and kissed it. 'My brave Judy,' he whispered. 'I'm very sorry.'

Bending over him, she kissed him warmly. 'There's no need to be. Just keep getting better. That's what I want.'

On the Thursday evening she came back to the flat feeling exhausted and depressed. Tom seemed to be making little progress and she knew that Mr Davis was still concerned about him. Fergus had prepared a tasty hot meal for her but even that brought only momentary relief. Like a blank wall in front of her was the horrifying thought, What shall I do if Tom dies?

When she thrust that away there were other more immediate problems which she now felt unable to solve. Although she hated the thought of leaving Tom, she knew that she must return to St Stephens on the Sunday in order to return to her teaching on the Monday. But how was she to convey this to Tom in his present state? And when she returned where was she to live? She shrank from the idea of asking for a room in the school, imagining only too clearly the gossip this would start. And then there was the question of the future. She must soon give a month's notice if she was to be free to leave at the end of the term and start a new life with Tom. And this, of course, brought her back to the original question, What would she do if Tom didn't recover?

The sudden, harsh ringing of her phone cut through these thoughts. Immediately, she was terrified. Who could possibly be calling her? She was afraid to answer it. But that was stupid, she told herself. She could not be shot over the phone, even though some hostile message might be delivered. Forcing herself to be sensible, she picked it up and spoke as normally as possible. To her immense relief it was Paul who answered. At first she hardly listened to what he was saying, until she realised that he was asking her whether or not she was returning on Sunday.

It was the first time she had spoken to him since she had rung him to say that Tom had survived the operation. 'If Tom is well enough, I will,' was all she managed to say.

'How is he? I hope he's making reasonable progress.' His tone conveyed friendliness but nothing more.

She was relieved and felt able to explain some of her difficulty. First of all, she told him, as if she were talking to a friend, of Tom's worrying lack of progress, as it seemed to her. Paul was reassuring. 'You mustn't expect too much too soon. He was badly wounded and lost a lot of blood.'

'I suppose you're right but it seems so slow and no one says anything encouraging.'

'You must remember that doctors are always afraid these days of being too positive, in case they might be sued.'

'Isn't that the lawyers fault?' This was an old discussion of theirs.

He laughed. 'Perhaps. But to return to my first question; what are your plans if you do return this Sunday?'

'I haven't any. I suppose I can get a room in school?'

'Don't be ridiculous.' He sounded very positive. 'You must obviously come here. It would be stupid to waste time moving your computer, your files and your books and God knows what else. Surely, you agree?'

'It would be more sensible but—'

He interrupted immediately she hesitated, wondering how she could express herself. 'I hope you're not trying to say that you're not sure that I will behave in a civilised manner? To put it bluntly I have already moved my things into the spare room and I propose to stay there. Surely we can meet twice a day for five days without too much difficulty? It will give us a chance to talk too and we must do that some time. What do you say?'

Impressed though she was by his apparent generosity, she was reluctant still to commit herself. 'You're very kind, Paul, but I must see how Tom is before I finally decide.'

'Do you mean that you have to ask his permission?' There was a touch of sharpness here.

'Of course not. I don't want to leave if he is very ill. Surely, you can understand that?'

There was a slight pause then he answered in his former friendly tone. 'Perhaps you'll be able to let me know by Saturday evening if I am to expect you?'

'I'm sure I can,' she replied quickly. 'And many thanks, Paul, for the offer.'

'Good. I'll expect to hear from you then.' He was gone, leaving her with mixed feelings.

After a restless night Judy did not go to the hospital until the early afternoon. As she came through the door of the little ward, she was amazed to see Tom sitting up and looking much restored. 'You do look better!' She was so astonished that she stood still for a moment staring at him.

'I am much better.' For the first time his voice was firm and clear. 'But don't stand there. Come and kiss me. I've been waiting most impatiently to see you.' As she moved towards him, he said, 'I want something better than your usual quick kiss. Sit on the right side of the bed then I can put my right arm around you.' As she followed his instructions, he immediately embraced her firmly and, pulling her towards him, kissed her very thoroughly. Smiling happily, she returned his kiss. 'Stay where you are,' he commanded her. 'I am in need of a little comforting. You're much later than I hoped. What happened?'

'I spent half the night worrying and then I overslept.' She kissed him again. 'But obviously I was stupid to worry about you.' She rested her head on his shoulder. 'But what's happened?'

'I'm not quite sure. A miracle perhaps? I woke up early feeling much better and then Mr Davis came in to give me a thorough examination. He was pleased and removed my tubes as you can see. He's a strange man. He said that someone must have been praying hard for me. There was no other explanation. I tried to thank him but he wouldn't listen. What do you make of that?'

'I think he's right. And I'm so glad.' She relaxed happily in the comfort of his embrace.

After a few moments he said suddenly. 'You didn't come to see me in the operating theatre, did you? No, of course you couldn't have done. But I had this extraordinary dream that you came up to me, took my hand and promised to fight with me and I immediately felt stronger.'

She sat up staring at him. 'Tom, that's almost frightening! I was praying for you and I had the same dream. It was so vivid that I thought it must have happened!'

'It seems that you helped to save my life. I owe you a lot.'

'You helped to save mine years ago. So now we're quits.' As he tightened his arm around her, they kissed again.

They were happily unaware that the door had opened and someone had come in until a familiar voice said cheerfully, 'I'm pretty sure that's not the right way for a visitor to behave and definitely not for a patient. What would sister say?'

'Bill!' Judy exclaimed. She tried to remove herself but Tom would not allow it.

'No other,' Bill replied, coming towards the bed. 'I've tried before but they wouldn't let me in. They gave me the impression that you were at death's door but you seem pretty fit to me.' He grinned at them both. 'Mind you, I'd be fit if I had a visitor like Judy.'

'If you intend to stay,' Tom said, 'sit down and be careful what you say.'

'Don't be horrid, Tom,' Judy protested.

'He's not being horrid, don't worry, Judy. He only wants to know in what capacity I'm here. That's right, isn't it, Tom?'

'Friend or foe?' Was Tom's somewhat uncompromising reply. 'Don't worry, Judy,' he added as she looked at them both anxiously. 'We understand each other. So what is it, Bill?'

'Friend,' was Bill's instant and cheerful reply. 'Lesser mortals will try the interviewing and be baffled, as they deserve. I have only come to see how you are and to give you my news.'

'As you can see, I am improving, although not quickly enough for me.'

'Every patient says that,' Bill replied imperturbably. 'It's what's expected of them. Good for the macho image and all that, but I don't believe you can't enjoy the first rest you've had for years, especially when you have the comfort of such a delightful visitor. Admit it, Tom, you do really. I know I should.' He smiled at Judy.

For the first time Tom smiled at him. 'I'll agree to the last bit but I don't recommend being shot.'

'Perhaps not. Which brings me to a question.'

'You said you had some news. What is it?' Judy interrupted quickly, feeling sure that Tom didn't want that question, if it was what she suspected. 'Don't keep us in suspense.' She felt Tom's arm relax again and knew that she had been right.

Bill gave her a sharp look but nevertheless he answered readily. 'My news? Ah, yes. Well, that's quite surprising. At least it was to me. It's just the change I've been wanting.' He grinned at them both. 'The paper is sending me on an assignment to the Far East for several months. I shall be visiting all sorts of exciting places from Beijing to Borneo or something like that. What do you think?'

'It sounds fine, if that's what you want and it obviously is. When do you go?' Tom was genuinely pleased, it seemed.

'Pretty soon. That's one reason why I was anxious to see you.'

'What about Katy?' Judy asked, then wished she hadn't.

'Katy? She's decided to take that job in California for a year.

She wants to see more of the world too. We're not the settling down sort, Katy and I.' He smiled and spoke casually but Judy was not convinced.

'Is she going soon then?'

'Early January, I think. Some time after Christmas before the next term starts.'

'I'd like to meet her again,' Judy said impulsively.

'I don't see why not but you'll have to make it soon as she plans to put in a visit to Belfast before then.'

'Belfast!' Judy was shocked. 'Why ever should she want to go there?'

Bill laughed rather bitterly. 'She doesn't know it as well as some of us do.'

'What's her reason?' Tom asked. 'Don't tell me we have roused her curiosity.'

'We may have done but that's not her real reason. She's arranged to see our old friend, Lawrence. Apparently the two of them have embarked on some kind of mystical relationship.'

'Mystical relationship?' Tom was obviously puzzled. 'What is that supposed to mean?'

'I'm not sure I can tell you. Being a cynic, I think it means at the moment that she wants to mother him and he's enjoying it. Perhaps Judy might understand it better?'

'Mystical relationship means nothing to me. I've no experience of any such thing.' She was puzzled.

'Perhaps I should have said "spiritual". It's all the same to me. All I know is that it appears to be something I'm incapable of achieving.' For a moment Bill sounded quite bitter. 'Even a serious offer of marriage hasn't deterred her from this adventure.' He shrugged. ' So what? The Far East is still tempting.'

'Perhaps that's just what it is, an adventure before she's ready to settle down,' Tom suggested. 'What do you think, Judy?'

Judy hesitated. There was much she could say but she wanted to be truthful. Finally, she said, 'I'm sure that Lawrence needs a good friend at the moment and Katy understands his feelings. It may lead to something else but not necessarily.'

Bill grinned at her. 'Maybe you're right but I'm not the sort to stand around and wait. She can always reach me if she wants to.

Which reminds me of Paul. Is he standing around and waiting? Or have you both conveniently forgotten him?' There was a hint of malice in the look he gave her.

Judy sat up. 'Paul and I have agreed to part,' she replied sharply. 'Like you, Bill, he has no particular desire to understand.'

Bill laughed. 'I asked for that, I suppose. You always were a bit of a spitfire, Judy.' He stood up. 'I guess it's time for me to go. I was told not to stay too long. You may not believe it but I hope you'll both be happy.' He turned to Tom. 'I'll see you again, I hope, before I depart.' He moved towards the door, then stopped. 'Forgive the old journalist, Tom, but there is one thing I'd like to know before I go. Have you any idea who shot you?'

'None at all,' Tom replied coldly and calmly.

'I'm not asking as a reporter but as an old friend.'

Tom smiled slightly. 'The answer's still "no". I have no idea. I told the police as soon as I was able to speak to them. Hearing the bell ring, I hurried to open the door, thinking it was Judy. Instead there was a masked man who, before I could react, fired three shots at me and immediately made off. I think I heard a car drive away. The next I remember is Fergus leaning over me.' His voice was still calm; his manner unemotional, only Judy could sense the increased tension in the arm which was still holding her.

Bill came a little nearer. 'But you must have some idea, Tom, surely?'

'Perhaps.'

'Then why don't you do something?'

'Because I don't want to know.' Tom's voice was steely now. 'Stop meddling, Bill. It will do no good.'

'I know we've been on different sides but I'm speaking now as a friend. Surely, you understand that?'

'I do but you on your part must understand that I have no intention of being drawn again into that vicious circle of hate and violence. I withdrew several years ago and I don't want to be sucked back. So, please don't try to tempt me. Let it be.' His dark blue eyes flashed at Bill with much of his normal fire. Judy felt a certain sympathy for Bill but she knew from the tension in his body that Tom was deeply affected.

'I'm only thinking of you, Tom,' Bill protested. 'I might be able to help. Don't you care about your safety?'

'Of course I do. But I don't think there's any further danger. There are others who can deal with that.'

'Oh, I see. I didn't know that—' Bill began but Tom interrupted him before he could finish.

'All the same I'm grateful for your friendly concern. As for me,' Tom suddenly sounded very weary, 'let's just say that I'm quite flattered that someone should still think I'm worth killing.' He gave Bill a friendly but slightly mocking smile, closed his eyes and leaned back on his pillows, relaxing his hold on Judy. 'I'm sorry,' he murmured, 'I really am tired.'

'I'm sorry, too. I should've had more sense. See you soon.' With a quick wave and a friendly grin, Bill was gone.

Since Tom was no longer holding her, Judy moved off the bed on to the chair. 'Do you want me to go?' she asked sadly, unable to hide her disappointment. There had been so much she had been going to say.

Turning towards her, Tom opened his eyes. 'No, I don't want you to go unless you want to. It's very comforting to have you here but I must rest for a while. I didn't realise I was still so stupidly weak. Can you bear to wait?'

'Of course I can.' Swallowing her disappointment, she took his offered hand in hers. 'I'll have a rest too. Just tell me when you feel able to talk. I have a few things to tell you.' The time seemed to pass very slowly, perhaps because of her impatience to tell him of her plans. But it was probably no more than twenty minutes before he spoke again.

'What is it you want to tell me? Poor Judy, you haven't had a chance to talk yet.'

It seemed best to be straightforward. 'I have to return to St Stephens on Sunday. You see,' she continued quickly before he could say anything, 'I must go back to work. The mock exams start soon and my students need my help. I wouldn't think of going otherwise. You understand, don't you?'

'Of course,' he said, smiling lovingly at her. 'It's what I would expect you to do. I would be surprised if you didn't think like that, although I shall miss you very much.'

'I shall come back every weekend. And the term will over in

about a month.'

'That's not very long. In any case, we shall have the weekends. But won't the travelling be rather a lot for you?'

'No. I shall get my car when I go back and that'll make it much easier. I shall continue to stay in your flat because it's convenient for the hospital. You don't mind that?'

'Don't be silly, darling. It's your home too, if you want it.'

'Do you know when you'll come out of hospital?'

'I'm afraid not. Mr Davis said it was much too early to give a date. But I think we can hope that'll it be before the end of your term.'

'Good. But I hate leaving you.'

'I don't enjoy the thought of your going but I've had you when I most needed you and now I'll be glad to know you're doing what you think is right, although I expect it will be difficult for you to go back. But it won't be for long.'

'It will be difficult but it's not for long, as you say.' She could not make herself say what she ought to say.

'Judy,' Tom asked suddenly, 'what is worrying you?' She stared at him. 'Don't deny it,' he said gently. 'I know you well enough to know that something is. Sit on the bed and let me put my arm around you again. Perhaps you'll find it easier then.'

Without a word more she did as he suggested. Resting her head on his shoulder, she enjoyed the comfort of his understanding. 'Tom, I don't know how you do it but you always seem to know what I'm thinking.'

'It's because I love you. Unless you tell me, however, I can't know exactly what it is. Come on, don't be afraid.'

'I don't want to upset you.'

'You can't upset me by being honest with me.'

Quickly now, she told him about Paul's phone call and her agreement to stay in her old home with him. 'Do you think I was wrong?'

'It seems a sensible arrangement to me. Don't worry any more.' Carefully, he bent his head and kissed her. 'There'll be temptations, Judy, but you'll have to meet them some time.'

'Paul doesn't tempt me – not now.'

'Perhaps not. But your old life might. It's wiser not to be too confident, Judy.'

'I won't go if it upsets you.'

'It doesn't upset me. I think it has to be done. Just be honest with me, as you have been now.'

'I promise I will, Tom. I love you very much.' For a while they stayed quietly together, then she said, 'I think I ought to go. You must be tired. I'll come early tomorrow, I promise.'

'I think I'll have to agree.' In spite of his efforts to be normal, he sounded very weary. 'One last kiss and then you can go.' For a moment they clung together, then gently releasing her, he closed his eyes and she went quietly away.

Later that evening when she had done all the little tasks she had deliberately set herself, Judy had to admit that she felt dissatisfied and worried. She felt that she had left Tom too readily and too quickly. She could so easily have stayed longer and talked to him more when he had rested. She felt now that there was so much more she could have said to make clearer her feelings about Paul. Tom had been so understanding that she had allowed herself too easily to be encouraged to leave. He could, however, have asked her to stay, she told herself, if he needed to hear more. He needn't have accepted her suggestion. But then she knew that Tom would never plead with her.

Did that mean, she wondered, that he was simply too proud or to aloof to share all his feelings? Suddenly, a part of his dialogue with Bill came unasked into her mind. Tom had stopped Bill from saying something, she was sure, when he said that others would deal with the problem. Bill had apparently understood but she had certainly not. Did that mean, as Paul had suggested, that Tom had not yet told her all the truth? She couldn't really believe that for she was convinced that Tom had told her everything that was important. She was being ridiculous, she told herself. If she could only talk to Tom, everything would be quickly settled. It was too late, however, to go to the hospital again.

Going to the kitchen, she made herself another coffee and took it back to the living room. As she was sipping her coffee, the phone rang. It was Paul apologising for bothering her but wondering if it were possible for her to let him know now if she was returning on the Sunday. Quickly she told him that as Tom was much better she could definitely say that she would be arriving on the Sunday.

'Good,' he said instantly, 'then I hope you'll let me pick you up in the car.'

'There's no need for you to make such an effort,' she answered quickly. 'I can manage perfectly well on the train.'

'Normally you could, I'm sure, but I've just discovered that there are going to be bigger delays than usual this Sunday, line repairs or something.'

She did not want this but as they talked she found it almost impossible to refuse. And when she finally put the phone down, she realised that somehow he had persuaded her to agree to all his suggestions. Why? she asked herself. Why was she such a weak fool? Perhaps that was what Tom had meant when he spoken about temptations. Once more she wished she could speak to him and reassure herself.

She went back to her now somewhat chilly coffee, wishing she had a piano so that she could comfort herself with music. When they had been together twelve years before Tom had actually borrowed a piano for her, before she had even asked. But then he had always understood her. As she sat before the fire feeling sorry for herself, unexpectedly the phone rang again. Unbelievably, it was Tom.

'I thought you only wanted to sleep,' she told him.

'I have slept well but now that I'm awake and feeling better I just want to say goodnight to you properly. I'm ashamed that I let you leave so easily.'

'You needn't be,' she quickly reassured him, 'I could see you were very tired and probably still are.'

'Perhaps,' he replied, 'but not too tired to try to tell you how much I love you and how much I wish we could be together. I don't want you to feel lonely or worried. Simply pretend I'm holding you in my arms and kissing you, as in a few weeks' time I will be.'

The tears came into her eyes. 'Oh, Tom darling, I love you so much! That's just what I needed! Now I shall be able to sleep.

'Then I'll say goodnight, my love' he said. 'We'll both sleep now and look forward to tomorrow morning.'

Chapter Twenty-Seven

'If we're not to be late for the concert, you at least should start to get ready now.'

Judith, who had just finished dealing with intricacies of a Bach fugue, looked up startled. As usual when playing she had been lost in the world of music, delighting in the difficulties and in the skill of her hands. Paul who had been listening comfortably in a near by armchair, smiled. ' It's already six fifteen and since you're one of the chief performers, you need to arrive by seven fifteen, suitably gowned, so I think you'd better start, don't you?'

'You're right, of course.' Standing up, she regretfully put away her music and walked towards the door. 'What about you?'

'Fortunately, I don't need to take so long but I promise not to disgrace you, especially as this is the last time.' He hoped she might respond but she only smiled as she left the room. This was the sixth school concert he had attended with her, delighted to be the husband of this gifted and attractive woman.

Just before the end of the Christmas term, the boarding school in the village gave a grand concert in which the most promising music students and one or two members of the staff performed. Judith had always been the only person outside the music department who took part and this year she had a star role. This was one of the reasons why she had spent this weekend at St Stephens instead of in London visiting Tom. The other had been the need to finish her exam marking. He wondered not for the first time what Tom had thought of this. As usual Judith had scarcely said anything.

As soon as she was in her bedroom, Judith methodically began her preparations with a shower and a shampoo. Sitting before her mirror brushing her hair, she began to reflect on the last three weeks. At first it had been like living two lives but during this last week which was not ending in a visit to London, she seemed to have slipped quite easily back into the old routine. This surprised and frightened her. For the past seven days she and Paul had lived together in exactly the same way as they had for nearly six years, except that they never made love. They were pleasant acquaintances who lived comfortably together without making undue demands on one another.

Was this all she really wanted, she asked herself? Where did her love for Tom fit in? During the two weekends she had spent near him there had been little chance for serious discussion and planning, chiefly because, soon after she had left, Tom had had a relapse and needed further surgery. The last weekend she had seen him he had been much better and full of hope of coming out of hospital before too long. He had definitely not been fit enough, however, for a serious talk about their future plans and she had not attempted it. He had, in his usual rational way, accepted the necessity for her to be in St Stephens this weekend. And yet, as she travelled home, she had felt dissatisfied with herself and still did. The reason was, she now admitted as she put the final touches to her make-up, the feeling she had that he had expected her to say something which she hadn't said. And what troubled her more was her reluctance to think what it might be.

After slipping into the simple but elegant black taffeta dress, she picked up the golden necklace she intended to wear with it.

'Are you ready? It's nearly time to go.' Paul put his head round the door. Seeing her struggling with the clasp of her necklace, he came across the room towards her. 'Let me help you with that. You've never been able to manage it yourself.' She felt his fingers touch her neck gently. It was the first time since her return that they had been close. 'There that's it!' he exclaimed, his fingers lingering on her neck. Feeling herself tingling, she turned to face him. They were suddenly very close. 'You look beautiful. That dress reminds me of the one you wore when we first met.' There was a slight tremor in his voice. She looked up at him, smiling. Slowly, he bent and kissed her. She didn't resist him and only after a moment did she move away.

'You're quite right,' she said as calmly as she could. 'We shall be late if we don't go now.'

Without a word he helped her into her jacket and then followed her down the stairs.

'What sort of a woman are you really, Judith?' Paul's sudden question startled her. At his suggestion on their return from the concert they were having a drink together in the sitting room before she went to her study to finish her marking.

She looked at him. He was obviously serious and waiting for her reply. 'I don't know what you mean,' was all she could think to say.

'Don't you? Or does that mean you that you don't want to talk about it with me? Do you realise that it's been three weeks since you came back to this house and I don't believe that I know any more about you now than I did then.'

'You do know more than you once did. You know about my past life and about Lawrence and Tom.'

'I wouldn't have learned any of that if circumstances hadn't forced you to reveal it. Since then, you have added very little. I know you have given in your notice at school and will be leaving in about ten days' time. What then? Have you made any plans? You certainly haven't mentioned any to me. I am still your husband. Surely, it isn't unreasonable for me to expect you to tell me something?'

Putting down her glass on the little table standing near to her, she looked at him with her beautiful dark eyes. 'You know that I intend to go to Tom after the end of term.'

'But how certain is that? When we last talked about it the night when Tom was shot you told me that he wanted you to return to Belfast with him and that you hated the idea. Isn't that right?'

'Yes, you know I said that.'

'Have you discussed that with him?'

'No. It hasn't been possible. He hasn't been well enough for that kind of discussion.'

'So you have allowed him to assume that it's all settled? Is that fair? It seems very like some of the things you have allowed me to assume in the past.' They looked steadily at each other. There was a tension between them. He considered going over to her on the settee and taking her in his arms. He wondered if she would resist him.

Before he could move, however, she stood up. 'I really don't want to discuss these matters now, Paul. I must finish my marking.' She moved towards the door.

'How long do you expect to be?'

'About an hour and a half.'

'Fine.' He looked at his watch. 'I'll bring you a drink at about eleven and we can finish our chat then. There are some things which must be said and the time is getting short.'

She frowned slightly but went out of the room without any protest.

It was just after eleven when Paul came up the stairs carrying a tray with two hot drinks and a plate of biscuits. Noticing that the light was on in the bedroom, he went there. Judith, who had changed into a jade green velvet housecoat, was sitting on the bed looking at some papers. She put them down as he came in and watched silently as he put the tray down on the bedside table near to her, then went to sit on the stool in front of the dressing table with his own drink.

After he had taken a few sips he realised that she was not prepared to begin the conversation, so he decided to challenge her again. Surely there was something that would disturb that unnatural calm? 'Have you ever cared about anyone?' he asked her, looking straight at her. 'Or more important still – do you actually care about anyone now?'

After putting down her mug carefully, she answered him coldly, 'Why do you ask me that? You know I do.'

'Do I?' He put down his own mug on the dressing table. 'Oh, I suppose you mean Tom? Yes, I do remember your saying some time ago that you loved Tom. Tom whose greatest virtues seem to be that he's never there, except when you want help and who is never jealous or possessive. A useful fellow for a woman like you.'

He wanted to rouse her and it seemed that he had, for she stood up and came towards him. 'What are you talking about? Why do you say that?' Her eyes flashed at him.

He stood up and confronted her. 'Perhaps you've already forgotten that only about five hours ago you allowed me to kiss you and you seemed to enjoy it. Even your saintly terrorist Tom might find that a little upsetting, don't you think? Particularly at this time, when he's pretty ill.'

He had roused her, although she still tried to hide it. 'How dare you say things like that? You think yourself so good but you only seem good because you've never been tested, have you? You've always had the things you wanted so easily. You never needed to struggle. Whatever I am, Tom is a good man.'

He laughed. 'A good man! A terrorist, a man of violence! Isn't that what you really mean? And he still is. Why do you think he was shot recently?'

Moving right up to him, she raised her hand as if to strike him. He seized her arm before she could. He had never seen her more beautiful or more desirable. The continual frustrations of the last month were not to be borne any longer. He wanted her and he would have her. He pulled her close to him and began to kiss her ravenously, while with one hand he pulled down the zipper of her coat and began to caress her breasts. She tried to push him away but he was too strong for her.

He forced her back until she was lying on the bed and he was on top of her, continuing to kiss and caress her. He knew all that would most arouse her. Suddenly she pushed his face away. 'Do you intend to rape me, Paul?' she asked bitterly.

He smiled at her. 'There's no need to pretend any more, Judith darling.' He could tell that her body was beginning to respond to his. 'You can't deny it. You love me as much as you've always done. Perhaps you'd like it to be different but it isn't, is it? Tom's forgotten. You can't help loving me, can you?'

With a tremendous effort, far greater than he had thought her capable of, she pushed him off her and sat up. Her eyes were blazing in her pale face. 'You're right, but you've used the wrong word. It isn't loving, is it? It's lusting. And don't flatter yourself, Paul. Any attractive man would do just as well when I'm feeling vulnerable. Many have before you. There was a time when I thought you were better but once again you've proved me wrong.'

Utterly outraged, he stared at her. They were standing, facing each other now. He looked into her defiant dark eyes and wanted to hurt her for what she had said. Deliberately, he slapped her face as hard as he could. 'You bitch!' he exclaimed.

She staggered and sat down on the edge of the bed, one of her cheeks turning a violent scarlet. As she covered her face with her hands, she bowed her head but she neither cried nor spoke.

Appalled at what he had done, he sat down on the stool. 'Oh God, Judith, I'm sorry. I never meant to do that.' She made no reply but remained silent with covered face and bowed head. He began to feel angry again. 'Why don't you say something? Curse me or hit me?'

At last she reacted. Slowly uncovering her face, she looked up at him. 'You'd like that, wouldn't you? It would make you feel better, more justified.' Her voice was quiet. She wasn't trying to mock him.

He felt utterly weary and miserable. 'I don't understand myself or you.'

'Poor Paul,' she said, almost gently, 'you never realised before how easy it can be to hate and be violent. How much you can want your victim to hit back so that you don't have to blame yourself. That's how all violence starts. You feel hurt, deprived of your right and so you hit out and the other person hits back. And so it goes on escalating.'

He sat silent for a few moments. This was a very hard lesson but the red mark on Judith's face forced him to speak the truth. 'What can I say? I always considered myself so civilised, so superior, instead of understanding that I was just lucky. But now I see that given the right circumstances I can be as violent as any other man. I might even be a terrorist if I were brave enough.' He looked at her. 'That is what you mean, isn't it?'

'We all have to learn that we're all sinners. As for me I'm a bitch as you said. I married you rather than become a whore.'

'But you say you love Tom.'

'I do love Tom. That's the best of me.'

'You may believe you do. But it doesn't always look like that.'

'Tom knows about my weakness. He understands how it came about.'

'I wasn't thinking about that. I was thinking how indifferent you can become to everyone when you're immersed in your mathematics or your music. I suppose that's why hours ago I asked you what sort of a woman you are.'

'What do you mean?'

'When did you last speak to Tom?' He was still determined to make her speak the full truth about herself. She should have no refuge in this supposed love for Tom.

'Why do you ask?'

'Does it matter? It's a simple question. Surely, you can answer it?'

'If you insist. I spoke to him on Friday during the lunch hour for about half an hour.' She seemed quite calm again.

'Do you really mean that you haven't spoken to him since? That you have let the whole weekend pass without your getting in touch with him again. Haven't you somewhat neglected him? I know I wouldn't be happy in his position.'

'Tom isn't like you. He knows that I have a lot of work to do this weekend with the marking, the reports and the concert. He doesn't need continual reassurance.'

'Like me, you mean? But then you were very good at reassuring me whenever I felt worried, although it must have been a nuisance to you. How splendid for you that Tom doesn't apparently need anything.' He smiled at her.

'What are you getting at?' She frowned at him. 'Why are you talking like this?'

'It was stupid of me. I'm sorry. You'd better put it down to my jealousy and forget it. How was Tom when you spoke to him?'

'He said he felt much better and he thought that the doctor might allow him to come home on Monday or Tuesday.'

'It would surprise you then to know that he's been home since Saturday.'

She stared at him. 'How can you possibly know? I don't believe you. You're just saying it to upset me, to make out that I'm...'

'Indifferent?' he suggested as she paused. 'No, I'm afraid not, Judith. It's true.'

'Then why hasn't he let me know?'

Paul laughed. 'He's tried several times, I think. But you, as you're so busy, have left your mobile switched off. In fact, you left it on the table in the sitting room where I found it this evening. I spoke to Tom this morning when, in desperation I suppose, he rang this number. I could only tell him you were very busy at school and wouldn't be back until this afternoon when you had to practise for the concert.'

'Why didn't you tell me?'

'He told me most definitely not to bother. He said you would be in touch when you were ready. I don't think I could have been so philosophical in the circumstances.'

'Were you unpleasant to him?'

'Of course not, don't be silly. When I met him I quite liked him. In any case I felt sorry for him. He didn't say much but I gathered that he felt pretty rough. It is rough when you come out of hospital. Everything is so much harder than you thought it would be. I suppose your lack of concern about him was one of the things that urged me on tonight, not that it excuses the way I behaved. Still you taught me a lesson, didn't you? I know now how violent I can be. You seem to be good at teaching people lessons. Perhaps it's time you learned one yourself.'

'About loving, you mean?' She was deadly pale and as she bent her head to avoid his gaze, he caught a glimpse of her tears. 'You're right! Oh God, I didn't mean it to be like this! I really didn't!'

'How did you mean it to be?'

'I meant to get everything done this weekend, my reports and everything so that I could leave early before the end of term, when he came out of hospital. I've already spoken to Mrs Hardy about it and she was very understanding. Oh God, how stupid I am! I never thought about my phone. I was concentrating so much on what I had to do. I can't understand it.'

'You didn't think about anyone much,' he could not refrain from saying. 'Did you intend to tell me before you finally left or was I to be allowed to find it out by ringing Tom? Still, that hardly matters now, does it? You and I are finished. You've made it perfectly clear that it never amounted to much as far as you were concerned and now it's over. I have to accept that. But what about Tom?'

'I don't understand you.'

'If you can put him so completely out of your mind how much do you love him? I have a suspicion that during the last week you have been wondering whether life with me might not be better than life in Belfast even with Tom. Certainly that thought encouraged me. Wrongly, it seems, for you seem finally to have rejected life with me but does Belfast still bother you? You've got to decide. Tom's not me. I imagine he expects you to be honest.'

Reaching out for a box of tissues on her bedside table, she took several and wiped her eyes before she answered. 'You're right,' she said at last, 'Tom is honest and he expects me to be the same. I was planning all I've just told you but I think I instinctively kept myself out of touch because I wasn't sure and he would want to know.'

'What are you going to do?' While he was waiting for her to reply she stood up, walked over to the cupboard and took out a couple of suitcases, then she turned towards him.

'I shall go early in the morning so I can get there by breakfast time. I still hate the thought of Belfast and I shall tell him but I shall also tell him that if he truly thinks that is the best for us, I'll go with him. Although I hate the thought of Belfast, I hate the thought of anywhere else without him much more. We've had to waste so many years already. I think it's time I started to live my real life. I'm sorry, Paul, but that's it.' She began to put her belongings into one of the suitcases.

Accepting the finality in her words, he did not protest. 'You're right. It's obvious that he's the only man who can deal with you. We never were suited. It was just a dream but I enjoyed it, while it lasted.' He went towards the door. 'Let me know if you want any help, at least have a coffee with me before you leave.'

'I will, I promise and thank you.' Before he left, she had already returned to her packing.

Chapter Twenty-Eight

Everything was going to be all right! Judy happily realised this a few minutes after she had arrived in Tom's flat. Throughout the long and difficult journey she had been worried by what Paul had said. Had she in fact neglected Tom when he most needed her? Would he be angry and perhaps even jealous? Was Paul right when he said that when she was busy with work or music she forgot about everyone?

She entered the flat with her own key, thinking that Tom might still be in bed. Instead, she came across him unexpectedly in the kitchen. Unshaven, hair tousled and wearing his bathrobe, he appeared to be contemplating the coffee percolator. As she called out, 'Tom,' he turned quickly.

'Judy!' He moved towards her. 'What are you doing here?'

Her first thought was how pale and thin he looked. The next moment he was hugging her and she was clinging to him.

'I've come to see you, of course. What do you think?' she said breathlessly. 'When Paul told me he had spoken to you and that you had come out of hospital on Saturday, I decided to come this morning early and surprise you.'

'You've certainly done that.' He smiled but she wasn't quite sure what that smile meant.

'I'm sorry I was such an idiot about my phone,' she hurried on, 'I was so busy that I forgot about it. I actually left it in the sitting room. Paul didn't tell me until late last night.' She looked up at him and met his penetrating glance. She still felt unsure. Paul's words had been so harsh. Did Tom think the same about her?

'I knew you were busy. You told me you would be and you told me why. What is worrying you, Judy?'

'I thought you might be annoyed with me. You might think I'd forgotten you or that I didn't want to bother to speak to you.'

'Why should I think anything so stupid? I think you really

know me better than that.' It was then when he smiled lovingly and kissed her that she knew her worries had been unfounded. Of course, Tom wasn't like that. She returned his kiss.

'When do you have to go back?' he asked.

'I don't. I'm a free woman now. I'd been given permission to leave early on Tuesday so when I heard you were already out, I came straight away. I've packed all my portable belongings into my car. Anything else can wait. I'm so happy now I'm here with you.' She moved back a little to look at him. 'You are pleased, aren't you?'

'What do you think?' Pulling her close to him again, he kissed her. 'I couldn't be happier. If I don't sound quite as enthusiastic as you might expect, you must remember that I only came out of hospital less than two days ago.'

'I know. I'm sorry. I'm being very selfish.' She looked around the suspiciously tidy kitchen. 'Have you had any breakfast yet?'

'No. I was thinking of making some coffee when you arrived.' Releasing her, he sat down on one of chairs at the kitchen table.

'Coffee! That's not enough for a convalescent! Surely Fergus could have given you some breakfast?'

'You mustn't blame Fergus. He would certainly have done so. He and Joe fussed around all day Saturday until I told them that I could manage on my own and would let them know if I needed anything. I warn you I'm not a languishing hero but simply a grumpy convalescent.'

She laughed. 'I think I can put up with that! But I'm certainly going to get some breakfast, not just for you but for me. I've travelled one hundred and forty miles on nothing but a cup of coffee. I'm famished.'

'In that case, I'll submit.'

'Don't just think you can sit there. Go and have a shower, a shave and comb your hair. You'll not only look better but you'll feel better. Breakfast in fifteen minutes. Can you manage that?'

'I think so.' He stood up slowly but he was smiling.

'There seem to be plenty of eggs. Would you prefer boiled or scrambled?'

'Definitely scrambled.' He made his way to the door. 'I'm glad you're here.'

Some twenty minutes later when they were seated at the breakfast table, Judy decided that things were not simply all right but splendid. She smiled happily across at Tom who was obviously enjoying his first satisfactory meal for some time. Ignoring the several more serious matters waiting to be decided, they talked cheerfully of some of the happier times they had shared in the past before events had forced them to part. Now, it seemed almost as if they had never been apart for it was all so easy and relaxed. They prolonged the breakfast with second cups of coffee and extra slices of toast but were at last forced to admit they must move on.

As Judy began to stack the dishes Tom said firmly, 'Leave all that until later. There are a lot of things we must talk about and decisions we need to make. The sooner we do all that, the sooner we can be happier.'

Reluctantly, she stopped what she was doing. She knew he was right but she shrank from his suggestions. Supposing they could not agree, she wondered, remembering his plan about returning to Belfast. Of course, she had told Paul that she was ready to accept even that but she preferred to put it off a little longer. 'I thought I could sort the kitchen out and start my unpacking while you had a rest. You must remember you're still very much a convalescent.'

Regarding her with that familiar mocking smile of his, he replied calmly, 'And you must remember, Judy, that I'm still the same Tom, even though I've been shot, so don't try to manipulate me. Your consideration is charming but all it really means that you want to put off this talk. Right?'

'Right. It's horrible the way you always seem to know what I'm thinking. I only wanted to go on being happy. It's such a change.'

'I think we'll be even happier after we've talked.' He stood up. 'Let's go to the living room, put on the fire and relax on the settee.'

Admiring his firmness as he walked away, she followed him. It was very comfortable she had to admit a few minutes later as she sat close to him, resting her head on his shoulder with his good arm around her shoulders.

It was naturally he who spoke first. 'I'll begin with a question which I've wanted to ask since I first looked at you this morning. What have you done to your face? There's quite a nasty bruise on your left cheek. Have you had an accident?' He touched the bruise gently with his fingers.

It was a relief because it enabled her to tell him what she needed to tell him about her last day with Paul. 'Not an accident, more a punishment, I suppose you might say.'

'Whatever do you mean?' He leaned towards her and kissed the bruise gently. 'I think I might begin to guess but it'll be better if you tell me.'

'Promise me you won't be angry.'

'How can I promise you that before I know the truth. Don't be afraid, Judy darling.'

Slowly, clearly and as accurately and honestly as she could, she told him the story of her last few hours with Paul. Tom was frighteningly silent when she had finished. 'I know I was rather weak and perhaps encouraged him more than I should have done but you're not angry with me, are you? Even though I didn't phone, I never forgot you.'

'How could I possibly be angry with you? I was simply trying to find the right words. I can't begin to understand how he could have forced himself on you, knowing about your unhappy past as he does! Oh God, I hate that sort of violence to a woman! I saw too much of that when I was a small kid and heard my father force himself on my mother.'

She spoke quickly sensing, that he was struggling with very strong emotions. 'He was just desperate. Looking back, I realise that he had planned all the time to get me back. Every day I was there he tried to prove to me that everything could be as it had been before. He didn't believe he could fail but at the end he was beyond reason. He was desperate and hated me for the wrong he was convinced I'd done to him. But he learned a bitter lesson. You should be sorry for him. I didn't mean to but I suppose I did wrong him.'

'No, I won't agree to that. He had what he thought he wanted. He simply wasn't mature enough to realise that it couldn't possibly last. No man should behave as he did. Don't try to make me accept that, Judy.' He kissed her cheek very gently. 'You'll never have anything like that to put up with again.'

'We parted on quite friendly terms. I felt he was very sorry. Do you think that was weak of me too?'

'No. It was right for you to forgive him and much happier for you.'

'He actually helped me to make up my mind, too. When he challenged me about going to Belfast, I told him that, although I didn't really want to go to Belfast, I'd rather be in Belfast with you than anywhere else without you. That suddenly became absolutely clear to me.'

She waited for him to answer. He seemed to be considering, then he said slowly, 'You couldn't have said anything more loving and I love you all the more for it but I think there are perhaps other things that should be said about that, but I'd rather leave it for a little while. There is something else I'd like to tell you first if you don't mind being patient.'

Puzzled, she remained silent, only pressing his hand to show her willingness to listen.

'Do you remember when Bill came to see me hospital and you were there?'

'And he asked you if you knew who had shot you? Yes, I certainly remember that conversation because I was rather annoyed.'

'Annoyed? Why?'

'Because I felt that Bill knew more than I was allowed to know, especially when you said that others would take care of it and then shut Bill up. I felt excluded.'

'That was never my intention. I didn't know what Bill knew, if anything, but I only had my suspicions which have recently been confirmed.'

She sat up, giving him all her attention. 'Tell me what you mean.'

'I don't know if it has occurred to you but there were several happenings in those days before I was shot which have never been explained.'

'You mean,' she said, excited now, 'the three men who seemed to follow Paul from our home to London and finally attacked him and the man who had obviously frightened Maeve?'

'Yes, that's exactly what I mean. It was clever of you to notice.'

'I didn't. It was Paul who pointed it out to me that Monday evening just before we heard you'd been shot. I think his intention was to show that you were involved in some way.'

'That would naturally occur to him as the best explanation.' Tom smiled a little bitterly. 'It must be correct since I was a terrorist and am clearly capable of all evils. The truth, however, is very different. It is really quite ironical and, even I, the victim, can begin to appreciate the comedy of it.' He paused for a moment and smiled at her. 'I think you may be able to appreciate it too, Judy.

'Two days before I left hospital I had an unexpected visitor. I had no idea who he was. He introduced himself as "John Green". No rank, no title. I summed him up quickly – English, public school, Oxford, then some kind of government department. He was about fifty, I should think, pleasantly spoken, very polite but with that touch of arrogance which many English officers have. I said, "I'm afraid I don't know you."

'He smiled almost apologetically, I thought, and spoke courteously. "It's not important that you should. I'm only the messenger boy, as it were. I have come to bring not only my apologies but also those of my superiors. I'm afraid, Mr Farrell, that you have been treated most unkindly. Certain over enthusiastic members of my department took it upon themselves to decide without proper investigation or authorisation that certain rumours they had heard about you were true. As a result they threatened Mr Paul Tempest, deeming it advisable to force him to abandon his wife, while she, they were convinced, would eventually lead them to you. Then, most heinous of all, they decided that they would be justified in shooting you."

'"Fortunately," I replied, "they didn't succeed. You really should teach them to shoot more accurately. In their situation I know I could have done a better job."

'He seemed to appreciate the humour and gave me quite a broad smile. "I don't doubt that but I suppose we must both be grateful for their lack of skill. You may be sure that they have been severely disciplined. It was their obvious duty to find out, as they could easily have done, your true position as a peace negotiator. It is not our wish to kill our allies. My superiors, therefore, have asked me, as I have already said, to convey their sincerest apologies and to offer you any compensation you may require."

'He stopped then. I looked at him and he looked at me. What was there to say? In the end I accepted the apologies and told him that I was relieved to know that it was not "my friends" but only my allies who had tried to kill me. I needed no compensation. He thanked me, said he admired my attitude and so we parted good friends. He actually thanked me for making his job so easy.'

He stopped then and closed his eyes, rather exhausted, Judy thought, by the effort he had made. She was so amazed that she scarcely knew what to say. 'It's a dreadful story,' she said at last, 'and almost unbelievable. I don't know how you could take it so calmly. I'm sure I should have been angry. You certainly did make his job easy. Why did you?'

Smiling, he opened his eyes and gave her one of his penetrating looks. 'What else was there to do, Judy? You know as well as I do that anger is usually futile and often dangerous. It took me many violent years to learn a measure of control, even a certain detachment. There are times when one must see the irony of events or despair.'

'I suppose you're right but I'm not sure that I'm quite equal to that.'

'Don't worry about it. I told you the story so that you would know the truth, as I understood you wanted to know it. Even now, however, I'm not sure that it is the whole truth nor even where Mr Green actually comes from but I'm quite sure that it is meant to show that I'm now free from danger.

'But now I have something else, in some ways even more important to tell you, because it concerns our future. I had another visitor after the mysterious Mr Green, an old friend this time. His name is Ed Collins and he was my boss in New York. He had heard something about what had happened to me and, since he was in London, he came to visit me wanting to know the full story.'

'I'm glad you had someone pleasant at last. Was he sympathetic?'

'Very, but more than that for he had a few practical

suggestions to make. He didn't think I should stay here and told me that my former job in New York was still open if I wanted to come back.'

'And I suppose you immediately told him you didn't want to? And being Irish, as I suppose he is, he was impressed by your heroic dedication. Am I right?'

'Only partially. I said I didn't want to go back to the States. He could understand that but he was not impressed by "my heroic dedication", as you term it.' He gave her a slightly mocking smile. 'His answer was, "Give it up, Tom. After twenty-one years working for the cause, they reward you by practically killing you. Doesn't that tell you something? The politicians have taken over now and it's better to leave it to them. We straightforward folk only get in the way and they've no compunction about getting rid of us, if it's necessary. Get the hell out of it while you can and live your own life. I guess you can say you've earned it."' He stopped waiting for her comment.

'Did he have any ideas as to what you might do?' she surprised him a little by asking.

'Yes, that too. The firm is extending their operations in Southern Ireland. He offered me a good job in Dublin, one that would just suit me, he said.'

'And what did you say? Did you turn him down? I suppose you did.'

'No, I said it sounded very interesting and I said I would let him know in a few days. He was pleased and will get in touch by Wednesday.'

Judith was silent for a few moments, then she said slowly, 'I don't understand. I thought that Belfast was all settled, that you thought it was the only right thing for us to do. Am I wrong?'

'No, I did say something like that. But many things have happened since then. I was shot and very nearly died. In fact, I came closer to death than I've ever been, although I've been in some dangerous situations. But even more important than that I had a lot of time to think and I'd already begun to believe that what Ed later said was right. Men who believe in forgiveness and justice and all such romantic notions are an embarrassment to the politicians. They have their job to do. Mine must be done now in the background. I must say that Mr Green's visit strengthened this belief.'

'Thank God for that!' Judith took hold of his hand. 'I'd much rather have you alive than heroically dead!' She hesitated, then continued, 'But can you really be sure, Tom, after all these years?'

'I am sure. I'm tired, Judy.'

'Of course you are! You've been seriously ill. You're over the worst now, however. You should soon start to feel much better.'

'I hope so, in fact I'm sure I will but I don't just mean physically tired. After twenty-one years of first fighting for justice as I believed it, then working for peace, I've had enough. I want to have time for myself, for us, before it's too late. Can you understand?'

'I think so.' Nevertheless, she still looked unconvinced.

'I told you recently,' he continued, 'that when I went back to the States I had two loves, you and Ireland. You suggested that I should have said Ireland and you. Perhaps you were right then but you wouldn't be right to say so any longer. I wronged you then and I was wronging you again when I insisted on Belfast. Our decisions from now on should be joint ones. I would like to go to Dublin and I want to start my new life there but only if you are willing.'

She smiled happily at him. 'You know I am happy to go to Dublin where, I expect, I shall quickly find some suitable work. But I can't accept all you say, Tom. After all you've done, you'll never be able to give up the fight for peace and justice. You'll have to do something, even if it's only in the background.'

'You're becoming very wise, Judy. And, if you're right, would that upset you?'

'No, because I shall be there working with you. It's time I too did something for what I believe in. I want our children to be able to respect me as well as you, don't I?'

'So there are to be children, are there?' Laughing, he kissed her.

'I hope so. That is, if you agree. Do you?'

'Very much so, but I think we should be married first as soon as your divorce comes through.'

'I'll accept that as the best proposal I'm likely to get. But could we be married twice, do you think? Perhaps it's old-fashioned but I would prefer it.'

'Twice? Oh, you mean in church too. I think that should be possible. A priest who visited me in hospital said he would advise you to apply for an annulment. It would be more satisfactory since we're both Catholics, if sinful ones.'

Judy smiled. 'I was sinful but I don't feel sinful now that we are firmly committed to each other. In fact, I think this is perhaps the least sinful time of my life since I was eighteen! All this is very good but I would still like a little romance. I know you said you were not a romantic hero but...' As she was speaking she was smiling up at him and twining her fingers in his.

He seemed to consider the matter seriously. 'You've reminded me,' he said at last, 'of a small thing I've forgotten to mention.' He paused deliberately. 'Ed has offered us a three-week Caribbean holiday in his house there in January. He thought it would be a sort of honeymoon for us. Does that make a difference?'

'You know damn well it does. It's about time you came clean. I knew there was something else, you sounded so smug. I suppose you wanted to see if you and Dublin had any charm. Well, you have but this is a definite improvement. So what's your plan? You always have a plan, don't you? I need to know because I have to unpack. To put it bluntly – do I move into the spare room or in with you? Don't answer, I think I know. We start our love life together in January.'

'That could be the plan,' he said very cautiously.

'Well, I suggest an improvement, since we're supposed to discuss arrangements. I move in with you straight away and we see how it develops. After all, my Florence Nightingale skills may bring about a more rapid improvement. What do you think?'

'I hope so, my darling. I really do. But you won't be upset if they don't?'

'Why should I be? All I want is to be close to you. Years ago you comforted me by hugging me all night. I can now do the same for you and make myself happy as well. What do you say?'

His only reply was to draw her as close to him as he could and kiss her long and lovingly, until at last she came up for breath. 'It's very difficult,' he said, 'to make love with only one arm and a sore chest.'

'You're doing very well,' she murmured. 'Why not try again? You might get really good at it.'

Printed in the United Kingdom
by Lightning Source UK Ltd.
116112UKS00001BA/8